SECRETS
of an
IRISH
HOUSE

BOOKS BY ANN O'LOUGHLIN

The Irish House
My Only Daughter
Her Husband's Secret

SECRETS
of an
IRISH
HOUSE

Ann O'Loughlin

bookouture

Published by Bookouture in 2023

An imprint of Storyfire Ltd.
Carmelite House
50 Victoria Embankment
London EC4Y 0DZ

www.bookouture.com

ISBN: 978-1-83790-276-7
eBook ISBN: 978-1-83790-273-6

To John, Roshan and Zia xxx

ONE

Manhattan, New York

'What do we do now; live happily ever after?'

Katie didn't answer. Maggie's voice was a white noise crackling inside her head.

Slipping out of her seat she moved to the window, squeezing in behind the attorney's desk. She couldn't make sense of any of this; the will of the man she loved had been read aloud and none of it had registered; it was all just words, bloody words. Suddenly, she jumped back when she saw a bunch of strangers staring at her.

The attorney coughed and swivelled around in his leather chair.

'The tourists on the High Line; worse than the paparazzi. Do you want some time to consider the contents of Mr Flint's will?'

Katie didn't answer, but peeked out the window at the holidaymakers, their cameras trained on a cherry blossom, growing where once there had been railway tracks. She heard a jumble of more words as the attorney attempted to read out the will a second time. Her head hurt, Maggie's outraged voice piercing through her brain. 'Can we just decide here and now to sell the goddamn place?' Maggie's loud voice intruded on the room.

The attorney shook his head.

'It may not be as simple as that,' he said quietly.

'Put it on the market and flip it to the first buyer who comes along. We are two women who have been left practically penniless.'

Katie flinched, wanting to scream at Maggie to shut up. *What place? What was she even talking about? Wasn't it enough that Harry was dead?*

The attorney cleared his throat.

'For the avoidance of doubt, I would like to read to the end one more time the last will and testament of Harry Flint. Mr Flint leaves his estate in equal parts between the two of you, his ex-wife, Maggie Flint and his partner, Katie Williams.'

'Yes, we know that, and it's all gone; Every bank in Manhattan has a stake on the properties that are rightfully ours,' Maggie snapped.

'In relation to the Irish property there is a—'

'Stop; what are you talking about?' Katie said. She pulled up a chair to the attorney's desk and sat down. Her head was thumping and her stomach was queasy.

'Wake up, darling, Harry Flint conned both of us,' Maggie screeched.

She turned to the attorney: 'Full marks to your Mr Flint, he continues to ruin my life even when he's dead. What's with the Irish angle?'

'Ms Flint, please let me continue.'

Katie reached out to Maggie, who pulled fiercely away then slumped on her chair; her hands on her lap; her fingers bunched into fists.

'Go on, hit us; what does it matter? He's left me saddled with so many loans no one knew he had taken out against our homes and also in my name. Our apartments are being sold off. The consultancy firm died with him – and who would give me work now? I'm just a stupid woman who didn't know the crap her ex-husband was pulling. I'm the silly copywriter who thought Harry was taking care of business. To think I was so proud my name was on the company documents and I was a co-signatory. He cheated me out of my future,' Maggie said, her voice fading in defeat.

'Let the attorney finish, please,' Katie said.

'What's he going to tell us, that there's millions at the end of the rainbow in Ireland, just for us?'

Maggie shuffled in her chair, crossing and recrossing her legs. The attorney shunted aside the file containing the will and gazed directly at both women.

'When Mr Flint made this will, he of course intended the property portfolio would be much bigger. However, there is the house and estate in Ireland.'

'Harry never said anything about a property in Ireland,' Katie said.

She suddenly felt foolish and angry that she had never been told about this place.

'He was very clear in his instructions,' the attorney replied, his voice clipped.

Maggie made to say something, but he put his hand up to stop her, and began to read from the will:

'Kilcashel House is very dear to me. There is a magic there; it is my special place. I bequeath this house and the estate, including the gate lodge, to my partner Katie Williams and my ex-wife Maggie Flint. They are each to have a fifty per cent stake in the property.

However, to inherit they must live in Kilcashel for a duration no shorter than ten months, starting in spring, and residing there at the same time.'

Maggie jumped up.

'Is this a joke, a sick joke?'

The attorney rapped on the desk with his pen. 'Ms Flint, you have to stop interrupting.'

'Wait,' Katie sat up and eyeballed the attorney. 'We have to go live there... together?'

'Yes, it's stipulated in the will, and it is the only way either of you will inherit.' The attorney spun his pen between his fingers as he continued: 'We spoke about this. Harry considered the purchase of Kilcashel House and its renovation and restoration to be the most important thing he would ever do in his life.'

'OK, but why all the way over there?' Maggie said.

'He felt a connection to the place. He said his ancestry was Irish and he wanted to move there eventually; become somebody in the community.'

'He was Boston through and through,' Maggie said, her voice full of indignation.

'His grandparents, I think, were Irish,' Katie said.

'Who the hell cares! So are mine, but I never knew them. And you have Irish in you too. Doesn't half of Brooklyn?' she said. Maggie put her hands across her face and dragged them down her cheeks. 'Good old Harry, he never said anything to us about this place and now he wants to interfere in our lives from the grave.'

'Do we have to do this?' Katie asked quietly.

The attorney pinched his shirt cuffs to straighten them.

'If you want to be the new owners of the house and estate, then yes, it is what you must do. He has added another codicil.'

'What does he want from us, to start a Harry Flint commune over there?' Maggie said, rolling her eyes to the ceiling.

'Not quite. You are free to do what you want in Ireland as long as you live at Kilcashel House for ten months and at the same time. However, Mr Flint does continue:

'"If I die in the springtime, I want them to leave straight

away so they can enjoy the best of Kilcashel. The house is so special, it should only end up with the person who wants to live there full-time through all four seasons. Maggie and Katie will need to be in Kilcashel together to decide what happens next. The person who can stay the course inherits Kilcashel House. And if they both do, I would ask they take some time before selling up."'

'The arrogance of him! And what bullshit. Who does he think he is, dictating to us?' Maggie shouted.

'Ms Flint, you're going to have to keep your opinions to yourself. Please let me finish,' the attorney said.

'Pardon me, this may just be an appointment on your schedule today, but for us this is huge; it's about our lives,' Katie said.

The attorney stared from under his eyes at the two women and continued to read from the will.

'"If I die in autumn or winter, they have to take up residence by the following spring."'

Katie looked around the room. A dingy fluorescent strip light buzzed, the walls were painted a dull coffee colour.

'When did Harry make this will, and why would he want us to go so far away – and why together?' she asked.

'Please, let me finish. I think he wanted to make sure the Irish estate is in good hands. I only know he wished for you to experience all four seasons there, so as to come to an informed decision,' the attorney said. Dipping his head, he continued to read:

'"After the ten months, both will be free to make their own arrangements in relation to the property as they will be the owners. If only one person decides to take up the challenge of living in the house for ten months, then that person will automatically be the sole owner."'

The attorney looked directly at Katie and Maggie.

'The very sad thing about all this is that Mr Flint only

purchased the property less than a year ago. The will was made quite recently. Nobody expected the tragedy that happened.'

Maggie leaned across the desk.

'How much is this place worth?'

'I would imagine millions, possibly two million or more.'

Maggie kicked back her chair as she stood up.

'This piece of shit property in a small country is the bloody reason I have lost the life I know in New York; that's what you are really saying, isn't it? That's why Harry borrowed all that damn money. That bloody place is why we are in all this trouble.'

'Ms Flint, I am merely conveying the last wishes of my client.'

'And he expects, having made me jobless and practically homeless, to uproot my whole life to live in a hovel.'

'You don't have to, Ms Flint, but if you don't, you will not inherit half of the property. This is no hovel. I very much doubt Mr Flint expected it to be such a problem and the only large asset which he left in his will.'

'Or he's laughing his socks off at us from the grave,' Maggie said before storming out of the office and down the stairs.

Katie scooped up Maggie's handbag, which was still on the floor.

'Aren't you supposed to give us the address, and some details of the property?'

The attorney handed over a small card with the name Kilcashel House, Bohilla Lane, Kilcashel, Co Wicklow, Ireland printed on it. She flipped the card and read: *Brendan Devlin Solicitors, Kilcashel, Co Wicklow for all your legal needs.*

'I have liaised with the attorney in Ireland. He is holding the keys to Kilcashel House for you. He will also be reporting back to me in relation to the occupancy of the house and estate.'

Katie slipped the card into her pocket.

'Spying on us, you mean.'

'Ms Williams, that is not correct, but the conditions of the will are very important, and we cannot have a situation where either of you think it is OK not to live at Kilcashel House.'

'Is that it? Can I go?'

'Yes. Contact me once you have completed the ten months and we can finalise the paperwork.'

Scrunching Maggie's bag under her arm, Katie got up. She was halfway out the door when she turned back to the attorney.

'Do you know why Harry did this?'

The attorney stretched his long arms and got up from his chair.

'I don't know. He must have had his reasons – maybe it was the pull of his ancestors – but he didn't discuss that with me and I never pressed him on it.'

He held the door open for Katie.

'Good luck over there,' he said as she made for the elevator.

Easy for you to say, Katie thought, making her way to the street.

TWO

TWO WEEKS LATER

Kilcashel, Co Wicklow

It was a cold, bright morning. Katie slowed down and pulled her car in close to the ditch; the tree branches scraping along the side. She didn't want to make a fuss by driving up the avenue, but she wanted a glimpse of Kilcashel House before collecting the keys. Walking along the road, she craned her neck for a glimpse of the house, but could only see fields with a scattering of daffodils as if somebody had thrown a lot of bulbs in the air, and planted them where they landed. A blackbird sounded a warning call and broke out of the briars, darting in front of her. A cat sitting on a stone wall opposite remained tucked up, watching her. Katie quickened her pace, the eyes of the cat tracking her as she made her way to the high, wrought-iron gate. It was padlocked.

Faded, dirty leaves and discarded sweet wrappers were caught in the thick mud around the bottom of the gate. Spent pink petals from the nearby cherry blossom trees had heaped up in one corner, where a strong squall of wind had deposited them. Katie pushed against one side of the gate, but it didn't budge. She nudged it with her knee; nothing.

The place was still. A butterfly fluttered over her shoulder, flitting over the top of the gate. Katie wanted to follow as she saw it weave up the avenue, which was overgrown with grass and speckled with yellow dandelions.

In the distance, she heard a dog bark before she saw a golden Labrador, its tail wagging, bolt across the field towards her and throw itself at the gate. Barking and whining, its tail repeatedly batted the padlock, making it clang.

Katie took a step back. A woman scurried after the dog. When she got as far as the gate, Katie could see she was out of breath; her headscarf had glided down the back of her head.

'What can I do for you? This is private property,' the woman said stiffly as she hissed at the dog to quieten down. A tall woman with a long nose, Katie thought it gave her a haughty look. The woman pushed her long grey hair back behind her ears, tightened the belt on her cream trench coat and stood waiting for Katie to speak.

'Is this Kilcashel House?' Katie asked quietly.

The woman sighed loudly. 'Yes, Kilcashel House and gate lodge.'

'How do I get in?'

'You don't. Like I said, it's private property and no, it's not for sale.'

'I just wanted to walk up the avenue and look at the old place.'

The woman straightened her headscarf.

'You and one thousand others; if I got a euro for every time I was asked that, I would be a rich woman,' she said as she turned towards the cherry blossom trees, sharply calling the dog to follow.

'But I've come a long way,' Katie said feebly.

The woman swung around. 'Nothing I haven't heard

before. Now get along, before we have a falling out,' she said, her voice kind, but firm.

It was only then that Katie noticed the gate lodge tucked in behind the cloud of cherry blossom flowers. A small quaint house with tiny windows at the front; it was run-down looking, but Katie thought that gave it an air of mystery. The cat, its tail up, ran across the road and slid between the rungs of the gate, creeping under the blossom to settle down on a front windowsill.

Katie felt so alone. Had she been crazy to come all this way on a whim? The incredulous voices of her friends when she told them she was leaving New York repeated over and over in her head. Grief plucked at her heart as she turned away from the gates of Kilcashel House. A huge part of her wanted to bolt; head for home, except she didn't have a home; not anymore. There was nothing left for her in New York. She walked briskly to her car and got in. Her phone rang, but she ignored it. She couldn't face another call from Maggie, hissing her complaints down the line.

Maybe she was crazy to have left the comfort of the familiar in the big city. Gripping the wheel, Katie shut her eyes tight, willing the flashbacks to disappear. Breathing deeply in through her nose, she counted one gunshot, two gunshots, and the third gunshot. Tears engulfed her as she imagined Harry's pain and a lonely death. Her phone rang again.

This time, she answered it in the hope of diverting away from the awfulness playing over and over in her head.

'Ms Williams, it's the office of Brendan Devlin solicitor here. Can you tell us if you are collecting the keys to Kilcashel House today?'

Katie straightened in her seat.

'I'm on the way; I should get to you shortly,' she said, her voice deliberately flat as she attempted to hide her upset. She had no idea what she was doing here, only that Harry was dead and she had nowhere else to be. She was nervous of being constantly around Maggie; she was almost afraid of her, especially since she had taken over the running of their lives since Harry died. Katie remembered back to that day after the reading of the will as she left the attorney's Manhattan office, and she shivered.

Maggie, her long black hair loose around her shoulders, was standing on the pavement, dragging on a cigarette.

'Did you pick up my bag?' she asked urgently.

Katie handed it to her.

Maggie quickly looked around her in case anyone was watching, stubbed out the cigarette with her fingers and pushed the butt into a bed of purple crocus under a tree on the sidewalk. Rifling in her bag, she pulled out her own brand and lit up, inhaling deeply.

'I had to ask a random person on the street for a cigarette. This dude stopped; it could have been weed; I didn't care.'

'It wasn't marijuana, it didn't smell like it,' Katie muttered.

Maggie sniggered.

'And how would you know that?'

Katie's face reddened, making Maggie laugh out loud.

'Come on, goody two shoes; if we don't laugh, we will bloody well weep for the whole of the United States.'

'What are we going to do? Katie asked.

'Go for a bloody drink, that's what.'

'It's only lunchtime.'

'So? I know a place.'

She tottered down the street on her high heels. Katie followed a few paces behind.

The hotel looked dingy from the outside, but Maggie didn't

falter, nodding at the doorman and passing into the hotel lobby and veering left to the resident's lounge. Sitting on a stool, she ordered a bourbon on the rocks. 'Get the same for my friend,' she snapped.

'Hey no, it's too early for me.'

'After that news? Come on, if we have to live together, there has to be some give.'

'Are you going to do it?' Katie asked.

'And you're not? I am not going to miss out on an inheritance for the sake of a few months. Thanks to Harry, I have nothing left here in New York except a few bars who won't turn me away.'

'Why did Harry do it?'

'Because he always wanted control. You lived with him for six years, you surely know that.'

Katie gave no answer, and nervously sat down.

Maggie raised her glass. 'To the next ten months, may they pass quickly,' she said, and they clinked glasses like two old friends who were used to sorting out the troubles of life at a hotel bar.

Maggie gulped her whiskey and nudged Katie with her elbow.

'Keep up, girl; drink it down.'

Katie took a sip, but the ice hit her teeth causing a mini brain freeze.

'You're taking this way too calmly,' Maggie said as she called for another round of shots.

'I wouldn't call this calm. I'm so angry, I can hardly talk,' Katie said, knocking back her shot so fast, she spluttered and coughed.

'Good for you,' Maggie said, gesturing to the barman for another two shots. 'This house better not be haunted. When do we have to go?'

Katie opened an email from the attorney. 'He's set a date for when we must take up occupancy: April first.'

'You're kidding, right?'

'No, that's what it says,' Katie said, pushing her phone across to Maggie.

'April Fool's Day! Harry would love this.'

'It's two weeks away. I can be there for then.'

'Of course, you can. I must pack up two apartments and sell off everything. My whole life is going to have to be packed into just a few suitcases. I'm going to need more time.'

Katie knocked back another whiskey. 'You're not the only one with problems. I was planning on opening my own business, a café with homemade cookies and bagels. That's gone now.'

'So, transfer the idea to Ireland. You're lucky; I have nothing except an option to spend idle months in some godforsaken place with you – no offence.'

'None taken,' Katie said, raising her glass again.

They clinked glasses and and fell silent, each wrapped in her own thoughts.

Katie shook away the memories and started up the car engine. She had to look forward, not back, she thought as she drove down the narrow road towards the small town of Kilcashel reciting 'left, left' over in her head. When a tractor trundled into view she braked, thinking she was on the wrong side of the road. The farmer waved to her and slowly inched past the car.

After a mile she reached the town and was on the main street almost immediately. Parking her car, she walked to the solicitor's office.

She was shown directly into Brendan Devlin's office, a large room with bookcases filled with files and a circular table in the middle of the floor which was used as a desk.

'Please take a seat; Mr Devlin won't be long,' the assistant said, closing the door behind her.

Feeling nervous, Katie walked to the window overlooking the lane, which was used as a shortcut to the local secondary school.

Two boys held tight to the wall, bending over their cigarettes. A number of girls passing by giggled. Katie smiled, feeling envious of their carefree attitude.

She didn't hear the solicitor come into the room until he cleared his throat.

'Ms Williams, welcome to Ireland,' he said, extending his hand and encasing hers in a damp grip, before directing her to sit at the table.

'You are taking on a very big challenge at Kilcashel House, but at least after the ten months ye can get rid of it. It should earn a good few bucks when the Kilcashel land is eventually re-zoned for development.'

'Mr Devlin, we intend to live at Kilcashel House for the required time and it is our business what we do with it after that.' Katie stuck her hand across the desk. 'The keys, please. And when you have all the necessary legal papers relating to our ownership of the property ready, can you forward them to Kilcashel House?'

He scrabbled in the drawer and took out a bunch of keys.

'I'm afraid I don't know what's what. But just so you know, you're definitely stuck with Anna Walker in the gate lodge; she's not going to leave Kilcashel House without a fight.'

Katie pushed the keys into her pocket.

'Anna Walker?'

The solicitor guffawed out loud. 'Harry, your, your...' He stopped to clear his throat. 'Mr Flint never took my advice on the matter; when he bought the place, he allowed Mrs Walker to stay there.'

'I think I might have met her earlier. Harry knew her?'

'Not exactly, but he liked the old dear. She spun him a tale or two and he thought she was harmless. Anyone who has been on the wrong side of Anna Walker will know she is anything but that.'

'Is she still there?'

'Lives in the gate lodge.'

'Why did nobody tell us before now?'

The solicitor shrugged.

'It's not as if you can do anything about it,' he said, leaning back in his chair, making it squeak.

Katie got up to leave.

'Don't take any guff from Anna; be firm from the off,' the solicitor said as she stepped out into the corridor.

Half an hour later, Katie pulled her car up in front of the gates of Kilcashel House. She didn't get out; she couldn't move. She could drive away, forget about this place, but that would only bring a temporary respite. Was she mad to think she could live here with Harry's ex-wife? Why did he have to do this to her? Anger surged through her; it wasn't as if he didn't know what Maggie was like. When she first hooked up with Harry, Maggie pulled her aside and told her to get out while she could. Katie had not liked her since that day, never tried to know her better though they had death-bonded in the days after Harry's murder. Anyway, Katie knew she had no choice but to come to Kilcashel House; she had nothing left in Manhattan. She just wasn't sure that it was a good enough reason for this move. Then again, she had to make a go of it here. If she didn't, regret would overwhelm and eat her away from the inside out.

She sat staring at the gates. The Labrador bounded from around the side of the house, snuffling around the weeds at the base of the gate, whining as she went.

Afraid the dog would alert its owner, Katie jumped from

the car, hoping if she spoke softly the Labrador wouldn't kick up a racket, barking.

Whispering soothing words to reassure the curious dog, she pulled out the bunch of keys, shuffling through them in the hope of figuring out which one to use for the padlock.

Excited, the Labrador joined her, its paws scratching across the gate as it watched her pull up the padlock to straighten it before trying the first key.

Pushing one key after another into the rusty lock, she cursed under her breath as the dog began to bark and growl excitedly as if it had suddenly dawned on it that she was trying to gain access. Prancing about, and alternating between howling and tail-wagging, the Labrador wasn't going to let Katie steal up to the big house undetected.

She was bent over trying the fourth key when a woman's voice punctured the barking.

'Be quiet, you stupid dog,' the woman with the scarf shouted out the open window.

The dog was howling when she came out the front door.

'You again! And this time you're intent on breaking in,' she said as Katie nervously stood back.

'I have keys,' she faltered. 'Do you know which key is for the padlock, please?'

'None of those. Those look like the big house keys.'

'I don't understand.'

The woman moved closer, pushing the dog out of the way.

'That makes two of us. Why on earth are you trying to get in here? And why do you have those keys? Is the place being put up for sale – or has it already been quietly sold off?'

Katie heard the sharpness in the woman's voice as she hid the bunch of keys back in her pocket.

'Not sold, not being put up for sale. I can come back another time, if you prefer.'

'You're American?'

'New York.'

The woman moved closer, her hand extended.

'Are you a friend of Harry's?'

Katie nodded, the tears rising to choke her voice.

The woman roughly pulled back the bolt in the gate. The old iron bars squeaked loudly as she tugged the gate fiercely, forcing a path through the mud until it was open wide enough for a person to slip through.

'Don't tell anyone, but the chain and padlock are only for show. Make it look difficult and you deter most of the day trippers.'

Katie's face crumpled as she tried to fight the tears. Turning away, she noticed the other woman continued to blather to cover the awkward moment.

'If I didn't put on some sort of show and make it hard to get in, I would have a constant stream of nosy parkers, particularly local people, since Harry bought the place.'

Katie smiled and crept through the gap.

'Was Harry a close friend?' the woman asked kindly.

Katie nodded.

The woman reached across and took her hand.

'I was so sorry to hear about his passing. He was a good and decent man. Not that I knew him very well, but he did right by me. I last heard from him the day he died; he said he had to meet me. I am Anna Walker; in case he ever mentioned me.'

Katie nodded, her fingers hurting under Anna's tight grip.

'Why did Harry have to meet you? Did he say?'

'No idea, but he said it was important. Would you like to see the house?'

Katie didn't have time to answer before Anna fiercely pushed the gate back into position and began walking up the avenue.

The Labrador ran on ahead as they moved at an easy pace

on what was once a gravel driveway, but was now covered in grass and dandelions.

They walked side by side, Katie dropping back a little to take in her surroundings. The fields came right up to the path's edge, where a wooden fence had been erected. The patchwork of daffodils was interspersed in places with yellow dandelions.

'It's so beautiful,' Katie whispered, and Anna stopped.

'Spring at Kilcashel is the best time of year. Poor Harry, he never made it back and I kept telling him, "Just hop on a plane and stay a few days."'

'Did you know Harry well?' Anna smiled. 'I was just getting to know him. He was only over at Kilcashel a few times, but our paths didn't cross. I was away a lot, helping a sick relative. We emailed a fair bit though.'

Katie shivered and they walked on a little faster to the bend in the avenue.

'Who was to know what was going to happen? I now wish I had met him; I considered him a friend. He loved Kilcashel House too, that I do know,' Anna said.

Rounding the pink azaleas and a tall rhododendron, yet to unfurl its buds, Katie gasped when she saw the house.

A high three-storey red-brick building with a sweep of granite steps to the front door, Kilcashel House may have once been imposing but now it looked worn and dilapidated. She could see that shutters were drawn across all the main windows. The window frames were painted a dark colour that stood out against the red-brick facade. Only the top floor was unshuttered, the window glass glinting in the faint sunshine.

A crow flew up and landed on the roof, carefully monitoring their approach.

Anna sighed loudly.

'Harry had such plans for this place. That dream is dead in the water.'

'Had he done work on the house?'

'The important things you don't see or appreciate at first glance. He sealed the place; rewired; patched the roof; gave it a new front door – an exact copy of what had once been here.'

That sounded like Harry, Katie thought: a stickler for detail. How could he have kept all this from her? He was serious about this place, yet he'd never so much as hinted about its existence or his plans. She squeezed the velvet box in her pocket tight as they walked on.

Katie swept her eyes across the facade, resting on the front door. It stood out, shining new and freshly painted white.

Pots of daffodils and tulips not yet in flower were clustered at the top of the steps, making it look as if somebody might be home.

'I don't like the old lady to look neglected, so I threw those pots there,' Anna said. She broke off to shout at the Labrador, who was furiously digging in the front flowerbed. 'My gladioli,' she explained, turning back to Katie. 'She saw me working on that bed a few days ago, and she has been mithering me ever since with the digging.'

Katie turned away. Tears were bursting through her. Staring across the fields, she wanted to scream Harry's name loud; call back his presence to comfort her.

Anna pretended not to notice, making exaggerated swipes at the dog to stop her tunnelling into the flower bed. After a few moments, she gently pressed Katie's arm.

'Do you like the view? Let me bring you around the back. The front is nothing in comparison. This is a slow-reveal house. Apologies for sounding like an estate agent,' she guffawed loudly, setting off around the side of the house.

Katie swiped away her tears as she rushed to catch up.

A narrow, worn path ran beside the long, shuttered side windows of what Katie figured was a drawing room or dining room. The path, which was covered in sea stones, wound under the canopy of the overgrown rhododendron, some blooms here already unfolding in shades of deep pink and white.

'I told Harry to cut down those rhododendrons, but he was having none of it,' Anna said, adding quickly that it was her job to keep an eye on the place.

Katie noticed a hesitancy in Anna's voice. 'He was here a few months ago, but only for a few hours. I am sorry now I didn't make more of an effort to meet up. He skipped over from London...'

If anything else was said, Katie didn't hear it. She remembered complaining because he'd gone silent and did not contact her. She'd given him such a hard time about it. Why couldn't he have told her about Kilcashel? Why keep it secret?

Katie stopped dead. They had stepped onto a wooden deck overlooking a flower garden which ran down to the sea.

'I had no idea,' she said, her voice hoarse with emotion.

'I think it's why Harry bought the estate. Pity he had no time to enjoy it.'

Anna broke off when she saw Katie's face change.

'He was something to you?' she asked gently.

Katie nodded as Anna led her to two old armchairs on the deck.

'I had these chairs put here; it seemed a pity to have this beautiful view and nowhere to sit and enjoy it.'

Katie sank into a chair. She didn't bother with the view but closed her eyes. She heard Anna mumble that she had a few things to do; she would be back in a while.

Katie settled into the softness of the armchair. The air was cool on her cheeks, the rhythmic sound of the sea loud in her ears. The waves thundered in and dragged back. The sound calmed her brain. This was not her home by choice, but it would do, Katie thought.

THREE

THREE WEEKS EARLIER

Manhattan, New York

Katie went to bed when Harry died. Friends left messages and came to the door with food care packages. She checked after midnight every night, and filled the fridge with lasagne and sliced pot roast on paper plates.

When she was feeling silly, she threw slices of roast beef at the front window overlooking the street, just to hear the thud as the meat hit the glass, before bouncing onto the floor, where she left it to turn into a grey, congealed mess.

Most people rang the bell and waited a polite length of time then turned away from the apartment door, no doubt relieved not to have to comfort the grieving partner. She didn't go to the funeral; she didn't want to see Harry in his coffin; she didn't want to be surrounded by well-wishers.

She was angry at Harry for dying, for taking the subway, for being the one who was shot to bits; for not walking away like everybody else, with a story to tell about how the city was on a fast track to the bad old days.

A week after the funeral, Katie woke up to the constant

buzz of the doorbell. She stuffed the pillow over her head to block out the noise, until the visitor shouted her name and pounded on the door.

'I know you're in there – open up, girl.'

Katie hid under the duvet for ten minutes, but the caller wouldn't give up.

She recognised Maggie's voice. Slowly, she got out of bed and opened the door a fraction with the security chain on.

'What do you want?'

'I have to talk to you.'

'No offence, but I don't want to talk to anyone.'

'I have something that Harry meant for you.'

Katie pulled back the bolts and opened the door a little more.

'You look like shit, girl, and why are there so many ready meals piled up in the hallway?' Maggie said as she shoved against the door. 'Release the chain; I'm coming in,' she snapped.

Katie unhooked the link and stared at the white food cartons.

'People keep thinking I need to eat more, I guess.'

'And what is the damn awful smell? This place stinks, like some sort of animal died,' Maggie said, waving her hands as if she could clear the air. 'Katie, I know it's tough, but you can't live like this.'

'I know.'

'You don't know – we are both screwed,' Maggie said.

'What do you mean?'

Maggie wiped away tears pushing from under her eyelids. 'Wonderful Harry emptied out the accounts then remortgaged this apartment. So now I have to sell it to pay back the bank. Without my knowledge, he did the same to our old place, so my home is taken from me too.'

'What?'

'A lot to take in, I know, but soon neither of us will have a place to live. And he somehow made sure I was a signatory to all this stuff I knew nothing about. Now, I owe millions of dollars.'

'I don't understand.'

'There's nothing to understand. The reading of the will is on Friday, and we have to be there.'

'Why?'

'God knows. What's left to give us, only bad news on bad news.' Maggie shook her head and turned towards the kitchen. 'I need coffee and so do you.'

'What am I going to do?' Katie asked.

'How the hell do I know?' Maggie said, her voice booming around the room as she popped a pod in the coffee machine. 'Go get dressed; then we can talk,' she barked.

Katie did as she was bid. There was something about Maggie that made her nervous and on edge. When she returned to the kitchen wearing a tracksuit, Maggie threw her eyes to the ceiling.

'Don't you have any real clothes?'

Katie shrugged and sat on the couch, her legs tucked under her. When a mug of coffee was handed to her, she knew her stomach was too sick to even take a sip, but she mumbled thank you.

Maggie sat down where Harry liked to sit and read the *New York Times* on a Sunday morning.

'I won't have anywhere to live if you sell the apartment,' Katie said.

'Join the club. Harry has screwed us over, plain and simple.'

'What are we going to do? I can't make any decisions right now.'

'And you think I can? At least you still have your job.'

Katie didn't say anything.

'Shit, what did you do?'

'I hated that job. I handed in my notice just before Harry—'

'What?'

'I was waiting to tell him. I had big plans to follow my dream...'

'Oh crap.'

'Yeah, it does not seem much of a dream now.'

'Looks like we have more than Harry in common. We're both nearly homeless and both jobless.'

'But you have a job.'

'No, because my ex-husband didn't leave a Plan B. With the debts he racked up, nobody is going to do business with the company now. Everyone thinks I was involved; I have to get out of New York.'

'I don't want to be here either, not now, without Harry.'

'I wish the son of a bitch could come back, just so I could give him a piece of my mind.'

'Telling off a dead man? That's dumb,' Katie said.

'I know,' Maggie said, her body shaking as she let giggles take over.

Katie joined in and they laughed and laughed, until Maggie leaned over so close to the floor, she spied a piece of dead meat.

'You're so disgusting, Katie. I wondered what the cringy smell was,' she screeched, and they both chuckled; their laughs momentarily masking the pain in their hearts.

Maggie reached into her handbag.

'You know they gave me all his personal effects – clothes, everything.'

Maggie placed a mug of coffee in front of Katie.

'Slurp some, you're going to need it,' she ordered.

Her voice softened as she continued: 'Among the crap Harry had in his pockets – and there was a lot: change, little notes with numbers scribbled, receipts – and this...'

She pulled a dark-green velvet box from her handbag and gently placed it on the coffee table in front of Katie.

'It didn't feel right, keeping it; we both know it was for you.'

Katie didn't move.

Maggie stood up and said she had to go, she had to collect a ham at Lobel's Butchers down the street.

'I refuse to give up on the little pleasures, not yet anyway,' she said, but Katie didn't reply.

Maggie hesitated at the apartment door.

'Katie, there's something else. It floored me and I wondered whether to tell you, but full disclosure is probably best.'

Katie stared at Maggie. 'Don't tell me the two of you were having an affair.'

'Good God, no! Harry had cancer.'

'What?'

'It got me in the gut too. The autopsy revealed it; he had stomach cancer.'

'He never told me,' Katie said.

Her head hurt and her vision was foggy. She heard Maggie walk across the floor and place an arm on her shoulder and squeeze it hard.

'He may not have known. Or maybe he did and just didn't know how to tell you.'

'It makes no sense,' Katie said.

Maggie sighed. 'It makes some sort of sense that he was trying to trace ancestors.'

'What do you mean?'

'The Irish connection; maybe the diagnosis made him want to delve into the past?'

Katie began to cry.

'Why has Harry left us like this?' she said.

'I don't know. Poor man didn't know he was going to lose his life on the day he planned to pop the question.'

Katie let the tears flow down her cheeks and closed her eyes tight.

'This is all too much,' she said.

'I know,' Maggie whispered.

Katie sat rigid on the couch, unable to speak; she could hardly think.

She knew Maggie stood by her for a while, but when she heard her steal from the apartment, Katie was glad. She didn't stir when she heard the door shut. The smell of the coffee made her nose twitch, but she still couldn't reach for the velvet box on the table. She kept her eyes on it as if it might disappear if she didn't stare at it continually. Her back hurt, but she didn't care.

If Harry knew he had cancer, he should have told her. And if he knew he had cancer, why was he proposing without telling her?

Darkness crept all around her. She knew she should get up and switch on a light, but if she did, she would have to open the box.

The lights from the streets and the apartment blocks around dipped into her space, creating designs across the floor, but still, she didn't move.

The sound of the street, the sirens and the traffic wafted up to her, pulling her slowly back to her own reality. When the night faded, and daylight began to stream through the window, she had her decision made. She needed to move away from the city where she had been so happy. Anywhere, as long as it was far away from New York.

Anna Walker urgently calling her name over and over broke Katie away from the past. For a moment, she thought she was still sitting in the dark, afraid to look in the ring box.

'I thought we had lost you. How come you're still here? I thought you would have wandered down to the sea,' Anna said, her voice grumpy.

'It seemed like a nice spot to stop and think.'

'That type of thinking won't do you much good, if it's the thinking you want to be doing in a windy, cold spot.'

Katie didn't say anything.

If Anna noticed she was upset, she didn't let on. 'Did you want to see the inside of the house?'

'Can I?'

Anna guffawed out loud. 'You hardly stole those keys. Are you going to tell me the real reason you're here?'

Katie shook her head as if she had been found out. When she spoke, Anna had to lean close to hear her.

'I am, along with my friend, the new owner of Kilcashel House.'

Anna gasped and jumped back.

'What? What are you talking about?'

'Harry left us the estate.'

Anna's face soured.

'Oh Lord. This is a bit fast.'

'I'm moving in.'

'When?'

'Now, today.'

Anna sat down beside Katie.

'What sort of madness is this?'

'Harry intended us to live here eventually, I'm sure of that. Well, here I am.'

'But you haven't even viewed the property.'

'Harry wanted me to come here; that's enough for me. I have to believe everything else will work out.'

'You're not selling up?'

'I know everybody expects that, but I want to live here.'

'But, darling, you don't know anyone in the country, never mind Kilcashel.'

'I know you,' Katie stammered as she set off towards the house.

Anna scooted ahead to block Katie's way.

'That house is bloody cold, it needs to be aired out. For

feck's sake, you need beds, mattresses; there's none of that stuff in there. It hasn't been lived in for quite a while.'

'I can get a sleeping bag.'

'Don't talk daft, girl. Harry had a lot of work done on the house, but there's no heat from any living there. That takes time to build up.'

Katie didn't answer but made to push past.

Anna touched her arm and spoke softly. 'Let me air out the house and get a proper bed and mattress, at least. The place needs to be freshened up. Just give me a few days.'

'I don't have a few days; I want to stay here tonight.'

Anna looked oddly at her.

'Take it easy. If it means that much, we'll have to make do, since you're so determined,' Anna said as they walked beside each other on the wide path past the bank of white and pink camellia to the front of the house. At the bottom of the granite steps, Anna pulled back.

'Do you want me to skedaddle and leave you to it?' she asked quietly.

'I don't think I can do it on my own,' Katie said, her voice shaking.

'The impossible can always be made possible,' Anna said, and climbed the granite steps.

At the top, she turned to Katie and smiled.

'I usually enter through the back door – much more convenient – but since this is your first time, you might as well have the grand tour,' she said.

Katie tentatively stepped into the tiled hall. Painted a deep grey with a number of wooden doors leading off, it looked almost forbidding, she thought. Anna switched on the light.

'It's nice when the chandelier lights up the place. The one bulb contraption that used to be there didn't throw out much, making the hallway too dark for my liking.'

Katie peeped into the front drawing-room. It was bare

except for a leather couch on the polished oak floor and a marble fireplace at one end of the room. The walls were painted a soft teal, the curtains a deeper shade of the same colour. The silk drapes were ruched and bunched, partially blocking the view of the fields beyond and the camellia walk to the gazebo.

Katie slowly paced the room as if, by treading the boards, she would somehow get answers to the questions in her head. Anna hung back.

'Do you know why Harry bought this house?' Katie asked after a few moments.

Anna shifted from one foot to the other.

'I thought you could answer that. He didn't reveal his inner thoughts to me,' she said, beckoning Katie to follow her to the kitchen.

Katie expected to see a traditional farmhouse wooden kitchen.

'Maybe you can tell me why this room looks like it should be on a spaceship,' Anna said.

Katie walked across to the industrial ovens, the special units for baking multiple trays of pastries or biscuits. Everything in this huge kitchen was shiny, even the worktops, which were large sheets of stainless steel. The double sink was industrial in size, the tap like a powerful hose.

Stroking the stainless steel, her hand tingled, but she felt cold in her heart.

'I never did understand why Harry insisted on such a big kitchen; it cost a fortune,' Anna said.

Katie pulled at an oven door. It was stiff as if just out of the showroom. She placed her hand inside, touching the floor of the oven. Tears pushed through her. Trying to compose herself, she slammed the oven door shut, leaning on the handle.

'Harry was important to you?' Anna asked.

Katie nodded, but she could not get the words out.

Anna put her arm around Katie's shoulders. 'Plenty of time for talking; you don't need to say anything right now.'

'You think I'm nuts.'

'Maybe, but what do I know?'

'He was my partner for six years.'

'Oh hell, I'm so sorry, why didn't you say earlier?'

Katie shook her head. 'It's hard making those sorts of introductions; hard to listen to the sympathy. It's all too soon.'

'I understand. But how come you've moved to Kilcashel?'

Katie smiled.

'There was nowhere else to go, it's as simple and as complicated as that. Will you stay on and help me?'

'Of course, but help you with what?'

'I'm going to have to make a living, if I want to keep this house.'

Anna groaned.

'Darling, the only way you will make a living here is to sell the place. And I can't say I want you to do that.'

Katie stepped into the tiny lean-to conservatory and sank into a squishy couch. From here, she could see across the gardens and out to sea, where a cargo ship was tracking across the horizon. Loneliness streaked through her.

Anna turned back to the kitchen, not sure what to do. Katie heard the whoosh of the kettle on the boil. A few minutes later, Anna arrived with hot sweet tea.

'You look like a no-milk person. Am I right?'

Katie nodded.

'Thank God; there was only the few teabags and sugar left over from when the builders were here.'

Katie sipped the tea and grimaced.

It was sickly sweet, but it was also strangely comforting.

'You think the grief is making me talk silly?' Katie asked quietly.

Anna took her hand and pressed it lightly.

'Grief always makes us talk silly, but sometimes we have to follow the gut and see where it takes us. Give yourself plenty of time.'

'I suppose.'

'Let me show you upstairs. It's just a whole load of empty rooms. Harry hadn't got around to having much done up there after he cleared out the place. He didn't like the old, big, heavy wardrobes and beds; said they gave him the spooks.'

Anna's face reddened because she knew she was babbling and she was afraid she may have caused offence.

Katie smiled and followed her up the oak staircase to the first return.

'This is the only modern en suite room; he had the good sense when the plumber was in to have it plumbed. There's also a free-standing bath in the bedroom.'

Anna walked across the room to the big window, which looked out over the front gardens.

'A bath with a view, if you like that sort of thing. Me, I would be afraid that anybody snooping about down in the road might see me in my nip,' Anna said.

'Pardon me?'

'Nothing. He planned to have a dividing wall here, between the windows, so he'd have a bathroom filled with light. Waste of a perfectly good view, if you ask me.'

'I prefer the view to the sea,' Katie said, crossing the landing to a much smaller room overlooking the back gardens and down to the sea.

'I always liked this one. I remember, when I was young, if you were up here you could hear anybody arriving to the house, because everybody and his uncle came to the back door,' Anna said, stepping into the room.

Katie swung around.

'You knew the house years ago?'

Anna looked flustered.

'When I was a child,' she said, as she made her way back out to the landing. 'There are two more bedrooms on this floor, and more on the floor above. And then there's the old servants' quarters in the eaves which has been used as a storage space. You'll hardly be interested in seeing that.'

'Did Harry clear it out?'

'No, he was moving up the house, floor by floor. He stopped last month, gave the builders notice and said he would call them when he had his finances sorted.'

Katie shivered.

Anna tapped her on the shoulder.

'Maybe we could leave the rest for another time. All this is probably a lot to take in. The house is secure, the roof and all the necessary things are tip-top; the rest can wait.'

Gently, she led the way downstairs.

'Why did Harry go for such a modern look?' Katie asked.

'He didn't spare any expense; he got an interior designer from near Dublin to advise on the decor. He had all the furniture that was here taken out,' Anna said, looking around her and shuddering. 'At least they never got as far as the bedrooms – that interior designer was talking about fur eiderdowns.'

She suddenly stopped. 'I shouldn't be gabbing on about things I don't know. I would never get full marks for my sensitivity; plenty of people will tell you that.'

'It's OK; don't worry about it.'

Katie walked back to the kitchen. It was her favourite room in the whole house. The light was streaming in the window. A wagtail on the windowsill was startled but defiantly remained standing and listening before flying off into the cover of the rhododendron.

She missed her New York morning. She should be dropping in at Bagel Boss for a plain bagel with cinnamon cream cheese and freshly squeezed orange, en route to her own downtown kitchen. She wanted to feel the sound of the city, the buses whooshing past, the sirens, the snatches of conversation as people talked on their phones, the pounding of the pavement and the sound of hurrying footsteps and business about to be done. There was none of that here. Loneliness coursed through her, chasing the fear through her veins, making beads of perspiration form between her shoulder blades and on her temples.

'Don't worry, we will find somewhere you can stay for a few nights, until we get the house aired out and a bed set up for you,' Anna said.

Katie turned on the sink tap, letting her fingers cool under the pummel of water, then dabbing some on the back of her neck.

'Let's go. I think you have done enough for one day,' Anna said kindly.

'I will stay somewhere else, but just for tonight. I want to move in here as quickly as possible,' Katie said as Anna steered her down the hall to the front door.

Katie stopped to look into the drawing room.

She knew Harry had not picked any of the pieces.

'I think the interior designer forgot she was doing up a period property and not a New York loft apartment,' Katie said sharply, and Anna laughed.

'She was trying to impress Harry. And he lost the run of himself, plain and simple – though this interior design is neither,' Anna said.

They walked down the driveway together, each lost in her own thoughts until they reached the gatehouse.

'I only have the one bedroom operational at the moment, but I can ring Triona McCarthy in town. She has a guesthouse and she can put you up.'

Anna beckoned at Katie to follow her, and they walked around to the back door, which led into a big kitchen with light blue units and a wooden countertop.

'I got Harry to do up the kitchen for me, He was a darling,

said it was no bother, that it was an investment in the future,'
she said as she switched on the kettle.

'The solicitor mentioned you have a special arrangement to
live in the house...'

'Until I pass on. Harry was a good man. People don't understand why he did that, but it's none of their business. Don't be
believing everything you hear about me in the town; I am a good
neighbour,' she said, and Katie noticed Anna stiffen as if she
was ready for a row.

When Anna spoke next, her voice was just a little bit
stronger.

'Harry and I understood each other; nobody needed to
know more than that.'

Katie waited for a longer explanation but there was none as
Anna fussed with her mobile phone and dialled Triona
McCarthy, wandering into the hall as she talked.

When she came back, Anna looked flustered.

'Unfortunately, Triona has a group of hillwalkers in tonight
and tomorrow, and does not have space, but she is driving down
with a single fold-up bed, and I was thinking you could have the
front sitting room for a few days.'

'I'm sure there is a hotel nearby—'

'And what would that look like? You're not staying
anywhere else,' Anna said firmly.

FOUR

Katie couldn't sleep. Her back hurt and Anna's house was too quiet. She shut her eyes, but the silence crept around her, taunting her, whispering in the shadows and the corners that she had made a mistake. The word mistake repeated over and over in her head. When her phone rang; she jumped on it because she didn't want to wake Anna.

'Tell me, does it stink?' Maggie said.

'You do realise it's five in the morning here.'

'Shit, you needn't have answered, but tell me.'

Katie dipped under the duvet to muffle the sound.

'The house is beautiful, big and old.'

'And you think that's going to make me feel better? Send me pictures.'

'There is a lot of land and Anna lives in the gate lodge, and she is pretty great.'

'I hope she pays rent.'

'Not exactly. She and Harry had a legal arrangement.'

Maggie groaned loudly. 'What was Harry doing in Ireland anyway; why not buy in Montana or even Minnesota?'

'You will fall in love with it. You just need to get over here.'

'I know, I know, I fly over in a few days. Maybe I can stay a while and nobody will notice if I slip back to the States. You won't tell on me, will you?'

'I guess not.'

Katie smiled. Maggie was so loud, everybody noticed when she wasn't around.

'Send me photos, lots of photos. I've been approached to write a one-off article for a magazine. It could mean I have some bucks to start me off in that old dump.'

'Not a dump, it's a pretty fine house.'

'If you say so. Send me your best shots of the outside.'

'I don't want everybody coming looking for us.'

'You are overestimating my power as a writer or the reach of the publication,' Maggie chortled heartily. 'Just send the pics,' she snapped as if she were talking to a member of her staff.

After the call, Katie couldn't get back to sleep. Dawn was breaking, light spilling into the room through the net curtains. Easing herself slowly out of the camp bed, she gingerly opened the sitting room door, and stepped into the kitchen.

The Labrador sat up, wagging its tail, and began to circle around Katie with excitement. When she sat at the kitchen table, it came over and brushed against her, nudging her and looking at the door. When she tried to ignore it, the dog sat at the back door, alternating between sighing and whining. Not entirely sure what to do, Katie slowly opened the back door. The dog pushed past her in a flash, scooting off around the house and under the cherry blossom trees. Unsure, Katie stood in the doorway waiting and worrying if she had done the wrong thing.

She listened intently until she could hear the dog snuffling about. Tiptoeing to the side of the house, she watched the dog's bulky frame throwing up old petals as it checked the garden perimeter.

A bird sounded a throaty call, designed to wake up the rest. Katie stood and listened as, one by one, other birds joined in, some chirping, some showing off, others briefly adding their song notes to the chorus before fading away. She reached into her pocket and ran her fingers along the velvet ring box. She wasn't able to wear the engagement ring Harry intended for her, but she liked to have it near.

The dog scooted back, but when it saw Katie it ran off again, this time heading to the front paddock.

Worried she had scared it away, she followed it out on to the avenue.

The Labrador Anna called Lola stood as if waiting for her. Gingerly, she approached it, gently calling its name, but it continued up the driveway to Kilcashel House.

Pulling the fleece dressing gown Anna had lent her the previous night tight around her, Katie slowly followed. She made sure to walk on the grassy middle line, because the slippers Anna had loaned her had such thin soles.

She called Lola's name, wanting her to stay close, but the Labrador ignored her, pushing on to the main house. The dew on the grass seeped into her slippers and she wondered would Anna get cross about that. The dog became excited and started barking as they approached the rhododendron bend. Katie felt nervous. She stopped, wondering for the first time if it was wise to be out so early on her own. Two pheasants, noisy and flustered, half walked, half flew across the path then disappeared under the dark green rhododendron canopy, with Lola in excited pursuit.

Katie, her heart pounding, laughed out loud, the sound making the starlings lining up on an old clothes line regroup and fly away in a collective swoop towards the house roof.

Feeling a little foolish, she strolled on. Kilcashel House

stood silent, immersed in a cacophony of birdsong. The first bright rays of sunshine streaked gold across the top windows.

The drawing room, where Anna had the day before opened the shutters, was also lit up by the morning sunlight. Katie wished she had her keys, so she could go in and pull back all the other shutters in the house.

The dog scooted around the back as if it knew where it was going. Katie hesitated, feeling she was in some way intruding.

She was about to turn back down the avenue when she heard somebody calling her.

'Excuse me, you will need to bring the dog home or Anna will go mad.'

The woman, who was wearing a black dryrobe with a bright pink lining, had a rolled-up towel in one hand and the Labrador's collar gripped in the other. Her curly brown hair was falling across her face as she struggled to hold the dog.

'I'm sorry but it wouldn't come back when I called.'

The woman walked towards Katie, her hand still on the dog's collar.

'My friend and I go swimming in the sea at dawn and the dog has a tendency to nose around our clothes. Once it ran off with our sandwiches. We like to have a flask of coffee and a snack when we get out.'

'Nice.'

'Are you staying with Anna?'

'Just for now.'

'If you like to swim, you should join us some morning. We swim and maybe gossip.'

'Thanks, but I don't think I could face the water at this time of year – too cold.'

'Are you visiting from America?'

'Yes, Anna is letting me stay with her.'

'Good. Well, think about the swim; it's a great start to the day. We might even be able to rustle up a wetsuit for you. Just don't bring the dog.'

She handed over Lola to Katie.

'Drag her down to the bend and she will run home from there. She knows the drill. I think she does it on purpose, so she has a bit of company in the morning. She knows what time we're here and starts whining to get out for a widdle.' She laughed and stuck out her hand. 'I'm Nora.'

'Katie, Katie Williams.'

'Will you be staying long?'

'I'm moving here.'

'Oh lovely. We have a few ladies from the village come out every morning – you can join us for afters, even if you're not swimming. They have to park at mine and tramp across the fields, because the American that owns this place has made it very clear he doesn't want strangers near his fine home. Little does he know we like to have tea in the garden gazebo after our morning dip.'

'Why object to a few women parking and going for a swim?'

'Some legal nonsense and – no offence – very American. Said he didn't want a right of way being established over the years, and then everybody would use the avenue for easy access to the nicest beach on the coastline, which he insists is strictly private.'

She emphasised the last two words and threw her eyes upwards.

'Is it a private beach?'

'It is for us – the guy has never stayed here, only got the place done up right smart. You know he got my Tony to take away all the old furniture that has been in Kilcashel House for yonks and said he wanted to sell it. Up until last month, he mithered Tony rotten, asking if anything had sold.'

She leaned closer to Katie.

'Eeejit wants to set up a fancy pants hotel and restaurant –

in Kilcashel, of all places! He was into his modern furniture. We weren't going to throw out the history of Kilcashel House just because one fool of a man wanted to get rid of it. Our American didn't know the old furniture was never put on the market. It's stored in the old stables down off the second paddock.'

The dog yanked fiercely, and Katie said she had to go.

'If you can, call up to the gazebo in about an hour for a cuppa,' Nora said as she set off down the garden path to the sea.

Katie said she would try as the dog dragged her away.

When Katie got back to the gate lodge, Anna was up and making tea.

'I thought you went swimming.'

'I had to come back with Lola, but I thought of re-joining Nora and the other women. Introduce myself properly.'

'You know Harry had no time for them.'

'I don't see what the problem was.'

'Because around here, if you give an inch, they take a mile. Those ladies, I think, have already taken two miles.'

'Nora seemed very nice, and I would prefer to get off on the right foot.'

'Go on then, but don't say I didn't warn you.'

Katie quickly got dressed and tidied up her camp bed, then made her way down to the sea. There was one woman in the water and one about to get in.

'Will you join us for a quick dip? It's freezing at first, but it's just about bearable after that.' The woman was pummelling the water with her feet as she plaited her blonde hair.

'I don't have a swimsuit, so I might paddle instead. I'm Katie, by the way.'

'Leonie. You've met Nora, that's her in the water.'

'We won't be long. The water is bloody freezing this morning,' Nora shouted.

Leonie ran into the waves, squealing at the top of her voice.

Katie kicked off her shoes and socks and moved across the wet sand, the cold seeping up through the soles of her feet. Slowly, she stepped out into the water, but almost immediately bolted back to dry sand.

The cold was both painful and exhilarating.

'You just need to dive in, get the blood racing. If you stop to think, it will be worse,' Leonie said.

Katie shook her head. 'Maybe another day.'

'You don't have to be mad to do this, but I suppose it helps,' Nora said, sprinting from the water.

Pulling on a towelling robe, she called out to Leonie, telling her to follow them to the gazebo.

'There's coffee, and Leonie made choc-chip biscuits, if you're interested? Leonie loves baking biscuits for our after-swim cuppa.'

Katie nodded and fell into step beside her as they made their way to Kilcashel House.

'We always scoot up the side by the camellia bushes, so we can't really be seen from the deck. Anna reports back on everything to the American; the less she sees, the better.'

They pushed past the big ferns sprawling across the path and the crocosmia plants, not yet in flower.

At the gazebo, Nora threw a rug on the wooden seat and took a picnic basket from under the table.

'Just in case Anna tries to intercept us en route, we don't want to show our hand. Tea or coffee?' she asked, pulling out two flasks.

'Coffee, please.'

'Thought so; you're not known to be great tea drinkers.'

'Maybe not,' Katie said as Leonie came up the path.

They poured out tea and coffee and grabbed some biscuits.

Katie sat for a moment, enjoying the chatter.

'So how come you're here. Are you on holiday with Anna? OMG! Are you related?' Leonie asked.

'No, not related.' Katie put down her coffee mug on the rickety wooden table. 'But I do have a connection to Kilcashel House.'

'Oh shit, you're the wife or the sister or the significant other,' Nora said.

The women sat down on the blanket and stared at Katie.

She cleared her throat, not sure what to say. Tears pricked at her eyes, and she suddenly felt vulnerable and foolish.

'We have put our size nines in it, haven't we?' Nora said.

Katie wiped away a tear.

'Not really, it's just, Harry, who owned this place is dead and—'

'Oh, hell no! And we were saying terrible things about him – please forgive us. We certainly didn't mean for anything bad to happen to him,' Nora said.

Katie's shoulders slumped. 'It was very sudden. He was shot.'

'Christ, no,' Nora said, grabbing her into a big hug.

'Yeah, forget everything we said; we didn't really know him; we never even knew his name.'

'So what will happen to Kilcashel?' Leonie asked, oblivious to Nora signalling in an attempt to hush her.

Katie pulled free from Nora's hug.

'It's OK. I, along with my friend, are the new owners of Kilcashel.'

She looked from one woman to another. Nothing was said. Leonie, who was dunking her biscuit, forgot it and let it drift across her mug until it turned into a soggy mess and sank.

'I didn't mean to startle you. I think it's great you use the gazebo after a swim, and I hope you will all continue.' Katie paused and looked at the two women. 'Maybe, one day soon, I will be brave enough to get fully into the sea.'

'You don't mind us walking through the gardens and down to the Kilcashel House beach?' Nora asked.

'No, not when it's only a couple of locals. But if there were a lot of day trippers, it might be different.'

'No fear of that! Anna has put the fear of God in most people; they wouldn't dare try to come on Kilcashel House grounds,' Leonie said.

'Anna's heart is in the right place,' Katie said, and the other two nodded in agreement.

'Is it just going to be your holiday home?' Nora asked.

'No, I intend to live here.'

'Wow, that's something. Being so near the sea in winter can be quite a challenge.'

'I'm sure it can't be worse than a New York winter,' Katie said a little too brightly.

'Why haven't you moved in?' Leonie asked.

'Anna says we need to air out the house and we need to get the furniture sorted.'

Nora's face reddened.

'You should have stopped me rattling on about the furniture. It's all there in the stables. I think my Tony would like to see it back in the house it was designed for.'

'It never left really; the stables are on Kilcashel land,' Leonie said.

'I would like to have a look at it. I could do with any help I can get, furnishing the place,' Katie said.

'Anna knows all about it. She never liked that Harry wanted to sell off the furniture, so she turned a blind eye. If I bring you over to the stables in the far paddock, she will only give out. She likes to be on top of everything at Kilcashel, even those things she's not supposed to know anything about,' Nora said.

'She's been so good to me; I would have been lost if she hadn't been here when I arrived,' Katie said.

'She certainly knows her way around the old place,' Leonie said, but Nora interrupted and said they had better get going. She threw the remains of her tea on the old crocosmia plant and took out her basket and told them to put their empty mugs there.

'We didn't have time to tell Katie how we got together.' Leonie's voice was full of disappointment.

'I'm sure Katie has more pressing things on her mind.'

'But that's it,' Leonie said. 'It might help.' She turned to Katie.

'I lost my husband last year. The stupid man went on a charity cycle and he had a heart attack when they were only ten miles out.'

Leonie's voice faltered. Nora continued for her:

'What Leonie's trying to say is that we helped her through, getting her out of bed every morning. The cold sea water kick-started Leonie every day – and us too. By the time she was able to start processing her grief, we had got into a routine, and the morning sea dip was the most important part of the day,' Nora said.

Leonie took one of Katie's hands.

'Come down with us in the morning; it will help, I can guarantee it. Dan, my brother, forced me down on the first occasion, but I look forward to each morning now. There are still days it's hard to go on, and some nights are unbearable. Come dawn, I always know I have somewhere to go, people who love me and a safe place where I can laugh or cry.'

Nora leaned in. 'Everybody else – especially Anna – thinks we're a bit loopy, but we don't care, it works for us. Each one of us was hurting and this simple act every day helps us to keep going.'

'Thank you, but I'm not sure. There's so much to do at Kilcashel House and...'

'You're afraid we're a bit mad,' Leonie tittered.

Katie blushed. 'Maybe,' she said quietly.

'Think about it and come for the chat, if not the swim,' Nora said.

'I will open up the front gates – please feel free to drive up and park at the side,' Katie said.

'Are you sure? Won't Anna have a checkpoint there?' Leonie laughed.

Katie smiled and changed the subject, telling them she had to get back because they were planning to open up the house ready for her friend and co-owner, who would be arriving in the next few days.

'If it's another woman, she can come along too, but we're early risers,' Nora said.

'I'm not sure she's a sea swimmer.'

Nora hugged Katie. 'Thanks for being so good about everything.'

'Thanks for letting me be part of the group,' she said, then set off down the path to the avenue, where Lola was patiently waiting for her. Katie's step was lighter. Maybe, just maybe she could fit in here, make a go of things.

FIVE

Katie read the text again.

> *Only 400 thread count Egyptian cotton linen for me. Can you get it there? None of the percale crap, please. I have to keep room in my luggage for my own clothes. See you soon.*

Katie sighed and put her phone away.

'Bad news?' Anna asked.

'It's Maggie; she acts like she's booking into a hotel.'

'When is she arriving?'

'Next Thursday.'

'I'll ring Michael Short Furniture and ask him to send over two double mattresses. He should be able to manage it in two days.'

'That'll be fine for me, but I don't think Maggie will sleep on a mattress on the floor.'

Anna smiled. 'Indeed, and do you think I would ask anyone to sleep on the floor? What do you take me for?'

Katie, detecting a cross note in Anna's voice, concentrated on buttering her toast.

'We'd best head up to the house straight after breakfast and get the windows open. You can decide what you are going to do after that,' Anna said, her voice softer.

Anna had two cups of tea for her breakfast and had to feed Lola and the hens before leaving the house.

'I run a tight ship here,' she said as she instructed Katie to load the dishwasher while she put a few bits out on the washing line.

'I can never come back to an untidy house,' she said, spraying the kitchen counters and wiping them with a damp cloth. 'With a bit of luck, Nora and her swimming buddies will be gone by the time we arrive,' she said.

'Nora and Leonie seem so nice. Why didn't Harry let them drive up to the house?'

Anna, who was busy changing the lining in the bin swung around.

'Harry was dead right. Once he bought the place, there were people around here who thought they could run riot and claim rights of way which had never existed. I advised him myself to show a hard hand from the off, or he would have loads of problems further down the line.'

'But it's only a few women.'

'Give that lot an inch and they will take a mile, mark my words. You know, they sneak into the garden every morning to have their bloody tea at the gazebo. Nora Cummins thinks she's lady of the manor.'

Katie smiled and Anna kicked the dustbin back into the corner.

'Harry was like you at the start. He emailed me and said he wanted to let the folks from the village have access to Kilcashel House. I told him off and I am doing the same to you now; don't be giving an open invitation to others to rob you blind.'

Katie, not sure how to answer, followed Anna meekly out the door on to the avenue.

It was a crisp, cold morning. A glimmer of frost overnight had deposited pockets of ice across the paddocks. Anna rushed up the avenue, but Katie held back, taking in everything around her. A few pigeons flew past, landing on the paddock fence and eyeing the two women. A robin watched them from the branches of a small hazel tree.

'Do we put anything out for the birds?' Katie asked.

'Only at the height of winter; there's enough around here for flocks to feast on,' Anna said, slightly miffed to have to slow her pace for Katie to catch up.

'It's so different here; I still can't get used to the country sounds.'

'Give it time. Put me in New York and I wouldn't know what to do either,' Anna said as they rounded the rhododendron bend. Anna stopped on the path.

'Isn't it just beautiful?' she said, sweeping her hand wide.

'I can't believe I'm even here, never mind that I'm a part owner of this house.'

'You'll know soon enough, when the bills start pouring in. Come on, we don't have all day to be dawdling on the avenue,' Anna said.

Katie stood gazing out to sea as Anna unlocked the back door.

'You should be the one doing this. I have no say in this place anymore,' Anna said.

'I should have asked, did Harry pay you for your caretaking duties?'

Anna straightened up.

'We had an understanding. I supervised the builders, made sure that everything was carried out to a proper standard and kept everything shipshape, and I have the gate lodge rent-free. I like gardening, so I also look after the roses at the front, but Harry always got Dan, who has the farm next door, to keep the grass down, and keep the hydrangea and camellia tidy. Nobody bothers with the agapanthus or crocosmias, they look after themselves.'

'And he didn't pay you at all?'

Anna stepped into the kitchen and immediately set about opening the windows in the glass conservatory.

'It's a privilege to be here at Kilcashel House and to have the gate lodge to myself. It's all I want.'

Katie did not enquire further as she suspected that Anna would become quite cross if she did.

'I will turn on the immersion and get started in the kitchen. Why don't you walk through the house, opening every window right up to the top floor,' Anna said in her businesslike voice.

Katie went to the drawing room first. She shivered as the damp cold seeped through her. Walking across to the bay windows, she tugged at the bottom of the sash frame, but it wouldn't budge.

'Don't forget to unlock the top part first,' Anna called from the kitchen. Katie pushed back the lock and pulled on the bottom part of the window again. It gave way easily this time, letting a light breeze enter the room, making the curtains billow. Katie looked around. The walls of this room were full of history; the history of the family who had once lived here and the history of the locality. It needed good antique furniture to complement the antiquity within its four walls, she thought, not the cold leather sofa which spanned the width of the fireplace, where a television had been set up over the mantelpiece.

Harry had given the interior designer free rein and she had decided to make this high-ceilinged, characterful room look like a minimalist New York loft. It was so Harry to think he could slip New York vibes into an old mansion down a country lane in Ireland.

She moved on to the dining room, which was long and narrow with a window overlooking the rhododendron grove. It was a pity, she thought, that there was no way through to the kitchen. Shaking her head, she suppressed a giggle. She could open up the wall, if she wanted; she could do anything because this grand house was hers now. Never before had she owned a property and she felt excited, even if she had to contend with Maggie.

Wandering into the hall, she stopped to examine the dark, grey walls. She hated the colour; it made her feel uneasy. Walking quickly upstairs, she stopped on the first landing to look out over the front fields and down the avenue. Horses in blue rugs were grazing in one of the far paddocks. She saw a man walk across the grass and clip a lead rope on one of the horses then lead it to the gate and walk towards the house. She must ask Anna about that, she thought as she continued through the rooms; all empty, bare, freshly painted and devoid of character. Upstairs, the master bedroom was at the front. It was a cavernous room with two deep windows overlooking the countryside and one looking out on the side of the house. This had a modern en suite bathroom, so best to assign it to Maggie, who would no doubt have a lot to gripe about once she arrived.

Leaning against the fireplace in the master bedroom, Katie wished it didn't have to be like this, being drip-fed this other life of Harry Flint. His flight was once rerouted to Dublin, or so he said. He decided to stay a few days and he brought her home a beautiful gold Celtic-inspired bracelet. She had no idea where it was now and she was glad. She took the velvet box containing the engagement ring from her pocket and placed it on the mantelpiece. She would decide about it later, but it no longer brought her comfort.

She continued up to the next floor. Neither Harry nor his designer had set foot here. There was still flowery carpet on the floor and each room was furnished with old, dark mahogany furniture.

There was a big bedroom at the front which was exactly the same size as the one on the floor below, but the walls were covered in a delicate silver wallpaper with tiny pink and purple roses. Drapes of plain silver fell at either side of the window. Running her hand across the wall, Katie thought this could be her room, but it was a pity there was no view to the sea. The bathroom had an ugly green suite, but the taps worked. Katie walked as far as the bed and sat down, making the frame shake.

She had no idea what she was doing here; where she was going to start, but she had to make it work.

'We will have to tighten the frame up if you want to use it. The mattresses will be delivered tomorrow. There's a mahogany sleigh bed for your friend, if she doesn't mind something antique,' Anna, who was standing in the doorway, her arms folded, said.

'I am sticking to the back bedroom with the sea view,' Katie said.

'I didn't think you would bother coming up to this floor,' Anna stuttered.

'It's so strange, it's like they walked out and never looked back. Was the rest of the house left furnished as well?'

Anna kicked at the old rug on the floor.

'It was, but your Harry had no time for it. He was quite annoyed it was not cleared out; the only thing that stopped him having the whole placed pulled apart was the cost. He couldn't find anyone to clear the rooms.'

'Nobody wants dark furniture anymore, I guess.'

'It was more to do with loyalty than anything else.'

'What do you mean?'

'Loyalty to all that went before. Look, we had better get on and stop this gossiping,' Anna said, swiftly turning on her heel.

Katie was about to ask more, but she knew from the stride of Anna down the corridor that it was something she would only dare to pursue at a much later stage.

She caught up with Anna on the landing.

'Do you think we could get the furniture out of storage?'

'You know about that.'

'Nora told me it's in the stables near the far-off paddock.'

'Do you want to have a look?'

'Can we?'

'You're the boss; it's a bit of a walk from here.'

'You never told Harry?'

'He never asked.' Anna smiled. 'We could walk up there while the rooms are airing out – if you're interested. I thought you city types liked your stainless steel and modern furniture; pieces that don't look one bit comfortable.'

'Anna, if there is free furniture and it's already linked to the house, what are we waiting for?'

'You'll need a pair of wellingtons to make it across the fields,' Anna said, already making her way downstairs to a tiny room off the kitchen. 'Harry never bothered to clear this out – we should find a pair in your size, no bother,' she said.

Within five minutes, she had a pair of wellingtons for Katie and another for herself.

'You certainly seem to know your way around the place,' Katie said.

'Down this neck of the woods, you won't get far in this weather if you don't have the wellies.'

Katie glanced at Anna, but she couldn't read her face and as soon as they got outside she set off in the direction of the seashore at a brisk pace.

She didn't speak until they turned inland, approaching the far paddock.

'There's a new stables here and an old piggery. In the olden days, all the work animals came in and out this way – there never was anything up around the house – but now everything comes through the entrance on the Kilcashel Road.'

'Did Harry ever come up here?'

'I don't think he cared much about the land, only the gardens and the beach.'

They tramped side by side across a field to another paddock, where the two horses wearing rugs up to their necks ambled over to them. Katie hid behind Anna.

'Just ignore them. If you give them anything, they will plague you every time they see you,' Anna said, raising her hands to shoo the horses away.

'Are they my horses?' Katie asked uncertainly.

'Dan keeps them here in return for the bit of gardening and doing a few odd jobs. It's an arrangement that has worked well for all sides.'

'So, they're here for free.'

'And you get your grass running down to the sea cut for free and the gardens tended. Those shrubs don't look that good without a little bit of expert help, you know. He has green fingers when it comes to camellias.'

'I didn't realise.'

'Why would you – but now I have told you,' Anna said briskly as they walked over to the stable block.

'Dan, is he the tall guy I saw walking along the avenue the other day and cutting across the fields?'

'Probably, he's always doing something or other on the estate. He's some sort of university lecturer so he has a lot of time on his hands.'

Katie giggled and Anna looked at her sharply.

'Don't be relaying anything I say about Dan to Leonie either. Brother and sister are pretty tight,' she said as they arrived at the stables.

Two stables were obviously used by the horses they had met in the field. Shavings were neatly spread and swept up the sides of each stall, a bucket of water in each.

'In the winter they often have to stay inside, but this time of year Dan only brings them in if the weather is fierce,' Anna said as she walked to a wide area which had been closed off with a heavy tarpaulin.

'Look at the size of Kilcashel House – and two floors of it can be stored in here,' Anna said as she pulled back the sheeting. 'This is it, the heart and soul of Kilcashel House, and it's all yours,' she said, her voice quivering with emotion.

Katie stepped into the stable for a closer look. Mahogany bed ends with an intricate inlaid design were stacked against one wall. Tall wide wardrobes were stored up against each other while dressing tables were placed on top of each other, so that the furniture pile went all the way to the ceiling.

Katie pulled out a heavy mahogany bedside locker.

'I really don't know how anybody could throw away this stuff,' she said, opening a drawer and taking out a small box filled with old-fashioned buttons. She scrabbled around, picking out a mother-of-pearl button which shimmered in the light.

'What was Harry thinking? We have to get all of it back to the house.'

'Everything is here, the sitting room suite is wrapped in plastic. I brought a leather armchair from the old library nook back to mine, if you want it.'

'And the books?'

Anna smiled. 'Stored in boxes in the attic at Kilcashel.'

Katie stared at Anna.

'You made sure all this happened, didn't you?'

'No harm admitting it now, I guess. What about the chair?'

'Somehow, I think you more than deserve it. We're going to have to get everything moved back before Maggie arrives. I suspect, like Harry, she would favour the minimalist look. I think to present her with a fait accompli might be the best course of action.'

'I'll get on to Tony straight away, and maybe Dan can help too.'

Katie put the mother-of-pearl button in her pocket and they walked back across the fields to the big house.

. . .

Within two hours of Anna sending out the call, Tony pulled up in a heavy truck with Nora in the cab.

'An extra set of hands,' she said.

'Anything to be in on the action,' Anna muttered under her breath. 'Dan will meet us up there,' she added, as they waved off the truck and she and Katie set off across the fields to the stables.

The others had already taken off the tarpaulin by the time Anna and Katie arrived.

'Anna, do you want every last stick of furniture brought or do you want to pick and choose?' Tony called out.

'Katie here is the owner of Kilcashel now; we'll let her decide,' Anna said primly.

Katie, not sure how to respond, smiled weakly at the group.

'We can see the wardrobes and bed frames; will we start with those?' Nora asked.

Katie nodded gratefully and stood aside as the men wrestled with a large mahogany wardrobe and staggered, carrying it to the truck. Running her hand along the end of a brass double bed, Katie could not fathom how Harry could have thought it was right to get rid of these pieces.

Anna picked up an end.

'Come on, ladies; we're not here to look pretty,' she said gruffly, and both Nora and Katie grabbed the other end and pushed it on the castors as far as they could, until Dan helped them lift it on to the truck floor. Katie watched as he effortlessly manoeuvred the bed end in beside the wardrobe. Once it was safely in place, he turned around to her.

'We weren't introduced properly. Dan Redmond; your neighbour and I do a bit of work in your garden for Anna.'

Katie noticed his grip was strong and his eyes were warm.

'Anna told me about you. Thank you,' she said.

Tony called for assistance and Dan jumped off the truck to

help move the wardrobe for Maggie's room, which Katie noticed was much bigger.

'That one fits the front bedroom and the other one is for the back room. You did say you liked the sea view,' Anna said.

Nora pulled some sheeting off a dressing table.

Katie gasped, floating her hand over the rich, inlaid mahogany.

'It's so beautiful,' she whispered as she delicately took a brass handle and pulled open one of the tiny drawers under the bevelled oval mirror. 'I feel you would need to have fine jewellery and wear silk to have a vanity such as this,' she said.

'Nonsense; we all need a bit of good furniture, and particularly the dressing table,' Anna said, instructing the men to be careful and make sure it went into the back bedroom.

Katie smiled and said they had better find something equally good for Maggie.

Anna took a blanket off a sturdy mahogany dressing table.

'Not a fine Edwardian piece, but adequate and big. I imagine your friend would prefer big to delicate,' she said.

'It's a good solid piece with spacious drawers; it just doesn't have the allure of the very old furniture,' Nora said.

'It fits that room perfectly, and your Maggie sounds like a woman who is high maintenance and will need all the space she can get,' Anna said.

Nora made a face behind Anna's back and Katie tried not to laugh.

They worked hard for the next hour, picking bedside lockers to complete the bedrooms, along with bedside lamps, which were wrapped in plastic and stored in a thick box.

Katie stopped to examine a blue velvet wingback armchair, which had been wrapped tightly in plastic.

'There isn't a couch, just four or maybe five of those velvet armchairs,' Anna said.

'I really like them,' Katie said, using her fingers to dig a hole in the plastic. She pushed her hand in and rubbed the velvet.

'It isn't damp, so they're good to go.'

'Of course it isn't! Didn't I wrap it myself for storage?' Anna said, as if she were offended.

Tony and Dan set off in the truck with a full load for Kilcashel House, leaving the women to walk back across the fields.

'Did you hear that Katie has said we can use the avenue when we're going swimming?' Nora said.

Anna pretended not to hear, until Nora began to repeat the sentence.

'I don't know why you're telling me this. Me? I think it's madness,' she said.

They tramped along in silence until Katie asked how they would get the furniture upstairs.

'We'll show the lads where everything goes and then we'll slip away to mine and make the tea and sandwiches. With any luck, they'll have got the worst of the heavy lifting done by the time we make it back to the big house,' Anna said.

'But shouldn't we try to help?'

'And listen to all the drama which will come with a task like that? I don't think so,' Anna said, and they all agreed.

SIX

APRIL

Katie slapped down her laptop and walked off the deck and down the garden path where the pink and white tulips were waving in a gentle breeze. She sat on the stump of a large tree, her finger tracing the curve of years long gone. She couldn't believe what she had just read. Why the hell had Maggie written about Harry's murder, setting out all the details for everybody to read? Had bitterness and resentment driven her to write about this? Was this the way it was going to be with Maggie Flint; every struggle to be dished out, when she fancied? Katie hardly knew her and now this, an invasion of privacy.

Anger surged through Katie, but she tried to suppress it. Anger that Harry had left her alone; anger that he had taken the subway, when he had promised to go by Uber; anger that he had robbed her of a future in Manhattan.

When he didn't turn up on time, she texted and said she was enjoying the sunshine sitting out at Bryant Park and listening to live music. As news of the subway shooter popped up on her newsfeed, she texted and said he had better rush up from downtown, in case neighbourhoods were closed off by police. When he hadn't arrived one hour later, she began to worry. She paced the park, because she didn't know what else to do. Two hours further on, she was in a panic; she could hardly breathe. When Maggie rang, Katie was already ground down to nothing, and that was where she remained.

Harry Flint was dead on arrival at hospital. Four bullets were pumped into him, one piercing his heart. The love of her life bled out on the cold, pockmarked floor of the subway car while others cowered for cover and the gunman cursed the world.

When they allowed her in to see his body, she was surprised that he looked so peaceful. The only sign of anything amiss was a graze on his right temple.

Katie stood up. Still, she could feel the stark coldness of his hand, the only part of him she was allowed to touch. She thought that was the worst moment, but now she worried that Harry had left her completely in the dark and Kilcashel House was only the beginning.

Swiping away the tears, she continued on past a small bank of pink camellias to an overgrown track that led down to the shore. Scrabbling down to the sand, she lingered by a cluster of big rocks. Resting against a tall boulder, she stopped to take a deep breath. Fear crept through her. Shivering, she pulled her jacket tighter around her.

She heard someone calling out and looked up to see Dan walking towards her. He quickened his pace until he was standing in front of her. He was a good head and shoulders taller than her and it struck her that he had a quirky smile.

'Hi, I didn't get a chance to talk to you the other day about the garden and the horses.'

'I will have to check with my co-owner – she'll be arriving soon – but I think, if you're happy, we can continue with the arrangement.'

'I would like that.'

'You've done a marvellous job.'

'Anna asked me. She didn't like to see the place fall apart.'

'I didn't know.'

'I try to fit it in with the rest of my work. What are your plans for Kilcashel?'

'I wish I knew.'

She said she had to get back. She had turned away and taken a few paces, when she stopped to ask another question.

'Did you ever meet Harry?'

'No, but I knew of him from Anna.'

Katie stared at Dan. He wasn't much older than Harry, but he was dressed in old clothes; a sweater which had seen better days and jodhpurs and boots, like he had just been riding.

'You must call up to the house soon. We could do with advice on what to do with all this land. Maggie arrives next week and I move in properly today.'

'Sure, once you get settled,' he said.

She walked up the path. She knew Dan was watching her, so she maintained her speed.

When she got as far as the garden, she sloped off down a side path to the gazebo. Pulling out her phone, she checked her messages. She had one saved message.

Darling, don't worry I will get there; traffic is such a brute today and a bus broke down in the worst place. I'm at the subway station. I can't wait to talk to you. I have something important to tell you. I know you're going to love it. This can be the start of a new life together. Love you forever.

Was the gunman anywhere near him? Did he overhear; did he care?

Placing the phone down on the bench, she closed her eyes. In her mind she was playing and replaying the message. Life was so different now. What new life? She had no idea what he was talking about. Was he going to finally tell her about Kilcashel House? She loved Harry, but she hated him too for putting her through all this. What was he thinking, buying a place in Ireland without telling her? What was he thinking, risking everything they owned? Anger and tears surged through her. Did he know about the cancer? And if he did, was he going to tell her? She had been due to sign a lease on a café bakery premises in Chelsea Market; she had dreams and plans and every one of them had been shattered the day Harry was gunned down. It left her empty and alone in this small place in Ireland. There was Maggie, but she hardly knew her – and after reading that article she didn't know how they could live in the same house for even a small length of time, never mind the next ten months. It seemed such a long way away, and who knew what would happen between now and then.

SEVEN

Katie stretched in the bed. It was too early but the glare of the rising sun through the window had woken her up.

She listened. There was nothing but birdsong punctuated by quiet. She yearned for the old familiar noises, the bagel delivery to the shops across the way, the air conditioning clicking in too loud, the garbage truck spinning by too fast; the commuters emerging from the subway half a block down; the street vendor setting up and calling across the way to his rival and the police sirens, always the police sirens. She used to lie in bed and listen and marvel at the life that was going on around her. Here, life seemed to go on despite her.

Her phone rang. She wasn't surprised when it was Maggie; she was the only one who called her nowadays.

'The only hire car is like a tin box; it's so tiny and so expensive. I have too much luggage; what am I going to do?'

'I'm sure you are good at putting your foot down. The hire company tried that with me, but I just got all New York.'

'You think?'

'From what I know of you, you should get the best car on the lot.'

'I'm going to rest up in a nice city hotel in Dublin, shake off the jet lag and see you in the morning,' Maggie said. Then Katie heard her yell, 'Sir, sir!' to someone and a second later she was cut off. She wouldn't be surprised if Maggie ended up in a chauffeur-driven limousine once she started to complain.

Katie jumped out of bed. She went down to the front en suite master bedroom she'd decided to let Maggie have, in the hope it would stop her complaining about the facilities. She and Anna had worked hard getting the house clean, but they'd put the most effort into Maggie's bedroom.

Katie picked a soft duck egg blue for the walls and an old mahogany chest of drawers to match the dressing table and wardrobe. She paced the room, checking every detail.

'What will we do about curtains?' Anna had asked. 'Not that anyone can see in here anyway.'

Katie laughed. 'Maggie is as New York as you can get, she will want her blinds or nets as well as drapes.'

'And cut out this beautiful view – is she mad?'

'Probably, I just want her to be comfortable from the start. The less she has to complain about, the better.'

Anna had managed to get a bolt of upholstery fabric in cream and had made the curtains, sewing them up over two nights.

'I could have bought a pair,' Katie said.

'And have that friend of yours giving out? No, we want to make a good impression, if only to keep her in her place.'

Katie looked embarrassed.

'I haven't painted a great picture of her, have I?'

'You have said nothing about anything, but I have a head on me. They divorced, and Harry picked you. He was happy with you, Katie. He mentioned you once or twice; said it was the best thing he had ever done, asking you to move in with him.'

Katie pretended to concentrate on plumping up the feather pillows. She had jumped at the chance to move in with Harry, letting her own apartment go. On reflection, it wasn't the best decision she had ever made, but how was she to know a subway shooter would turn her world upside down like this?

Anna gently poked her in the back. 'We had better get a good shop in before Ms Fancy Pants arrives.'

'I'm not so sure about that; I have no idea what she likes. I'm going to put some bagels in the oven, and there's cream cheese.'

'Whatever you say.'

Anna sounded a bit offended, and Katie didn't understand why.

Soon after, Anna said she would run the Hoover over the downstairs and then she would be off.

'I will stay out of your way, until you think I should meet your visitor,' she said.

Katie put her hand out, to stop Anna.

'Maggie is co-owner of the house and will be living here for several months.'

'Oh.'

'It was in Harry's will; he wanted us to live here together until the start of next year at least.'

'What nonsense! Who in their right mind would do that?' Anna said.

'Harry Flint, and it's in his will so we have to do it.'

'That sounds like a fierce complicated arrangement. You make sure that one doesn't walk all over you,' Anna said, heading for the stairs. Katie followed.

'Have some tea before you go, and let me walk you down the avenue; it is dark out there.'

'Don't be silly, girl. Why don't you have a bit of quiet time and enjoy the house on your own for an hour or so and before going to bed. There's no one around these parts that would cross Anna Walker, and Lola will come up the avenue to meet me, once she hears my step.'

'I doubt Lola would be much of a guard dog.'

'She's fierce loyal and that's all that is required,' Anna said as she set off at a brisk walk.

Katie stood in the hall and watched her leave, then made her way down the hall to the kitchen.

Feeling jittery about Maggie arriving, she decided to finish getting a batch of bagels ready.

Kneading and rolling out her dough, she manoeuvred it into shape, pushing it back and forth between her hands to ease it into the ring shape she wanted. She did this ten times, placing each ring on a large tray with parchment sheet. Covering the baking sheet with plastic and a damp cloth, she placed the tray in the fridge to chill for a few hours before the boil/bake stages.

Gulping her wine, she waited for the bagels already in the oven to brown. How many times had Harry sat beside her on the counter at the bakery and waited for a hot bagel from the oven? Almost too hot to handle, he would roll the bagel around his hands, then deftly slice through the dough and smear the inside with butter. Harry liked cream cheese with cinnamon. He always slathered too much on, so that it melted and ran down his chin.

Why did she remember that? she wondered. The first time she brought him back to the bakery kitchen and she wiped the cream cheese from his chin, he had reached over and kissed her. He was still married, but she didn't care. He said he and his wife had already agreed to divorce, which made her feel happy.

Katie took the tray of bagels from the oven and let them cool slightly before slathering on the poppy seeds and crisped onion, then she popped them back in the oven for a final blast.

Two years ago, Maggie had come for breakfast and Harry insisted on a crisped onion topping. He said if the bagel was right, the brunch would go well too and Maggie would stay friendly.

Katie stayed in the kitchen until the early hours, because it was here she felt closest to Harry, the old Harry who loved

her. It was a little bit of the familiar, the life she knew. It was
her world, and not even Maggie, she hoped, could intrude on
that. But this world with the old Harry was only make-
believe. Now that she knew how Harry Flint had gambled
her life and dreams away, she was so full of rage she wanted
to go back and claim his ashes so she could flush them down
the toilet. Maggie had left Harry's ashes unclaimed and his
cremation bill unpaid. Katie was shocked and upset when
she found out, but a part of her admired Maggie too for
doing it.

Katie was on the deck, having managed only a few hours' sleep,
when her phone rang.

'I can't find the bloody place. Where are you?' Maggie said,
her voice anxious and loud.

'Did you turn off the highway?'

'Highway? If you want to call it that, yes.'

'And did you drive through Kilcashel?'

'Yes, and turned left, but I can't find the place. We will have
to put up a proper sign.'

'Did you pass the small house with the large cherry blossom
trees?'

'I'm parked outside. God don't tell me this is it. I'm going
home; it's yours.'

'That's the gate lodge. I'll come down to you.'

Katie got as far as the rhododendron bend when a BMW
appeared, speeding up the avenue. Maggie sounded the horn
and waved out the window.

'This house looks more my style,' she said.

She pulled up beside Katie.

'Hop in. I struck a deal on this baby for a month and maybe
longer.'

Maggie continued at speed up the avenue, throwing gravel

on to the field edge. Parking at the bottom of the front steps, she let out a low whistle.

'From the outside, it looks as if old Harry had taste. But then, we know he did; he picked the two of us.'

Without waiting for a response, Maggie got out and ran up the steps.

'Why couldn't it have been a city pad?'

Katie pushed the front door open, and stood back to let Maggie enter.

'We can do the bags later. I'm starving,' she said as she stepped into the hall.

'I have your favourite bagels.'

Maggie wrapped Katie into a tight hug. 'You didn't have to do that, but thank you.'

Katie switched on the coffee machine while Maggie perched on a stool at the kitchen island.

'The house seems in good shape.'

'Only the rooms on this floor. Your bedroom and mine to a lesser extent.'

'That's enough for the next ten months. How are we going to do this, Katie? Do we share bills or live independent lives?'

Katie got two mugs and poured out the coffee. She deliberately didn't answer straight away. Placing a bagel on a plate and a little pot of cinnamon cream cheese on the side, she pushed it across the counter to Maggie.

'There's something I have to say to you.'

Maggie stared at her. 'Shit, this sounds serious.'

'It is.'

'You're not staying?'

Katie snorted.

'That was the second item on the agenda, but I want you to know I am going to do everything in my power to make a go of it here. I want to stay. There is nothing in the US for me and I don't want to go back.'

'Oh, and what am I supposed to do?'

Katie sat down opposite Maggie. 'Look, I want to you to know that I'm looking at setting up a business here.'

'I don't have anyone back in Manhattan, but I'm not staying here. So either I leave you to it, or you buy me out at the end. For the record, I ain't leaving until we reach the end,' Maggie said, emphasising the last words as she spread the cream cheese thickly on her bagel. She held the bagel with two hands, took a bite, chewing slowly.

'This is so good, we must get some more,' she said.

'I baked the bagels.'

'Is this what you're planning to do? Bring the New York bagel to the arsehole of nowhere?'

'Not in so many words, but yes, cookies, bagels, a small bakery. It's what I had been working towards in Manhattan, so it makes sense to transfer the idea to Kilcashel.'

'Here at the house?'

'Yes, this seems a good place to set up. In time, I was hoping to use the front room as a tearoom. We have a guest bathroom down the hall and this is an industrial-type kitchen; the pantry can be my storage area. Harry must have had some business idea for me because he obtained the necessary permits, so I'm good to go, even though he never saw fit to discuss it with me.'

'You have it all worked out. It would've been nice to be consulted.'

Katie blushed with embarrassment.

'I've been working on the plans the last few days; I'm telling you now.'

'Since we are straight-talking: I intend to return home to Manhattan; it's where I belong.' Maggie sipped her coffee. 'No amount of bagels can replace the feel and buzz of a city for me. As far as I'm concerned, the next ten months are a necessary evil until we sell up.'

'We have different goals.'

'Damn right, and that's not going to change. I have ideas too, real writing ambitions.'

'I didn't want to bring up this, but your writing is a problem. I read your article about the subway murder,' Katie said, shaking her head. 'I didn't agree to that. You never said you were writing about Harry and what happened. How could you do it and not even tell me?'

Maggie shrugged. 'I thought it read quite well.'

'That's not the point; you can't go public on what's so private to us; you shouldn't have done it. And you do not have permission to put our lives here at Kilcashel House in any published form out there.'

'You sound very legal all of a sudden.'

'I've had time to consider it. I just won't allow it.'

Maggie shifted on her stool.

'And I didn't agree to the world passing through our front room. You never bothered to mention the bakery idea.'

'I'm just trying to make a living.'

'So am I.' Maggie threw her hands in the air. 'Look, I'm jet-lagged; it sure as hell is not a good time for this conversation. Please show me to my room. It's not the way I intended this trip to begin,' she said, her voice shaking with emotion.

Katie swivelled off her stool to stand in front of Maggie.

'That's the problem. For you, this is a trip and for me it's a life change.' Her cheeks were flushed with anger and she knew her voice had risen in pitch.

Maggie opened her bag and slapped a bottle of champagne on the counter.

'For another time, if we ever feel we can toast each other and Kilcashel.'

'I suppose this is just fodder for another of your damn writing ideas,' Katie muttered.

Maggie walked out of the room to the stairs.

'First door on the right at the top of the landing, the master bedroom,' Katie called after her.

Maggie hesitated at the bottom of the stairs.

Slowly, she turned to Katie.

'Thank you. Just so you know, I never wanted it to start this way. I need some rest.'

Katie slowly let the kitchen door shut. She wasn't angry, but she felt let down. Harry always said Maggie was so confrontational, she would pick a fight with herself if there was nobody else around.

Grabbing the bottle of champagne, she pushed it to the back of the cupboard under the sink. If it ever had to come out again, Maggie could bloody well find it.

Next, she took down the stainless-steel bowls she had bought in Aldi the day before. It was time to make her raspberry cookies.

As it got dark, Maggie was still sleeping. Katie considered taking up a tray of tea, but instead put her head down, concentrating on her new cookie recipe. The weighing, the examination of the fresh raspberries, the preparing of the trays, fitting the parchment sheets, the kneading of the dough – it all calmed her down. To concentrate on one task was to exclude all others, particularly the arrival of Maggie.

She had been on the edge of Maggie's life in New York. Harry had worked with her, spent a lot of time on the phone to her and whined constantly about her; so much so that Katie sometimes wondered why they had ever split up, they seemed to enjoy their spats so much. Sometimes she felt an outsider, but Harry insisted she was his rock, that her calm, serene and quiet manner was what he needed and wanted.

Maggie, he said, was a blast, but not a person he wanted to

spend the rest of his life with, and that had been the mistake he made in marrying her.

'She's fantastic, but she tires me out,' he would say, and Katie always felt insulted that she could never challenge him in that way.

After she had put the trays of cookies in the fridge to prove, Katie grabbed her rain jacket and walked out on the deck. Every day she had to walk Harry out of her system. It didn't matter what time it was; when she had to walk, she walked. She was happier going out at night; she traipsed up and down the avenue, anxiety and grief pushing her on, making her concentrate on one step at a time; the focus helping her cloak the pain and loneliness searing through her. Sometimes, Lola heard her and barked, but more often than not, she turned before reaching the gate lodge, so as not to draw any unwanted attention. Anna was not likely to understand the depth of her grief, and anyone else who saw her would surely mark her down as mad.

On the driveway, with only the stars overhead and the swish of the trees for company, she felt safe.

Sometimes she stopped by the rhododendron, the branches of shiny leaves reaching out, pulling her in to encircle her and she felt safe in this new place. She breathed in the night air and hoped it would cleanse her, free the pain and deep-set grief and let if wither away.

Had she come to this, that the only time she found peace was walking up and down the avenue in the dark? If she were in Manhattan, she would slip into her local diner and have Louis prepare a half stack of blueberry pancakes.

It was at these times that she both loved Kilcashel and hated it. Loved the peace it gave her troubled brain, and hated that she had only found this place through the worst set of circumstances.

She turned back up the driveway towards the house. A light switched on in Maggie's room and Katie found herself tensing up, worried the other woman would see her on the driveway and goad her about it. Hurrying along, she made it to the back door seconds before Maggie got to the bottom of the stairs.

'My head hurts like hell; what time is it?'

'Near midnight.'

'Hell, I was tired. You know, since that son of a bitch died, I haven't had a full night's sleep. My body just gave in to the jet lag and then some.'

'I can make us some tea, or would you prefer coffee?'

'Heck no,' Maggie said, pulling a bottle of champagne from behind her back.

'I figured I had better bring down my spare in case you smashed the other one against the wall.'

'I don't think we have anything to celebrate,' Katie said flatly.

'Don't tell me you're one of those people who has to be celebrating to drink champagne?' Maggie turned away from her and began to open kitchen cabinet doors. 'There must be glasses in here somewhere,' she muttered.

Katie sighed.

'Look, whether we like it or not, we're stuck with this situation, so how about we start over?'

Katie took down two wine glasses from a shelf over the sink.

'You don't have champagne flutes?'

'Count yourself lucky to have any glasses; the house wasn't exactly at the lived-in stage.'

Maggie popped the cork, allowing some of the champagne to spill over on to the counter.

'A glass is a glass, and this is good champagne,' she said, carelessly pouring, so some ran down the side. She wiped the base of the glass stem along the counter then handed the glass to Katie.

Katie held the glass in her hand, not sure what to do. Maggie held hers aloft.

'Let's get through the next while without killing each other,' she said.

Tentatively, Katie clinked her glass to Maggie's, and they sat down at opposite sides of the counter.

Katie noticed Maggie's mascara was smudged and she looked as if she had been crying.

'I was a bit of a bitch earlier, but so were you,' Maggie said.

'Neither of us wanted to be in this position.'

'Too right. I still don't want to be here. Look, I got paid well for that feature article and I needed the money.'

'So, you intend to write about our private lives at Kilcashel and make money on it?'

Maggie made to speak, but Katie put her hand up to stop her.

'It's not only your life that's going public, you're putting my private life out there too for all of America and the world to read, because you need the cash.'

'What's the big deal? If you have business plans, I'm sure the publicity won't go amiss.'

Katie put her glass down and stared at Maggie. 'That is so selfish. Don't I have a say in this?'

'What say? It's my private life I'm throwing to the wolves here. Yours will just be a walk-on part, when I have to mention you.'

'That's so reassuring,' Katie said, her tone sarcastic.

Maggie threw back the last of her champagne and poured another glass.

'Look, Katie, it's shit what has happened to us, but we both have to get through this the best we can. What about starting over?'

'What would you like me to do, congratulate you on what you've written? This is such crap, Maggie,' Katie said as she whipped out of the kitchen and to her room.

She heard Maggie opening and shutting cupboard doors in the

kitchen, followed by the sound of her making her way out to the deck. From her bedroom window, Katie could see Maggie in the pool of light from the kitchen window, flopping into an armchair, lighting up a cigarette and blowing rings of smoke to the night sky. It made Katie feel even more angry. She moved away from the window and took down her high ponytail. When she was baking, which was practically always, she wore her hair up. She always calmed down when she brushed her hair out, letting the bristles slowly move down her thick brown mane until it felt silky smooth.

What did Harry want them to do? Fight it out, like they were competing for his affection? If she let this situation fester, they would spend all the time spatting over stupid things. Suddenly, she felt foolish as if she were participating in a weird powerplay from beyond the grave.

Without thinking too much, lest she change her mind, she tore down the stairs and on to the deck.

Maggie didn't budge, but continued to blow her smoke rings.

'Your hair is nice down; you don't look so serious,' she said.

Katie pushed her hair back behind her ears and took a deep breath.

'I don't know what Harry wanted and to tell you the truth, I don't care. This property is the only opportunity I have of making a future for myself, so if you can put up with me, I sure as hell can try and put up with you.'

Maggie blew a last ring which shimmied over the garden before dissolving into the air.

She held out the champagne bottle to Katie.

'Always best when slurped,' she said.

Katie took the bottle and slugged a long drink from the neck, letting it fizz down her throat and the front of her pyjamas.

'This stuff is good.'

'It should be, it cost me my last hundred-dollar bill.'

Katie looked aghast at Maggie.

'Oh, don't you start; we'll do fine. We have all this land, we just have to get it working for us – and the house too,' Maggie said.

Katie leaned against the balustrade, listening to the waves hitting the shore and throwing up fine stones.

'But you want to sell up at the end?'

'Sure do. But if this place is thriving, we'll get a better price. Or you can buy me out. It's win-win either way.'

Katie didn't answer but continued to lean against the deck balustrade looking at the sky.

'I miss the sounds of the street,' she said almost to herself.

Maggie got up and joined her.

'Me too, and I've only been on this deck a short while. Can you imagine if we had this space in Manhattan – we would be millionaires or even billionaires.'

'But we're not.'

'Ever the practical one. We can always dream,' Maggie said. Katie ducked back inside the kitchen. She didn't know how to respond.

Anger against Harry surged through her. They'd had such a good life together. He'd pursued his business interests and, after years as a baker in Manhattan, she'd been on the verge of starting her own bakery and delivery service. A coffee house serving the best cookies and coffee was also on the cards. There was even talk about a weekend retreat in Connecticut; Harry had started to look at property there. She wanted a place within driving distance of Manhattan, but Harry always wanted to be far away from the city.

She heard Maggie get out of the deck armchair and she busied herself to avoid getting caught in more conversation.

When Maggie sauntered back into the kitchen and eased

the velvet engagement ring box in beside her, Katie burst into tears.

'It was in my room. I know it's yours,' Maggie stammered.

Katie, using a tea towel to wipe her eyes, looked at Maggie.

'It's all such a mess,' she said.

'Keep it, and one day you will be able to look at that ring and remember the good times together,' Maggie said.

Katie pushed it across the table.

'Will you hold it safe for me? I can't bear to even think about it now.'

Maggie nodded and shoved the velvet box in her pocket. Inhaling deeply, she smiled.

'It smells like a downtown bakery. You're serious, aren't you, about this?'

'Yes. I have no choice.'

'Let me help you with marketing and all that sort of stuff; you can concentrate on getting your collection of cookies right.'

'Aren't you going to be too busy writing that column of yours?'

Maggie took the bottle and guzzled down the last of the champagne. 'My career as a columnist is over before it even started. I woke up to an email. A new editor has been appointed and my column has been spiked. New chap says who the hell is interested in two Americans holed up in an Irish mansion. I will just have to make it on my own writing."

'I'm sorry,' Katie said.

'No, you're not. And to be honest, I kind of agree with the guy. I just don't know how I will get through the next months here.' She paused. 'Are you setting up a café? Do we need to get things moving around here?'

'I was thinking of a bakery. I don't have time to run a café, and where would I find premises in the town? I need to be here, baking and looking after Kilcashel House.'

'I can run the café. It might be fun. I write at night, so that would fit,' Maggie said as she took out a pen and notebook from her pocket.

Katie stared at the pen.

'Is there something wrong?' Maggie asked.

Katie walked over to the draining board where she had left her favourite pen along with her shopping list. She picked it up and held it aloft.

Maggie gawked at her and raised her pen.

'Snap,' she said gleefully.

'So we have the same pen. Mine was a present from Harry.'

'Don't tell me. Christmas four years ago?'

Yes, he bought silk pyjamas.'

'And it was in the pocket.'

Katie dropped her pen on the counter.

'Darling, maybe he got two for the price of one,' Maggie said.

'He told me it was so expensive and the two stones on the top of the barrel were diamonds.'

'Diamonds, my ass!' Maggie guffawed. 'He told me all that crap too, but after the divorce I had it valued in a jewellers. It's an ordinary piece of shit, but a nice piece of shit. I wouldn't say the same thing about Harry Flint.'

Katie turned away and walked out onto the deck.

Why did Maggie have to tell her this? Why did Harry think so little of her that he bought her the same present as Maggie? Pain engulfed her and a loneliness that she was grieving a man who was so careless with his love for her.

Her foot touched against a small rock the dog had left on the deck. Bending down, she scooped it up and fired it as far as she could. She heard it plop to earth somewhere around the blue agapanthus.

'Dior silk cream pyjamas, beautifully presented in a box with a ribbon bow?' Maggie asked quietly as she approached Katie.

'Please go away.'

'Darling, he had us both conned. All we can do now is move on.'

Katie swallowed hard before she spoke again. 'He probably wants us to be at each other's throats.'

'Damn sure he does.'

'Maybe our best revenge is to make some sort of go of all this.'

'Is that a yes to letting me in on the café with you?' Maggie asked.

Katie said she would think about it, and for the first time she felt a tingle of excitement that maybe all of this would work out.

Maggie slumped with disappointment.

'You don't want to be in business with me. You don't think I can do it, do you?'

'I don't know what to think. All I know is, this has to work for me here at Kilcashel,' Katie sighed.

'Go with the flow, girl, that's my advice. Can I have another bagel?' Maggie asked, in a vague attempt to change the subject.

'Yes, they were just out of the oven when you arrived, but we can toast them, and there's cream cheese.'

'And cinnamon?'

Katie handed the cream cheese and cinnamon in a bowl to Maggie.

'You mix, I'll toast.'

They worked in silence and when everything was ready they sat down together to assemble their bagels.

'We are going to have to set rules, aren't we?' Maggie said.

Katie reached for the champagne bottle. Pouring the dregs of the bottle into two glasses, she pushed one across to Maggie.

'Eventually, I suppose. But let's see how we do first,' she said.

'So, no rules? Not even about my writing?' Maggie asked.

'Just entice visitors here who will put their hands in their pockets, please.'

'I can certainly try.'

When they had finished the champagne, Katie rummaged in the cupboard under the sink and came back with a bottle of whiskey.

'To help us sleep,' she said.

She poured whiskey into two mugs, and they clinked like farmers with full pints.

'Does this mean you will consider the café idea?' Maggie asked.

'Yes, let the Kilcashel adventure begin, wherever it may bring us,' Katie said, and Maggie laughed nervously.

The next morning, they were sipping coffee at the kitchen counter, when Maggie let out a low whistle.

'Alert; rather handsome-looking man coming our way.'

Dan knocked twice before sticking his head around the back door.

'Just to let you know, I've had a lot of enquiries about the possibility of allotments. Would you consider letting people rent garden slots in the front paddock area? It's not as if that field is doing anything for you anyway.'

'Do you think it would be worth our while?' Katie asked.

Maggie cleared her throat loudly, and when Katie didn't react, she walked over to Dan and extended her hand.

'Maggie, co-owner of Kilcashel House. Wouldn't the allotment cars interfere with the bakery or café traffic on the avenue? The last thing we need is customers unable to make it up to the house.'

'Nice to meet you, Maggie. There's an entrance to the paddock further down the road, which we could turn in to a small allotment car park. It shouldn't interfere with the work going on in the house.'

'How many car spaces and how many allotments?' Maggie asked.

'Ten allotments and the same amount of parking spaces,' he said.

'Dan has a farm next door and helps out with the land here,' Katie said.

'So we will see a lot of each other then,' Maggie said, flashing Dan a wide smile.

Dan, red rising up the back of his neck, said he had provisionally marked out the allotments, but he needed their approval before leasing any out.

'I have to go and see Anna. I can walk down and take a look at the allotment area at the same time,' Katie said.

'I am interested. Mind if I tag along?' Maggie asked.

Dan looked at her red leather shoes with the two-inch heels.

'You might need to change your footwear; you don't want to ruin your shoes.'

'I have sneakers, let me go get them,' she said, rushing off upstairs.

Katie turned to Dan. 'You might as well sit down; this could take a while.'

'So are you really going to make a go of it with this bakery then?' he asked quietly.

'I don't want to make a big deal of it, just open up and hope people come along. I'm thinking they'll come because they're curious – and then they'll become regulars because they like the baking. Maggie, though, has other ideas.'

'I bet she has,' he smiled.

'Do you think those in the allotments will want trays sent out to them?'

'I rather imagine those that go for allotments will be the

flask of tea and homemade sandwich type. Anna should be able to spread the word for you.'

'If Maggie doesn't put her off.'

Dan looked his watch. 'I have to get back to work in an hour, do you think there's any chance she could hurry up?'

Before Katie had a chance to reply, Maggie came thundering down the stairs. Katie stifled a giggle when she saw her in jeans and trainers with orange and pink flashes, setting off her yellow raincoat.

'We're only going to the front paddock,' Dan said.

'I know,' Maggie said haughtily, slipping out the back door and sighing as if she had been waiting for Katie and Dan all along.

Dan led the way, Maggie half running to keep up with him. Just short of Anna's house he indicated to the fence.

'We can get over the fence here and walk across to look at the proposed parking area.'

Katie climbed over and jumped down the other side. Maggie stepped on the fence and immediately asked Dan for help.

'I don't want to hurt my ankle when I jump down,' she said.

Surprised, he put out a hand for Maggie to lean on as Katie walked over the grass.

'Do you think will there be much interest?'

'I already have a waiting list, but better start with ten decent plots and if it goes well, you can expand next year into the field at the side of the house.'

'We don't want it stretching too near the front of the house – too messy,' Maggie said.

'Surely it's only a good thing for the house. People love allotment gardening.'

'Providing our allotment owners don't scar the horizon with huge and unsightly plants or structures,' Maggie chuckled.

'You're right; we'll need to set rules and police it from the start; that means only letting certain people take up the leases,' Dan said.

'It sounds like very hard work; I was just going to let people at it and allow them to sow flowers and vegetable and enjoy our gardens,' Katie said.

'How did you ever survive in New York, girl?' Maggie said, taking Dan's arm. 'Why don't I liaise with Dan here while you focus on the baking? Sounds like a fair distribution of labour to me.'

When Maggie laughed, Katie thought it was more like a tinkle and it made her feel uncomfortable.

Katie said she had to get along. She moved away through the grass without the others noticing. She felt slightly miffed by Maggie and Dan, but she concentrated on trying to avoid the clumps of buttercups which had already soaked her canvas shoes through to her socks.

EIGHT

Katie was cross. Maggie had left her clothes in the dryer again and had not bothered to collect them. She wanted to throw them to the side, but instead she pushed them in to a basket and made her way upstairs to confront Maggie.

Last night they had sat down and thrashed out how they were going to continue for the next months. Maggie was under the impression that Anna should do all the housework and was quite annoyed when Katie pulled her up on it.

'I think we can ask her to do a few basic things, but surely we want to keep our privacy. Our bedrooms and bathrooms should be our own responsibility and, of course, our own laundry. Anna should not have to go upstairs.'

'If we must. I'm not used to this way of living; can't we get a cleaning service?' Maggie said, and Katie burst out laughing.

'Get used to it! Anna already thinks you are treating her a bit like a servant, and maybe you are. It's not fair – and if Anna turns against us, we haven't a hope of fitting in here.'

Katie stared at Maggie.

'And no, we are not hiring a cleaning service. We can't afford it. Please be nice to Anna.'

'Boo bloody hoo; you're the one who wants to fit in, not me. Am I correct, but doesn't Anna have the gate lodge rent-free?' Maggie said, flouncing off.

Now Katie wanted to dump Maggie's laundry basket in her room and have it out with her. There was quite a racket at the front of the house with a dog whining and barking excitedly. Peeping out the window, Katie observed Maggie, on the avenue with Anna's dog, Lola, a makeshift lead knotted to the dog's collar.

Katie watched as Maggie tried to cajole and then pull the dog down a part of the avenue, until Lola, all four paws digging in to the gravel, managed to pull free of her collar and bolt under the spread of the rhododendrons. Katie quickly dropped the bag of washing outside Maggie's door and made her way downstairs. When Maggie came back into the kitchen, she looked as if she had been crying.

'Is there something wrong?' Katie asked.

'As if you care. No, everything is peachy; I'm out of here,' Maggie snarled, throwing the dog collar on the kitchen counter.

Katie walked to the drawing room to watch Maggie march down the avenue; her upset obvious in every step. She was about to leave the room when she noticed Maggie's laptop was open on the seat of an armchair. Katie picked it up with the intention of closing it, but she couldn't resist sitting down to read when she saw the headline.

Trying to Fit in to Kilcashel

This very minute I would be strolling with my pooch at the edge of Central Park, his lead studded with Swarovski crystals in one hand, my chai latte in the other.

I would make sure to look over the heads of others and yes I could scoot quite quickly if Randolph pooped. I was the snooty lady who only let her dog crap under the bushes to one side of the Metropolitan Museum of Art.

It was good fertiliser, I think, and Maggie Flint wasn't made to carry poop bags. I only ever got caught once when a man politely told me to clean up after my animal. Randolph growled and I told him to piss off.

There are a lot of regrets about having to move here to Kilcashel House in Ireland and the loss of Randolph is one of them. A bit like myself, he was set in his ways, and he had, at most, just a few years left. It was an agonising decision, but I think the right one for both of us. A good friend gave him a home and he left for Long Island, three days before I flew out.

I was caught up in the last days of moving out of my home and leaving my life behind and I thought the loss of Randolph would, as a result be easier. How wrong I was. I braved it until I pushed the sitting room ottoman across the floor and the lid came off, his favourite toys spilling out.

The purple velvet rabbit he slept with as a puppy landed on my foot. Much the same as Randolph used to do all the time as I sat working at my home desk.

I shouldn't have stopped to pick up the rabbit; it held too many memories. It sits now at my feet almost as if I am trying to recreate the past.

I agonise whether it should be this way. I know Randolph would have hated it here, it would all be too earthy for him. It's that for me too, but I know there is an endgame. Maybe he would have loved the long, wet grass, but this was a dog who wouldn't leave the house without his bootees. Maybe he would have liked sitting in front of the Aga in the kitchen, but this was a dog who wanted his own heated basket, hang the cost. Randolph was a dog made for the finer things in life, and I pray I was right in my decision that he would have been miserable here.

Making that decision, I didn't factor in that I am wretched

and lonely without him. Randolph was my pal; he heard all my secrets and now it is the dark night and the stars that puncture their way through the inky sky around Kilcashel House that are privy to my inner fears and thoughts.

When I am feeling very low – and these early days that is most times – I imagine Randolph and Harry are the brightest stars in the sky and it gives me some comfort.

Katie has plans to put down roots here and open a café. She is a talented baker and her idea is a good one. I, on the other hand, have only a plan to survive the next ten months and come out of it with enough money to return to Manhattan and start all over again.

That difference of approach is a source of tension for both of us. Katie no doubt loved New York as much as I did, but she is trying too hard to fit in here and create a new life. I miss Manhattan, the sounds and smells, the brash New York attitude; the skyscrapers which block out the sun in places.

Here, the dawn chorus wakes me up and I am ungrateful, fed up with the early starts on long days in which I have little to do. It is a conundrum; I have to live here for ten months so I can rightfully earn what is mine from this property. I need that financial boost to start a new life and yet, for the next ten months, I am just a lodger in someone else's life, a person on the edge of someone else's dreams.

I am at sea here and the writing is the only thing I have to sustain me. At Kilcashel House, I feel very much forgotten by life. As prisons go, it's a beautiful setting, but a prison nonetheless.

There are times I wonder if I could have clung on for dear life in Manhattan and fought the banks. My heart tells me I should have, but my head tells me I did the right thing, no matter how bad it feels.

The thought of days on end here at Kilcashel scare me. I

wish I could be more like Katie; she sees a clear path through all this, whereas I am floundering.

But neither was I made to quit at the first hurdle. Every day I will write and write until I somehow know how.

Katie left the laptop as it had been. She didn't want Maggie to know she had read these musings. To cover herself in case Maggie noticed that the laptop had been moved, she pulled up one of the windows to air out the room. The wind was rustling the leaves of the rhododendron; she could hear the distant waves pounding the beach. The sun flashed gold across Kilcashel House. Katie too pined for the sounds of the city; the uncompromising, constant noise that makes up Manhattan. Her heart was still among the hard, concrete streets; the tall, architectural buildings; the avenues where traffic snarls can lead to loud flare-ups.

She was prepared to give Ireland a chance; to give Kilcashel, Co Wicklow a chance, and to give this elegant and beautiful old manor, Kilcashel House, a chance. Her grieving heart had to heal and now she knew so did Maggie's.

NINE

'Our friend is fierce hard on the inside of the cups; she should put milk in her coffee,' Anna said, gathering up the mugs and holding them under the hot tap to rinse them.

Katie smiled.

'Maggie is hard on everything; she thinks putting milk in coffee is one of the worst sins you could commit.'

'I imagine she has committed far worse,' Anna harumphed as she scrubbed the inside of a red mug fiercely with steel wool. 'Do you think she will last here?'

'I don't think she wants to be here, but Maggie isn't going to let the opportunity of inheriting this place pass her by.'

'Harry was a stupid man to put anything like that in a will.'

'He wasn't to know it would come into effect so soon.'

'He must have been raving; tempting fate is what he was doing. Why would he ever want the two of you to be cosying up together anyway?'

Katie stopped pounding the bagel dough and looked directly at Anna.

'That's simple, he loved us both and he knew that, whenever he was gone, we would be grieving him and maybe to do it together would help.'

'What piffle! Stupid, stupid man. I don't think you believe that either.'

'No, but it stops me overthinking it. Maybe it was just a whim. What does it matter? We're stuck with it now.'

'None of my business. All I'm saying is she needs to put the milk in her coffee,' Anna said as she got a teacloth and began to wipe brown from the inside of the cup.

'Look at that, a perfectly good tea towel ruined. Easily known Maggie isn't the one doing the hard work around here.'

'Anna, please, you're being unfair; Maggie may not do any housework—'

'She doesn't lift a finger, that one.'

'Housework was never her thing apparently, but she's helping me a lot towards setting up the bakery and a café and she's writing, though she doesn't talk a lot about it.'

'I never see her do any of the heavy lifting.'

'She's going to help with the finer details of the start-up and the marketing. I don't think I could do this without her.'

Anna threw the tea towel in the washing machine.

'She's good at all the arty, farty stuff, but the only thing that will make your venture a success is everything you do in this kitchen.'

'Teamwork, Anna, that's what will do it for us.'

'And too much champagne for madam. You know in the shopping list this week she asked me to get some miniature bottles of champagne or Prosecco. What would I look like, buying things like that with the meat and spuds? Is she a secret drinker or what?'

Katie didn't bother to answer. She knew Anna didn't want her input, only to feel the thrill of her own indignation. She concentrated on rolling out her bagels.

Anna took the cutlery box from the dishwasher and began

to empty it, noisily tossing forks and knives into the drawer. When she was done, she turned to Katie.

'Can I talk to you about something?'

'Yeah, of course,' she said, pulling out a high chair at the counter and sitting down, expecting Anna to do the same. 'Is there something wrong?'

Anna stayed standing, drumming her fingers on the countertop.

'I need to know who is in charge here; who has the last word?'

'You know the arrangement, Anna; it's going to be like this for the next while.'

'But who has the final say?'

Anna caught up a stray spoon and fired it in the drawer. Katie saw her clench her hands tight as she spoke again.

'It's hard for me; you know my arrangement at the gate lodge, whether ye are happy with it or not. I need some assurance it will continue, no matter what.'

'But neither of us have said anything to the contrary.'

'Maggie has been throwing out hints.'

'What do you mean?'

'She wants to change things at the lodge.'

'I know she mentioned about the entrance, pruning trees to make the entrance more accessible for visitors. We are going to run with opening a café. Maggie is helping me with that'.

'Nobody has ever complained to me about the cherry blossoms.'

Katie reached over to touch Anna's hand, but she pulled away.

'I don't want my trees cut down or interfered with in any way; I love those cherry blossoms. I don't know what I would do if anything happened to them.'

'I'm sure a bit of pruning could only be good.'

Anna flopped into the seat opposite Katie.

'Maggie is a woman used to getting her own way; I knew it the first time I met her. She's not one who takes no for an answer.'

Katie reached over and took Anna's hands.

'I will talk to her about it, I think you're worrying unnecessarily. We have to make the best impression to get people up to the café in the first place.'

Anna pulled her hand away.

'What are you saying, that my little cottage is taking from the grand enterprise?'

Katie shook her head fiercely.

'Anna, let's be clear, I said no such thing, but we're going to have to spruce up around the gate. There's someone coming tomorrow to paint the gates and get rid of all the weeds on the avenue. We were thinking of window boxes on the windowsill of the gate lodge.'

'And when were you going to tell me?'

'I didn't think it was such a big deal.'

'I have two cats and if you put window boxes there, they will only use them to crap in. They are lazy buggers.'

'I never thought of that.'

Anna stood up, her chair screeching across the floor as she did.

'Of course you didn't; you two think you can come in here and change everything. I am in the gate lodge until I pass on to the next life. You would do well to remember that.'

In two strides she was out the back door. Katie listened to her stomp across the wooden deck and go down the side of the house, the dog she knew was running beside her.

Katie wandered down the hall to the front drawing room. Standing watching Anna on the avenue, she wondered what Harry would have done about this. There was something about

Anna that had spoken to him, and Katie wished she knew why he had agreed to let her stay in the gate lodge, unless he knew he would not gain favour in the town if he didn't have Anna Walker on side.

Maybe keeping her there was the only way he could complete the purchase of Kilcashel House. It was a beautiful place, but Harry was always a businessman, and there must have been a reason he agreed to such a strange arrangement. If only Anna were a little more reasonable, she wouldn't mind; the cherry blossoms hardly fitted in with the image of a boutique hotel

She looked around the room. Once she'd given Maggie the all-clear to help with the café idea, she had set to work quickly, even managing to find a job lot of tables and chairs in a liquidation sale. There was little else that had to be done here, only get rid of the modern paintings. Dan had promised to bring around a ladder at the weekend, so they could access the attic, where Katie hoped to find a few antique pieces to set off the room.

Maggie had already found brass candlesticks on the third floor, and they were either side of the mantelpiece along with an old clock which they'd found in a box in the pantry.

Small tables with comfortable chairs upholstered in the same blue velvet as the curtains and armchairs were arranged at intervals. A glass vase was on each table waiting to be filled with fresh flowers from the garden.

A counter was set up in the wide doorway between the drawing room and dining room. It was good that customers could watch the cookies and bagels being made fresh, the aroma of fresh baking filling the café.

'They will come from all over, to see a genuine New York bagel being made?' Maggie said.

'Ah no.'

'Either you want to do well, or you don't. You have to

remember, darling, you need to be making enough to be able to get a mortgage to buy me out.'

'Is that why you're helping me?'

'Yes and no; but mostly yes.'

The scrunch of gravel outside indicated that Maggie had returned from her five-minute trip to town, which had actually taken about two or more hours. Katie sat down at a table, waiting to hear the front door swing back until it hit the wall.

'Darling, I have the most wonderful idea,' Maggie called at the top of her voice.

When she saw Katie sitting in the drawing room, she stopped and dropped her shopping bags.

'Uh oh... What have I done now, ordered too much Prosecco?'

'There's that, Anna was embarrassed doing the shopping, in case anyone thought she was an alcoholic.'

'Does the woman work for us or not? What complete nonsense.'

Katie smiled. 'That may be so, but Anna is upset, said you wanted to cut down her cherry blossoms.'

'Will that woman ever stop? They are crowding the entrance and I wanted to prune them, so we can have a proper sign there.'

'She doesn't want us touching the cherry blossoms and she doesn't want window boxes either.'

'Am I right, but don't we own the gatehouse?'

'Anna is a tenant for life.'

'Harry Flint, you miserable crud for landing us with her as well,' Maggie shouted and Katie sighed.

'Anna is all right, she just doesn't like change.'

'Is that it? I never knew. Seriously, why do we even have to consult her on any of this? She's lucky we don't just turf her out on her ear.'

'Maggie, everybody in this place knows Anna. I'm not sure if they love her exactly, but if we mess with her; they won't be on our side. Maybe that's what Harry realised too.'

'I should have written about her when I had a chance. Nobody would believe the nonsense she comes out with.'

'That wouldn't have been a good idea.'

'It might have made her back off.'

'Or the very opposite.'

'We could do with livening things up around here,' Maggie said as she pulled out a pile of fabric from a paper bag. 'Tablecloths are so chic, and I've found a lovely woman who will run them up for me.'

'They will only get dirty.'

'Thought of that, and I am arranging for glass cut-outs for each table.'

'That's a lot of fuss, when everything looks fine as it is.'

Maggie pirouetted across the room pointing to every corner.

'It's dark and dingy, blue velvet is so yesterday; we need pops of royal blue, gold and maybe green. As it is now, this room isn't somewhere where people will want to sit and chat. It's an eat and push setting. I don't think that is what you want. It needs ambience.'

'I will leave that in your hands.'

'I have a nice woman in the town who has agreed to stitch covers and cushions for us.'

'If I didn't know you, I would say you're enjoying setting up the café.'

'I want the café to work; it must, for both our sakes, and to do that, it must have a good vibe, be somewhere people want to linger; a place people talk about.'

'I thought my baking would do that.'

'Baking first, service second and décor third.'

'If you say so.'

'I most definitely do.'

'We need to spruce up the gate lodge, paint the windows and door and tidy up the front garden, get rid of the cherry blossoms.'

'Anna won't let us do that; they're important to her.'

'Well, if she wants to keep it, she's going to have to agree to everything else; hanging baskets or window boxes?'

'I'll call down to her in a while I have some new almond cookies, it might sweeten her up.'

'If she doesn't think almond isn't too exotic an ingredient for a Thursday,' Maggie said, gathering up her handbag and making her way to the kitchen to pour a Prosecco.

'And who cares what we order at the grocery store anyway,' she called out.

'Anna's arch enemy May Grimsby works there, and she is a fierce gossip,' Katie answered.

Maggie pushed her head around the dining room door.

'So what if everyone knows I only drink champagne or Prosecco; to be accused of expensive taste is always a good thing.'

Katie picked up the fabric Maggie had left on the table. A cream background with flowers of every kind, it was a riot of colour; purple foxgloves, daisies, blue bergamot and ice pink roses.

'You don't think the flowers are too much? I thought we were going for understated elegance.'

'Of course they're too much, but with the teal walls and teal velvet chairs it's the perfect contrast,' Maggie said a little too loudly.

Katie knew better than to argue and was glad when the postman arrived at the kitchen with his delivery.

Pushing open the door, he placed a large cardboard box on the counter.

Maggie tore at the cardboard.

'You're going to love these divine little cake boxes. There's even a teeny box with a ribbon for the skinflints who only buy one item.'

'I didn't order these,' Katie said as she took out the white carboard and popped a box into place.

On the lid was a drawing of Kilcashel House with the name The Drawing Room Café printed in deep blue and surrounded by flowers.

Maggie, her hands up to her face, peeped through her fingers.

'I knew you would never agree and were determined to use those stupid brown paper bags that look so dull...'

'But these must have cost a fortune.'

'You have to spend the bucks to get the bucks. Surely you know that.'

'But I don't have the bucks,' Katie said, her voice anxious and high-pitched.

'That's what credit cards are for.'

Katie traced the name with her finger.

'I hadn't picked a name,' she said.

'I know, but it's perfect, you have to admit.'

'It is, but this is too generous. I can't take your charity,' Katie said, pushing a box away.

Maggie laughed.

'Well, you're going to have to. I can't send them back with a nice drawing of the house on the front.'

She stopped laughing when she saw Katie's face as tears streamed down her cheeks.

'Hey, hey this is good. What's wrong?'

'You're being so kind...'

Maggie caught her into a tight hug.

'We are a team, an unlikely one, but a team. Take the gift.'

Katie whispered thank you.

'Now, off you go and deliver a box of cookies to Anna. No doubt she will complain it is all too ostentatious.'

'I'm sure she will mutter something about you having notions.'

Maggie poured two glasses of Prosecco and handed one to Katie. 'To the Drawing Room Café,' she said.

'I like it,' Katie said, clinking Maggie's glass.

'Just as well, because there are another five hundred boxes arriving later in the week,' Maggie whispered, then downed her Prosecco in one go.

TEN

Katie took a moment to look around her. Maggie was right, the entrance to Kilcashel House looked very shabby; the cherry blossoms blocked a full view of the gate lodge. It was a beautiful mid-May day but there was no doubt these trees took light from Anna's front sitting room as well. For a short period of time the trees looked magnificent in full bloom, but now they were beginning to look scraggly and tired; the green leaves beginning to block out the gate lodge.

Holding the box of cookies tightly, Katie wandered around the side of the lodge, picking her way around the flowerpots of gladioli to knock on the back door.

Anna came through from the front of the house.

'Is there something wrong?'

'A peace offering, and I would like your opinion on the flavour,' Katie said, trying to sound as if it were the most natural thing in the world that she should drop by with a fancy box of homemade cookies.

Anna opened the door wide.

'I presume this tomfoolery is Maggie's idea,' she said,

running her finger along the outline of Kilcashel House on the box.

'It was, it's lovely.'

'God bless your heart, Katie, but that woman has no end to fancy about her.'

'We're just trying to get the café and bakery off the ground; she has come up with some great ideas.'

'And some crazy notions; I think she forgets this is plain old Kilcashel and Bohilla Lane is just that, a tiny road leading into the town.'

'We all need a bit of crazy sometime.'

'I wonder does Dan need crazy; Maggie is certainly throwing herself at him.'

Katie sat down.

'Ah Anna, that's not fair. Give us a break. We're working our socks off.'

Anna slowly undid the blue ribbon, folded it neatly and placed it in a bowl on the dresser. Carefully, she opened the cake box without saying a word. She got a plate from the dresser and took out two almond cookies and two raspberry.

'They smell divine,' she said as she placed the biscuits on the plate. Slowly, she picked up each biscuit and took a delicate bite from one, then the other.

'So delicious, but then you don't need me to be telling you that. Why are you here Katie?'

'I know Maggie has upset you about the plan for around the gate and I wanted to talk more about it.'

Anna sat down opposite Katie.

'If she wants window boxes fine, and she can tart up the place, but nobody, and I mean nobody, is touching the cherry blossoms.'

'We could get a specialist in to give advice on pruning.'

'Not necessary.'

'I don't really see what the problem is; a tidy-up would do the trees good.'

Anna got up to let in the dog, who was scraping at the back door.

'I like you, Katie, I really do, and I don't want us to fall out.'

She stopped to concentrate on her breathing. When she continued, Anna's voice was shaky.

'This insistence about the cherry blossoms could bust us apart.'

'I just don't understand.'

'Those trees mean the world to me; I will never let anyone touch them and even when I'm dead and gone, I will haunt anybody who even attempts to touch the blossoms.'

'Maybe, if we could understand their significance for you.'

Anna shook her head.

'Isn't what I said enough? It should be.' She leaned closer to Katie. 'I can't move on this; please understand.'

Not sure of what Anna expected of her, Katie said she had better get back, that she had to work out prices for the cookies and bagels.

Anna grabbed her arm.

'Charge enough, make those cookies a luxury must have. They are both delicious and sinful. Make the women of Kilcashel and beyond yearn for them. Selling them off cheap will signal that nobody gives a damn. And don't you have to get back something on the fortune those boxes are costing you?'

Katie ducked out under the cherry blossom trees and strolled up the avenue.

It was a dull day but at this moment, she didn't feel the usual sadness. There was an excitement growing inside her for the Drawing Room Café. Harry had never been a part of her business plans, never asked how she was doing. Looking back now, she realised he was selfish, always talking of his own dreams, never considering she had a few of her own. Was she being disloyal, thinking of Harry like this? Some days she missed him so much, it hurt; but then there were days like today, when she was too busy to lose time reminiscing on a life that was entirely in the past.

Suddenly, she stopped. Leaning against the fence, she eyed the paddock where Maggie and Dan had used spray paint to roughly sketch out the allotments. Everything was moving forward. Katie felt they may be moving too fast, but if she brought this up with Maggie, she knew she would instantly dismiss her fears, telling her she needed to have faith, that this café and bakery was their only option.

Lola sat beside her and dropped a ball on her toe. Katie threw it into the field and stood watching the dog as it soared over the long grass into the creeping buttercup, hunting for the ball. Katie hurried on her way.

Maggie stomped into the kitchen directly after her.

'What is it with Anna? I told her I won't touch her precious cherry blossom trees, but she's standing sentry all the same. It's not a good look. She can't take her eyes off me or Dan.'

'Those trees are special to her; she's afraid of what might happen. She is on high alert.'

'That one has major trust issues, just saying,' Maggie said, taking a new bottle of Prosecco from the fridge. Katie sighed.

'She has heard about your writing; she's probably afraid she will end up in print.'

'I will be very stuck if I end up writing about that crazy old broad,' Maggie laughed. 'I'm off for my creative time, if anyone, especially Dan, is looking for me,' she called over her shoulder as she dashed up the stairs to her room.

Maggie was good with the excuses and at disappearing, Katie thought, resentment pinching at her. She remembered Harry bitterly complaining that Maggie was expert at telling the world what should be done, but she wasn't the type who would roll up her sleeves and pitch in, without announcing to the world that she was saving it.

Katie threw her mixing bowl and some cutlery in the sink and sprayed hot water from the tap over them.

The bright morning sunlight danced on the water, sending silver stars surfing towards her.

The last time she had seen that effect was the weekend before Harry died, when the two of them had got up early one morning and gone to the local park. It was a cool but sunny spring morning, the light peeping through the leaves and dancing on the fountain water, so that it looked like it was spewing out stars.

Harry often talked about them having children. She smiled to think of him chasing a little boy and girl around the stone fountain, and life at that moment was good. Children were now a long-lost dream, like all the plans that got thrown by the wayside once Harry decided to take the subway.

Her heart was full of pain, but mainly anger that he had left her like this, alone and sharing a house she never even knew about with his ex-wife. Her only hope now was to make her café work, though it was a far cry from the venture she had planned for Manhattan. In her dreams, her Chelsea Market coffee house was mentioned in the *New York Times* and a queue formed outside the door every morning, waiting for the trays of bagels and cookies to be taken from the ovens.

There was no chance of any of that here, though Maggie thought there may be a little interest in an American bringing big city food to a small town.

Dan knocked on the window as he passed and stepped straight into the kitchen.

'I need your help or maybe even both of you. Anna is going mad.'

'You didn't touch her cherry blossoms, did you?'

'No, but the cherry picker I brought in to reach the high rhododendron shaved past one, gave it a right tug and now she is convinced a part of it has been damaged. I think it's fine, but there's no talking to her.'

'Did you even try?'

'Yes, and I bedded the tree back in and watered it as well; I practically apologised to the bloody thing.'

'What do you want us to do?'

'Could ye come down and talk to her; she's got fierce upset and she doesn't want to even see my face.'

Maggie, who had heard all the commotion arrived in the kitchen.

'You go, Katie; I think my presence could only aggravate things further,' she said.

'Frankly, I could do with the support,' Katie said.

Maggie shrugged her shoulders and said she thought it was a bad idea, but what the heck, she would go along.

Dan said he would get on with work on the rhododendron and to call him if they needed help.

Katie marched down the avenue, Maggie tottering behind on her three-inch heels.

Every now and again, Katie stopped and waited for her to catch up.

'Maybe I should turn back; she hardly wants to see me,' Maggie said.

Katie linked her arm.

'You have to help, otherwise she will keep me for the day, giving out about you.'

'Nice to know I am an essential part of the team,' Maggie said, and they walked along together, Katie strolling at a slow place to fit in with Maggie.

Anna was on her knees at the cherry blossom tree, pushing

the earth in firmly around the base, when the two women came down the avenue.

'Dan Redmond is a coward. He has ruined my tree and he can't face me himself,' she hissed loud enough for Katie and Maggie to hear.

Katie rushed over to help Anna to her feet, but she pushed her roughly away.

'Just go away and leave me be, will you?'

Maggie stepped forward.

'Anna, this is really over the top. We're here to help, so let's go inside and talk.'

Anna stood up.

'I bet you put him up to do this; get rid of the cherry blossoms any which way you can.'

Katie reached out to place a steadying hand on Anna, but she pushed it off.

Stepping closer to Maggie, she pointed in her face.

'Nice fodder for one of your silly bits of writing, I imagine,' she said.

Maggie shook her head.

'Anna, I know you don't like me, but I own half of this estate and that means half of the gate lodge too, so I suggest we go and sit in my half of the kitchen and talk like civilised human beings.'

Anna looked at Katie.

'Is that what you think as well?'

Katie hesitated. Anna turned on her heel, flouncing off around the side of the lodge.

'Gosh, that woman has a mean temper. She has only months to change her tune, or she is out on her ear, even if I have to sell off half the land to pay the lawyers to get her out,' Maggie snarled as she turned back for Kilcashel House.

. . .

Katie waited a few moments before she followed Anna to the gate lodge back door.

Hesitating, she pretended to admire the garden. It was at complete odds with the front. The cottage garden perennial flowers were beginning to peep out of neat beds boxed in with railway sleepers; the rose bushes were showing signs of life, ready to start climbing along heavy wires trained around the windows. Rows of beds were dug out for the vegetable spring planting and terracotta pots were cleaned and ready to be used.

Lightly running her fingers along the glass of the back door, Katie whispered:

'Anna, can I come in?'

When there was no answer, she pushed the door gently.

Anna was sitting, her head in her hands, at the kitchen table.

'I'm sorry about all this with Maggie. I will ask Mr O'Malley from the garden centre to come and look at the cherry blossom trees to set your mind at rest,' Katie said.

Anna raised her head.

'And have somebody else condemn them? Nobody goes near my cherry blossoms. Why can't you understand that?'

'It was an accident; Dan is very cut up about it. He asked us to come down to explain that to you.'

'He and Maggie are pretty tight...'

'No conspiracy theories, Anna, please. It was an accident and Dan, who knows about these things, says the tree will recover quickly.'

'And if it doesn't?'

'Hopefully, that won't happen.'

Anna pushed her head in to her hands weeping.

'Jesus, Anna it's not that bad.'

She watched her shaking her head, her body convulsing with sobs. Feeling helpless, Katie edged closer to Anna, but was too nervous to reach out to her.

'I don't know what to do,' she whispered.

'Just pray the cherry blossoms stay alive, please.'

Katie pushed in on the bench beside Anna.

'I feel we have intruded on something, that we keep doing it. I am so sorry, Anna.'

'It's not you, sweetheart, but that other one is a trial.'

'Can you tell me why the cherry blossoms are so important to you?'

Anna shook her head.

'Get the man down from the garden centre if you want, but it has to be when I'm here. Hopefully the tree won't take umbrage. Just tell me Dan and Maggie are going to stay away from those trees.'

'I promise. I will talk to them about it.'

Anna stood up and put on the kettle.

'They are going to think I'm a stupid cow.'

'Does it matter?' Katie asked.

'It always matters,' Anna replied, not bothering with a teapot but throwing teabags into two mugs.

She poured boiling water from the kettle on the teabags and placed a mug, along with a sugar bowl and milk jug on the table in front of Katie.

Katie was about to reach for her mug when Anna, clearly changing her mind, whipped it away.

'Tea is no damn good. We need whiskey for the next conversation.'

Katie didn't object, but looked on as Anna fussed, taking down two crystal whiskey glasses, and wiping the dust from the insides with a paper towel. Reaching into the small cupboard in the corner, she pulled out a bottle of Midleton whiskey which was three quarters full. Without asking, she poured a good measure into each glass and pushed one across the table to Katie.

'What is all this about?' Katie asked.

Anna gulped her whiskey.

'I want you to know the cherry blossoms are my life; I can't have anybody interfering with them in any way.'

'Are they in memory of some event or somebody dear to you?'

Anna's grip tightened on her glass.

'I loved them deeply.'

'I don't understand.'

'The trees are old now, twenty years this May to be exact. I'm not sure how much longer they will last.'

'We could plant some more now, maybe somewhere else on the land to take over when the time comes.'

Anna shook her head.

'No, and if you don't mind, I can't talk about it anymore.'

Katie sipped her whiskey.

'You can talk to me anytime, I hope you know that.'

Anna nodded. They sat in silence as they slowly savoured the whiskey. The clock on the mantelpiece over the stove appeared to tick louder. Lola stretched out on the tiles and went to sleep. Katie heard a car in the drive, and she knew it was Maggie heading into the city.

'You're going to need help, I'll call up later if you like,' Anna said.

'That would be nice,' Katie said, draining the last of her whiskey and placing her empty glass in the sink.

Anna stood up and held the door for her.

Katie didn't turn up the avenue, but down the side path, which ran parallel to Anna's back garden towards the stream. The grass was long and still damp from the rain of the night before. The ferns sprayed water over her shoes as she passed by, but she persisted on the path to where the stream widened out to be a river. A makeshift wooden bridge over the expanse of water led to a leafy glade on the far bank, where a seat had been placed.

Gingerly, Katie stepped on the bridge, which swayed under her weight. She stepped out slowly; each step considered, searching for weakness. The old bench had been pushed against a bank of hawthorn trees. Katie sat down.

From here, she could see the gate lodge peeping over the high shrubbery at the back of Anna's garden, Bohilla Lane visible in part between the trees. Lola was snuffling through swathes of creeping buttercup in the nearby field. Yellow water irises stood sentry around the river; a heron flew to the far side of the bank, circling until it quickly dropped down out of sight.

She heard Anna call *chuck-chuck* to her hens as she threw handfuls of meal on the grass for them. The dog, thinking there may be titbits she could pick up, scooted across the field ready to snuffle in the grass once Anna went indoors. A robin flew in, pecking the ground at Katie's feet then suddenly flitted away. Katie closed her eyes and listened.

She knew she needed to give Anna time, but some day she hoped she would tell her of the great loss that clearly made her heart heavy. The water tickled slowly over the small stones, the sound low and soothing. Further along the river path, crows started up a racket. *Life continues, no matter what*, she thought.

Loneliness seeped through her. She missed her city so much, the brash loudness of New York city. Only Maggie was loud here.

A strange *cheekee* sound made her open her eyes and look about. Nothing. She was in such a constant state of flux here that, somehow, she was missing everything; that it all happened behind her back: that she was never automatically included.

Suddenly, a flash of blue and orange zipped across the water as a bird whipped up from somewhere beneath her feet then disappeared into the bushes at the other side of the bank. Excitement surged in her as she scanned the riverbank. When it swept low over the water again, she wasn't ready, but gasped in admiration.

'Ah, you've found one of my favourite spots,' Dan said, as he approached from behind.

Katie jumped.

'I apologise, I didn't mean to startle you. Did you see the kingfisher?'

'Is that what it was?'

Dan sat down beside her.

'Anna said you had come this way.'

'I thought I was hiding.'

'It's such a secluded spot; it's why the water channel was widened; for the delight of the otters and kingfishers.'

'Otters?'

'Not at this part of the river anymore, but they have set up home further down. Though at this time of the day, they're likely to be keeping out of sight.'

'I had no idea there was such wildlife.'

'You must have seen the heron flying in.'

'Heron?'

'Big grey bird; two of them have a nest further down the far bank.'

'How do you know all this?'

'Much the same way as you know where to walk and not to walk in New York.'

'That's easily acquired.'

'So is this, once you are interested.'

'It's all very new to me; I've always been a city girl.'

'At least you're prepared to wear the right shoes. What is it with Maggie? No matter how many times she sinks into the grass around the allotments, she refuses to reduce the size of her heels,' he said, and Katie thought she detected a certain softness in his voice.

'Did you talk to Anna about the cherry blossoms?' he asked.

'Yes. They're very important to her, I'm not sure why, but that's good enough for me. They stay and we try to help her to keep them in top shape.'

'I can get some good fertiliser for them.'

'I think that would make her happier – at least, I hope it will. I'm going to tell Maggie to lay off her too. Maggie can sometimes be hard to take.'

Dan laughed and Katie thought he was falling hard for the brash New Yorker.

Katie had set to work cleaning the kitchen when she got back to Kilcashel House, and she was bent over scrubbing her oven trays when Maggie came tearing in the back door.

'Who is responsible for this?' she shouted, pushing a ball of dirty torn fabric in Katie's face.

'What are you on about?'

'I hand-washed my dress and put it out on the washing line and it has been shredded. Somebody or something has attacked it.'

Katie put down her scrubber and wiped her hands on a tea towel.

'What, do you think I went out with the carving knife and slashed your precious dress?'

'I don't know; it was probably the stupid dog. This designer garment is worth thousands of dollars.'

'You're kidding?'

'No.'

'Why were you even washing it? And what were you doing, hanging it out to dry in a field?'

Maggie sat down at the counter.

'The dry cleaners in town, when they heard the value of the dress, refused to take it.'

'So you decided to wash it yourself... nice.'

'I asked Anna and she recommended a hand wash in washing up liquid and hang it on the makeshift washing line between two trees in the side paddock.'

'And you did that?'

Maggie nodded.

Katie took the dress and shook it out.

It had once been a straight shift dress made of the finest tulle, with embroidery flower detail and lace inserts on the front and side and little semi-precious sparkly stones sewn into the tulle.

'Could you always see through it?' Katie asked.

'That's the design, very cutting edge.'

'More totally unforgiving,' Katie said, holding what was left of the dress up to her. 'How exactly would you wear it?' she asked.

'We will never know now, because of that bloody dog,' Maggie snapped.

Katie did a twirl, but more sparkly stones fell off, floating across the floor; the tulle separating where the dog had grabbed it, sinking in her teeth and swinging from it as it flapped in the wind.

'I don't think even Anna can do anything with this,' Katie said.

'It's her bloody dog that did this.'

'There's no point blaming Lola, she probably couldn't resist it flapping above her in the wind.'

'I don't want to see that bloody dog again.'

'Maybe we can cut the bottom from the dress. It would make a nice top for under a jacket, but you would have to keep the jacket closed,' Katie said.

Maggie fisted the counter.

'You don't get it, do you? It cost thousands of dollars. I mean, it cost Harry thousands of dollars. When am I going to be able to afford such a designer dress again?'

'Thank goodness Harry paid for it,' Katie said.

Maggie couldn't help but smile.

'And I'm glad he never got me one,' Katie said.

Maggie shook her head.

'I only picked it out because it was so damned expensive; it was not long before we separated.'

'But why bring it here?'

'Hell, I don't even know.'

Katie giggled, making Maggie laugh as well. Soon both of them were laughing that Harry had paid so much for a bit of tulle and sparkly beads.

'I never even liked it,' Maggie guffawed.

Anna, looking flustered, walked into the kitchen. 'What have ye done to the dog? She came back and her mouth is all swollen. What have you given her to eat? The inside of her mouth is full of sparkly stuff.'

She stopped talking when she saw the remains of the dress.

'I guess Lola will be crapping sparkles for a day or two,' Maggie said, and she and Katie began to laugh again.

'Very funny, I'm sure,' Anna said, giving them both a strange look.

ELEVEN

It was 6 a.m. Katie looked at the clock again. Somebody was hammering on the front door.

'What the hell, who even knows we're here?' Maggie shouted as she pulled on her dressing gown.

'The whole world if they read that one column,' Katie answered.

'Shit, you don't think it's a stalker?'

'It's probably Anna,' Katie said, slipping on a hoodie and making her way downstairs.

'Let me go to the door. That woman has to learn good manners. This is way too early for me,' Maggie said as she pushed past Katie.

Maggie yanked back the door with a flourish.

'Good morning, just want to tell you I'm bringing equipment into my allotment, so don't get worried if there's a lot of noise,' a woman they had never met before said cheerily.

'But it's six in the morning,' Maggie said feebly.

When Katie got to the door, there were two women wearing wellington boots and long wax jackets standing on the top step.

'Which of you is the baker?' the woman wearing a blue knitted hat said.

'That's me,' Katie said.

'We are expecting to get preferential rates on tea and scones, and will you be able to send a tray down to us? We can set the times later.'

'I would be delighted, but I won't be doing scones.'

The woman, who had black hair tinged with grey, eyed Katie up and down.

'Look, I love what you are trying to do here at the old house, but if you go down the fancy pants route, you're only going to push away the people who could be your most loyal customers.'

'Oh, that's nonsense! Katie here is a fantastic baker. Why don't you ladies come in and have a fresh bagel; and a raspberry cookie to follow. Come on in,' Maggie said.

'We haven't been in Kilcashel House for a very long time – not since we were young girls, in fact. I suppose we could just let the tractor and rotavator men get on with it,' the woman in the blue hat said.

Her friend, who was wearing a red scarf tied tightly around her neck, stepped into the hall. Maggie knotted the belt of her silk dressing gown and led the way down the corridor to the kitchen.

'I bet you are tea drinkers, but we have the most divine coffee from India. Do you think you would like to try it? If we were in New York right now, it would be coffee and bagels with your favourite filling.'

'I think it would be nice to have coffee for a change,' the woman in the red scarf said.

They inched their way into the kitchen, oohing and aahing as they moved.

'This must be what you call a state-of-the-art kitchen,' one of the women said, whistling under her breath. She turned to Katie and Maggie.

'My name is Muriel Falvey, and this is my sister Rosie. We live in the big house near the scout hall. Our garden is only a tiny east-facing patch at the front and we have a little courtyard at the back. That's why we wanted an allotment.'

'Muriel and Rosie, welcome to Kilcashel House. You are our first guests,' Maggie said.

'If we had known we were going to be invited in, we would have dressed up more, put on the slap and the lippy. But working in the garden does not require any level of fashion,' Muriel said sadly.

Maggie took down her china cups and saucers, while Katie sliced the fresh bagels.

'I reckon you are butter and jam ladies, maybe another time for the cream cheese filling,' she said.

'Butter and jam forever,' Rosie answered, and the two sisters chuckled like young girls.

Maggie sat at the counter opposite the sisters.

'You ladies can get me up on the gossip in the town. It always helps to know the connections.'

'We don't do gossip, it only brings trouble,' Muriel said.

'Anyway, the only thing people are talking about is you two and what you are doing here. Everybody wants a gawk.'

Maggie laughed. 'That may happen, because as well as a bakery, Katie is opening a stylish café. They will be beating a path to our door.'

Rosie blushed.

'Stack up the breakfast rolls; that's where you will make the money,' Rosie said.

'Breakfast roll? What's that?' Maggie asked.

'You know, breakfast – bacon, sausage, egg and a dollop of tomato sauce in a white roll; nothing like it,' Rosie said, and Muriel nodded enthusiastically in agreement.

'We won't be doing anything like that,' Katie said, her voice clipped.

'Not to worry; everybody is so interested in how you are doing up this place. The word was Mr Flint wanted a very modern interior. We were hoping you ladies would have more sense.'

Muriel slapped her sister on the wrist.

'Now hush, Rosie, it's entirely their own business what they intend to do.' She looked at Katie and Maggie.

'We just want the old Kilcashel House. This was once the best house in the area. When Anna was in charge, she let the whole town picnic down at the sea and we had community events here.'

'Anna?'

'Yes, Anna Walker. She owned the place until the American came along.'

Katie, who had placed the toasted bagels on small china plates, stopped what she was doing.

'Anna, who lives in the gate lodge?'

Muriel elbowed her sister.

'We have said too much already. We're not gossips, but we can't help it if we know the town and everybody in it like the back of our hands.'

Maggie poured the coffee.

'Ladies, you have started, so you may as well finish. This is the best thing since I arrived, real juicy gossip – and about Anna, no less.'

'I think if Anna wanted us to know, she would have told us herself,' Katie said sternly.

'Oh, come on Miss Prissy Pants,' Maggie chuckled. 'Can't we have a bit of fun for once?'

Rosie and Muriel giggled as Katie sat down on the edge of the group.

'When we were growing up, Kilcashel House was the best house in the region. Anna's mum always had the finest parties and there was a piano in the front drawing room. They took the big table out of the dining room and pushed back the chairs and that was the dance floor. If you hadn't danced at Kilcashel House, you were a nobody for sure,' Muriel said.

Rosie interrupted: 'It was a thriving farm too, with fine horses in the front paddocks and cattle in the far-off fields. Mrs Walker was the one who grew all these beautiful flowers. She was multi-talented; she could sing, dance and had green fingers to boot.'

Muriel leaned forward. 'It's why we jumped at the chance to have an allotment here. The soil at Kilcashel House is the finest.'

'But the estate house seemed very run-down and I understand Harry...' Katie stopped because her voice was shaking.

'She means my ex-husband.'

'We thought you were sisters,' Muriel said, nudging Rosie with her elbow.

'There you have it: ex-wife and partner, holed up in this grand old place. Harry has turned it around, done all the necessary work.'

'And thrown out the character with it. This was a lovely old farmhouse kitchen.' Rosie stopped. 'I am sounding too critical. I don't mean to. It's just, the place meant so much to all of us. We left from here to our first dance. We got ready up there in the front first-floor bedroom. Mrs Walker used to send up trays of sandwiches and squash. We poured the vodka in from a naggin Catherine hid under her bed.'

The two women tittered, their heads together.

'Catherine?' Katie asked.

'Anna's younger sister. She was a wild one,' Rosie laughed.

Maggie pushed a plate of cookies towards them.

'Try the cookies and you will never want another dry scone again. Now, please do tell us more.'

Katie got up and let in Anna's dog, Lola, who was scratching at the door.

'Yes, tell us more about the Walker sisters,' Katie said.

Rosie was about to say something, but Muriel cut across her.

'Maybe Anna is the best one to talk about all this. It was all a long time ago. We might have overstepped the mark.'

'Did Anna live here, and did she sell it to Harry?' Katie asked.

'Anna has lived at the gate lodge for a long time now. She was rattling around this old house on her own, so it was best she move out. Your Harry might have torn the guts out of the place, but at least he let Anna stay in the gate lodge. It would have killed her, if she had to move away altogether.'

They were interrupted by a man knocking on the kitchen window.

'Can ye come out and direct me exactly where I should be? I don't want to get it wrong,' he said, and the sisters got up from the table.

'Can we take a few of the cookies to nibble on as we work?' Muriel asked. Katie nodded and got a little box for them.

'This is so fancy, nobody is even going to care about scones anymore,' Rosie said, as they rushed up the hall to the front door, calling out goodbye and thanks as they went.

When they heard the front door shut behind the Falvey sisters, Maggie reached for two glasses.

'It might be early, but I imagine this calls for an alcoholic beverage.'

Katie didn't disagree, but sat down.

'It's so weird that Anna never let on she owned Kilcashel. I wonder why.'

'Pride,' Maggie said, 'the woman has it in spades.'

'But what do we do now? Do we wait for her to tell us or what?'

Maggie poured her drink and slurped it quickly.

'We pretend we never knew.'

'It's just that Dan never said anything either.'

'Maybe he thought we knew,' Maggie said as she pushed a glass towards Katie. 'I can't help thinking of good old Harry with his big boots tramping all over history.'

'But why? What made him buy the property in the first place and write into his will this ridiculous thing he has us doing? A posh hotel was never going to work in these parts.'

Maggie clapped.

'Finally, you agree with me.'

'I don't like thinking that the local people hate what has been done to the place. What if they boycott the café?'

'We will have to make sure they don't. The sisters are a good start. Anyway, we didn't make the decision to throw out the furniture and make this into a modern pile.'

'Anna must hate everything that has been done to Kilcashel House,' Katie said.

'And she probably hates even more that we are opening a café. She is such a private old bat. Is that what the hoo-hah about the cherry blossoms was about? It still doesn't make much sense.'

'Maybe a little, Anna has had to put up with a lot of change in a short period of time,' Katie said.

'And three mad Americans,' Maggie snorted, making her way back to her room with her glass of Prosecco. Katie pulled an old tracksuit from the laundry basket along with a well-worn pair of socks and put on her clothes and wellingtons.

Calling the dog to follow, she set off down the garden path to the sea. It was still too early for anybody to be about. Pushing her hands in her hoodie pockets, she dipped her head and set off across the sand. This was her beach now, but it didn't feel like it. She wanted to be tramping the streets of Chelsea, people jogging by her, others already talking on the phone and rushing to work. She needed to feel the city around her; she so badly pined to be back in New York, it hurt.

She was conscious of the power of the sea every day, the

rhythm of the waves was a constant backdrop. The salt in the air greased across the window glass. When they parked the car at the back, the sea brine built up thick on the windscreen, so they had to get a kettle of warm water to remove it. Sometimes too, she took her cue from the plants, cowering down as if they knew the sea wind was ready to blast them.

Standing, she held out her hands towards the oncoming waves as if to stop them; the water rolling towards her and crashing around her feet. She ran backwards, but was drawn again to the water's edge. Her hood fell back and she let her hair tumble around her, pummelled by the strong breeze.

When Dan called her, she didn't at first hear him. When she saw him jogging along the shore, she thought he was exercising.

'The otters are just up the coast a bit, at the mouth of the river, I thought you might like to see them.'

'How did you know I was here?'

'I saw you from my garden,' he said, pointing to a bungalow further along.

They walked briskly together, the wind on their backs, until Dan indicated that they climb some rocks and over a wall into a field.

'Time you got to know your own land anyway. This is the field you have leased to a farmer from Rathdrum, he grows pota-toes here.'

'Wow, I didn't know about that.'

'He paid Harry upfront for two years to make sure he secured the land.'

They skirted along up the side of the field and across the top, towards the river, where the water gathered in a large pool then ran down to enter the sea.

Dan put his finger to his mouth and inched closer to the water.

'We will stay here; there's an otter and her pups. They

should be out and about shortly; she brings them to the river and pool edge. I'm hoping to see their first swim.'

They didn't have long to wait before the female otter appeared, surrounded by her young. The otter looked cautiously about as her pups tumbled over the grass to the pool edge. Katie moved closer, stepping on a tree branch, which cracked loudly.

The mother otter made a squeaking noise, gathered up her young and they disappeared into the undergrowth.

'Have I frightened them off?' Katie asked anxiously.

'Yes, but don't concentrate on that; think of the few minutes we were able to watch them unobserved. We can walk back to the house through the fields, if you like.'

He led the way along the side of the potato field and into another field where cows were grazing.

'They are not mine, are they?'

'No, they are my cows; I rent the field from you, and again I paid Mr Flint upfront as well.'

'I am beginning to feel I know nothing about the Kilcashel estate.'

'How would you? You're a New Yorker.'

'My New York survival skills aren't doing me much good now.'

'You have a lot on your plate. Starting up a business is not easy, and doing it all in a place you don't even know...'

'...is madness, but baking is the only thing I know, and Maggie makes good coffee.'

'That's a start.'

'You never told me Anna lived all her life at Kilcashel before selling it to Harry.'

'Not my story to tell. It's Anna's business, not mine.'

'But you could have given me the heads up. I feel a fool about all this.'

Dan stopped walking.

'It was for Anna to reveal that story, not me,' he said, kicking the sand with his boots.

'She has been so good to me; I feel bad, I had no idea.'

'It's been a long road for Anna; she lost her home and land and somehow managed to keep that gate lodge. I imagine there were times she was terrified she would be chucked out on her ear.'

'I would never do that.'

'I think she probably knows that, but what about Maggie? She's ready to flog the estate to the highest bidder.'

Katie looked at him.

'She can't do it without me. I am determined to make this home. I might be a city girl, but my future is here.'

'I didn't mean to offend.'

'You didn't; you said it as it looks. Guess I have to prove to everybody, and especially Anna, that I mean to bring Kilcashel back to its glory days.'

'Take it slowly and you will get there, but be careful of the Falvey sisters. They insist they aren't gossips, but they're full of it and they twist everything. Don't be looking to them for help. Anna will be fierce mad when she finds they are churning up her front paddock.'

'If she had only told me...'

'She will, all in her own good time.'

They rounded the rhododendron.

'I'm off to make sure the Falveys don't take too much ground for their allotment. I reckon that's why they wanted to get in early.'

Katie shook her head.

'One day I will get up and I will feel everything is under control at Kilcashel.'

'That will be a boring day,' he said as he jumped the fence and set off down the avenue to reach the allotments.

Katie turned to the house.

The glass on the window flashed gold, the brickwork looked mellow in the morning light. The pots of flowers at the front were budding, and the dog was asleep on the front step. How did Anna walk up this avenue every day and see her former home? Katie's heart tightened for her and the conversation they must have someday soon.

TWELVE

Katie was surprised when Maggie came into the kitchen as she and the other two swimming ladies prepared for their morning dip. Usually she went out of her way to avoid the kitchen as the swimming group met for their dawn dip, but this morning apparently Maggie's desire for an espresso drove her downstairs. Katie was putting the last trays of bagels in the oven, ready to bake when she got back, and Nora was laughing and trying to get into her wetsuit, when Maggie swept into the room in her silk dressing gown.

'It rained buckets last night; won't it be unpleasant down at the sea this morning?' Maggie asked.

'Unpleasant getting there sometimes, and maybe this morning is one of them, but once we get in the sea, it's a different world,' Leonie said.

'Bloody freezing and half crazy,' Maggie said.

'How do you know? What are you basing that criticism on?' Nora asked, her voice high-pitched, because she was annoyed.

Maggie swung around to her. 'I am entitled to my opinion. Going for a morning swim in the Pacific Ocean, I could understand, but this' – she gestured across the room where the women were in various stages of undress – 'this is madness getting into the bitterly cold Irish Sea.'

'I tell you what, you are entitled to your opinion when it is an informed opinion. Why don't you come with us this morning? And if you think it's madness after that, so be it,' Nora said.

The other women clapped and Katie, feeling they were trying to railroad Maggie, pointed out that she didn't have a wetsuit.

'I always have a spare set in my car,' Leonie said, shooting out the back door before anyone had time to respond.

'Give it a try, you might end up loving it,' Katie said, and Maggie laughed and said she would, but just to prove her own point.

They all came around and helped Maggie into the wetsuit, Nora insisting she wear special shoes to protect her feet, and a swimming hat.

'To me, swimming is wearing a bikini and feeling the sun on my back, not this survival course,' Maggie grumbled as they playfully pushed her out the back door.

Katie took her hand as she stumbled and slipped in places as they made their way through the garden and down the narrow path to the beach. The first birds were singing as the sun inched over the sea, throwing pink gold streaks across the sky and water.

The sound of the waves was all around them as they walked on to the shore.

Katie made them stop to take it all in.

'I never realised it was so beautiful down here,' Maggie said, squeezing Katie's hand.

'We are all so glad you came,' Nora said as she persuaded Maggie to take off her coat and walk towards the sea.

Leonie took her other hand.

'Let yourself go, just run in, and let the water take over,' Katie shouted after her.

When she tried to pull back, Katie and the others propelled her forward, only letting go as the waves came crashing in around them.

Katie stood and watched Maggie as she let the sea take charge. She knew the pain of the cold water was searing through her, chasing her grief away, making her concentrate on nothing else but the power of the waves. She saw Maggie steal further out, swimming parallel to the shore. Katie joined her. When a wave came over their heads, they welcomed it, treading water, willing the next one to come along.

Nora hollered that it was time to get out, but they both shouted back that they didn't want to ever leave this sea, which cleansed both body and her mind. Nora swam to them.

'We always get out together.'

'But—' Maggie said.

'Come on; we never leave anybody behind,' Nora said, and both Katie and Maggie obediently followed.

The women marched back up the strand, laughing and chatting.

When they got to the garden, Maggie ran in front of the others.

'OK, I admit it, I was wrong. I bloody well loved it and, if you allow me, can I please come again tomorrow morning?'

Nora grinned from ear to ear.

'Of course you can, silly goose,' she said.

Later in the kitchen, Katie expressed surprise that Nora had not gloated over her win.

'There are no winners; this is all about being together. Now, Maggie is one of our tribe; we look after each other, and the sea, it looks after us,' Nora replied.

Katie added an extra mug as Maggie sat up to the counter for coffee and bagels. Katie was about to turn on the ovens when Maggie said they should all have a glass of Prosecco to celebrate.

'Celebrate what exactly?' Katie asked.

'My first day where I actually feel part of Kilcashel House,' she said, taking down a bottle of Prosecco and easing off the cork.

Nora quickly placed some glasses in front of her and Maggie poured the bubbly then raised her glass high.

'A toast to the swimming ladies; my tribe,' she said, and they all laughed, clinking glasses.

Katie said they had better rush as Anna would soon be arriving.

The others gathered up their belongings and hugged both Katie and Maggie before leaving.

Maggie, her eyes bright, said she was off to shower and change.

'Thank you, Katie, I can honestly say that, since this terrible thing happened to Harry, this is the first time I have felt a reason to be alive.'

'I know,' Katie said, and she didn't resist when Maggie enveloped her in a big hug.

Katie smiled as Maggie climbed the stairs, humming a tune to herself. She had been equally reluctant when first asked to join the swimming ladies, but now, it was the only start to the day she wanted to contemplate.

Nora, she knew, had said the same words to her as she did to Maggie: 'Be yourself; don't be afraid.' It was a good maxim, she thought.

All this time, Maggie had been hiding behind a facade. Maybe now she would find, from the healing power of the sea, the strength to be herself.

Maybe here at Kilcashel House, they had both finally found their tribe.

Anna didn't come to the big house that morning and by noon, Katie was worried. The dog hung around the kitchen at Kilcashel, looking forlorn.

'She's probably avoiding us, because she knows the Falveys have spilled the beans,' Maggie said.

'Do you think I should call on her, in case she's ill?'

'That's why she has a cell phone. Doh.'

'She doesn't text and never answers her phone.'

Maggie put on her coat.

'I'm off to see the local newspaper about publicity for the café opening. If I see the old bird, I'll tell her you're looking for her.'

Katie couldn't settle. She took down her steel bowls to try out her cranberry cookie recipe, and gathered up the ingredients, but left them on the table untouched.

Calling Lola, she took her raincoat from the hook on the back door and set off down the avenue.

Muriel Falvey was in the car park lugging a big bucket from the back seat of her car.

'We're planting extra spuds. Maybe it's a few weeks late, but we'll take our chances. Are you looking for Anna?'

'I was going to call in.'

'She went out early.'

'She never said.'

'Anna is her own woman; you should know that by now. She does things her way.'

Katie made to turn away, but Muriel called her.

'Grab the other side of the bin; help me drag it up to the allotment.'

Katie did as she was bid, and the two of them half dragged and half carried the bin up to the top of the allotment.

'Your friend doesn't want the spuds in front of the house; she has stipulated that one quarter of each allotment has to be wildflowers. Did you ever hear such nonsense?'

'It's good for the bees and butterflies.'

'And an absolute mess, but she's the boss. Comes around every day to see what we're doing. I will be glad when we have a few more allotment owners. We will be able to shout her down.'

Katie shook her head.

'I wish you luck with that.'

Muriel pulled a flask out of a bag which was straddled across two wooden chairs.

'I can offer coffee. I'm sorry, but we're pensioners, we won't be able to afford your coffee prices all the time. We bring the flask for the early morning. Your café will be our treat for elevenses, when you open your doors.'

'I'll hold you to that.'

She sat down on a chair, letting its legs sink into the earth until it became steady.

'Will you guys be able to do all the heavy lifting?'

Muriel poured the black coffee into two china mugs and handed one to Katie.

'The beauty of an allotment is that there is always a little man who wants to be helpful. We are learning a lot at the moment. Dan won't be helping us for much longer. He doesn't look like an allotment man. He will head for the hills.'

'He's just lending a hand; I'm sure he has his own life.'

'I don't know, I see himself and Maggie chatting. They look good together, but she'll have to lose the heels; that man is a country man through and through.'

Katie giggled.

'Maggie is all New York. She's on the way back there, and I don't think anyone will get in the way of that.'

'Love works in mysterious ways. Now, we just have to find somebody for you.'

'I'm too busy with setting up the café.'

Muriel got a small hip flask out of the bag and poured some of the contents in her coffee.

'Brandy. It's very good in the coffee and it keeps me off the sugar. You're silly, if you think you're too busy for love.'

Muriel reached over and, without asking, sloshed some brandy in Katie's mug.

'At my age, I can say anything, and I do,' she said.

'I like your spirit, Muriel,' Katie said as she downed her coffee.

'Seriously though, what good is life if we don't let ourselves fall in love?'

'I'm still grieving for my partner.'

'Maggie's ex? Was that ever going to work out?'

'We loved each other. When he was killed, he was on his way to ask me to marry him.'

Muriel stared at Katie. 'You poor thing, and you let me blather on.'

'It's OK.'

Muriel coughed to hide her embarrassment. When they both saw Anna turn in at the Kilcashel House gates, Muriel threw her hands in the air.

'Maybe I should just go home to bed; I seem to be getting everything wrong today.'

Katie waved at Anna, who didn't look towards the allotments.

'I had better go and talk to her.'

Muriel stood up to walk Katie off the allotment as if she had been entertaining in her front room.

'We let the cat out of the bag, didn't we?'

'We were going to find out eventually, I guess,' Katie said.

Muriel stopped by the potato bin. 'Could you do me a favour and not tell Anna it was the Falveys who told you she once owned Kilcashel?'

'Sure, but I don't see what the big deal is.'

Muriel moved from one foot to another.

'It's a very big deal, but I have said enough. Anna is a very private person and when she wants to let you in, she will.'

'Are you friends?'

'We were the best of friends once, a long time ago. Until Catherine left. We're only passing acquaintances now.'

Katie detected a sadness in Muriel's tone.

'Anna's sister, can you tell me more about her?'

'Emigrated to the States, never came back after that,' Muriel said, her voice flat.

'You're kidding.'

'Unfortunately not. Do me a favour please, Katie; don't let on any of this to Anna. She would go mad if she thought I was talking about her.'

'Don't worry,' Katie said, making her way along the allotment path to the avenue.

When she got to the lodge, Anna was in the kitchen. Katie tapped lightly on the open door and stuck her head in.

'Hi Anna, I just called down in case there was anything amiss?'

Anna, who had just set up her ironing board, made a face.

'Can't a person take a day off without somebody sending out a search party?'

'No search party; it's just me and I was worried about you, that's all.'

Anna rifled through her wash basket and pulled out a white blouse and placed it on the ironing board.

'No need to worry, I'll be back to the big house as usual tomorrow morning.'

Feeling nervous, Katie fiddled with a tea towel which had been left on the worktop.

'It's very busy at the house right now, Anna, so if you need another day off, I would appreciate if you would let me know in advance.'

Anna plugged in the iron and set it on the ironing board.

'Today is May twenty-seventh and I always take that day off. I go to Mass and there are other things I have to do.'

'Which is fine, but you could have let me know—'

Anna caught the iron and slapped it on the sleeve of the blouse. The iron made a thudding noise as she banged it across the fabric.

'It is not my fault or my responsibility if you, as the new owners of Kilcashel House, are not aware of the terms of my contract. Considering you intimated that everything was going to go on as before, I presumed you had read the contract and the provision for this day off.'

'Everything happened so fast. I didn't know about you until I got here, and I certainly never knew about a contract. I agreed to continue with the arrangement because we needed the help, and I didn't want you to think I was taking over and going to change everything.'

She noticed Anna slump a little and place the iron upright.

'Do you really need me at the house today?' she asked.

'No, of course not; you do what you have to do. I'll see you tomorrow.'

'Thank you.'

Katie left by the back door and quickly walked back to the avenue. She did not dare ask Anna the significance of this date and she shouldn't ask the Falvey sisters. Harry should have left a handbook on how to negotiate life here at Kilcashel, she thought, and she felt angry that he had set herself and Maggie up without even an explanation.

Lola stopped and stooped down, her ears back, growling into the allotment paddock. Nervously, Katie stood behind the dog, peering across the allotments. She froze when she saw a fox, his head in Muriel's canvas bag. Muriel was busy nosing around somebody else's garden. Katie watched the fox for a few moments before deciding she should do something. Clapping her hands loudly, she hoped the fox would run away. Muriel turned around and gave a friendly wave. Retreating from the bag, the fox ambled across the Falveys' allotment, throwing a sideway glance at Katie and the dog and then disappearing behind a polytunnel. Katie called the dog to heel and continued back to the house.

THIRTEEN

Katie was too busy to join the swimming tribe. She heard Maggie get ready upstairs as she slipped out on to the deck for some quiet time. This was her favourite part of the day, when she could stand alone on the deck and listen to the waves crashing to shore. There was a strength in the sea that both frightened and exhilarated her, making her heart race. Pulling in the cold morning air, she shivered, tugging her cardigan tight around her.

Soon Maggie would come downstairs and fill the place with her chatter and the swimming women would arrive in dribs and drabs. Most of the time here at Kilcashel she felt she was fire-fighting, but in this early morning, waiting for the other women to arrive for their morning dip, she was happy.

Katie giggled when she saw Maggie, her wetsuit under her robe, and a bright red swimming cap, which Nora insisted she wear.

'It's the hat, isn't it?' Maggie said.

'They will definitely be able to find you if you go missing.'

'If I sink, a fat lot the hideous hat will do then!' Maggie said, but Katie wagged a finger at her and said in a good imitation of Nora's voice:

'You'll tread water and try to stay alive. We'll find you.'

Nora, who was coming up the path, laughed out loud.

'Not bad at all, but you need to work on your Irish accent; sounds a bit too fake yet.'

Katie jumped back embarrassed.

'Gosh, we were just having a laugh, no disrespect intended,' Katie said, her cheeks burning red with embarrassment.

Nora smiled. 'No worries, we're swimming buddies. Why aren't you dressed? We want to get going straight away,' she asked Katie.

'I have so much to do. I'm just taking a moment sitting out on the deck. Thinking time.'

'Aren't you the lucky one to have the luxury of thinking time?' Nora said.

Maggie said they should get going and Katie smiled that the girl who never could see beyond Manhattan was now, every morning, looking forward to the dip in the cold Irish Sea with these women, who had something to say about everything.

She so wished she could join them. Sometimes they ran into the sea and other times, they tiptoed in and washed their face and hands before plunging into the waves.

They talked a lot. There was something about feeling the movement of the water all around them and the freedom of whispering secrets across the waves. In the sea there was no need to hide anything. These women were good listeners too.

About forty-five minutes later, Katie had all the bagels and cookies in the ovens and was sitting having her morning cup of coffee when Maggie burst in the kitchen door, tears streaming down her face.

'What happened?' Katie rushed to Maggie, who side-stepped her and ran for the stairs. Hesitating in the hall, she turned around.

'I lost Harry too, you know.'

Nora and Leonie ran in, without knocking.

'Where is she, is she all right?' Nora asked.

'What happened out there?'

Nora sat down at the counter.

'I opened my big mouth and said what everybody is thinking; that she's just swanning around here and you're working so hard.'

'You had no business saying any of that. Maggie has been very generous with her time.'

Leonie threw her wet clothes on the floor and pulled a stool out to sit down.

'That's not the whole story; we sort of implied you had it worse, losing Harry.'

Katie clenched her hands into fists and pounded the counter.

'You had no right.'

'We know; she asked and we told the truth; a bloody stupid thing to do. Maggie sure isn't as tough as she makes out; we know that now,' Nora said, hanging her head so she didn't have to look Katie in the eye.

'Dan is going to be so cross when he hears this. He always says we are too direct and we don't think things through,' Leonie said.

Katie got up and poured coffee into Maggie's favourite china mug.

'I'm going upstairs to talk to her; please help yourself to coffee and bagels,' she said, her tone clipped.

Maggie was lying on the bed crying. Katie placed the mug of coffee on the mahogany bedside table.

'Do you want to talk about it?'

Maggie pushed further into her pillow.

'I'm sorry for what happened out there.'

Maggie suddenly sat up. 'Are you really? Doesn't this suit nice, popular, grieving Katie, who is so brave coming to Ireland and setting up a business; while I am the wicked witch from the Big Apple.'

'That's not true.'

'Of course I'm grieving; I just don't go around looking like a mopey dog all day.'

'You didn't bother to claim Harry's ashes.'

'Really, you're going to throw that at me now? You didn't bother to go to his funeral.'

'You know I was too upset to go,' Katie shouted.

'And I was too upset to collect the ashes of the man who'd robbed me blind. Pardon me if I didn't want to put him on the mantelpiece.'

'It wasn't right, Maggie.'

'Maybe, but it's done.'

Katie tried to stifle a giggle.

She saw a smile touch the corner of Maggie's mouth.

'I want to throw slices of cold beef at windowpanes, but all there is around here are bagels and more bagels.'

Katie put her hand up. 'We can't afford to repair any broken glass.'

Maggie sighed.

'It would have helped so much.'

Katie pulled her hand.

'Get some clothes on and come downstairs; I have an idea.'

Are the others down there?'

'Yeah, but it's OK.'

'I yelled at them.'

'So? They're big girls, a bit of shouting is not going to put them off. Five minutes.'

When Katie got downstairs, Nora and Leonie stood up, ready to leave.

'Maggie is coming down, please stay.'

The two women sat back down, nervously picking at the bagels on their plates but not eating. When Maggie came into the room, she was wearing a black velvet dressing gown and carrying a handkerchief. Her eyes were red from crying.

Nora was beside her in two strides and grabbed her into a hug.

'We're so sorry, we shouldn't have opened our big mouths.'

'Yeah, meet the insensitive clods,' Leonie said, and Maggie smiled.

'We're good.'

Katie reached into a cupboard and pulled out a big refuse sack.

'The Japanese smash bottles, but all I have is a lot of hard, stale bagels, I thought we could have a throwing contest, fire them into the sea.'

Maggie stared at her.

'If this is your big idea, you need help.'

'It might be fun – come on,' she said, pulling on her coat and making for the door.

Nora and Leonie laughed, and Maggie tied her dressing gown tighter around her as they followed Katie out the door.

'I will ruin my slippers,' she said, but Katie dragged her down the path.

'Who cares, come on,' she shouted.

Maggie kicked off her slippers and they raced to the shore, skipping past each other and whooping loudly as the sun rose high over the water. Katie upended the refuse sack, spilling the bagels out on the sand.

'They're like footballs,' Nora said.

'I don't always get it right. I forgot these were in the oven and hadn't set a timer when I went for my bath,' Katie said, going for an underarm pitch.

The bagel whizzed through the air, plopping down to be drowned by a wave.

'Pathetic,' Nora shouted, throwing two in an over-arm pitch which sped through the air and landed fifty feet out.

Maggie kissed her bagel before sending it off, but it dropped into the shallows.

Leonie pulled her aside and coached her as she made another attempt; this time extending her arm as if she were executing a baseball pitch.

The bagel whizzed through the air, diving into the water, landing the furthest out, surfing a wave before finally sinking to the bottom. Maggie jumped up and down, punching the air and whooping. Leonie clapped and Katie and Nora pitched harder to try and beat the record. When all the bagels were gone, they trooped back to the house, invigorated and happy.

'Prosecco time,' Maggie announced, getting down four champagne glasses.

The others didn't object.

Katie asked to make a toast.

'To the women left behind by Harry, may we always be friends,' she said, turning to clink glasses with Maggie first.

'Thank goodness we got over that,' Nora said.

'Yes, be sure and have a stash of hard bagels ready for when we next need them,' Leonie said, making the others giggle.

Nora and Leonie said they had better get along, but they would be around first thing the next morning.

When they had gone, Maggie poured two more glasses of Prosecco.

'I think it's time we had a talk,' she said, and Katie sat down opposite her at the counter.

Maggie twirled the glass stem between her fingers as she tried to find the words. Katie fidgeted with a cake box, pulling at the sides until it collapsed.

'I think maybe we got off on the wrong foot. It's my fault. I have been against everything here and in truth, this is my home now too, and I want to make a go of the bakery and a café too and anything else we do. So I thought, if you don't mind, we could work together,' Maggie said rapidly and all in one breath.

'But what would you do?'

'Like I said, you need an expert eye to oversee the setting up of the café and I am, pardon the modesty, the queen of marketing.'

'But you have already helped with the boxes and so many other little details, I would never have imagined.'

'The boxes are a gift. Now I want to be a full partner in charge of presentation and marketing.'

'That's a fancy title.'

'Darling, I work best when I have a big title; it drives me to think big.'

'But what about the hard graft every day; are you ready for that?'

'I'm not afraid of work. We need a warm, welcoming café; a place where people want to linger and celebrate occasions. You must have a lunch, snack and treat takeout service as well.'

Katie suddenly felt nervous. 'Do you think there will be a demand for something like that in Kilcashel?' she said.

'We'll have to create a demand,' Maggie said firmly.

'Easy to say.'

'And for me, to do. I am also willing to invest some savings as well as time. I want to be part of this, Katie.'

'We're taking a massive leap.'

'True, but let's work to our strengths and create something wonderful.'

Katie drank down her Prosecco. 'You do realise I want to stay on here; I don't want to go back to Manhattan.'

'If this is a success, you can buy me out.'

'I can see what you're gaining from the arrangement, but will you put in the work to get us to that stage?'

'There has to be a certain level of trust. I want to be bought out, so it's in my interest to make the new venture a success. You get my expertise and I get your talent.'

Katie looked at Maggie.

'Can we draw up a written contract?'

'We can, but my word is good, Katie. I know Harry may not have painted me in the best light, but I don't go back on a deal.'

Katie took Maggie's hand and shook it.

'Welcome aboard, Maggie.'

'Good, partner; this is going to be such fun,' Maggie said, smiling broadly.

'I know Anna won't be happy.'

'Anna is going to have to learn her new position around here.'

'I don't want to alienate her, Maggie. She's a valuable asset for us in the local community.'

'If you say so. Now let's have a look at this café room.'

The builder had already created an opening in the wall and was due to plaster the arch later that day and install a granite-topped counter as a divider between the bakery, kitchen and the café.

Maggie walked out into the middle of the room.

'Tables for two along the centre and velvet armchairs at the fireplace where an open fire will be lit. We must have little nooks with velvet armchairs at the bay windows. Longer tables for groups with benches along the back wall, to the side of the door.'

'Won't the armchairs take up too much space?'

'They will, but customers will fight over what they think are the best seats in the house.' Maggie stood at one of the bay windows, her hands on her hips, surveying the terrace. 'And we need a few tables outside with parasols.'

'I thought it might cheapen the place, and the weather is never very good here.'

'Benches will give too much of a pub feel, but classy rattan chairs and tables outside will look the business. And parasols too.'

'That all sounds too expensive.'

Maggie shrugged. 'You have to spend the bucks to get it the bucks, darling, I saw a set the last time I was down at the stables. We can ask Dan and Nora's hubby to get it up here. One set will do to start.'

She spun around to take in the room.

'The teal can stay on the walls. I'm thinking a rich velvet gold or bright blue on the armchairs; we can cover them ourselves. We're stuck with the tables and chairs, but the table-cloths should be lovely. We must have a focus over the fireplace. Maybe there is something in the stables store.'

'No, it's all furniture, unless you want to try the attic rooms.'

'Sounds like a plan.'

They heard Anna push open the back door and pause to shake out her umbrella.

'Have you seen the beach? It's destroyed; somebody must have gone through your rubbish and taken the stale bagels. They're all over the shore. I had to forcibly drag Lola away. I'm sure she's going to get sick,' she called out.

'What's going on? Have I missed something?' she said, eyeing the champagne glasses after she hung her coat on the backdoor hook.

'We have decided to become partners in the café and bakery,' Katie said.

Anna looked from one to the other. 'I see. This means I really do have two bosses, I suppose?'

'It means we are going to share the responsibility and the work and bring our own strengths to the table to make the house and café a success,' Maggie said, her voice unusually firm.

'Whatever you say,' Anna replied, opening the dishwasher.

'Thanks for the vote of confidence,' Maggie snapped.

Anna straightened and looked at Maggie.

'This is none of my business; you do what you have to do. I am, at this moment, more interested in the beach; it's destroyed. Somebody is going to have to clean it up, and my brief doesn't extend that far,' Anna said, putting on her apron and gathering up the champagne glasses and putting them in the dishwasher.

'Ah the tide will sort all that,' Maggie said.

'Well you may laugh, but that's a hazard. What will happen to the baby seals if they eat bagels?'

'Next we will have them queueing at the back door looking for bagels with cream filling,' Maggie said, and Katie burst out laughing.

Anna said she had to hoover the stairs and flounced out of the kitchen. Maggie and Katie laughed until they cried. Embracing, they held each other, letting the laughter tears turn to sobs of grief for a shared loss.

FOURTEEN

'Come on up here and see what I've found,' Maggie hollered.

Katie ignored her; if she answered every time Maggie shouted out, she would never get any work done.

'Worth the climb up, you have to see this.'

Katie concentrated harder, tying ribbons on the boxes of cookies for display beside the till to tempt customers.

It was just two days to the opening and the finishing touches needed to be made to the Drawing Room Café.

Maggie had said she was going to drive into town to buy flowers for each table, but first, she disappeared upstairs. Katie was annoyed. How many times had she done that: say she was going to do one thing and then wasted time on something entirely different? It meant that someone, usually Anna or herself, had to take up the slack, and they were both tired of it.

She picked up her mobile phone and rang Anna, who was in Bray buying sugar, milk and extra spoons.

'Maggie has decided today is a good time to rummage in the attic and we still haven't got any flowers for the tables.'

'Surprise, surprise. What do you want me to get?' Anna asked.

'Roses, but not expensive ones. Go to Aldi and buy a few bunches.'

'I'll hop in there on my way home. What is Maggie doing up in the attic rooms? I thought she had pulled enough out of there and the stables already.'

'Who knows?' Katie said, quickly ending the call when one of her ovens pinged, signalling the latest batch of biscuits was ready.

She was rolling the heavy trays from the oven when Dan stuck his head in the door.

'I've tidied up around the front gate and trimmed the grass edges up the avenue. Is there anything else you want doing?'

The blast of heat from the oven hit her in the face as she wheeled the trays out. Wiping off the sweat with a tea towel she always kept on her shoulder, she turned to Dan.

'What will I do if nobody bothers to turn up?'

'That's not going to happen.'

'We sent out over one hundred emails and got ten replies, and nothing from all the invitations I hand-delivered myself.'

'Everybody is coming. All you need to worry about is that you have enough to feed the hordes of Genghis Khan.'

'I don't understand.'

'Who's going to answer an invitation? What would they say?'

'But it's rude not to answer; I have been so worried.'

He laughed. 'You don't realise that this place has been the talk of the town for quite a while. Wild horses won't keep them away, and once they taste what's on offer, they will come back again and again.'

'I wish I could be so confident. Muriel said the other day that another café has opened up in Kilcashel, where the old bank used to be; they're offering full lunches, meat, two veg – and a doggy bag if you can't clear the plate.'

'And there will be people who will like that, but the rest of us will love sampling downtown Manhattan just a mile out of Kilcashel.'

She grinned. Dan really was a glass-half-full sort of guy, and she loved that about him.

'Come on, take a break; I'll show you what I've done on the avenue.'

He caught her by the hand and she let him guide her out the back door and around the house.

'What am I supposed to be looking at?' she said, scanning the avenue as far as the rhododendron.

'Close your eyes and let me lead you.'

She tried to peek through her hands, but he tapped gently on her wrists.

'You will see soon enough.'

Leisurely, he led her along the driveway, stopping every few steps to ensure she wasn't peeking. At the rhododendron grove, he angled her body very deliberately.

'You can open your eyes now,' he said, taking away his hands.

Katie blinked in the light. On the grass verge was a sign on a dark green background which said:

Welcome to Kilcashel House and the Drawing Room Café.

Further on, at the entrance to the path running across the wildflower meadow was another smaller sign:

Gentlemen won't, and others must not pick the flowers.

'There's another sign at the gate for the house and café. Do you like them?'

Katie walked over to the big sign and ran her fingers across it. Delicate paintings of wildflowers edged the writing.

'I love it; who thought of this? It's beautiful, just like the boxes.'

'Maggie, of course; she has such an eye for detail and the small sign was her idea as well, though I think she may have stolen that from a picture on the internet.'

'Anna will say it's more of her notions, but I adore it. We look like a proper country house now.'

They heard a window at the top front of the house being pulled up and opened.

Maggie waved to the two of them.

'Don't they look great?'

Katie gave a thumbs up.

'Dan, can I borrow you? I've found something interesting, and I want you to carry it downstairs,' Maggie said.

Katie patted him on the back.

'Madam has called; you had better help her or we will never hear the end of it.'

Katie watched Dan turn back to the house, then she set off along the avenue to look at the main sign at the gate. It was a warm June day; the roses planted along by the field fencing were in bloom and a jasmine she had picked up at a super-market was creeping along thin wires attached to the planks. Dan, she thought, must have done that. The avenue had been weeded and gravelled and the edges sharpened. As she turned the corner approaching the main gates, she could see the gate lodge. Anna had allowed them to repaint the windowsills, window frames and front door, and the area around the cherry blossoms had been mulched.

The house didn't look neglected anymore, she thought, but she doubted Anna was happy with the transformation. Two signs had been erected left and right of the gates for the benefit of approaching traffic. Opening times were hanging separately from the main signs. Katie crossed the road to view the entrance. The gates had been painted silver and the entrance looked well.

Lola wandered on to the road as Anna stepped out of her house, a shopping bag and bunches of roses in her hands.

'They won't miss us now with those signs,' she said.

'They're not in your way, are they?'

'No, but you do know nobody will pay a blind bit of notice to anything written there. We'll be plagued by those wanting to go up the avenue morning, noon and night.'

'When the café is closed, the gates will be shut.'

'As if that will stop them! They'll come sniffing around the gate lodge then.'

'I don't think it's anything to worry about, Anna. If we can make a go of the bakery and café, things will be easier around here.'

Anna shrugged her shoulders and said she had better get on and do the last few bits in the café.

Katie pointed to the rose bushes running along beside the stone wall to the one side of the avenue.

'I never thought of them,' she said.

'No good to us; once we put that particular rose in the vase, it will start dropping the petals. Best to have them for show along the driveway. Have you thought of where people are going to park?'

'Dan is going to mark out half the field nearest the entrance, and hopefully, people won't try to drive up to the house.'

'You're expecting too much. With all your fancy signage, you should have made that clear,' Anna said, setting off up the avenue at a quick pace.

Katie trotted along beside her.

'You don't like the house being opened up, do you?'

'My opinion doesn't count.'

'You think, despite our hard work, it's going to fail.'

Anna stopped walking.

'I think your baking is phenomenal and I think you will be full the first week or so, but after that, who knows. It worries me, because if you can't keep Kilcashel House going, I don't know what I'll do.'

'Word will get around and we won't be so dependent on the town for business. Maggie is pretty sure of it.'

'I hope you're right; there's too much hanging on it,' Anna said, her voice fearful.

Maggie was at the front door as they rounded the rhododendron bend.

'Quick, come, have a look,' she said, gesturing wildly at both of them.

'Another find from the attic,' Katie said.

'Probably some godforsaken stuffed animal,' Anna muttered.

As they approached the front steps, Maggie ran out to greet them.

'I have found the perfect piece for the café; it pulls everything together and you're going to love it.'

She threw her arms wide as Dan lifted a framed painting over the fireplace.

'Isn't it perfect? Help me decide how high.'

Anna stepped in front of Maggie.

'What makes you think you can have this painting on display?' she asked, her voice trembling.

Maggie looked directly at Katie.

'Is this not our home and the contents too? I could throw it out or burn it even, if I so wished.'

'You can certainly do that,' Anna said as she turned to Dan and ordered him to take it down.

'It's such a beautiful piece of work. It's probably something to do with the history of Kilcashel and we want to respect that,' Katie said.

Anna shook her head and walked from the room.

Maggie looked at Dan. 'What's her beef?'

'I shouldn't say anything; it's up to Anna to talk about it.'

Maggie grabbed the painting from Dan and leaned it against a chair.

'I am so fed up of her doublespeak. How are we to know about the past, unless she tells us. The colours in the painting match the décor; it's perfect.'

She turned to Dan. 'I need a break from this house and from her. Have you time to go riding with me? I can change quickly.'

Dan sighed and told Maggie not to take all day; it wouldn't take him long to tack up the horses.

Katie examined the painting. It was a happy family scene, mother and father with two girls sitting in front of the fireplace in the drawing room at Kilcashel.

The woman's hair was blonde and she was wearing a deep purple dress pleated from the waist down. On her fingers were expensive-looking rings, which matched the richness of her choker necklace. The man looked older and his attire was more casual, but no less expensive.

The girls were sitting on the floor at their parents' feet. They looked about ten or twelve years of age, Katie thought, and a little uncomfortable in what were obviously their Sunday best outfits.

Placing the painting out of the way behind an armchair, Katie steeled herself before making her way to the kitchen, where Anna was loudly moving pots and pans.

It was so near the café opening and she wished Maggie had not created a drama. It was not the time for conflict, but Maggie had managed to do it. They had planned a vase of roses with some fennel to give height on the mantelpiece along with the old clock and the brass candlesticks either side. Why couldn't she have been happy with that? But then, Maggie was always striving to go bigger and better.

Cautiously, Katie pushed the kitchen door and called Anna's name. Anna jumped up from the counter.

'I can't talk about this, Katie. I need some air,' she said, rushing out on to the deck.

'It's your family, the Walkers, isn't it?' Katie said.

Anna gripped the balustrade and looked at the sky, tears wetting her cheeks.

'Can I help you set up the rest of the café and we can talk after? Just not right now, please.'

'Do you promise?'

Anna nodded.

'I'm sorry about Maggie.'

'Don't be. If you start apologising for that one, you'll never stop. Can we just get on with it?' she said, grabbing a paper towel to pat her cheeks dry.

'OK, you do the flowers; they should be fine for the opening. I'll fold the napkins and finish off the cookie boxes,' Katie said.

Anna squeezed Katie's shoulder.

'Thank you,' she whispered. They walked back into the kitchen, where Anna immediately busied herself with arranging pink and yellow roses in small vases for each table.

Katie carefully placed different flavoured cookies into the gift boxes, tying them with pink and blue ribbons and then stacking them at the cash register.

At one stage, they heard Maggie come downstairs. She seemed to hesitate in the hall. Both Katie and Anna stopped what they were doing, but neither uttered a word until they heard the front door bang shut.

'She will be gone a few hours,' Katie said, and Anna frowned.

They worked side by side polishing the tables, arranging the chairs and making sure the presentation trays and baskets for the bagels were spotless. When the last glass and cup had been polished and the cutlery had been laid out in the trays beside the till, Anna said she was going home; the chat would have to wait for another time.

'But you promised.'

'And I meant it, but I can't do it right now. What is there to tell? They're all gone.'

'All the more reason to have the painting on display,' Katie said, but Anna turned her back.

Katie was cross, but she tried not to show it. Instead, she said she had to finish off a few last bits in the café. When she heard Anna on the gravel outside, she pulled the painting from its hiding place and dragged it up to the second landing, where she leaned it against the back wall of the spare room.

FIFTEEN

Katie was sifting through all her invoices from suppliers when she heard Maggie stamping across the hall and into the café the next morning.

'That Anna is some piece of work, she has only gone all dramatic because I was talking about her precious cherry blossoms.'

'What do you mean talking about them?'

'I was in Mulgraves' supermarket and a few of the ladies were asking me how I was settling in. It was kind of nice to be asked. I told them it was a bit difficult, that I had been invited to The Hamptons this weekend and instead I was going to be trying to figure out how to keep the cherry blossoms at the gate of Kilcashel House in check.'

'Oh no, Anna hates anyone talking about her business. If she pulls her support for our café, our life here will be so much harder. This could ruin us.'

'Oh stop being so dramatic; she's all antsy and I didn't even say anything bad. In fact the women were more interested in a weekend in The Hamptons than Anna and her stupid cherry blossoms. They wanted to know everything.'

'I bet they did.'

'Katie, you weren't there. It was nice that someone was interested in my previous life. There was a time if I got an invitation like that, I would have danced around the room, immediately contacted my hairdresser and manicurist. I would have rescheduled my appointments and probably bought a whole new wardrobe. My reply would have been considered and grateful, with just a little bit of humour. That invitation made me feel like somebody, and the ladies being impressed, well, it was nice.'

'So where does Anna come in to all this?'

Maggie threw her eyes to the ceiling.

'I might have said that unfortunately this weekend I was going to be wrestling with the great Anna Walker, to see if we could finally get rid of those trees that were blocking the entrance to Kilcashel.'

Katie jumped up.

'You said what?'

'Look, I got carried away in the moment, but unfortunately Anna was shopping in Mulgraves' and she heard it all. The other women tried to warn me, but you know me, when I start telling a story.'

'That explains why she came back with only half the shopping, and was so crotchety all morning,' Katie said.

Maggie suddenly sat down, her face grey and gripping her side.

'Is there something wrong?'

'That woman is causing such stress and I'm not feeling great.'

'You're the one who has caused a stress in Anna's life.'

Maggie put her hand up as if to stop Katie talking.

'Just leave it,' she said, pouring an espresso into a takeaway cup and flouncing out of the kitchen.

'I'm off to find Anna to attempt to talk to her,' Katie said loudly.

Anna was making her way out the front door when Katie came up behind her.

'What has Maggie done?' she asked.

'She has been talking all over town about me and my cherry blossom trees. She has no right. When will she learn to leave well alone?'

'Come back inside so we can talk, Anna.'

Anna dithered on the doorstep, but eventually turned back into the hall and walked to the kitchen, where she perched on the edge of a stool.

Katie noticed her eyes were red and puffy.

'I am so sorry; Maggie can be insensitive. She obviously has no idea how much those cherry blossoms mean to you. I don't think I do, either.'

Anna sighed.

'I don't mind telling you, but I don't want that one knowing,' Anna said, her voice stiff.

'All right,' Katie said, sitting opposite her.

'I couldn't bear if any of this appeared in print; she's always looking for ideas for her writing,' Anna said, looking around the kitchen as if she were afraid somebody was eavesdropping.

'I hated the kitchen; I don't like this one, but I was so glad when the old one was ripped out,' Anna said, dabbing away the tears which were gathering under her lashes.

Katie got up and spooned instant coffee and sugar into two mugs, then filling them with hot water.

She placed a mug in front of Anna.

'I put in a second spoon of sugar.'

Anna nodded and smiled.

'You know me well.'

She slurped her drink. The aroma of the coffee curled

through her kitchen, making her straighten up and concentrate on what she was going to say.

'You understand because you lost your Harry on what should have been a normal day. I lost my family on what should have been a normal evening. I had two girls, Ciara and Siobhan, twins, they were twenty years old and I was lucky they were still living at home and commuting in and out of Dublin to college. They were talking of moving out to rent a place with friends, so in a way, it was their last time staying at Kilcashel. There was a shindig in the town, a twenty-first birthday bash for Johnny Ruane's son and they asked their father Bert to collect them at 1 a.m. He was out playing cards; there was nothing unusual about that.

'I always stayed up for my girls, but when it went to 2 a.m. and nobody, not even Bert was answering his mobile phone, I knew in my heart something was wrong.

'I remember I cleaned out the cutlery drawer, wiped it out and then dropped the forks, knives and spoons in place; the ping of the metal hitting the drawer was suddenly too loud. I switched on the kettle, but I don't remember if it boiled. The backyard was illuminated by the old light, I switched on, so they could see where they were going, when they got home. I remember the yard was almost empty, except for a few pots thrown in the far corner that had toppled over in a strong wind, and nobody had bothered to straighten. Ciara's bike was parked against the far wall, and I was a bit cross she hadn't put it in the shed.

'I got tired of the kitchen and made my way to the drawing room, standing in the dark inside the bay window, watching for the glow of Bert's headlights as the car came up the avenue. The house was silent, the dog asleep on the couch. In that hour I came to detest the silence. I wanted to hear Siobhan's loud music vibrate through the house, to hear Ciara moaning on about something or other. I knew something was wrong and the house was adjusting, filling every room with an eerie silence, which made a din inside my head.

'When I saw the beam of a car fall across the rhododendron, I slumped in relief, berating myself for my foolish ramblings and worry.'

Anna pushed her mug in a tight circle, letting the coffee spill out of her cup.

'Sorry, I don't know if I have ever really spoken about this before.'

'Don't worry,' Katie said, reaching for a tea towel to wipe up the coffee stain. A part of her was afraid to hear this sad story, but she knew how difficult it was for Anna to share her deepest thoughts and she steeled herself for what was to come.

'It was only when the car pulled into the front, I realised it was a garda car. Somebody ran up the steps and pounded on the front door. For a fleeting moment, I thought of not answering. I wanted to shrink into the corner and pretend nobody was home. I knew it could only be bad news.'

Katie reached out and squeezed Anna's hand.

'You don't have to go through every detail like this, you know.'

Anna shook her head. 'After twenty years it's about time I was able to talk about it. I want you to know.'

Katie got up from the counter and took down the bottle of whiskey and poured a measure into a square glass.

'This might help,' she said.

Anna took the glass and gulped the whiskey.

'I felt sorry for the garda; he was so young; I knew him, had met him a few times in the town. This was probably a defining moment in his career, poor lad. He could hardly get the words out. I ended up bringing him in and sitting him down on the couch.

'I spoke to him sternly, like you would to a boy found

stealing apples from the orchard. I said, "Tell me clearly, are they dead?"

'He said my Ciara and Siobhan were pronounced dead at the scene, but Bert was in hospital with life-threatening injuries.'

She took another gulp of the whiskey.

'There and then, my life changed, changed utterly.'

The poor garda was crying. He knew the girls. It was a bloody drunk driver, just ploughed into them two miles up the road. They were dying in that mangled car just two miles away, and I didn't know. Bert tried to go up the ditch, but there was nowhere to go. Poor man, I was glad he didn't wake up to the news of his daughters lying on cold slabs of marble in the morgue. Once the garda had finished telling me the news, he got a call. Bert was pronounced dead on arrival at hospital. I had lost my entire family.'

Katie put her head in her hands.

'Anna, I didn't know. I am so sorry. Why didn't anyone tell me?'

'Because they knew it was my story to tell and only mine. They say I started to scream, lashed out at the poor garda. I remember sitting on the couch, a glass of brandy in my hand and wondering how it got there. A doctor was called and neighbours turned up to sit with me. The garda told me to drink the brandy; it might dull the pain momentarily.

'I wasn't very patient or polite. I didn't know why people I barely knew were walking through my home. Siobhan and Ciara were only starting out in life; they couldn't be dead. Bert, who I'd known since we were both at secondary school together, could not be dead. It's strange, the only thing that helped was to press my sore head against the cold windowpanes in the drawing room; the cold seeping through my skin made me concentrate for a moment on that glaring pain and nothing else. When I pulled away from the glass, I was thinking clearer.

'I said I wanted to see my family. The garda called the sergeant in charge, who advised against it. I created quite a fuss, and I don't regret it. How would I ever believe they were gone unless I stood and held their cold hands and kissed their hard, cold cheeks?

'The sergeant who drove up to the house to talk to me said I could see my daughters, but he shook his head in relation to Bert.

'"Don't do it to yourself, Mrs Walker. I saw your husband on the way to hospital. You are better sticking with the memories."

'"And my girls?" I asked him.

'"We will drive you there," he said, clicking his fingers at a garda to take the wheel.'

Anna shifted on the counter stool and rearranged her skirt.

'I went to the morgue in my pyjamas. I grabbed my coat from the hook in the front hall. I remember as we left Kilcashel House, the lights were still shining in the girls' rooms. Kilcashel looked warm and welcoming, a family home. They drove around the long way, so I didn't have to pass the crash site.

A nurse met me at the hospital and brought me through corridors to the morgue. She was kind and I asked her was I doing the right thing going to see their bodies.

'"Do what feels right, it will help later," she said. And you know, she was right.'

Katie sighed loudly and Anna stared at her.

'I'm being too intense, I know. Nobody ever wants to listen, because I can't help being searingly honest about all this.'

Katie shifted uncomfortably on her stool. 'It's not that; there's so much pain for you, I don't know how you keep going.'

'Not sure I have, in any meaningful way. Every night, I think of my two girls in that morgue, and I still find it hard to believe they're gone. Sometimes, when I wake up in the morning, there's a moment when, in my mind, it hasn't happened, and I am for that brief time at peace. When my heart thumps heavy, I know I am in the same old world, and all alone without my family.'

'You will always have us here at Kilcashel House.'

Anna held both of Katie's hands.

'You're such a kind person, and Maggie isn't half bad either, when she hasn't got the airs and graces. I am lucky to have both of you here.'

Tears flowed down Anna's cheeks as she continued her story without enquiring of Katie whether she should.

'At the morgue, the young garda said there was no harm backing out.

'But I wasn't going to do that. I pushed in the double doors. The nurse stayed with me but she knew, when I saw my girls, I wanted to do it on my own.

'She pulled me close and said each of my girls was laid out on a trolley and covered with a white sheet. An assistant would pull back each sheet, and ask me to identify first Siobhan, and then Ciara. He would then leave the room.

'She told me to take my time – all night if I wanted – and she would wait in the corridor.'

Anna picked up a biscuit and rolled it between her hands as she continued to talk.

'I wanted to touch them, to whisper in their ears and just to say goodbye,' Anna stopped for a moment, her voice low and raspy. When she spoke again, her voice trembled.

'Somebody had combed Ciara's hair. I know, because they had placed her hair over her ears and she always liked to tuck it behind. There were only a few cuts on her forehead. Siobhan looked so beautiful, her eyebrows in a perfect arch, which she had asked her friend Betty to shape just three days previously.

'There was a gash across Siobhan's forehead, which had been stitched together; her hair was still in a messy bun.

'I held both their hands and kissed them on the forehead. I didn't know what else to do.

'Somebody brought a chair for me, and they let me sit for a while, between the two trolleys. I burrowed my head into the sheets of each one and tenderly held the girls in my arms.

'I wanted to stay there all night, but I knew I couldn't. In truth, I wanted to stay there forever. I had no idea how I could continue without the three most important people in my life.'

When Anna stopped talking, they sat in silence for a few moments.

'But you carried on,' Katie said quietly.

'I planted the cherry blossoms and I willed myself to see them bloom together every year.

'Which is why you don't want them ever to be removed.'

Anna nodded.

'You have my word; nobody will touch those cherry blossoms, ever,' Katie said.

'I am a silly woman who probably attaches too much significance to those trees, but they have given me solace all these years. For so long, I was an empty shell.'

'But you kept going.'

'Barely. You know how difficult it is to run a big house. All I had were the animals on the farm, no income and mounting debt, not to mention the well of grief in my heart. I soldiered on and many people helped me on the way, but the time came when I'd had enough. I was tired and sold the house to an American. And look at me now.'

'I think we have brought a lot of aggravation into your life.'

'That's true, but for the first time in a long time, there has also been friendship, and a few laughs.'

They heard Maggie on the stairs. Anna hurriedly got off the stool.

'You have my story. I am fond of Maggie, but I can't face an inquisition. Let me go home.'

'Are you sure you're OK?'

Anna turned and smiled at Katie.

'Surprisingly, I feel good. Nobody has ever let me talk so much about that night or the aftermath. Thank you.'

She left without giving Katie time to answer.

Maggie came in rubbing her eyes.

'Did I hear Anna?'

'Yes, but she had to rush off, something about playing bridge in the town.'

'That woman never ceases to amaze me; who would have thought she plays bridge?'

Katie peered closely at Maggie.

'You don't look well, are you all right?'

Maggie appeared flustered.

'I think I have a fever. Nothing an early night and a few Advil won't cure,' she said, snatching a bottle of Prosecco and making for the hallway.

'I'm not sure you should mix Prosecco and pain medication,' Katie said.

'All right, all right; you're not my mother,' Maggie shouted as she climbed the stairs.

Katie poured a whiskey and walked out on to the deck. The waves were crashing on the shore, the sound breaking into the still night.

Harry certainly could pick them, she thought as tears splashed down her face. She saw an aeroplane move across the sky and she wondered where it was going. How many times had she looked for the very same air route and wished she could go home to Manhattan, to a past life, a time before Harry was shot.

She cried back then to fill the silence. Now, she cried because she loved Kilcashel House so much, and she badly needed to make it work out here.

When she heard a step on the deck, she jumped.

'Who's there?' she called out.

'I'm sorry, I didn't mean to scare you; I saw the light and I was passing,' Dan said.

'It's OK, I'm a bit jumpy; Anna was telling me what happened to her family and...'

Her voice wavered. Quickly, Dan crossed the deck and put his arms around her.

'It is a dreadful story, and it was a terrible accident. Anna is an incredible woman to be able to keep going.'

'But she has lost her home. How can she live there in that gate lodge and see us turn her former home in to a bakery and café? Not to mention that we are American.'

Dan laughed.

'Anna has always been a practical woman and I think to be part of Kilcashel House is a help. She tried to live here, but she couldn't keep up with all the bills. I often did work here for free, and the local farmers cut the grass and saved the hay each year without her even having to ask, but when rain poured in on the roof and the heating system broke down, I think that was the last straw. She only lived in a few rooms anyway; the drawing room and the bedroom mainly. The rest of the house held too many memories for her, so maybe it was all for the best.'

'I just wish I could make it up to her.'

Dan let Katie go and gently let her drop down to the seat. He took the chair beside her.

'She hadn't much to do with Harry; they never seemed to meet up, but she defended him because he let her stay on in the gate lodge. However, you have made her part of Kilcashel House again, and that for Anna, is gold.'

'I hope so, because we couldn't manage here without her,' Katie said.

'Is Maggie about?' he asked.

'She has retired for the night with a bottle of Prosecco. Why do you ask?

'We were supposed to bring the horses out on a hack this evening, but she didn't turn up.'

'I thought when I saw her earlier she didn't look well, but she said it was just a headache.'

Dan got up.

'I'd better be going. I have an early start in the morning.'

'You will come around, won't you? There isn't ribbon cutting or anything, but it would be nice to see a friendly face.'

'Don't worry, everybody will come for a gawk; you won't have time to even notice me.'

'I hope you're right,' she said, her voice croaky.

'Remember, nobody is going to give up on a chance to see what you have done here. And once they taste the food, that will be enough to keep them coming back.'

'I hope you're right,' she stuttered. Dan leaned down and softly kissed the top of her head.

'Remember, you and this café are exactly what Kilcashel House and the wider Kilcashel area needs.'

She turned to look at him and smiled. She liked him a lot; his quiet strength and kindness. She didn't know Dan well, but she knew he never said anything if he didn't mean it. For the first time in a long time, she felt good about herself. She felt maybe she could make a go of this crazy idea of hers and she finally had a good friend here too. Tomorrow would come; the café would open, and...

She would have to add to that later because her stomach was feeling queasy even thinking about the café. Closing her eyes, she listened to the sound of the waves hitting the sandy shore; curling back, pounding on the beach once again.

Her dad had always told her every seventh wave was the biggest, so she waited until she heard the loudest thud and counted one, two, three... until she got to seven.

On her way upstairs she peeped into the café. The moonlight through the windows was the only light, skimming over the tables and the empty chairs, picking out the flowers on the tables and on the mantelpiece. She stepped into the room. Taking a deep breath, she twirled between the tables, coming to a halt in front of the fireplace.

This was once a beautiful drawing room and she hoped that the café would bring this old mansion back to life and, maybe, also bring her back to living a good life again.

Harry was gone, but what he had left her was magnificent and she was going to work night and day to make it succeed.

She heard Maggie shuffling about her room and she went up the stairs on tiptoes, for fear she would get pulled into a silly drink-fuelled conversation on the eve of the opening of her café.

SIXTEEN

Katie only had four hours asleep and was in the kitchen before dawn. When she heard a step on the cobbled yard and the back door open, she assumed it was Anna.

'There was no need to come so early; it's just about the baking at the moment,' she said without turning around. When she didn't hear a caustic comment as was Anna's norm, she stopped what she was doing and turned around.

Dan was standing in the kitchen looking at her, a silly grin on his face.

'I was thinking you could do with a bit of company. I can just sit here, if there's nothing you want me to do.'

'I'm sorry about my wobble last night. Didn't you have to be somewhere, that we wouldn't see you until later?'

'Everything else can wait. I am the friendly face to help keep up the spirits; you can't really rely on Anna for that.'

'True, if Anna was nice to me all the time, I would be seriously worried.'

'And we know Maggie will be down much later and try to take the limelight, when all the hard work is done.'

'A little harsh, I think. She does a lot behind the scenes.'

Dan laughed and took a seat at the counter.

'I know, I know, but she's quite a handful.'

'I'm sure it's nothing you can't handle,' she said, turning back to her trays of biscuits and pushing them into the oven as she continued: 'Maggie is a New Yorker; it's hard to get through the brash exterior, but underneath I have seen glimpses of her soft side. Anyway, I thought you liked all that loud brashness about her.'

Dan shuffled on his stool. His voice was hesitant when he finally spoke.

'It certainly has its allure, but...'

He would have said more, but they heard Anna and Lola walking across the courtyard.

When the kitchen door opened, Lola ran in, a ball in her mouth.

'We had a bracing walk down by the sea; there's a beautiful sunrise,' Anna said, but stopped when she saw Dan.

'Am I interrupting something?' she asked.

Both Katie and Dan laughed.

'Dan came to keep me company, it being opening day.'

'It's not sightseers we need but people who will roll up their sleeves,' Anna said as she shooed the dog outside.

'I can go if I'm in the way, but I thought Katie here could do with all the support she can get,' Dan said.

He made to get off the stool, but Katie rested her hand on his shoulder to stop him.

'I would like you to stay; it can get lonely here in the kitchen, just rolling bagels and cutting out cookies. The silence can leave too much time for worries to push in around me.'

Anna clicked her tongue impatiently as she emptied the dishwasher.

'You can get the boxes ready for the biscuits. Are you good at tying a bow?' she asked.

Dan said he would give it a go and Katie felt herself blush

when he winked at her. She dipped her head and tried not to look interested. She and Maggie had enough on their plate without competing for the affections of a nice-looking man.

Anna sighed loudly and pushed a big cardboard box across the counter.

'Every box in there has to be assembled – you surely can do that. And when you're ready, I'll show you how to do a bow.'

'I think I can run to tying a bow,' Dan said, and Katie stifled a giggle.

Katie rolled out her bagels while Anna got the cream cheese fillings made up. Dan worked quietly beside them, stacking each box on top of the next.

'Don't go any higher; it's not a competition and we don't want them to hit the floor,' Anna said as if she were chastising a child.

'It's pretty labour intensive, all this. You're going to need help full-time,' Dan said as he popped another box into place.

'We'll have to see how it goes; in the meantime, Katie needs all her friends to help out. There's no point throwing stupid wages about when a few friends can put in the elbow grease,' Anna said, snorting loudly.

'Just trying to think ahead.'

'Time to start thinking about filling those boxes with biscuits and tying proper bows,' Anna barked, taking out the biscuits which had been made the day before.

'Five per box. Raspberry biscuits get pink bows and the chocolate chips get blue.'

'What do I do, tie a bow and stick it on the box?'

Anna looked out under her eyes, and Katie, feeling her disdain, disappeared to check the temperature of the ovens.

Slowly, Anna took a box, filled it with five raspberry and white chocolate biscuits and closed it. She then pulled the thin pink ribbon from a big roll at the end of the counter, and tied it around the box, finishing with a small, perfectly formed bow.

'Do you think that male brain of yours can get around that?' she said, pushing a box towards Dan.

Katie tapped Anna on the elbow.

'I think you're forgetting Dan is a volunteer and you have to be nice to him.'

'I can't help it if I'm a stickler for doing things right.'

They both stood as Dan filled a box with the chocolate orange biscuits and expertly tied the blue ribbon in a big blousy bow.

'Nice. I think you might have done this before,' Katie said.

'When I was at college I worked in a pharmacy, and I was the gift-wrap guy at Christmas time.'

'That bow is too big; we have to economise, so the less ribbon used the better. A small bow next time please,' Anna said.

Dan did a mock salute and continued to work.

Anna announced that she was going out to check the café and dust the mantelpiece and around the windows.

'There will be a lot of people calling in just to find fault; we won't give them anything bad to talk about,' she said.

'She loves me really,' Dan said, and Katie giggled.

'I used to get upset when Anna growled at me, but now, if she doesn't, I get worried,' Katie said.

'Everything is topsy turvy with Anna, but there are reasons for that.'

Dan stopped talking, when they heard a step in the hall.

When Maggie walked in, wearing a bright red top and black leather jeans and big jangly earrings that looked as if there were cakes hanging from her ears, Katie burst out laughing.

'What are you wearing?'

'Hey, I have managed to get the local paper and photographer down this morning, and I thought I would dress up.'

'You never told me.'

'I'm telling you now.'

Katie stared at Maggie.

'What time are they coming?'

'I invited them to have breakfast with us and a chat at eight, and the café opens at nine, so we can concentrate on the customers then. There will be a bit of a buzz because everybody wants to be around the media.'

Katie slapped down a tray of cookies too hard on the counter.

'Maggie. I really appreciate it, but it's now seven thirty – why on earth didn't you tell me earlier? I haven't even washed my hair and I still have to take a batch of bagels out of the oven, and Dan has to fill all the boxes.'

'Keep your hair on, darling; it'll be fine.'

Katie banged another tray on the worktop, making the bagels hop in the air.

'Maggie,' she protested, 'that's easy for you to say because you're looking so—'

'Beautiful, I know. You will too. Come on, let me take you upstairs and give you a little makeover.'

Katie was cross and frazzled and, at that moment, she wanted to shout at Maggie, but she didn't want a row so near to opening time.

'I have to wait for the bagels,' she said stiffly.

'I can take them out of the oven, if you have it set to make some sort of noise to alert me,' Dan said.

'Yes, it's on a timer, and you must put them out on the cooling grids straight away. Don't let Lola into the kitchen or she will help herself.'

Katie was grateful for Dan's intervention and allowed herself to be dragged up the stairs by Maggie.

'Have you an outfit picked out for today?' Maggie asked as she swept into Katie's room and flung open the wardrobe doors.

'I hadn't got around to it.'

Maggie looked aghast at her.

'But that's so important for photographs.'

'Pardon me if I thought the baking and organising of the café was more important.'

Maggie ignored the sarcastic tone of Katie's voice and began pulling out clothes from the wardrobe.

'You're a casual gal, I can see. Don't you have anything dressy?'

'I never usually need to wear dressy in the kitchen.'

'There has to be a life outside the kitchen, darling. Let's go to my room.'

'I don't want to wear your clothes.'

Maggie swung around on the landing.

'Darling, you have to; your clothes are... Well, they're perfectly fine for working in the kitchen.'

Katie stood looking out the window as Maggie rummaged in her own wardrobe.

Waves of different colours drifted across the allotments; the cornflowers and poppies the brightest, with the sunflowers in the Falveys' plot adding height. One allotment, planted with potatoes, onions, cabbage and lettuce, was awash with green.

She could see Muriel sitting out in her chair having a morning coffee from her flask as Rosie staked the sunflowers. In the far-off field, the horses had their heads down munching the grass. Another allotment nearest the house was a riot of colour and a mixture of different dahlias. Another was solely a supermarket mix of wildflowers with borage. She wished it could always look like this, but she knew that, once winter blew in, the front fields would look dejected and bleak.

'I found it,' Maggie said, triumphantly pulling a slate-blue silk dress from a box in her cupboard. 'Don't worry, I've never worn it. It's a vintage piece that I borrowed for a photoshoot and oops, I never returned it. It looks your size and it's so pretty with a nice hang to it.'

The dress was a simple, silk day dress with a slightly ruched bodice and sleeves that ended at the elbow. The fabric had a faint floral design picked out in light pink and grey.

'If you put your hair up in a bun, it will look very sweet.'

Katie touched the fabric.

'It's beautiful, are you sure?'

'Does that look like my style? I have no idea why I kept it, to be honest. Come on, try it on.'

'I don't want to leave Dan too long.'

'Pooh; give in, you know you want to try it.'

Katie pulled off her hoodie and jeans and slipped the dress over her head. It slithered down her body and she immediately felt good. Standing in front of the mirror, she let the silk waft around her knees.

'Perfect fit, what did I tell you? A little eyeshadow and lipstick and you're ready.'

'I have some sandals I can wear with it.'

'A kitten heel, I hope.'

'No, I don't need kitten heels in the kitchen.'

Maggie sat on the bed.

'Darling, you have to make an effort. Lucky for you I have a silver, strappy pair that will be perfect, and some silver earrings too. You do have your ears pierced, I hope?'

Katie laughed.

'Yes, I do, but I don't know when I last wore earrings.'

'Don't worry, I have a conservative but stylish pair here for you, nothing to jangle about.'

Katie put her hand out for the earrings, but then stopped.

'Don't tell me they're too conservative,' said Maggie. 'I didn't think we could reach that point with you.'

'I have a pair exactly like that.'

Maggie shut the box and sighed.

'The bastard Harry, just when you think you're getting over him, he crawls right back into our lives.'

Katie walked over to the window. Tears were streaming

down her face. This was the last thing she needed. Harry had bought her those earrings as a surprise gift last Valentine's Day. They never gave each other Valentine gifts and he had come home and handed her the perfectly packaged box.

She was delighted and embarrassed at the same time, because she did not have anything for him, not even a card. When he died a few weeks later, she had taken the earrings and cried over them, chiding herself for not showing him how much she loved him on such a special day.

'I've been a fool,' she said.

When Maggie answered, Katie realised she had spoken out loud.

'I got mine from him last February.'

'Valentine's Day?'

'The creep, yes, but he said it was a gesture of friendship.'

'He told me they were to tell me how much he loved me.'

Maggie came up behind Katie.

'We are a pair of idiots, both thinking we were somehow special to this man.'

'At least he wasn't cheating on us.'

'No, but this nonsense over the house and inheriting it, and putting us together – what did he think he was doing, planning to observe us from hell?'

'That might be going a bit far.'

'Harry was such a shit.'

Katie couldn't answer. She still loved Harry, missed him and needed his memory to be untarnished so that she had the strength to go on. She wanted him to be here, to pop his head around the door, his hands in the air and come out with a long-winded explanation as to why he had given them both the exact same present on Valentine's Day. No doubt he would have persuaded her to forgive him.

Down in the allotment, she could see Rosie and Muriel

tidying up in preparation to make their way to the house. Katie looked at her watch.

'Shit, it's after 8 a.m. I have so much left to do.'

'You will put on make-up or I won't let you out of this room. Everything is ready, don't worry,' Maggie said firmly.

Gently, she led Katie to the dressing table and told her to sit on the stool.

'I'll just get your foundation from your room, but I have a nice eyeshadow and a new lipstick, which will be just right for you,' Maggie said.

When she was gone, Katie looked across the dressing table. There were all sorts of bottles and perfume. She took the Chanel No 5 and sprayed it on her wrist and neck. As she returned the perfume bottle to the dressing table, a small plastic bottle of prescription tablets toppled over. Maggie had not mentioned she was unwell or that she had seen the doctor. When she heard her on the landing, Katie pushed the bottle in behind the Chanel perfume.

'You haven't a great deal of make-up either. I suppose you don't have to wear it in the kitchen,' Maggie said.

'When you're sweating over a hot stove, the last thing you want is any of that.'

'So, buy a specific brand for the job, silly.'

'I don't think those things are as important as you do.'

'OK, so I'm the shallow one; tell me something new.' Maggie stopped for a minute. 'You think I'm going too far about Harry. It's just, sometimes I can hardly believe what has happened to us.'

'At least we're not buckling under all of this; we're trying to make a go of it.'

Maggie gently blobbed some foundation on Katie's face and began to massage it in with a sponge.

'Harry has left us with no choice but to make a go of it.'

Katie made to answer but Maggie told her to be quiet while she concentrated on doing her make up.

When she had the eyes done, she handed a pink lipstick to Katie.

'It's more your colour than mine; far too quiet for me.'

Katie slicked on the lipstick and looked at herself in the mirror. Maggie had done a good job. The make-up gave her a natural glow and the dress highlighted the blue of her eyes. She stood up.

Maggie held out her hand.

'Are you ready to open the Drawing Room Café?'

'I'm as ready as I'll ever be,' Katie sighed, letting Maggie lead the way downstairs. Dan and Anna waved from behind the café counter.

Dan whistled when the two women walked in.

'Wow, don't you two look beautiful?' he said.

Anna eyed Maggie up and down.

'Very you,' she said. Then turned to Katie. 'I used to wear dresses like that a long time ago.'

'They're vintage now, Anna, very trendy,' said Maggie.

'If you say so,' Anna grumbled, turning away to check on the coffee machine.

Dan said he was off to open the gates. Maggie told him to wait a few moments. Whipping off to the broom cupboard in the kitchen, she came back with a big banner which said 'The Drawing Room Café, Open All Day, Every Day.'

'When did you get this done?' Katie asked, examining the rainbow-coloured sign.

'There's a man in Kilcashel who is very good at making all sorts, so we put our heads together.'

'They certainly can't fail to see it,' Anna observed as she rubbed a cloth over the café counter.

'Why is it she can never ever like anything I do?' Maggie asked.

'Because she's Anna,' Katie said.

Maggie poured an espresso coffee for herself and sat inside the bay window watching for the local press to arrive.

Katie paced between the counter and the fireplace, until Maggie told her to stop.

'Come sit down, we don't want to appear so anxious.'

'What if nobody comes? Maybe we should have put signs up in the town or put a notice in the newspaper.'

Anna, who was loitering, waiting like the rest of them, snorted.

'The world and her husband will be here; they're so damn curious about what you have done to the old place,' she said.

A car pulled up to the side of the house and two men got out, one with cameras hanging from both shoulders.

'What are we going to say to them? I haven't rehearsed anything,' Katie said, shaking out her sleeves because she was afraid the perspiration would seep through from her underarms.

'Just follow my lead and hopefully the crowds will arrive early, so the café looks busy.'

'Maybe you should have invited the press for later in the morning,' Katie said, her stomach churning with nerves.

'Don't worry so much; the swimming ladies and the Falveys promised to be here bright and early,' Maggie said.

'I'm not sure if having an audience will help at all. Maybe all this is over the top and a low-key opening would have been better.'

'Don't be silly,' Maggie said, grabbing Katie's hand and squeezing it hard as they watched the two men pause at the foot of the granite steps to take in the view of the allotments.

Maggie scooted to the front door and pulled it back just as they arrived at the top step.

'Welcome to Kilcashel House and the Drawing Room Café,' she said ushering them inside and propping the door open with a heavy metal door stop.

The photographer walked in and whistled.

'I like what I see,' he said, turning to the reporter and giving a thumbs up.

The photographer said he wanted to take his pictures first and he positioned Katie and Maggie either side of the fireplace, and later in the bay window holding a plate piled high with bagels and cookies. When Katie made to move away after the first few photographs had been taken, the photographer shook his head and said not so fast.

Picking up two bagels and pulling them apart, he asked Katie and Maggie to hold them to their eyes.

'Why?' Katie asked.

Maggie gave her a sharp elbow.

'Let the photographer be creative, Katie; it could be the one that gets the front page,' she said, holding up the bagels as if she was looking through a ship's porthole. Katie did the same, but a tension headache was forming at the back of her head and spreading upwards.

'Perfect, all done,' the photographer said, and the reporter immediately corralled the two of them with a lot of questions.

Nora and Leonie, the first to arrive, tiptoed around the huddle to make sure they got the armchair seats at the bay window. The Falveys, dressed up in their Sunday best, made a grand entrance announcing that everything looked fabulous.

'Are there going to be speeches?' Muriel asked.

'And free coffee, I presume,' Rosie said.

Dan rang from the gates to say the car park there was full and there were a load of people walking up the avenue. Katie swallowed hard and took a deep breath.

'This is really happening,' she whispered.

'Go, and do what you do best,' Dan said, tapping her lightly on the shoulder as he went back out front to direct customers to the café.

Soon Anna was overrun at the counter and Katie had to

step in and help her as more and more arrived, ordering coffee, bagels and boxes of biscuits to take home.

At one stage, Nora and Leonie stepped in to help out. When there wasn't enough room to sit, some people took their coffee outside to the steps and the front gravelled area.

Just over an hour in, Maggie clapped her hands loudly and asked everybody to gather around. Everybody stood up and crowded around Maggie, those outside pushing in at the doorway.

Gesturing to Katie to join her, Maggie told people to make way for the star baker. Those around the entrance to the bakery stepped back, forming a corridor for Katie, who despite feeling embarrassed, made her way to join Maggie.

Dan called for quiet, and Maggie began her speech.

'We are so glad to see you all here today and especially for the welcome you have given to two Americans at Kilcashel House. We know how important this house is to this community and we thank Anna here for all her help in bringing us to this day, where we can open the Drawing Room Café.

'This café is so important to us, and we hope it will become significant in your lives as well. I know you will come to love this wonderful baking of my dear friend Katie. She has, after all brought the best of New York to Kilcashel, County Wicklow.'

Maggie craned her neck to see Dan, Leonie and Nora and pointed to the corner, where they were huddled in a group. 'Those three have been our dear friends, our rocks, and we thank you so much,' she said.

Nora and Leonie beamed and Dan bowed awkwardly. Maggie raised her hand for hush as she continued: 'This is opening day. We want you to come back on more days and bring your families. Come for the food and stay for the conversation. We are so proud to be a big part now of Kilcashel,' she said.

There was a huge round of applause and both Katie and

Maggie bowed low as if they were on stage. People grabbed both women and took selfies and photographs, holding up bagels and cookies for social media shots. Katie disappeared into the kitchen, but Maggie held court, standing in front of the fireplace calling each person by their first name.

'How does she know everybody?' Katie asked.

'Because while you have been working your socks off to get this place off the ground, that one has been swanning around Kilcashel, like she is lady of the manor,' Anna said fiercely.

The café stayed open well after four. Once the last person left, Anna closed the front door.

'It won't be like this every day. Thank God,' she said as she started clearing off the tables. 'I can't believe we ran out of food. I thought I had made enough cookies for three days,' Katie laughed.

'You might as well get baking and get Dan back to do the boxes, because we're going to need a hell of a lot more,' Anna said.

Maggie announced she was beat after all the talking and the standing and would anyone mind if she had a quick nap?

'That's the last we'll see of her until she gets hungry later. Wouldn't you know Lady Muck would leave as soon as all the excitement was over,' Anna muttered, but Katie ignored her.

Dan carried a pile of plates into the kitchen and began stacking the dishwasher.

After they had cleared all the café tables, Katie asked Dan and Anna to join her for a moment.

Taking down the bottle of whiskey, she poured three measures.

'Let's toast to a very successful opening of the Drawing Room Café,' she said, and they held up their glasses, clinking loudly.

'Shouldn't Maggie be a part of this?' Dan asked.

'She should, but no doubt she is knocking back the Prosecco upstairs. However, she made a very fine speech.'

'To the speech,' Dan said.

They clinked their glasses again.

'Do you think should we check on her? I thought she looked a bit pale,' Katie said.

'Surprised you could notice under all the make-up,' Anna mumbled.

Ignoring Anna, Katie put down her glass and went upstairs.

Knocking lightly on Maggie's door, she peeked into the room.

Maggie, still in her clothes, was curled up on her bed, fast asleep.

SEVENTEEN

It had been a hectic few weeks at the café and Katie was tired. It was still dark when she started baking in the kitchen ahead of a promised busy weekend. An hour later, Maggie joined her. They usually had their set routine and didn't need to talk much, but Katie knew by the look on Maggie's face that she wanted to talk cake.

'Have you noticed that the chocolate and orange biscuits were all left the last few days? It's only been a few weeks and the interest in any of the cookies is practically nil.'

'Do they even realise all the work that goes into them?' Katie asked.

'That doesn't matter; what matters is they are not selling well enough to be a main product. You need to start thinking cake.'

'And how do you know that?'

'You know it too; customers keep asking for cake.'

'But these cookies are delicious; maybe if I add some more variety.'

Maggie threw her hands in the air.

'You know I don't think much of Harry Flint, but one thing

he said does ring true. Fail to listen to your customers and face failure in business.'

'But they only want big fry-ups, breakfast rolls and now cake.'

'So, let them eat cake, Katie,' Maggie said, waving her arm in a theatrical fashion as if she were on stage.

'I don't know any good cake recipes. This is a disaster; I don't have time to do the research,' Katie said. Her head hurt; she was exhausted and the last thing she wanted was to have to perfect a cake recipe.

'Don't be so dumb; cake is cake,' Maggie said.

Katie slapped her hand on the counter making the flour puff into the air.

'Cake is not cake! I can't put an inferior product out there.'

'You're just going to have to accept that they want cake. Cookies – or "the biscuits", as they call them – are nice, but not substantial enough. And frankly, they're too expensive. We can still have them, but we need cake as well.'

Katie pushed the stainless-steel bowl full of cookie mix away from her.

'Why don't I just shut up shop?'

'Hey, this is a blip and only a blip. Some ideas work, some don't; that's the way the cookie crumbles. Pardon the pun.'

Katie got a paper towel and dabbed the sweat from the back of her neck.

'It's summer. I want to have picnics and swim in the sea. Even this early in the morning, it smells as if it's going to be a lovely day.'

'It's too early for me to be even thinking about the rest of the day. Promise me you will think about the cake,' Maggie said.

Katie nodded. There was no point arguing with Maggie. She heard her prepare the till before sneaking back to bed. She said she needed her beauty sleep to be ready for the lunchtime rush.

Katie felt sick. She knew Maggie was right. Muriel had cornered her the other day and offered her cake recipes and told her if she didn't start serving what people wanted, they might start frequenting elsewhere. Yesterday, not all the bagels sold and Muriel said the new place in town was offering coffee and a bun for a fiver.

Tears pricked at her eyes and she wanted to shout at Harry Flint that it was all his fault. She wanted to be in Chelsea Market serving people who were prepared to put their hands in their pockets for an artisan product.

When she heard Anna arrive, Katie escaped to the café floor and pretended to be checking over the tables.

'So now you have to do all that work as well. What's Miss Fancy Pants doing? Sleeping, I suppose.' Anna snorted and Katie smiled weakly. If Anna noticed anything off about Katie, she had the good sense not to say it, but she made a cup of instant coffee and pushed it across the counter.

'We have time for a quick cup,' she said.

Katie sat down, her finger circling the rim of the mug.

'Maggie says we need to serve cake or people will stop coming.'

'Overly dramatic, but that's her style and yes, you need cake.'

'I thought everybody loved the cookies.'

'They do and they will always tell you they do, but Irish people never tell the full truth.'

'Excuse me?'

'They don't want to offend.'

'I don't understand,' Katie said, shaking her head.

Anna took her two hands.

'It means, give them cake. A slice of sweet cake with a cuppa. What could be easier?'

'Easy for you to say,' Katie said, and pointed at the clock.

'Let's hope we have any customers left,' Katie said as Anna

tapped her gently on the shoulders as she made her way to the front door to open it.

Katie stayed away from the café floor and concentrated on getting orders ready in the kitchen. She was glad there was a steady trickle of people in. Everybody ordered bagels, but the majority of the cookies stayed on display.

There were moments she wanted to rush out and shout out loud that these were the best damn cookies in New York and no, they weren't just biscuits, but instead, she knuckled down, determined to quiz Maggie about favourite cakes when the café closed.

It was noon when Maggie came downstairs. Katie rolled her eyes when she saw that Maggie was elaborately made up and wearing a quirky outfit that would have fitted in better with the streets of Manhattan.

Katie only felt slightly jealous that most people decided to descend on the café when they knew Maggie would be sitting on her velvet armchair ready to chat and to listen. They asked for her opinion on the most serious personal matters, whispering in hushed tones, hoping nobody else would hear. Katie would not dare try to solve the problems of others, but for Maggie it was a challenge. So successful were her 'meet and greets' that queues started forming sometime after eleven, with everybody looking for the seats closest to Maggie. It wasn't that they wanted to divulge their own problems, but they were very happy to earwig on the strange and bizarre worries of others.

Katie slaved behind the scenes and people grumbled about her cookies, but Maggie's straight talking and nuggets of advice even ended up on TikTok when Leonie's teenage niece shared a video of the café online. Katie didn't want the café on TikTok, but Maggie insisted it would be good for business.

Maggie had the starring role and made sure she was wearing

her best jewellery and extra make-up for the video, because the camera lens was so draining.

'This is more like a consulting room than a café – and don't get me started on all the hangers on who order the bare minimum,' Anna complained bitterly. Katie raised her hand to stop her.

'Ssh, somebody will hear you. They come to talk, sure, but if they keep putting their hands in their pockets, we're all happy. They might even buy cookies,' she laughed.

When Maggie ran into the kitchen, her face beaming, Anna threw her eyes to heaven.

'What now, are they offering you your very own TV show?'

'That's for next week, Anna,' Maggie sniggered. 'A local tour bus company has offered to drop off a busload of American tourists every Monday and Wednesday. That's fifty tourists each time. And the first group is tomorrow.'

'How did you manage that?' Katie asked.

'They saw me on TikTok and the travel agent said US tourists keep asking to meet me and to visit the café.'

'Jesus, where will we fit them all?' Anna asked.

'I didn't think of that, but I'm sure they won't mind wandering along the avenue and maybe looking at the allotments as well.'

'Well, they are not welcome to be peering in my windows, I want that made clear,' Anna said as she piled biscuits into boxes. 'And tell me,' she added, 'how are we going to feed so many people?'

'I'm sure they will love cookies, so we can offload all the extras to them.'

'They won't demand cake,' Katie said, her tone sarcastic.

Maggie walked over to Katie and hugged her and pushed a note into her hand.

'My grandmother's chocolate cake, the recipe to get the ball rolling,' she said.

Katie opened up the page and looked at the recipe hastily written down in Maggie's writing.

'I don't want to give you the original, because Granny has little notes made at the side, but I have written down everything precisely,' Maggie said nervously.

'I can give you my lemon cake recipe. I always got great compliments on that cake,' Anna said.

Maggie clapped her hands loudly. 'Sounds wonderful to me,' she said.

Katie wanted to scream that she didn't want their recipes; that she was shit at making cakes and she wanted to do her own thing, but instead she smiled and said thank you, she would look at the recipes later.

'Now what about the bus tours? Can we do it?' she said in a feeble attempt to divert the conversation away from cake.

'We have to do it. We can't afford to turn it down. The tour bus menu will have to be very simple; two of either tea or coffee with four cookies for ten euros and, if they want something more substantial, they can pick from a limited lunch menu on tour bus days,' Maggie said.

'You're asking a lot of just the two of us,' Anna said turning to Katie.

'Don't forget me; I brought in the new business,' Maggie said, her tone betraying that she felt offended.

'Yeah, but when are you going to put in the hard work?'

Katie told both of them to hush, but they ignored her.

'Why don't you ever give me credit? You do know there wouldn't be a huge queue of people waiting to be served right now, if it wasn't for me,' Maggie said, her voice raised.

'You're not the one expected to get her hands dirty,' Anna replied.

Katie slammed her fist on the counter so hard the two others jumped back.

'Can you both please stop. We have to figure out how we're

going to do this and there is a café of customers out there waiting to be served.'

Maggie put her hand up like she was a child in the school classroom. 'Why don't we ask Rowena to help? She's looking for a summer job.'

'Who?' Katie asked.

'Paddy Carthy's girl; her mum died about six months ago,' Anna said.

'She sat beside me most of yesterday. She hopes to go to college in the Fall,' Maggie said, biting into a raspberry biscuit.

'As long as she's a good timekeeper and honest, I guess we could give it a go. We can only afford the minimum wage though, but she can have a free lunch here,' Katie said.

'Sounds good,' Maggie said.

'OK.' Katie clapped her hands loudly. 'Let's get back to the job in hand; we can work out the details about the tour buses and Rowena later,' she said firmly, so that Maggie went back to her seat, where a number of people were waiting to talk to her, and Anna started taking orders again.

It was several hours before Anna and Katie sat down to talk about the tour bus menu, and to make a list of what ingredients they needed.

'Are you sure they're even coming, and this is not some pie in the sky idea from Maggie?' Anna asked.

'You're being unfair, you know how excited she was.'

'She has a tendency to believe everything she's told. Some-body could have just been pulling her leg.'

'I think we should give Maggie more credit. She practically ran Harry's business in Manhattan.'

'And look what happened to that,' Anna said in her marbles in the mouth voice.

Katie shook her head. Maggie-bashing was almost a pastime for Anna.

When they had the list done, Katie said she was going for a walk.

It was a warm evening, so she headed down to the beach. A girl and her dog were the only others around; the dog running after a ball and barking. When the girl saw Katie, she called her dog, but it would not leave the water.

As Katie got closer, she was happy to see it was Rowena.

'I'm, sorry, I couldn't resist setting the dog free. She's been cooped up in the car too long. I hope you don't mind.'

'You're Rowena, aren't you?'

'Yes, have I done something wrong?'

'I wanted to talk to you. Maggie said you were looking for a vacation job, and I wonder would you like to work in the café?'

'Are you serious?'

'Yes. The work will be hard, and I can only pay minimum rate, but we're a nice bunch, and you can have lunch from the café menu; that is, if you like bagels.'

'I love bagels, but I haven't worked in a café, or worked anywhere really.'

'You will soon pick it up. Just don't drop anything or over-charge and you'll be fine.'

'Do you want me to wear a uniform?'

'No, come as you are. We have blue aprons – and tie your hair back, please. But I'm afraid you must leave the dog at home.'

'Will do. I can't wait to be working alongside Maggie.'

'I'll tell her,' Katie said, making her way along the beach.

She walked beside the waves, letting the water crawl up almost to her shoes. Somewhere over the fields a red kite called out and she tried to smile, to think that here she was in the most beautiful place in the world, realising her dream of a bakery and café. She felt the note in her pocket. She took out Maggie's recipe. There was no harm trying it out, she thought as she turned back to Kilcashel House.

EIGHTEEN

Katie took Maggie to one side a few days later.

'What's the big secret?' Maggie said, looking around to make sure Anna had not seen them slip into the conservatory.

Katie went to the cupboard in the corner and took out a tray with a small chocolate cake on top.

'That isn't Granny's cake, is it?'

'The great thing about the recipe is it's a no flour cake; it's a chocolate almond cake and if I have done everything right should be quite delicious, but I want you to be my taster.'

Maggie picked up a knife and let it run through the cake, cutting out a thin slice on to a plate. She cut off a triangle and popped it in her mouth.

'I am back in Granny's brownstone in Brooklyn, the walls covered with black-and-white photos of ancestors in Ireland she could hardly name. The balance of chocolate and almond is just right.'

Katie sampled a piece.

'You're right, delicious.'

'We have to let everyone have some; make a big deal of it,' Maggie said, making to whip the cake away to the café.

Katie put a hand out to stop her.

'I would like to perfect it a little. Maybe in the next few days.'

'Come on, Katie, the sooner we get people talking about this cake the better.'

'We will have it on the menu for the weekend, I promise.'

Anna walked into the conservatory.

'I know we have Rowena working for us but that doesn't mean you two can take it easy.'

Katie pushed the cake back in the cupboard and said they would be along in a minute.

'Why didn't you give her any?'

'I tried out her lemon cake, but it's too heavy. I think I might have found a nice lemon and poppy seed cake instead. I just have to broach the subject carefully.'

They heard Anna give out to Rowena and both rushed back to the kitchen.

'I know she has only been here a few days but the girl needs a bit of direction and you lot are way too soft,' Anna said as Rowena went back to work on the café floor, her shoulders slumped.

'Go easy, she's young,' Katie said.

'No reason she shouldn't learn the right way,' Anna replied.

Rowena accepted every correction from Anna, but Katie noticed she only brightened when Maggie came into the café. Grinning, she asked to work on the counter and Katie hadn't the heart to say no. Anna was miffed at first to be delegated to kitchen duty, but she passed it off, saying she was happy not to be listening to all the nonsensical chat.

Katie noticed Rowena straighten up as if she were going to answer back, but she reconsidered and turned her back to concentrate on the next push of customers.

Maggie, for her part, was very kind to Rowena, often telling her she could leave early.

'I hope everyone is taking a note of when that young girl punches out,' Anna said.

'Oh Anna, were you ever young? The last hour is clock-watching; it's not very productive holding a person here until the last minute,' Maggie said.

'All I know is you should work the hours agreed,' Anna sniffed.

Katie laughed out loud.

'We're lucky to have Rowena; have you not noticed her friends come to the café as well? I'm sure if it wasn't for her, they wouldn't have bothered trying the bagels in the first place. Now, they're doing silly TikToks and asking me how I make them.'

'And don't you be telling them that either,' Anna scolded as she took a bowl of scraps and wrapped it in cling film then put it in her bag.

'My hens love the stale bagels,' she said, and both Katie and Maggie burst out laughing.

'Full of the compliments, Anna, aren't you today?' Maggie said.

Anna clicked her tongue loudly, pulled on her raincoat and left.

'She's getting very cranky. Best keep her behind the scenes,' Maggie said.

'Everybody knows Anna, she's a sweetheart underneath it all.'

'Oh right, like when she refused to fill Muriel's flask with coffee, because Muriel had only paid for one cup, and the flask probably took one and a half.'

'She's snappy and sharp, but isn't that part of her charm?'

'Katie, you always see the best in people, but this is ridiculous. That old bat is going to say something to one of our visitors and we could lose a lot of business.'

Katie shook her head. Maggie was right, but maybe she

didn't know Anna so well. Anna would do nothing to jeopardise the future of the café, because she knew it was essential to the future of Kilcashel House. 'I don't think she likes being front of house anyway,' Katie said.

'Yeah, let her stay in the kitchen and grumble about me instead,' Maggie said.

'She loves you really,' Katie laughed.

'I'm thinking of going riding, do you fancy trying it out?'

'Not for me, I just want to curl up with a book for a while.'

'Time enough for all that boring stuff. Honestly, if you're not careful, you'll end up an old lady all alone except for bagels and cookies.'

Katie got her teacloth and slapped Maggie smartly across the back.

'That hurt,' Maggie said rubbing her back as tears came to her eyes.

'What's wrong?' Katie asked.

'I think you may have hit a nerve, it's just painful. I'll be OK,' she said, turning away.

'I'm sorry; I was only joking.'

'I know that, silly; we're good,' Maggie said, wiping her face as she turned, smiling to Katie.

'Remind me not to do that again; I'm so sorry. I had no idea, and I certainly didn't mean for it to hurt,' Katie said.

'We're good, I'm just a little tender in my lower back.'

Maggie said she had to go and change, and Katie was left in the kitchen feeling strange. She wouldn't be able to concentrate on a book right now, so she headed out on to the deck and the garden, making for the gazebo.

She felt unsettled. Maybe Maggie had fallen off the horse but didn't want to admit it. She had only whipped the teacloth, but this reaction was disturbing. Suddenly Katie felt down. It was hard, living here surrounded by all these people she hardly knew. She sat down at the gazebo. She was an only child, and her parents were dead. Harry had been her person and now he was gone too. She had always been closest to her father. He believed you never got to know somebody unless you lived with them, and she was beginning to find that out now.

If they could get over the hump with the café she might be able to apply for a bank loan, and get some work done on the living quarters upstairs. Maybe in time, she could let out rooms to paying guests. Why then did she feel that her world was so small and somehow, there was no escape? She was happy here, but she wondered if it was enough.

Katie was about to set off on the path to the sea when she saw Rowena sitting on a rock beside the agapanthus, looking towards the horizon.

'Do you like the place so much you can't leave it?' Katie asked, her voice bright.

Rowena scrabbled to pick up her things and attempted to hide her face.

'Rowena. What's wrong. Has something happened?'

'No, I'm OK.'

'Did Anna say something to you?'

'No, I don't care about Anna,' Rowena said as she tried to get past Katie.

'Look, I know we don't know each other very well, but you can talk to me.'

Rowena dropped her bag.

'I'm OK, I was just taking some time out before going home.'

'Come on up to the house. I didn't see you eating at lunchtime. I'm sure we can rustle up a few bagels.'

'No, thank you. I have to get home; I have to...'

Her face crumpled.

In two steps, Katie was beside the young girl and put her arm around her.

Rowena attempted to shrug off her grip, but that made Katie hold tighter.

'You're upset, now spill,' she said kindly.

Rowena smiled.

'Maggie says you're the strong one.'

'I'm not so sure about that, but I can be bossy, when I have to be.'

'It's stupid, I've built this problem up in my head and I know it's silly, but...'

'Do you want to talk about it?'

'I have a Debs coming up and I don't know what to do.'

'Debs?'

'It's like a graduation night. We all dress up; it's a chance to wear a glitzy dress.'

'Hey, that's a special life event for you.'

Rowena shivered.

'I haven't got anything to wear, it's tomorrow night and this great guy has asked me to be his date.'

'Tomorrow night! Rowena, what were you thinking?'

'I didn't have the money.'

'Do you want an advance on your wages?'

Rowena shook her head.

'My dad is depending on those wages. Two months after Mam died, the bank took our house. We live in a caravan now at the other side of Kilcashel.'

'I had no idea.'

'It's not something I go shouting about.'

She suddenly stopped and jumped up to go. 'I'm sorry; I'm sure you don't want to be hearing my troubles.'

Katie took Rowena by the elbow.

'Come with me, I have the person who can at least solve the fashion crisis.'

She led Rowena up the path towards the back of the house.

Maggie was having a cigarette on the deck, blowing rings up to the sky.

'Rowena here needs your fashion help,' Katie said.

Maggie quickly stubbed out her cigarette with her fingers.

'Intriguing, how can I help you?' Maggie asked.

'I'm invited to a Debs – it's tomorrow night. My father thought he would have enough money for a dress, but he lost his job a few weeks ago and the bank repossessed our house.'

'Hey, slow down, deep breaths,' Maggie said.

'I didn't realise your dad lost his job as well,' Katie said.

'We're just about making ends meet. It's only me and my sister and my dad.'

'Oh, honey, this is such bad news,' Maggie said.

Tears streamed down Rowena's face.

'Don't cry, I have a treasure trove of dresses. I'm sure we can find something. Does it have to be evening wear?'

'Yes.'

'I have a really nice designer slinky dress, but we may need to take it in. Your hair is so thick and beautiful, we'll get away with a good blow-dry.'

'I shouldn't be asking for your help. My dad will kill me if he finds out.'

Maggie got up from her seat and put her arm around Rowena's shoulders.

'Don't you worry about any of that; you shall go to the ball.'

She ordered Rowena to follow her upstairs.

Katie was surprised when she followed them inside to see Anna back in the kitchen.

'I was a bit hasty, and I thought I would come back and get the boxes ready for tomorrow. I can't be piling everything on the young girl. Why is she back? I thought she would be gone home by now,' she said.

'Maggie is helping her pick an outfit for her Debs.'

'Somebody should tell Maggie what is required for a

Debs, otherwise she will have her all dolled up for the Met Gala. Anything Maggie has will be too big, I can offer my services as a seamstress. I'm a dab hand with the sewing machine.'

Anna left the boxes and disappeared upstairs. When she got as far as the bedroom, she stood lingering in the doorway watching Rowena and Maggie.

Rowena was wearing a pink satin gown.

'It's a bit low, your father won't be happy with that,' Anna grumbled.

'We know, we're just trying to work out how to get around that,' Maggie said.

'I have a sewing machine back in my place and a wide red ribbon, which will clash well with the pink. I know the fashion types like colours to clash. I can attach the ribbon, if you wish.'

'You can do that?' Maggie said.

'I have a lot of hidden talents. It looks like I will need to turn it up as well. What footwear are you wearing?'

Rowena made to answer, but Maggie interrupted.

'Rowena is a small size – a four – so I can't help her and I don't think Katie can either.'

'I can,' Anna said. 'I didn't always go around in these flats. If you don't mind wearing my dressy gold sandals, the heel is about an inch or so?'

Rowena beamed with delight.

'Would you do that for me?'

'Why wouldn't I? I'm not a complete dragon, young lady,' Anna said in her mock cross voice.

Maggie gave Anna a thumbs up and said by tomorrow she would have hunted out some sort of jacket or stole to go over the dress.

'None of your fancy stuff; this girl wants to be hip, not a hippie,' Anna said, stepping back on to the landing as Maggie playfully hit out in her direction.

Rowena laughed, looking from one woman to the other women.

'I don't know how to thank you.'

'Work hard in the café, that's all we ask,' Anna said gruffly as she led the way downstairs.

In the hall, Katie was talking to Rowena's father at the front door.

'Your dad was passing and called in to see did you need a lift? I was saying to him you should get dressed here after your café shift tomorrow. There's a lot of preparing to do; it makes more sense to leave from here.' She turned to Rowena's dad. 'You're welcome to come over around six thirty, to see her off.'

'I would like to do that, maybe bring her sister. Thank you,' he said.

Anna turned to Katie as the car drove off.

'You're so kind; she's lucky to have met you.'

'And what about me?' Maggie said.

'You constantly surprise me,' Anna replied, taking her coat and asking Maggie to get the dress, because she wanted to work on it when she got home.

Anna and Rowena arrived at the same time the next morning.

'I think you'll like what I did to the dress, but that's for later. We best concentrate on the work for the next few hours,' she said.

Katie noticed that Rowena never slacked, clearing tables within minutes of customers leaving and managing to take orders, and completing payments in double quick time.

When Maggie came downstairs, she was wearing a midnight blue, silk vintage Dior dress which complimented her eyes, but Katie thought it drained her face of colour. She had her long hair in a chignon and a chunky piece of jewellery at her neck.

When she sat on the blue velvet armchair, she looked as if she were the lady of the manor.

The tour bus drove slowly up the avenue, pulling into a special bay Dan had organised at the side of the house.

'Why do they have to look so American?' Anna said, and Katie giggled.

'American and proud of it,' Katie said.

'I just don't like tourists; no offence to the present company intended.'

'OK, none taken. But it's not so long since we two Americans were tourists in Kilcashel,' Katie said as she walked with Maggie to the front door to greet her guests.

The next few hours passed in a blur of work. Katie had made one hundred bagels the night before, and every one of them was eaten. Of the fifty boxes of cookies Rowena had filled, only one was left by the time the café closed at 4 p.m.

Locals mixed with tourists and, at one stage, Katie stopped and listened to the happy hubbub of conversation and the laughter coming from around the fireplace, where Maggie was holding court with her stories of the days when she'd rubbed shoulders with celebrities.

'Do you think she ever even met any of these people?' Anna asked.

'I don't exactly know, but she sure can tell a good story,' Katie said.

Maggie, she thought, looked tired when she closed the front door after waving off the last customers.

'Time for the Debs makeover,' she said, but Katie thought the lilt had gone from her voice.

Anna, who had the dress hanging in the pantry and covered with a sheet so nobody could have a sneak peek during the day, brought it into the kitchen. The red satin ribbon had been lightly ruffled about the round neck of the dress, so that it looked as if it always had been that way.

Around the waist was the same colour ribbon but in a thinner width.

'Entirely up to you, Rowena, but I thought the ribbon at the waist sets off the dress beautifully,' she said.

Rowena said it was fab and she hugged Anna tightly.

'Go on, get ready; I'll look after the café and the kitchen. Sure, I only have to fill the dishwashers and wipe down the surfaces,' Anna said gruffly.

When Katie put her arm around Anna, she shrugged it off.

'Off ye go; I have work to do.'

The others went upstairs, but Katie from the hallway watched Anna wipe away tears from her eyes with the end of her apron.

Maggie and Rowena were chatting and laughing when Katie joined them.

'I think she should wear the earrings Harry gave me,' Maggie called out.

'I can't, they're too precious to you,' Rowena said.

'Turns out there's a second pair if you lose them – right, Katie?'

Katie nodded and sat on the bed, watching Maggie curl Rowena's long hair.

At one stage she saw her arch her back and rub it fiercely.

'Is something hurting? Katie asked.

'It's been a long day, that's all. I will have a bath, when Cinderella here has gone to the ball,' Maggie said, flashing a big smile.

It was another half hour before Rowena was ready.

Anna called up the stairs that her dad had just arrived.

The bedroom door opened.

Both Katie and Maggie grinned in delight at the young girl in the designer pink silk dress and the gold strappy sandals. The dress hugged around her hips and Katie noticed she wasn't wearing the ribbon belt. Rowena with her long hair curling down her back, looked both beautiful and sophisticated.

Anna called up the stairs that a very nervous young man in a tuxedo was at the front door.

'Let us walk down first; we need a picture of you descending the Kilcashel stairs,' Maggie said, and she and Katie hurried on ahead.

When Rowena arrived on the landing, her father let tears stream down his face and her young sister clapped in excitement. Katie saw Anna slip away into the kitchen as Rowena made her way down the steps to be presented with a corsage and be led to a waiting limousine. Before she got in the car, she stopped to hug her father and wrapped her arms around both Katie and Maggie.

'Thank you,' she whispered, and they hugged her back tightly.

'Go and enjoy yourself, make memories,' Maggie said.

'Where's Anna?' Rowena asked.

'Grumbling to herself, no doubt, that she has been left to do all the work,' Maggie said.

When the limo had bounced its way down the avenue and Rowena's Dad had left, Maggie said she was beat and went upstairs for a long soak in the bath and then to bed.

Katie knocked on the kitchen door. When there was no answer, she pushed the door ajar, just a little. Anna was sitting at the counter, her head in her hands. Katie knew she was weeping.

She dithered over whether to give Anna her privacy or to go and comfort her. She was still trying to decide, when Anna gestured her to enter the room.

'I'm all right, it was just such a beautiful moment,' she said, blowing her nose into her handkerchief.

'It reminded you of your girls.'

'It did, but not in a bad way. All the good memories came back and overwhelmed me.'

Katie grasped one of Anna's hands.

'I am glad you two have brought life back to Kilcashel House,' Anna whispered, and Katie pressed her hand.

'It has been a privilege,' she said quietly, pushing a small plate of cake squares towards Anna.

'Can I ask you to try our new cakes?'

'Did you go for my lemon cake?'

'Yes, thank you; I modified it a little and added poppy seed,' she said, indicating the trays of chocolate cake and lemon poppy seed cake, cut into small squares.

'Try them and tell me what you think.'

'I'm no fan of poppy seeds, they get stuck in the dentures,' Anna said, taking a tiny bite of the lemon cake. She swallowed and looked at Katie.

'That's not my recipe.'

'I did modify it.'

'Well, whatever you did, it's a heck of a lot better.'

Anna took big bite of the chocolate cake.

'That's divine, not even the café in the town can beat that.'

'So, they have your seal of approval?'

'Definitely.'

'Great, they're both on the menu from tomorrow with a cake and coffee special for a fiver just for the first week.'

'No doubt Ms Fancy Pants wanted a price special.'

'Yes, and a very good idea it is to take on the town café head on,' Katie said.

NINETEEN

Muriel and Rosie Falvey rushed around the side of Kilcashel House and banged on the back door.

'I know it's early, but do you think we could come in?' Muriel asked Maggie, who was on her way back from her swim.

'The café opens at 9 a.m., but if Katie doesn't mind, I don't.'

'We're in a bit of bother.'

'Oh, is there anything we can do to help?' Maggie asked as she pushed open the back door and let the two women into the kitchen.

'You don't mind, do you, Katie? Muriel and Rosie here are in difficulties.'

Katie, who was boxing up cake squares didn't look up from what she was doing, and just gestured for the women to come in.

Maggie bundled her canvas swim bag under the counter.

'I was just going to have some bubbly, but I guess you ladies would like tea.'

Muriel cleared her throat and looked around as if checking to see if anyone was within hearing distance.

'To tell you the truth, we could do with something stronger and more than that bubbly stuff too,' she said.

'Whiskey, if you have it,' Rosie piped up.

Katie stopped what she was doing and swung around.

'Has something happened? Are you all right?'

Muriel threw her hands in the air and sighed loudly.

'We're not all right; we could be arrested any minute.'

'What have you done, murdered somebody?' Maggie laughed.

Rosie took a tiny plastic bag out of her pocket and carefully put it on the counter.

'Is that what we think it is?'

Katie stole a glance at Maggie, who was trying her best to suppress her giggles.

'Where did you get it? Don't tell me you bought it?' Katie asked.

'What do you take us for, a pair of old druggies? We found it in the allotment next door to ours,' Muriel said, her face grim.

Maggie picked up the bag and opened it.

'That's weed.'

'Close it before it pongs out the place,' Katie snapped.

She reached into a drawer and took out a large zip-lock bag and threw it across the counter to Maggie, who slipped the cannabis inside, folding the bag over several times.

'What do we do now?' she asked.

'We throw it in the sea; get rid of it. We can't keep it here,' Katie said.

Maggie stuffed the zip-lock bag into the pocket of her dryrobe and poured the whiskey.

'Nora and the others will be here shortly; I got out early today; I just didn't have the stamina for a full swim this morning.'

'Mother of divine Jesus, they can't know! They'll make a laughing stock of us all over Kilcashel,' Muriel said.

'What were you doing, nosing around someone else's allotment anyway?' Maggie asked.

Muriel gulped her whiskey. 'We weren't nosing around; we were investigating the bloody awful smell that keeps wafting over to our lovely spot, spoiling our enjoyment.'

'Yeah, and when she asked that fellah McDonald, he said it was some foreign cigars that a friend brought back from Cuba, but we're no fools. Our father used to smoke the best cigars and no Cuban cigar stinks that bad,' Rosie said.

Maggie burst out laughing, but she quickly put her hand over her mouth when she saw Rosie's face crumple.

'It's all right for you to laugh, but this was our one piece of heaven and that fellah has turned it into hell.'

Muriel stood up as if she were about to leave.

'We're obviously bothering you when you're busy. We will have to sort this out ourselves. Thank you for confirming our suspicions,' she said, her tone formal.

Maggie stood in front of her.

'I'm sorry, ladies, but it's just a teeny bit funny. You know we want to help.'

Katie poured hot water into a teapot and placed it on the counter.

'Sit down and we'll work out how to deal with this.'

Rosie sat, but Muriel hesitated.

'Come on, Mu; you know we can't fix this on our own,' Rosie whispered to her sister.

Maggie put some chocolate and lemon cake squares on a plate and pushed them across the counter.

'I'm sorry, I shouldn't have laughed, but I honestly didn't expect to come across this problem in Kilcashel. Times Square maybe, but not Kilcashel.' Maggie snorted loudly in her attempt to stop her sniggers.

Rosie put her hand up to stop her.

'It said in the papers last week that there are drugs, even cocaine, in every village and town in Ireland. I think we've just proved it.'

'What are we going to do?' Muriel asked, gripping the mug of tea her sister had edged towards her.

'Dan is in charge of the allotments; I just help out. I will get him to have a look,' Maggie said.

Muriel shook her head.

'Couldn't we just leave it between us? Dan Redmond knows too many people in Kilcashel.'

'You can trust him, he won't go blabbing to anybody,' Katie said.

Rosie shifted on the counter stool.

'It's just, we think McDonald is trying to grow cannabis as well. There are strange plants in his polytunnel and there is more of that stuff in plastic bags.'

'Now that's serious,' Katie said.

'How do you know? What does cannabis in its raw state look like?' Maggie asked.

'We googled it and it's cannabis all right. The summer has been kind this year and this August has been so hot, the plants are growing well,' Rosie said.

'I thought that guy said he was using the polytunnel for delicate herbs he was going to supply to a restaurant in Dublin,' Maggie said.

'He probably said it to sound fancy,' Muriel said.

'Or as a cover,' Rosie piped up.

Nora and Leonie walked into the kitchen, but stopped a few paces inside the door.

'Has something happened? You lot look so serious,' Nora said.

Muriel stood up.

'I was pitching an idea to Maggie and Katie; maybe ye

should set up a proper swimming club for everybody in Kilcashel. Your swimming gathering is a bit exclusive and by invitation only from what I can see. I notice we never got an invite.'

'You two are hardly going to risk getting into the Irish Sea and freezing your rocks off,' Leonie said.

'It would have been nice to be asked,' Rosie said quietly.

'Yeah, maybe the ladies would get a high from it,' Maggie said, her voice very serious.

Flustered, Nora said she couldn't stay for coffee as she had to rush off and if Leonie wanted a lift, they had better choose coffee to go.

Katie filled takeaway cups and they left quickly.

Muriel chuckled.

'I knew that would work. Nora never really liked me.'

'Maybe we should go to the gardai and tell them the truth,' Rosie said.

'No,' both Katie and Maggie shouted. Katie plonked herself directly in front of the Falvey sisters.

'If you do that, they will be here in their police cars and the cannabis find will be linked to the house and café. Our business could be ruined. Can't we find some solution ourselves?'

They stopped when they heard the clop of horses on the cobbles of the backyard.

'Shit, it's Dan, he said he would tack up the horses and meet me after my swim,' Maggie said.

'You can't leave in the middle of this,' Katie said, her voice firm.

Dan knocked at the door.

Katie got off her stool and opened it.

'Can you tie up the horses somewhere? We need your help.'

Katie watched as Dan tied the reins to an old hook on the outside wall. When he saw the Falveys, he looked puzzled.

'Is something wrong at the allotment?' he asked.

Muriel pointed to Katie and mouthed to her to tell him.

Dan listened intently, shaking his head.

'That chap swore to me he was sowing herbs; he had a contract to supply a well-to-do restaurant in Dublin. I even gave him a lower rate just to help the business along.'

Muriel clicked her tongue and her face reddened with anger.

'You gave him a lower rate than two old age pensioners. May God forgive you, Dan Redmond, because I'm not sure that I will,' she said.

Rosie put a hand on her sister's shoulder and told her to calm down.

'Are you going to help us?' she asked.

'I will have to take everything out of his allotment and burn it. Tell him to hop it or else I'll get the law involved.'

'But if you burn the weed, won't it stink?' Maggie said.

'I will take it away and burn it at my place tonight.'

'Please be careful, I see him at the allotments before ten each morning. He's an oddball,' Katie said.

'He's always down to ventilate, as he says, his special herb room,' Rosie said.

'I will go there now,' Dan said.

Maggie jumped up.

'Just let me pull on some jeans and I'll come with you.'

Katie was annoyed when Muriel and Rosie said they would go as well, and she was left to open the café on her own. She dialled Anna and asked could she come in as soon as possible.

She heard the others hurry down the avenue and she felt a little jealous that she was left behind. It was only then she remembered the zip-lock bag in her pocket. Taking down the ornamental ginger jar from the top of the fridge, she popped the bag in.

Walking into the café, she unlatched the shutters on the windows and let them swing into place.

She could see the little group on the allotment, forcibly pushing the grow house over. Dan filled a wheelbarrow with the plastic sheeting and carefully placed the cannabis plants on it, wrapping them up as if they were fragile cargo. Muriel and Rosie helped him dig out the earth, to make sure every last piece of evidence of the plants was destroyed.

Maggie stood guard at the fence, watching. Katie checked the time on her phone. Fifteen minutes until they opened. She didn't want anybody getting a whiff of what was going on in the allotment. She rang Maggie.

'Tell Dan to get out of there,' she said urgently.

'Don't worry, he's steering the load out now.'

'Anna will be on the avenue shortly; we can't have her suspecting anything.'

'Relax, it's all under control; don't worry,' Maggie said, making Katie feel even more nervous.

Dan pushed the wheelbarrow of cannabis plants quickly up the avenue; Maggie and the Falvey sisters scurrying behind him. They diverted to the front door while he went around the back.

Katie saw Anna coming up the avenue and called out that she was going around the back to talk to Dan, and could Anna serve tea to Muriel and Rosie in the café?

Anna snorted her displeasure but told Katie to take her time.

'I'm going to bring this lot down to the far stables,' Dan said when Katie caught up with him.

'Are you sure you want to be mixed up in this?'

'Don't worry, I was thinking I will take it out of the plastic and sink it deep at sea. That way, it won't get washed up and haunt us further.'

'Thanks for helping us out.'

It's OK, I was thinking of going out for a spin in the boat anyway. Would you like to come, be my accomplice – I mean, guest.'

'I have to do a lot of baking for tomorrow.'

Dan stared at Katie.

'Get the baking done and we will go out about 5 p.m. Bring some bagels and we can eat on board.'

'I didn't say yes.'

'But you didn't say no, either,' he laughed. 'I have a little pier at my place; come over for around five. I am correcting a lot of exams, but I should be finished by then.'

'OK,' she said, and she was annoyed at herself, because she knew she was blushing.

'Hey, we will have some fun,' he promised, and she nodded, turning back to the house.

When she got back to the kitchen, Anna was slapping cups onto saucers.

'I hope you're going to charge those Falvey sisters. They ordered tea and biscuits, like I'm here to serve them.'

'They've had a funny morning; it's on the house.'

'I don't know how you're going to make any money; you're way too soft,' Anna said as she carried the tray to the café counter. Rather than walk to the table, she called loudly for Muriel to collect her order.

Katie poured herself a coffee and sat down.

'Can you give it a rest, Anna, please? It's been such a long morning. I have to go upstairs for a bit. Can you hold the fort until I come back?'

Katie didn't wait to hear Anna's grumbles but escaped up the stairs as three people arrived at the café. She needed to escape Anna's mood. She needed to get away from Kilcashel for a while. She didn't know what to wear going out to sea on a boat.

Rooting in her wardrobe, she pulled out her pink sneakers and a white pair of trousers she had never worn. She pulled a fresh white T-shirt from her chest of drawers and a red hoodie she'd she bought in Macy's sale, just a few days before Harry died.

Maggie no doubt would look beautiful and chic if she was asked onto a sailing boat, but she could not compete with her flamboyance. She wasn't even sure if it was a date, though she hoped it was. It had been so long since she had been on a date that she felt nervous. If Maggie knew, she would mock her for sure, so best to keep it to herself and dress up in a nice date-not-a-date sort of way, Katie thought.

From her window, Katie could see all the way down to the sea. Maggie and Dan were at the edge of the waves, exercising the horses. It was good that Maggie was finally beginning to make friends, she thought, but she so wished that it didn't have to be Dan Redmond.

Katie jumped when Anna hammered on the bedroom door.

'I know you lot think I'm superwoman, but there's a queue a mile long in the café – you have to come down,' she said.

Katie followed her downstairs and took over at the counter as Anna got the orders ready.

When the ten people in the queue had all got their food and there was a nice buzz of conversation in the café, Anna pulled Katie aside.

'Maggie is nowhere to be seen. She's leaving us high and dry every day. You were mad to ever let her into your business.'

Katie would have answered, but a tall man came into the café and shouted that he wanted to the talk to the person in charge.

Katie stepped up to the counter as Muriel and Rosie came

behind the man, gesturing frantically to the allotment and back to him.

'I am David McDonald; somebody has dug up my allotment and stolen all my plants. Do you know anything about it?'

Katie walked around to the front of the counter and asked the man to follow her to the front door.

'You do know something about it, don't you?' he asked.

Katie led the man by the elbow down the front steps. Leaning in close, she whispered in his ear:

'I know that you were growing cannabis and that it has been taken away. My advice to you is to leave this place before the gardai come to arrest you.'

'Are you saying the cops took it? What did you tell them?'

'I only saw the plants being taken away; I didn't tell anyone anything.'

'It was those interfering biddies, wasn't it? Why can't they let a man live in peace?'

'I'm not sure you were letting them live in peace.'

McDonald pulled away from Katie and kicked a pot of flowers on the top step. Muriel and Rosie appeared at the door. Anna marched down the hall carrying a sweeping brush.

'We would like you to leave now, Mr McDonald; you are causing a nuisance,' Katie said.

Anna advanced with the brush.

'Get the hell out of here,' Muriel said.

'And don't come back,' Rosie shouted.

McDonald stared at the group of women, cursing under his breath as he ran down the steps and jumped in his car.

'I hope that's the end of him,' Katie said.

'If he has any sense he won't come back here. Now, will someone tell me what the hell is going on?' Anna asked.

Muriel dug her in the ribs.

'We would have to kill you, if we told you,' she said as she skipped down the steps and called her sister to follow.

Anna looked severely at Katie.

'I suppose this has a lot to do with some madness this morning?' she said.

'It's done and dusted; you don't want to know,' Katie said, turning back into the café.

TWENTY

The weather had changed quickly. The sky was grey, the sea choppy and the wind cold. Katie was so disappointed they could not take the boat out to sea. Dan had moored the boat at the jetty, tying its ropes around two bollards, and they made their way across the beach.

'I intended to drop the cannabis and plants far out at sea. I have no idea what to do with them now; do you think we should chance burning it?' Dan said.

She didn't answer; she was too busy feeling self-conscious. She had a basket with bagels and a bottle of bubbly, and she felt rather foolish, that she thought she might have been going on a date.

'I'm sorry for getting you involved in all of this,' she said, her voice so low, he could barely hear her.

'It's not your fault; it's just a bit of a headache to figure out what to do. I certainly don't want to be accused of having anything to do with drugs.'

Anger pushed through her that the boat trip was nothing but a chore to him. She didn't know whether she was more frustrated and cross at herself or Dan. She felt like crying, but instead she pushed the basket into Dan's chest, and stomped off across the sand. She was fed up and angry and she didn't want a stand-up row. Harry always let her be when she got like this, so when Dan ran after her, she was surprised.

'Katie, please come back,' he shouted as she quickened her step.

'Please turn around at least,' he called.

She swung around ready to give out, but he was holding up the basket and laughing.

'Can't we feast on this while you help me come up with a plan?'

He had a quirky smile and soft eyes, and she had nothing better to do, she thought. Also, she knew she couldn't turn back to Kilcashel House; Maggie would know the date had been ditched.

Shrugging her shoulders, she said OK, and they walked along, side by side. The sound of the waves hitting the shore filled the space between them, until Dan reached out for her hand. She let him take it and he gently pulled her closer.

'I've made a mess of things, haven't I?' he said in her ear. She nodded.

'My house is nearby; let's go there; have this nice picnic and talk.'

'OK, just for a while,' she said.

She let him steer her across the sand and rocks to a path up through a field.

They didn't speak. She knew he was trying to think of something to say and she didn't help him one bit.

She'd never been to his house before, and she was surprised that, while it was not as grand as Kilcashel House, it was a beautiful bungalow with huge windows overlooking the sea.

He smiled at her reaction.

'It was my parents' place. My older sister – I don't think you've met her – inherited the smallholding; she has a vegetable-growing business. She lives in a farmhouse about a mile from here. I have an acre and the old bungalow, which I've been slowly doing up, and Leonie lives in the property next door.'

He opened the door and stood back to let her step into the kitchen.

'It's why I'm so glad to help out at Kilcashel and have my horses so close. My sister wouldn't have any spare land and Leonie only has enough for her garden next door.'

Katie took the kitchen in. It was an old-fashioned wooden kitchen which had seen better days, but she liked it. Running her hands along the wooden worktop, she sighed.

'I would love to have a kitchen like this.'

'It's from Kilcashel House. Harry didn't want it, so I took it out for him and put it in here,' Dan said sheepishly.

'Don't get me wrong, the kitchen at Kilcashel is perfect for the bakery and café and this would be a nightmare, but it's so lovely. I feel every little notch and groove and this worktop tells a story.'

'Yes, money was tight when I salvaged it, but I'm so glad I did.'

'So, I can't get it back then.'

'No. I'm afraid not,' he laughed, taking some glasses and plates from a cupboard.

'So, what are you going to do about the cannabis?' she asked.

'I thought of burying all of it, but at the rate Lola digs up Anna's bulbs, I would be afraid she'd get a whiff of it. She's always nosing around here.'

'I have an idea.'

'I'm all ears.'

'Why don't we flush what we can down the toilet and bury the plants on the Kilcashel compost heap?'

'And have cannabis-infused peat for the allotments? I don't think so,' he said.

'So, what are we going to do? I guess we can't throw them out with the garbage.'

'We're just going to have to sit this out and dispose of it at sea when the weather calms down,' Dan said, taking out his phone and looking up the shipping forecast. 'It says here that should be around 4 a.m. I'll go out and throw it overboard, and hopefully nobody will see me and think I'm dumping a body.'

'I can come along, if you like.'

'But what about the café?'

'I can ask Anna to open up.'

'OK, you're on.'

Dan took some plates from an open shelf. Katie placed the bagels on them and looked around for another plate for the biscuits. Dan handed her a blue plate then poured the Prosecco.

'It's nice to finally get you on your own and away from Kilcashel House,' he said.

'I guess it does consume rather a lot of my time, but at the moment, that's good for me.'

'Maggie told me about Harry.'

'She tells everyone about Harry; I think it helps with her grieving to talk her way through it.'

'What about you?'

'I don't see the need to be seen as poor Katie, left behind when her partner of six years was gunned down in Manhattan.'

They sat quietly, neither knowing what to say next.

Dan cleared his throat. 'It might help to talk it through.'

Katie twiddled the glass stem between her fingers.

'It's just that most people get caught up on the fact that Harry left us with a mountain of debt. I don't get to talk much about the Harry I knew.'

'What was he like?'

'I don't know. These days at Kilcashel, when I see the way

he cleared the house of its history and tried to throw away the furniture, I wonder did I know him at all.'

'I think maybe pick the version you want to believe and forget about everything else.'

'I want to believe he was the man I was going to marry. Now, I'm not so sure that would have been a good idea. Kilcashel Katie I guess is very different to Manhattan Katie.'

She got up and walked to the window.

From here, she could see all the way across the sea to the horizon.

'Did you know from my apartment in Manhattan I could just see the street below and a chink between buildings hinted there was a lot more out there. It was a beautiful night after Harry died, all the lit-up buildings made me feel so alone, so lonely. It was as if everybody was getting on with their lives and mine had stood still.'

'I hope you don't still feel that way,' he said, joining her at the window.

She smiled. 'These days I stand on the deck and look out to the horizon, and I feel a part of something bigger. Kilcashel has given me a sense of belonging. Now, I couldn't bear if I had to leave here.'

Dan put his arm around her and pulled Katie close.

'I couldn't bear if you had to leave. I like having you around. I like Kilcashel Katie,' he said, gently kissing the top of her head.

When her phone rang, Katie didn't want to answer it, but the caller persisted.

'I had better check,' she said.

Maggie's voice was high-pitched.

'Katie, where are you? The police are here, and they're asking questions.'

'Shit, about what?'

'You know, the allotment. Where are you?'

'I am over at Dan's.'

'Did you go out in the boat?'

'No.'

'Just come back home; I can't handle this on my own.'

Katie looked at Dan.

'Police are at the house, asking about the allotments.'

'Do they know?'

'I don't see how – unless Muriel or Rosie blabbed.'

'I doubt it, particularly since they were involved.'

'I have to go back.'

'I'll come with you.'

'No, we don't want any suspicion falling on you.'

'I will walk you back at least. And I want you to ring me, soon as they've left.'

They tramped across the sand. At one stage Dan tried to take Katie's hand, but she pulled away; her mind was too full of worry.

When they reached the path leading up to Kilcashel House, Dan pulled Katie into his arms and kissed her on the lips.

'Stay calm, everything will be fine. We've done nothing wrong,' he said. Katie snuggled into Dan's chest before reluctantly pulling away.

'Not yet anyway,' she said, turning to make her way to Kilcashel House. She stopped when she reached the garden path to compose herself. When she looked back, Dan was still standing on the beach, waiting to see her safely at the back door.

Maggie was sitting at the counter with two plainclothes detectives.

'I told you Katie would be back soon. She can answer any questions; she's the business head behind the venture; I'm just the creative one,' she said, her voice still high-pitched.

Katie took a deep breath and shook hands with both detectives as they introduced themselves. The tall skinny one sat back down, but the squat one with a beer belly overhanging his belt paced the kitchen and cleared his throat.

'Ms Williams, we understand you had a visitor to your café today, a man called McDonald, and that there was some sort of argument. Could we ask what that was about?'

Katie straightened up.

'He has an allotment and he said somebody had taken something belonging to him. He grows herbs for a restaurant in Dublin. We didn't know what he was talking about.'

'I very much doubt that he was growing herbs.'

'What do you mean?'

'Can we have a look at the allotment?'

'I told you, there's nothing there now, not even the herbs,' Maggie said.

'But there used to be plants there?'

'He had a polytunnel; we never went there.'

'But it's empty now?'

'Well, we had a look after he left, and it was bare. I don't know what he was talking about.'

The tall detective got up from the counter.

'You should be more careful who you allow to frequent Kilcashel House. McDonald is a drug dealer; he supplies half the cannabis in these parts.'

The other detective picked up a biscuit and bit into it.

'Oh, I've heard about these American cakes. My wife keeps saying we must drive out on a Sunday for lunch.'

Maggie picked up two boxes of cake squares.

'I hope you're able to accept these with our gratitude,' she smiled, pushing a box into the hands of each detective.

The tall detective turned to Katie.

'If that fellow McDonald comes around here again, give us a shout. He's a nasty piece of work.'

'We're not in trouble then?' Maggie asked.

'Not unless you're drug-dealing,' the stocky detective said.

'Bagels, cake and cookies are our game,' Katie said nervously, ushering the two detectives to the front door.

Pausing at the door, the tall detective swivelled around to Maggie and Katie.

'Don't forget to give us a call if that fella turns up again. He's not one to cross and he's usually not put off so easily.'

'We will, and thank you.'

'And if you ever want to vet anybody interested in taking up an allotment, give us call,' the other detective said. Katie and Maggie stood on the steps and watched the detectives drive down the avenue.

'Are we very bad people?' Katie asked.

Maggie snorted. 'We did what we had to do; nobody got hurt and they got a box of biscuits each.'

'What if McDonald comes back?'

'He's not getting a box of cake squares; we'll set Anna on him,' Maggie laughed.

Katie phoned Dan. When he answered, she could barely hear him.

'Where are you?' she asked.

'I decided not to wait; I'm bringing the boat out past the headland to get rid of the stuff.'

'But I thought conditions weren't good until the early hours.'

'It's not so bad and she's a big boat. I was afraid the detectives might swing down to my place.'

'Will you be all right?' Katie asked.

'Are you on the Kilcashel deck?'

'I am now,' she said, rushing through the conservatory and out the door.

In the distance, she saw a light flash on and off a few times.

'You do know that you could be arrested for very suspicious signalling from sea to shore. You will get us all into trouble,' she said.

'But I have made you smile.'

'Yes,' she said.

'Well then, it's worth it.'

Katie giggled and Dan said he would see her soon.

Maggie came on the deck.

'He likes you a lot.'

'Who?'

'Darling, we all see it; just don't let it slip away because you're still grieving a man who maybe didn't deserve you.'

'I don't want to talk about Harry,' Katie said.

Maggie shrugged. Katie said she had to get baking, pushing past Maggie on her way to the kitchen.

'I'm just saying, stay open to possibilities. Dan is one of the good guys, but he has only eyes for you, no matter how many times I try to turn his head,' Maggie said, following quickly behind.

Katie pretended to ignore Maggie and concentrated on her recipe.

Maggie went to bed soon after. Katie couldn't concentrate. She went out on the deck and scanned for Dan's boat. She dialled his number. It took him a while to answer.

'Sorry, I was tying up the boat. Mission accomplished.'

'It won't wash up on shore or anything like that?'

'You watch too many movies.'

'Maybe.'

'Are you working right now?'

'I was too worried; I couldn't concentrate. I can get up extra early tomorrow morning instead.'

'Are you up for a stroll in the moonlight?'

'That would be nice.'

'OK, see you in ten.'

Katie wasn't sure what to do. She ran upstairs and peeped in Maggie's room. She was fast asleep, so she tiptoed to her dressing table and sprayed the Coco Chanel on her wrists and neck.

When she got downstairs, Dan was in the kitchen.

'I was hoping you hadn't changed your mind.'

She was pulling on her coat when he wrapped his arms around her.

'I don't want to get it wrong again. I really like you, Katie.'

She smiled and she let him kiss her.

'I like you too, but what about Maggie?'

Dan smiled broadly at Katie.

'Maggie is a good friend, but that's it. She knows how I feel about you.'

Katie reached for her coat and put it on.

'I think it's time to go for that walk,' she said.

He followed her out the door and caught her hand as they made their way down to the sea.

They wandered along the sand, happy to be together. He pulled her close and asked did she want to go back to the bungalow.

She liked Dan so much, but she wasn't ready.

'I need time.'

He looked disappointed.

'I understand,' he said, offering his arm so she could link through and he walked her home.

'Are you OK with this?' she asked when they got to the back door.

Dan laughed.

'I'm going to have to be, but promise me you will tell me when you're ready.'

'I promise,' she said, and she kissed him quickly on the cheek then disappeared indoors.

TWENTY-ONE

It was a cool September morning and Katie had hidden herself away in her bedroom preparing for her afternoon meetings, before heading for the local market. She saw Anna out in the cobbled backyard, filling a bowl of water for the dog and chatting to Maggie, who was in the kitchen.

'So you're a bit of a fair-weather sea swimmer then?' Anna said as Maggie flopped on a stool at the counter.

'Excuse me?'

'I always said you would stop once the novelty wore off and the water started to lose its summer appeal.'

'The water is always cold and no, I just don't feel good today.'

Anna stole a glance at Maggie, who had poured a glass of water and was sipping it.

'You look a bit peaky.'

'I'll be all right, we New Yorkers are tough birds.'

Anna switched on the kettle.

'A cup of sugary tea should put you to rights. Are you staying up for Nora and her lot when they come back from their swim?'

'Shit, I forgot they are due, aren't they?'

Maggie jumped from the stool.

'I don't want them to think I just couldn't be bothered.'

'Why don't you tell them you're under the weather.'

'And face an inquisition? God, no! You're not to tell Katie either. She's finally agreed to take an afternoon off and I'm going to look after the café. Tell her I needed a lie-in. She'll believe it, if you make me out to be lazy.'

'Maybe you should see a doctor.'

'I just need to rest and I'll be fine.'

'Go on, go back to bed. I'll drop up the tea,' Anna said kindly.

Maggie made her way back up the stairs, stopping halfway to get her breath. Katie was on the landing, pulling a straw market bag from a cupboard. She nodded to Maggie as she went past then stood by the window to look out over the front paddocks. Dan was traipsing through the allotments, inspecting each one before the gardeners turned up. Since he discovered the cannabis operation, he patrolled the allotments weekly to make sure there was nothing illegal happening. The cornflowers were still in bloom and one allotment had a bank of purple blue borage which Katie loved. Tall sunflowers, which were beginning a to look a bit scraggly, had taken over another rectangular patch. Not realising Maggie was watching her, Katie quickly stepped back from the window when Dan glanced up at the house.

Maggie went on into her room and closed the door behind her. When she heard Anna coming up the stairs Katie asked was Maggie ill?

Anna, who was carrying a tray of tea shook her head in exasperation.

'Listen to that scrabbling,' she huffed. 'She's running around tidying up her room because I said I'd drop up her tea for her. As if I don't know at this stage what an untidy bugger she is.'

She was still giving out as she entered the room and placed the tray of tea on the bedside table and began to fluff up the bed pillows while ordering Maggie to get into bed.

When Anna placed a small plate of cakes beside the cup of tea on the bedside table, Maggie told her to take them away.

'My stomach isn't right, Anna, I'm afraid I will throw up if I eat.'

'I think you should go see the doctor this afternoon.'

'When did Katie last ask for any time off from the café? And even now, it's not a proper break; she's off drumming up new business.'

Anna didn't answer, but Maggie grabbed her hand.

'Not a word of this to her. If Katie asks or makes a big deal about me being bone lazy, it shouldn't be too hard for you to agree,' she said, sipping the sugary tea and grimacing.

Katie was on her way out the back door as the swimming ladies trooped up the path.

When Nora wandered into the hall and called out to Maggie to get up and face them, Anna, pretending to be cross, came scooting down the stairs to chastise the women for being so noisy.

'I just hope she can look after the café this afternoon,' Katie said, worried that Anna would end up running things on her own. 'The rest of us would soldier on regardless, but not Maggie.'

Anna's response was to shoo her out of the kitchen and tell her to be on her way, she could manage.

When she returned from the market that afternoon, Maggie still hadn't surfaced. Furious, Katie marched upstairs and knocked sharply on her bedroom door.

'Maggie, are you getting up?' Katie asked impatiently. 'You have to take over in the café in an hour.'

'I'll be down in a few minutes; keep your hair on.'

'You need to help me out here. The success of our business depends on us having multiple strands of revenue, and that means both of us pulling our weight.'

'I've got this, don't worry,' Maggie said.

Katie hesitated at the door, only turning to go downstairs once she heard Maggie stumble into the shower.

When Maggie finally made it to the kitchen, Katie was looking at her watch, in exasperation. Were you ever going to come down, if I didn't call you?' she snapped.

'Can't a girl have a lie-in?'

Katie put down the tray of bagels she had taken out of the oven.

'You promised to take over from one o'clock today, and that was almost an hour ago.'

'Shit, I'm sorry. Have I made you late for your meeting?'

'It's at 3 p.m., but now I'll have to rush and I didn't want that.'

'You're going to smash it. I'm sure the tourist board will love you.'

'And you are full of sweet talk. Table three's order is ready to go now, and five and six are waiting to order. There's also a queue at the till. Anna should be back shortly to help out.'

'Can't wait! What fun we will have,' Maggie said, placing a stuffed bagel on a small plate beside a cappuccino on a tray and sweeping out to the café floor.

Maggie, detecting a certain tension in the café, twirled around and clapped her hands.

'Ladies and gentlemen, I am on my own this afternoon and will try my best, so I ask for your patience. Please, in the meantime, help yourself to a plate of almond biscuits I will leave on the counter.'

There was a murmur of approval as she went in behind the counter and began taking payment at the till. Anna, when she arrived ten minutes later, called out from the kitchen that she would set up the orders.

'You must be feeling wrong in the head giving out free food. Katie won't be happy at all.'

'She won't know if you don't tell her. Besides, the almond cookies don't really sell.'

'I won't have to tell her. Once she does her sums, she will come to her own conclusions.'

Maggie reached for her purse on the top of the fridge and took out a ten-euro note.

'That should settle it. Can I rely on your discretion?'

'For this and anything else you want to share with me,' Anna said, but Maggie ignored the invitation to talk.

'Tables three and four want two lattes with their bagels,' Anna said gruffly, and Maggie snapped up the plates and rushed off to make the coffees. Relief coursed through Maggie that she didn't have to talk about the constant pain she felt at the base of her spine.

Nora popped her head around the counter.

'You missed Dan this morning. I think he was disappointed you weren't swimming.'

Maggie smiled.

'There will be other days. I'm sure.'

'Are you OK for tomorrow morning?'

'I don't know, I'll see.'

'Did we say something to offend you?'

'No, nothing like that. God, what are you, the swimming police?'

'It's all about turning up. Once you get in the water, you'll be glad.'

'I know; I love it, it just wasn't for me this morning.'

Nora looked slightly put out. 'You're not going to go all hoity toity on us, are you? We love you, warts and all.'

'When you put it like that, how can I resist,' Maggie said, waving Nora off as she served another customer.

When Dan knocked on the counter, Maggie knew she had to talk to him. She pinched her cheeks lightly to bring up the colour and hurried over.

'Dan, what can I do for you?'

'A mocha for takeaway, please, and the Falvey sisters have asked for a box of six raspberry biscuits and two cappuccinos, also for takeaway, please.'

'I knew they wouldn't be able to resist a daily treat from the café.'

'I missed you at the swim this morning.'

'Doesn't a lady need to get her beauty sleep at some stage?' she said, and he smiled.

'And what happened yesterday evening? Weren't we supposed to take the horses down to the beach?'

Maggie handed him the tray of drinks and the box of biscuits.

'I have to apologise; I completely forgot.'

She thought he looked annoyed, and she wished she could have come up with a better excuse. She waited until he had gone to make her way back into the kitchen and collapse on a chair.

Anna swung around.

'What is it, are you still not feeling well?'

'I'm just under the weather. Please don't tell Katie; she will only fuss.'

'There's only an hour to go, I can run everything from here, you get to bed.'

Maggie stood up. 'And have Katie think I'm too lazy to do

the job? No way,' she said, making her way back to the café counter.

There were about ten customers in the last hour and three phone calls for click and collect bagels and cookies.

Anna kept a watchful eye on Maggie, who insisted on chatting to everybody as well as handing out free lollipops to young kids.

When Katie's car pulled up outside, Anna and Maggie were ushering the last customers out the front door.

'You never turned the sign at the gate to closed and I think there are some cars after me,' she said.

'Well pardon me, but we've been pretty busy,' Maggie snapped and set off down the avenue to turn over the gate sign. One car had pulled into the side to let her pass, but she told them they must turn back.

When they had left, she walked across to the paddock fence and leaned on it to take a break.

Muriel Falvey saw her and waved, shouting out that they loved the raspberry biscuits.

'Thank you for the extra ones; we say you should be in charge all the time.'

Maggie waved back and leaned more into the fence, attempting to catch her breath.

Maggie heard Muriel call out and run across the allotments, not bothering about the pathways.

'Are you all right?' she shouted. Maggie covered her face because she knew her cheeks were puffed up and red.

'It's just some sort of stitch, I reckon it will go as fast as it came. I just need a moment.'

Rosie arrived with a bottle of water.

'Here, drink some,' she said, pushing the bottle towards Maggie.

Maggie gulped the water, some dribbling down her chin.

'Thank you.'

'You need to be checked over by a doctor. What are you trying to do anyway?' Muriel asked.

'I have to put up the closed sign. Eagle-eyed Katie spotted I hadn't done it.'

'Rosie will do that for you, you should take it easy for a bit.'

Maggie drank some more water.

'It's just been a long day, I'm OK.'

'I'll walk with you back to the house,' Muriel said.

'There's really no need.'

'Be that as it may, I'm doing it anyway,' Muriel said, quickly climbing the fence and taking Maggie by the elbow.

'You know you don't have to try to live up to your tough image all the time, girl.'

'What image?'

'Brash American and as tough as nails. We all know you're as soft as butter underneath. Me, I think Katie is a lot tougher.'

'You might be right.'

They walked up the avenue together.

'I should be fine from here,' Maggie said as they reached the rhododendron bend.

'It's no bother.'

'I feel a bit silly; I'm feeling much better.'

'You don't want Katie or Anna to see us; I understand.'

'I just don't want to face a barrage of questions,' Maggie said, kicking the gravel, making stones skate across the driveway into the grass verge.

'Tell me to mind my own business, but I really think you should get a check-up. It would do no harm.'

'Thank you for your kindness, but really, I'm OK,' she said, continuing alone up the avenue; Lola running out to greet her, her tail wagging.

Katie was sitting at a table in the café with Anna when Maggie passed by the door.

'We've been waiting for you; what took you so long?'

'I bumped into Muriel; you know what she's like,' she said, grinning broadly.

Katie jumped out of her seat and twirled, bowing low to Anna and Maggie.

'I did it! And I have you to thank, Maggie.'

'You did what exactly?'

'When I met with the tourist board people, they could only talk about Kilcashel, the café and you. They said tourists will love it and people are already asking is Kilcashel House part of the Wicklow tours on offer. It's going to be a winner all year round for us.'

'I never knew my musings from beside the drawing room fireplace had such a reach.'

Katie grabbed Maggie and danced her around the floor.

'It has put us on the map, business is going to be great – they're even talking about filming Kilcashel House for international advertising.'

'But we're run off our feet as it is, with the tour buses that Maggie arranged. How will you do it? Are you going to close to the locals?' Anna asked.

'No way. Rowena can take on more hours and we will all have to work harder,' Katie said.

'It's not going to be every day, is it?' Anna asked uncertainly.

'Sometimes, yes.'

'It's going to be crazy,' Anna grumbled.

'And they will all want to talk to you, Maggie; you're going to be our celebrity.'

Maggie sighed loudly. 'I can't wait.'

'Good,' Katie said, ignoring the lack of enthusiasm from the other women.

Maggie disappeared upstairs and Anna said she had to get home to feed the hens. Katie made her way to the kitchen to start making batches of raspberry, almond and chocolate orange biscuits.

She heard Maggie talking on the phone and she lingered, listening. She knew she was talking to Dan, the one person who was always happy for them and cheered them on no matter what. She liked that he watched out for them; his was a quiet presence they both were beginning to rely on.

TWENTY-TWO

The café was practically full, but Maggie only surfaced one hour after opening time. Anna told her she had to take over at the counter and the till, because Rowena was on a special leave day.

'I might apply for that myself; I need to recharge,' Maggie said.

'Why not, you must be desperately in need,' Anna said, her tone sarcastic.

There were a lot of new visitors in the café with the tourists ordering lunch and takeout boxes for later. When she saw Dan standing at the end of a long queue, Maggie pretended to ask him for help.

'We can't have you queueing. Come inside to the kitchen,' she said.

'If you're sure.'

Dan looked around at all the full tables, before turning to Maggie.

'I guess there's no point asking if you have time to go riding later today?' he asked.

'Don't you think you should be asking Katie, not me?' she laughed as she totted up a bill on the till.

'I would, but unfortunately she has never even sat on a horse and Millie isn't a horse for a beginner.'

'So you are just using me to exercise your beauty on four legs.'

'I wouldn't use those words exactly, but yes. And I think you love the freedom of cantering along Kilcashel beach.'

'I am damned if I'm not riding today. It's near closing time,' she said, slapping down her order book. 'Can you give me an hour? I would love to ride Millie.'

'Come down to the stables, I'll have her tacked up.'

He made to leave, but she called him back and handed him a paper bag.

'It's going spare; a cinnamon bagel, if you want.'

He took it, zig-zagging his way to the front door past the tourists who were lining up on the steps taking photographs.

When they had waved off the last tour bus of the day, Katie said they had better get on with the tidy-up.

'Dan was here earlier and he asked if I wanted to go riding on the beach. Can Anna manage the tidy-up?' Maggie said.

'But why go riding today – you know how busy we are.' Katie sounded cross.

'Katie, all work and no play...'

'Go on, it's better than having to listen to you moan about how tired you are,' Anna said, and Maggie squealed with delight, dashing off to change into her jodhpurs.

She was halfway up the stairs when she began to feel lightheaded.

Gripping the banisters, she tried desperately to stop herself falling, but the pain all over her body was too much and her hold slipped, her body falling back as two customers, who were chatting in the hall shouted out for help.

. . .

Maggie was attempting to stand up, but slumped back on to the steps as Anna and Katie tore down the hall from the kitchen.

'Don't move, we need to get help,' Katie shouted.

Anna took out her mobile and rang for an ambulance as well as the local doctor.

'Did she lose her footing? How could that happen?' Katie asked.

Anna sent the women out to the main gate to wait for the ambulance.

'That silly girl doesn't look after herself. She hasn't been well,' Anna said.

'What do you mean, she hasn't been well?'

'She's been very tired and trying to hide it from you. She wouldn't go to the doctor.'

'And I've been pushing her to help out more with the café.'

'Don't beat yourself up about it. You weren't to know.'

Katie put her head in her hands. She should have noticed, but she had been so focused on keeping the café going that she had excluded everything else. She felt she had let Maggie down.

Anna told the remaining customers they were closing early and she called Dan to bring Katie to the hospital after the ambulance.

Once Dan arrived, Anna volunteered to stay back in Kilcashel and prepare the café for the morning.

'I can take the bagel and biscuit batches out of the ovens and clean up the place.'

Katie hugged her. 'We'll ring as soon as we have news.'

It was several hours later when Katie rang Anna, who had wandered home to the gate lodge.

'She has broken an ankle, but otherwise has escaped injury. They're keeping her in for observation,' Katie said.

'But do they know why it happened? There's nothing wrong with those stairs that would make a person slip,' Anna said.

'I haven't been told anything else. I'm going to let Maggie rest and set off for home now,' Katie said.

Two days later the café was full of well-wishers when Maggie returned home from hospital.

Katie was standing on the top step with Anna when Dan pulled up in his Land Rover.

'There was no need for a welcoming committee,' Maggie said.

Katie ran down the steps and embraced her.

'I'm so sorry I worked you so hard. The others are here to welcome you home,' she said, shepherding Maggie into the café.

When she saw the swimming tribe and the Falveys, Maggie threw her hands in the air.

'I feel I should fall on the stairs more often, if this is the welcome I get,' she said.

There was tea and coffee and glasses of Prosecco, special chocolate biscuits and tiny rectangular sandwiches the Falveys had made.

Anna slithered in beside Maggie at one stage and whispered in her ear. Maggie nodded gratefully and made to get off her seat.

Anna announced that it was time for Maggie to rest up and she was going to help her upstairs.

Muriel Falvey, who had knocked back two glasses of Prosecco, grabbed Maggie in a hug and Rosie kissed her on the cheek as they made their way to the stairs.

Anna followed on the steps, her hands on Maggie's waist. When they got to the landing and Maggie knew she was out of sight, she let herself slump against the wall. Tears flowed down her cheeks.

Anna bundled her in her arms and inched her slowly

towards her bedroom, where she gently placed her on the bed. Maggie made to speak, but Anna hushed her.

'You don't have to say anything to me; I know the news isn't good.'

Maggie turned her head away and began to sob.

'I was going to tell you and Katie and Dan, but there was the party; I couldn't spoil the mood.'

'Nora is no fool, I saw her looking at you.'

'I don't want anyone to know until I absolutely have to tell them,' Maggie said.

'How bad is it?'

'Stage 3 cancer, cervical.'

Anna felt the tears rise up inside her.

'What can I do for you?'

'Please don't tell anyone. I'll tell Katie, but first I have to get my head around it.'

'OK, but make that soon.'

'I will.'

Maggie looked at Anna. 'I'm happy Katie has made such a success of the café, because now she is going to be the owner of Kilcashel.'

'That's hardly the priority.'

'But it's the reality.' Maggie sighed loudly. 'I know we didn't see eye to eye at the start, but I trust you, Anna. Katie is going to need your help. When I do tell her, she's going to take it bad.'

'I know.'

'Promise me you'll be there for her.'

'I'll do more than that, I promise to be there for both of you.'

'Thank you; it means so much. But now I'm tired,' Maggie said, her voice low.

Katie loitered on the landing as Anna tucked Maggie in. She watched from a distance, afraid to go into the bedroom and afraid to ask after Maggie, who looked so frail and small all of a sudden. There were bad times ahead very soon and Katie worried whether they would be able to weather the storm.

When she emerged on to the landing and saw Katie, Anna threw her hands in the air.

'Were you thinking of calling in on Maggie?'

'I just wanted a chat.'

'Let her sleep for now,' Anna said gently.

'What did the doctor say?'

'It's not my place to be chatting on the stairs about Maggie's health. Maybe talk to her later.'

They were interrupted by a squeal of laughter from the café, and Katie rushed downstairs to find out what was going on.

Nora, Leonie and the Falveys were all gathered around, watching something on Rowena's phone.

'The café has gone viral, whatever that means,' said Muriel, who was on the outer fringes of the group. The others pulled back so Rowena could show the Drawing Room Café on TikTok. Maggie was there, sweeping in and pulling exaggerated faces, pretending to be listening to a conversation at the next table while choosing a bagel from the menu. When the bagel arrived, Maggie flashed a winning smile, saying it was better than any bagel in Manhattan, while Rowena held up a sign with the café's name and address.

'It makes us look as if we come here for the gossip,' Muriel said.

'And don't you?' Anna quipped, taking up her position behind the counter.

'We will have to put you two in the next TikTok,' Rowena said, making Muriel scuttle away and Anna look cross.

Katie passed by the group by and continued through the kitchen as far as the deck. Her stomach was sick and her head was thumping. Maggie was a pain in the ass but she loved her like a sister. She needed her to be OK.

TWENTY-THREE

Katie pushed the bagels into the oven and sat at the counter. She was tired. It had been a busy weekend and now, with tour buses arriving every day, she could hardly keep going. She wanted to go at full tilt to make up for the expected fall off in tourists in the winter, but it was taking its toll. She was the one who only got a few hours' sleep every night. Maggie had gone to Dublin last night, supposedly to see a play with Dan, but Katie heard her car crunch across the gravel as she got up to make the first batch of bagels, sometime after 4 a.m.

It was now 6 a.m. and she still had to get the trays of cake and cookies in the oven. Maggie had promised to help, but when Katie knocked on her bedroom door, she hadn't stirred. A text buzzed on Katie's phone. She didn't need to check, she knew it was Nora, saying they would be down at the sea in thirty minutes. Nora sent the same reminder text every morning as if she were afraid she would end up down by the shore on her own.

Katie poured a coffee and texted that she wasn't going to make it, but to call to the house after their dip.

'Is there something wrong?' Nora asked.

'Life. Today is hard going.'

'Sounds like you need the sea more than ever, I'll call by in a few minutes to collect you,' Nora said, adding another quick message. *And I won't take no for an answer.*

Katie poured an espresso coffee and knocked it back. She felt like ringing Dan and shouting at him, but she knew she wouldn't. She sighed; even thinking about Maggie upset her; the hurt of betrayal seeping through her, making her rage in her head. Maggie knew how she felt about Dan, but still she went out and stayed with him until the early hours. Katie slapped down her coffee cup, concentrating instead on taking the trays of cookies from the fridge. She lifted them on to a trolley and wheeled them to the ovens where she set a timer. Damn it, she was going for a swim and Maggie could help out for once.

Nora was right, she needed the waves around her this morning, more than ever. She climbed the stairs to her bedroom, stopping along the way to knock on Maggie's door.

'I'm going for a swim. Everything is on a timer; can you get your ass up out of bed and take the trays out of the oven for me if I'm not back in time?'

She thought she heard a muffled yes, but she wasn't sure. Quickly changing into her wetsuit, she went downstairs to meet the others. Nora was first up the drive, followed by Leonie.

'It's the Monday blues; we'll soon sort it, but where is Maggie?' Nora said as she got out of the car.

'Just about awake; I think it's definitely the Monday-morning wobbles – she was out until all hours.'

'Strange, there was no holding her back in the cooler months and now, when the water has become almost bearable, she misses more often than not.'

Katie shook her head. 'Maybe she's tired of life here. Maggie always was the big-city type.'

'Come on, slow coaches, less of the chat and lift those legs,' Leonie called out as she set off down the path to the sea.

They followed in single file to the shore.

'Damn it, Dan is nearly here,' Leonie said, quickening her pace. Katie made to turn back to the house, but Nora stepped in front of her.

'Never let a man get in the way of something that is good for you. The ocean is big enough for both of you,' she said.

Leonie, who was a few strides ahead, turned around to the others.

'For God's sake, will ye hurry on! I put on a bet with Dan that we would get into the water first this morning.'

'Why on earth would you do that?' Nora asked.

'Can I explain later? Let's run into the sea, please,' Leonie shouted as she pulled off her robe and ran towards the waves.

The others followed, screaming and laughing.

'Is this some childish thing between sister and brother?' Nora asked.

'He bet me twenty quid he would be up before me and down to the shore, so I locked the front door from the outside to slow him down and parked his car out on the road, so he thought it was stolen.'

'You did all that for twenty quid?'

Leonie didn't answer until she'd swum a few lengths and come back to join the others.

'I did all that because I was tipsy and feeling good about myself. What more can I say? And maybe I wanted to put my perfect little brother in his place.'

'Oh, I don't know; he's quite nice to look at early in the morning. Put him in his place more often,' Nora said, and the others laughed, splashing her with water.

Dan swam up to the group. Katie moved away. She was still smarting that he and Maggie had been out together until all hours.

'Going to share the joke with a fellow swimmer?' he asked.

'If we did, we would have to kill you,' Nora said in a serious voice and the other ladies cackled.

'Leonie, race you to the shore,' he said, and his sister launched into the waves with long strokes as they raced the waves to the sand. Leonie kicked out hard, making a wall of water wash over her brother, who put all this strength into his stroke to reach shore first.

Katie floated, watching the sky turn from dark to grey with streaks of pink and gold as the sun crept up, filling the horizon with light which dappled across the water. She let the waves and the current gently bring her to shore. Nora was right, she needed this calm space to let her mind wander and the water wash her worries away. What would Harry think of her now?

There was a time she could have answered that question, but not anymore. Sometimes, and this was ridiculous, she could hardly remember the exact details of his face. It was like one day, she got up and Harry had somehow disappeared into her past. This was not a bad thing, but it was something she had never imagined possible. Sometimes too, Maggie mentioned Harry fondly and Katie was surprised that the pangs of jealousy she had once felt were no more.

Almost at the shore, she turned over on her stomach and swam the rest of the way.

Dan had already left.

'You should have invited him over for coffee,' she said stiffly to Leonie, but she didn't mean it. She wanted to scream at him, that he said he would wait, but he didn't tell her he was going to stay out all night with Maggie.

'I doubt if he would have said yes. He's grumpy and being all dramatic about me moving his car. He reported it stolen and then had to ring back and say he found it outside his house. He said it made him look like an idiot,' Leonie said.

'Walks like a duck and all that,' Nora said as they headed back to Kilcashel House.

. . .

Katie was surprised not to see Maggie up, and angry when she realised nothing had been taken out of the ovens.

All the cakes on four large trays were as hard as rocks.

'Uh oh, is Maggie in trouble?' Nora asked.

'Bloody hell, how much cake have you lost?' Leonie said, peering into the ovens.

'Four trays of twenty small cakes each. I'll just have to make another batch. Can you guys help yourselves to coffee and bagels?'

'We can, but first tell us what we can do to help you?' Nora said.

'That's OK, I can just get on with it.'

'Don't be silly, the cake is one of the main reasons people queue up. Let us help,' Nora said.

'All right, but only if you follow my directions exactly,' Katie said, getting down her big stainless-steel bowls.

'As if we would try to vary anything,' Nora said, pulling a face as if she were aggrieved at the suggestion.

Katie set up four of everything needed.

'Just follow my directions and everything will be fine,' she said, putting all the ingredients beside each bowl.

They were halfway through when there was a loud thud from upstairs.

Katie stopped mixing her batter.

They listened intently, but there was nothing else.

'I should check that out – back in a sec,' Katie said as she calmly walked towards the hall. She was standing wondering if she should go upstairs, when she heard muffled cries coming from Maggie's room.

'Come quicky, there's something wrong with Maggie,' she shouted as she took the stairs two at a time.

The others followed, getting to the landing as Katie opened

the bedroom door.

Maggie was on the floor beside the window, doubled over in pain.

'Quick, call for help,' Katie shouted.

Nora searched for her phone as the others attempted to lift Maggie on to the bed.

Maggie grunted and pulled Katie close.

'No ambulance please, just call my doctor and get everyone out of here,' she hissed.

Nora, who had heard the alarm and fear in Maggie's voice, shepherded the others out.

'We will be downstairs if needed,' she whispered as Katie got on the phone to the doctor.

Katie stood looking out at the wildlife meadow and the horses in the field, Lola sniffing among the roses under the café window as the doctor came on the line.

'I will be passing Kilcashel on the way in to the surgery in about fifteen minutes. I'll swing by, but Maggie is going to have to think about how she needs to handle the next stage,' he said.

'What do you mean "the next stage"?'

'I'm sorry, Katie, you're going to have to discuss this with Maggie. I cannot say anything further.'

When Katie got off the phone, she turned to face her friend.

'It's something bad, isn't it? Why didn't you tell me?'

Maggie sat up in the bed and arranged her silk dressing gown around her.

'Please, not now.'

Katie stamped across the room.

'Please tell me. I know you. This is why you've been missing in the mornings and sneaking off to bed in the afternoon. You're ill and you didn't tell me.'

Maggie threw her eyes to the ceiling.

'Which is worse: that I am sick, or that I didn't tell you?'

'What?'

Maggie rubbed a tear from her eye.

'Let's not argue, Katie; I can't cope with it right now.'

She turned away, pulling the duvet tightly around her.

Katie perched on the edge of the bed.

'It's bad, isn't it?'

Maggie nodded.

'Why didn't you tell me? I've been inwardly seething every morning because you weren't pulling your weight.'

'Don't beat yourself up about it.'

'What is it? Can it be treated?'

'Aggressively, maybe. I don't know. It's cancer.'

Katie stared at her.

'Oh crap, Maggie, no.'

'Totally crap, and yes.'

Nora shouted up the stairs that the doctor had arrived.

Katie leaned down and kissed Maggie lightly on the cheek.

'I'll be right outside,' she whispered as the doctor stepped into the room.

Dan was halfway up the stairs.

'How is she?' he asked gently.

'The doctor is with her now.'

He climbed the rest of the stairs and stood beside Katie at the landing window.

'Don't you have someplace you need to be?' Katie said. Almost immediately she was cross at herself for saying it.

'Why are you annoyed at me?'

She didn't answer. He reached out to take her hand. but she moved to the side.

'Maggie needed somebody to talk to, that's all.'

'Please, don't. It's none of my business.'

'I want to explain.'

'I don't want to hear it. I have enough to be worrying about right now.'

He made to speak again but she raised her hand, requesting him to stop.

'It's not even important anymore, so please leave it.'

'Neither of us wanted to hurt you, Katie.'

She thought she would scream, but instead she babbled on, ignoring his need to unburden himself.

'It looks so lovely out this morning. It's strange, isn't it? Inside, it feels like our world is going to explode, but outside, life goes on as normal. Millie is munching her grass; Lola is sniffing about, and the early-bird customers are making their way to the café. The café, oh crap, what am I going to do?'

Dan put his arm around Katie's shoulder. She stiffened under its weight.

'Nora and the tribe have everything under control. The bagels are on display, the fillings made and the cakes are ready to come out of the oven.'

'Cakes?'

'Nora directed operations. Everything is fine. They had me taste them. They followed your recipes: it's all good.'

'I should go and check,' she said, pulling away from his embrace.

He didn't let her go.

'But the gate?'

'I rang Anna, she pulled back the main gates and she's on her way to help behind the scenes.'

'I still need to check.'

'Maggie needs you here. The rest of us can manage the café today.'

Katie was too upset to argue; she slumped into Dan, and they stood silently watching the world outside the window go on as normal. After another ten minutes, the doctor called out to them.

'Maggie would like to speak to you both,' he said.

Slowly, they entered the bedroom.

She smiled at them both, gesturing for them to come sit on the bed. Katie walked around to the far side and sat on the edge of the bed. Dan sat beside Maggie, his hand resting lightly on hers.

'I certainly would have preferred to see you in my bedroom under different circumstances, Dan,' Maggie said, and he blushed.

'Just kidding, I wanted you both here because you're my dearest friends. Katie, I'm sorry for keeping Dan out until the early hours. He was a good friend and a good listener. When it was his turn to talk, he couldn't stop nattering on about you. He was worried how you would take my news. I should have told you earlier: I have cancer. It's Stage 3 and my chemotherapy starts in two days. Today's collapse hasn't helped, but my legs and balance are very badly affected, I just fell over. It was not as a result of my lovely night out last night. Dan, I thank you for a wonderful adventure.'

'Darling, I am so sorry,' Katie said, tears rising up in her.

'Please don't cry, I need your help, not your tears.'

'Anything,' Dan said quietly.

'Practical help is what I need. I will have a few days in hospital at first, then the treatment will continue with a portable contraption at home. We are hoping it will buy me time – long, short; who knows?'

'I can ferry you back and forth and come in during the day to help,' Dan said.

'It's not going to be pretty. Does Anna knit? Maybe she will knit a hat for me, because these lovely locks are on the way out,' Maggie said, patting her long black hair.

Katie sobbed loudly. Tears engulfed her and she ran to the window. How she wanted to be out in the meadow and as happy as Millie. How simple life was for Millie and Lola. Why couldn't she have the simple life and why couldn't Maggie be well?

Maggie called her name softly.

'Katie, I know it's not fair. Don't you think I have gone through all this already? What I need from you now is practical help; I know I have your love and affection.'

'I'll close the café, so I can concentrate on you.'

Maggie pulled herself up on her pillows.

'You will do no such thing. We have worked too hard to let the café shut down now. We will soldier on and, when the time comes, we will tell the others. Anyway, people drive for miles for Granny's chocolate cake; we can't close.'

'I just don't know what to do,' Katie said, tears strangling her words.

'You soldier on, just like me. Anna knows, maybe she will knit me some hats to hide my bald chemo head. We will tell the swimming tribe, but that's it. Josephine Soap and the allotment sisters can wait until I can't hide it anymore.'

'Don't say that,' Katie said.

'I have to be practical. Damn, you don't understand, do you?'

'I do, and we'll all work together to help you through this. It doesn't mean I have to like it though.'

Maggie smiled at Katie.

'Hate it all you like; but channel the energy into me and the café.'

'OK,' Katie gulped.

Maggie clapped her hands loudly.

'Now, that we have got that sorted, I want to go riding this afternoon.'

'Christ Maggie, you've cancer, you can't,' Katie said.

Maggie guffawed out loud.

'What are you afraid of: that I'll fall off and die?'

'We're just trying to look after you.'

Maggie threw back the duvet and swung her feet onto the floor.

'I know, but while I still can, you have to help me to do the things that give me pleasure. I'm relying on both of you to do that.'

'I've got you,' Dan said.

Katie collapsed into the armchair Maggie had placed by the window.

'Just give me a little time to take it all in.'

'I don't have time, Katie; that's one thing that is too precious to give away. Are you in or out?'

'In,' Katie said, without hesitation.

'Good, it's your job to tell Anna, just pretend you don't know I've told her already. She would prefer it that way and you have to tell Nora and Leonie, but nobody else. People will have their suspicions, but that's OK. Dan, stay with me while I get ready.'

Katie crossed over the room and hugged Maggie, noticing for the first time how thin she had become, and how fragile she felt.

'I'll go down now, before the café gets too busy.'

Maggie held on to Katie a little bit longer than usual.

'Who would have thought we would become such good friends, but I'm glad we have.'

'Me too,' Katie croaked as she rushed from the room.

On the landing, she listened to the drone of conversation from the kitchen and café. She dawdled for a moment, enjoying the happy buzz of Kilcashel House.

She must now step into that world and deliver bad news. Blotting the tears from her face with her sleeve, she set off down the stairs.

When she walked into the kitchen, Nora swung around, a bright smile on her face.

'I don't know how you do this, day in day out, Katie. I—'

Nora suddenly stopped talking.

Leonie reached over and took Katie's hand and led her to a seat at the counter.

'Maggie? Is it bad?' she asked gently.

Katie nodded and the others sat down beside her. Anna stuck her head around the door with an order.

'Why are ye all sitting around? There are customers to be fed,' she said. Then, noticing Katie's distress, she stopped in the middle of the room, looking around the circle of women.

'Come, sit down. I'll see to the customers,' Nora said.

Leonie got to her feet and offered her chair to Anna. 'I'll go give Nora a hand,' she said, heading into the café.

'Katie, what's wrong?'

Katie opened her mouth to speak, but nothing happened. She swallowed and shook her head as if she had to pull herself out of the trance that was enveloping her.

'You know Maggie has cancer.'

Anna got off the seat and began to pace the kitchen floor, going back and forth between the ovens and the sink.

'She doesn't deserve this,' she said.

Nora bustled back into the kitchen and slapped filling on two bagels and set out biscuits on a plate for table three. Leonie followed her in with a tray of cups and plates, sobbing quietly as she loaded them into the dishwasher.

'Do we know what happens next?' Anna asked.

'Yes, she starts chemo this week. She's at Stage 3, but she thinks it has already got worse and…' Katie's voice trailed away.

'The poor lamb, to get that bastard of a disease,' Anna spit out to nobody in particular.

'What can we do to help?' Nora asked.

The kitchen door was pushed open and Dan marched in, carrying Maggie.

'She is only insisting on talking to you all,' he said, tenderly placing Maggie on a seat.

'I'm begging you, please don't tell anyone else. I don't want my illness impacting on the café. That's all we have now and we must keep it going, so when I am no longer here, I'll have left some sort of legacy. The Drawing Room Café is more important than ever,' Maggie said softly.

She turned to Anna.

'I heard once that you're very good at knitting and I thought – if you feel you can – maybe you could knit a hat for me for when my hair falls out. I'm going to be bloody cold when that happens.'

Leonie sighed deeply and Nora stared fiercely at her.

Maggie put her hands in front of Nora to cut her gaze.

'There's something I want from all of you and that is good mood, good humour and, please, no tears, not even when I am gone. The giggles give me strength. And Anna, you can't be going all soft on me either.'

Anna snorted loudly as she tried to hide her tears.

Maggie clapped and turned to Dan.

'I want to ride Millie. I need to do it soon, while I still can, but first I will have a nap, if you don't mind carrying me back upstairs.'

'Your wish is my command,' he said loudly as he scooped Maggie into his arms.

'Well, at least that's sorted,' Anna muttered and Nora, who was within earshot, chuckled.

TWENTY-FOUR

The cold October winds swept in from the Irish Sea making the old windows at the back of Kilcashel House rattle and shake. Katie concentrated on the bakery and café, trying not to think what Maggie was going through at each chemotherapy session. She was able to walk slowly about the house, but the only way she could get downstairs safely was on her bum. It had been over a week since her last bout of chemotherapy, and she was still exhausted. Chemo exhausted and cancer exhausted, Katie thought; a terrible combination that left her slow in mind and body and overwhelmingly sad.

Anna never left her side. It was strange, they had fought like cats when Maggie first came here and now Anna was the one person she could talk to and above all, laugh with.

Katie called on Anna to talk to Maggie about losing her long hair. Maggie was embarrassed and hiding away, especially from Dan. Tasked with sorting it out, Anna marched in to Maggie's bedroom one morning and took out her measuring tape.

'I have a nice bolt of silk; I'll make one of those fancy turbans for you, but first I have to measure your head.'

Maggie pulled away.

'Why do you need to measure my head?'

'We all know the great American might have a big head, so I'm looking for the proof,' Anna said in such a matter-of-fact voice that Maggie burst out laughing.

'Are you sure the chemo didn't shrink it?' she asked.

Anna, who had the tape around Maggie's head, pulled back so she could see her face.

'I'm sure of one thing, not even mean old cancer is going to make Maggie Flint look bad, but she may have just forgotten that important fact,' she said gently.

Tears welled up in Maggie.

'And another thing: tears never helped anyone fight a battle.'

'What would you know about fighting a battle? The only one you've had is the cherry blossom scuffle,' Maggie said.

Anna sat on the edge of the bed.

'You can believe that if you like, or you have my permission to enquire of Katie. If lashing out at me gets you through some of these days, go right ahead, but I reserve the right to throw it right back at you.'

Maggie threw her hands in the air.

'Anna, I don't mean to lash out, but I'm bored sitting here and hearing the bustling in the café and bakery downstairs.'

'So, let's get you downstairs.'

'But I look shit.'

'You have cancer, it does that.'

'But I haven't told anyone.'

Anna snorted out loud.

'For God's sake, Maggie, how many months have you been here now? Sure, the whole place knows about the cancer and...'

'And how long I have left?'

Anna frowned.

'There's not a family around here that has not dealt with

some form of cancer. There's nothing but sympathy out there, for you.'

'I don't want sympathy.'

'Pity, because in these parts people are pretty good, when you let them.'

She opened up her handbag and whipped out a silk fabric in a myriad of blue and purple colours.

Maggie reached out, letting the shimmering silk slip through her fingers.

'Beautiful. Where did you get this, it feels so soft?'

'All the way from China. This is just a sample to show you. I had Mary Downes bring back a bolt from Beijing last week. She travelled to China with her daughter, who was adopting a child.'

'The things you get people to do for you,' Maggie said, shaking out the silk so that it caught the sunshine which was peeping in the window.

'You can't put that on your head until I hem the edges,' Anna said as she snatched the silk away and took out her sewing box.

'Don't rush, I can go down tomorrow. I have you to entertain me now.'

Anna, who had put on glasses for the close work, looked out over the top rim.

'Go and get dressed like a good girl. Wear your nice blue dress and cardigan; it will go lovely with the silk. It will only take a few minutes for me to hem the edges.'

'There's no point arguing with you is there?'

'None at all. You know I'm a bossy cow.'

Maggie, who was halfway out of the bed, stopped.

'How did you know I called you that?'

Anna laughed. 'How many months did you say you were here?'

Maggie got out of bed and started to rummage in the wardrobe.

'I need the iron, so I'll finish this downstairs; I'll be back in ten minutes or so,' Anna said as she went down the stairs and called Katie.

'I've persuaded her to come down. We need extra pillows on her armchair; she has a lot of pain.'

'She can sit inside the window, where she can see the comings and goings.'

'I have opened the top of one of the windows so she can hear the birds sing, though the starlings are making quite a racket at the moment; there must be a hawk nearby,' Nora said as she plumped up the pillows on the velvet armchair.

Leonie walked in with a bright blue mohair rug in her arms.

'To keep Maggie's knees warm,' she said.

Katie shook her head.

'If Maggie only knew how much everybody around here loves her.'

'She does, but she might need a bit of reminding,' Anna said as she headed off to the kitchen to get the sewing done.

The café was busy when Dan arrived to carry Maggie downstairs. He pulled Katie down the hall where they couldn't be seen.

'I feel I have lost you, just as we were getting to know each other.'

'Cancer is bigger than all of us. I can only give time to Maggie right now.'

He kicked out at the skirting board. 'It's not that, Katie. I want to know if you're happy for me to spend time with Maggie.'

Katie smiled. 'I want you to do anything that will make Maggie happy.'

'And us?' he asked.

'There will be plenty of time after...' Katie couldn't finish the sentence.

He reached over and brushed the tears from her cheeks.

'I'm going to carry her downstairs to the café,' he said.

'I'm not sure she will let you,' Katie said.

'I don't think she will have much choice. She hardly wants to bop down on her arse in front of onlookers,' Anna huffed as she emerged from the kitchen.

When they knocked on the bedroom door, Maggie was up and dressed.

She was wearing an LK Bennett navy-blue wrap dress with sleeves to just above the wrist. The colour accentuated her pallor, but also her fine features.

When she saw Dan, she shrank behind Anna.

'What is he doing here?' she asked.

Anna gestured to Dan to stay on the landing and gently pushed the bedroom door shut. She placed the silk in Maggie's hands.

'Go over to the mirror, there should be enough in it to tie a bow on top, or at the side.'

'At the side, I think,' Maggie said.

'Fat chance of that. You have never looked so beautiful,' Anna said.

'Wow, I must be dying, to wrestle a compliment out of you,' Maggie laughed.

'Something like that, but I still don't trust you with my cherry blossoms.'

Maggie reached over and hugged Anna.

'Come on, a selfie.'

Anna gently pulled away.

'Don't be silly, your audience awaits you downstairs.'

Maggie's face changed.

'I have the dress, the great turban and a bit of lipstick to try and brighten up my face, but I still have to use that goddam awful walking stick.'

She reached for the heavy walking stick; Katie had found in the attic.

'Katie said she found it upstairs. Do you know it? It's gross.'

Anna's face changed.

'It was my grandfather's and he used to push the chickens out of the way with it and, many the horse got a belt of it, when they wouldn't move.'

'I knew it; it's a farmer's stick. I could never be called a farmer, and the dress and turban, well they highlight how—'

She stopped when Anna opened the door. 'What have I said now?'

Anna didn't answer, but disappeared, popping back after a few moments.

'My friend just back from China did me another favour,' she said.

From behind her back, Anna pulled a long, elegant cloisonne walking stick in colours of blue, purple, pink and white.

Maggie reached for it.

'How did you know?'

'Don't I know you and the importance of a bit of style? It certainly suits the outfit.'

Maggie leaned on the stick, pushing her hip to one side.

'Cancer style,' she said, and they both laughed.

'You're a good friend, Anna.'

'And you're a terrible patient. Now, let Dan bring you downstairs,' Anna said, inviting him in.

He stood back and looked Maggie up and down.

'You look beautiful today,' he said quietly, picking her up in his arms and cradling her tenderly as he walked down the stairs.

At the bottom, he set her down gently, so she could walk on her own into the café.

Katie smiled a bright smile from behind the counter and

clapped as Maggie walked in. One after another, Nora, Leonie and Rowena joined in and the customers stood up to applaud, making a little welcome corridor as far as the velvet chair.

Maggie, shuffled along, nodding and smiling. When she sank into the pillows, she looked exhausted.

'Now we're going to let Maggie have a bit of quiet time with a nice cup of coffee,' Anna said loudly as the others pretended to get back to what they were doing.

Dan sat opposite her.

'I was thinking I could bring Millie around later and, if you can make it to the top steps, you could meet her.'

'I would like that.'

Gently, he rubbed her hand.

'I'm so glad you have made it downstairs and you can accept the friendship being offered by all these people.'

She didn't say anything at first but pulled her hand away.

'*These people* as you call them are very nice, but I feel a bit of a spectacle, to be honest.'

'I don't think anyone intends that.'

A little girl shoved a small book in her hand.

Maggie smiled and told her to come closer.

'My mum says you're famous. Can I have your autograph, please?'

'Famous around here, I guess,' Maggie said as she signed the notebook and added two love hearts.

The girl ran way excited, and her mother raised her china teacup in Maggie's direction.

'See, you're a celebrity already,' Dan said.

'Yes, I definitely need Anna to bring me down to earth' she muttered, putting her head back and closing her eyes so that Dan and everybody else would leave her be.

After a while she opened her eyes when she smelled her Coco Chanel perfume.

'You're talking about me,' Anna said as she pulled a chair up beside Maggie.

'I didn't know you wore Chanel,' Maggie said.

'Isn't it lovely? I stole a spray from your dressing table. Did it every day I tidied up in there too, when I didn't like you,' Anna said.

'What style! But stealing from a dying woman?'

'Leave it to me in your will.'

'Now, that's a bit low.'

'I've arranged a wheelchair; I thought you might like to be wheeled out to the deck, away from the inquisitive eyes in the café.'

'For that, you can have the whole bottle.'

Nora brought in the wheelchair and, between them, they managed to get her out on the deck.

Maggie sat back, listening to the sea.

'To think I hated the deck when I came here, and now...' she said, tears swelling up inside her.

Katie came with a smoothie and bagel and placed them on a table beside her.

'I would prefer a Prosecco.'

'Maybe, after you've had something proper to eat.'

'Why, what are you going to tell me? That the Prosecco is going to kill me?'

'Remember the last time you guzzled a glass – you threw up almost immediately.'

Maggie waved Katie away. 'Please, I want to enjoy the cool breeze, the sound of the sea and feel the tingle of the bubbles at the back of my throat. These days are no good to me if I can't do something I enjoy.'

Katie walked into the kitchen and took a bottle of Prosecco from the fridge.

Carefully, she opened it and poured two glasses.

'I don't mean to be a killjoy; it's just I hate to see you suffer.'

'Suffer is my middle name; I choose to ignore it. To Kilcashel,' Maggie said, holding up her glass.

They clinked and laughed.

Maggie let the Prosecco fizz through her mouth and, for a moment, she felt happy.

'Remember that first drink after the reading of the will. Weren't we different then?'

'I suppose we were. Have you told people back in Manhattan?'

'I'm not sure I have that many people to tell. When I'm gone, maybe you can send an announcement to a newspaper or post something online.'

'Isn't there anyone you want to talk to?'

'Before I kick the bucket?'

'Don't talk like that.'

'I need Anna here; she doesn't mind talking death.'

Dan came out on the deck and Katie got up and gave him her seat beside Maggie.

'How come you're around so much; shouldn't you be giving lectures?' Maggie asked.

'I've taken some leave and I'm doing some mentoring from home, so I have a little more time on my hands.'

'Not because of me, I hope.'

'If it means I can spend more time with you, then that works fine,' he said, filling the glass from the Prosecco bottle.

'Isn't he just the nicest man you have ever met?' Maggie said to Katie, who raised her glass and smiled.

Maggie coughed and tried to hide it, but her whole body began to convulse. Katie and Dan both ran to her, but she pushed them away as she threw up over her blue dress. Tears streaming down her face, she attempted to pull herself from the chair, but collapsed into Dan's arms. He carried her swiftly through the house and up the stairs to settle her on the bed.

'I will look after her from here,' Katie said as Anna suddenly appeared to help.

Twenty minutes later, Katie trudged downstairs to find Dan waiting for her.

'How is she?'

'Frail, embarrassed and very sick.'

'Can I see her?'

'She's falling asleep. Best let Anna stay with her for now.'

'It happened so quickly.'

'It's my fault; I should have known, but I hate to deprive her of the little pleasures,' Katie said, wiping away the tears, which she had only just realised were flowing down her cheeks.

'She wants to meet Millie tomorrow. She said she might be able to sit on her, but I don't know.'

'All we can do is play it by ear. She might be strong enough, she might not. The doctor said there will be good days and very bad days. Today was good, until it turned bad.'

Dan didn't answer. She knew he was too upset to talk and she let him go. She watched him cross the deck and make his way to the sea, his shoulders slumped.

She wanted to run after him and ask could they walk together for just a few moments; to forget about their troubles for a short time, but she knew she couldn't, not now. And who knew what would come afterwards.

She took down her stainless-steel bowls and began to make cake for the next day. Twenty minutes later, Anna peeped into the kitchen.

'I think she's asleep for the next few hours. She took her medicine, the poor lamb. You should try and take it easy while you can. I'm off home.'

Katie heard her go out the front door, pulling it shut behind her. The house was too quiet, she couldn't bear it. Grabbing her coat from the hook, she went out the back door and followed the sea path. When she saw Dan on the shore she thought of going another way, but she wanted to talk to him. She waved and he walked towards her. She sat on flat rock watching him stride across the sandy beach and she wanted more than anything to run to him and feel safe in his strong hold.

'Can we clear the air?' he asked.

'It's OK, Dan; I know now you were helping Maggie. I may have overreacted.'

She moved over on the rock for him to sit beside her.

'You know how much I like you, Katie.'

'I know, and I like you too, Dan.'

'But?'

'It's not the right time for us, not now.'

'With Maggie the way she is?'

'She really likes having you around her. That should be your priority now.'

'I don't know what we will do when she is gone.'

Katie felt the tears welling up inside her. Dan moved towards her but she shrugged him away.

'We owe it to Maggie to make this as uncomplicated as possible,' she said.

'Can we come back to all this after?'

Katie gulped back the tears.

'I can't go there, not yet. Let's do what we have to do now and let the future take care of itself.'

She turned away from Dan, who loitered for a few moments before he said he had to get home.

TWENTY-FIVE

The days merged and they got into a routine of sorts. Katie got up extra early to do the baking, then Anna, Nora and Rowena handled the opening of the café while Katie went upstairs to help Maggie get ready for the day.

'Can we walk across the field and look at the sea? Give me my cashmere sweater and hat, I think I can do it,' Maggie said one morning.

'But are you sure? I can call Dan and he could carry you down to the sea.'

Maggie shook her head.

'The doctor said I would have good days. This is one, I can feel it.'

'But where will we go?'

Maggie sighed loudly.

'Katie, what does it matter? Please stop wrapping me in cotton wool; I'm dying, for fuck's sake.'

'I suppose when you put it like that... And it is a lovely, mild morning.'

'That's the spirit. You could do with a break too.'

Maggie insisted on putting on make-up, spraying her

Chanel perfume high and wide and walking down the stairs without any help.

'At least let me go ahead of you.'

'No. If I fall, I'll knock you and that's you injured. No way.'

When Maggie arrived in the hall, Rowena ran and got Anna.

'What are you doing? Do you want to spend some time in the café?'

'No, Katie and I are going out to get some beautiful fresh air.'

'Out? Out where?'

Maggie walked past Anna to the kitchen.

'Nora, we need a small picnic basket, enough for Katie to carry on her own, and maybe two cushions?'

Nora began to pack some of their favourite bagels into boxes and cut two slabs of chocolate cake.

'Biscuits too, please.'

Let me come with you,' Anna said.

Katie shook her head.

'We need to do this, just the two of us. I'll ring if we need help.'

Katie took the basket and, linking her arm with Maggie's, set off slowly down the garden path.

Maggie, she noticed, walked as straight as she could while the others were watching, only allowing herself to slump after they had passed the camellia bank and they were out of sight of the group observing from the back door.

'How about we rest at the gazebo?' Katie asked.

'Yes, good idea.'

They sat down and Katie produced a bottle of water. Maggie drank gratefully from it.

'Isn't it strange what I miss most now is the open fields, Millie, and the feel of the sea breeze on my cheeks? Who would have thought that the woman who wore high heels walking her dog in Central Park could change so much?'

'We've both changed.'

Maggie giggled. 'I think it's a little more marked in me. I don't even want to return to Manhattan before I die. My fondest memory from there is my grandmother's chocolate cake, and you have recreated that for me. Can we call it Maggie's chocolate cake? When I'm gone, people will bite into it and have sweet memories of me,' she laughed, but soon she was doubled over coughing.

She stood up, holding on to the gazebo to steady herself.

'We had better move along. This burst of energy won't last forever,' she said, and Katie scrabbled to join her on the path, which ran along at the top of the field, edged by the sea.

Maggie tramped out to the middle of the field and twirled. When she felt dizzy, she let herself drop to the ground. Calling Katie to join her, she lay looking at the clouds collide in the sky.

Katie gingerly checked the grass for horse poo, then lay down alongside her.

'Let's watch the birds fly by,' Maggie whispered, inching closer to Katie.

'Last week out near the allotment, where Muriel set up a chair for me, I saw the bees still tripping between the flowers. Sometimes they were so heavy with pollen, they had to rest up before continuing with their task. The horses in the paddock looked like something from Mars, still wearing their fly rugs and masks. I could have cried, to think this time next year, I won't be here.'

She squeezed Katie's hand tight.

Above them a kestrel screeched, and they scanned the sky looking for him, eventually spotting him swooping down on his prey near the allotments.

'I never realised how much this place had got under my skin,' Maggie said. 'You will have to organise one last dip with the ladies for me. Tomorrow – or maybe later today would be better, because I don't know how long I have. I literally could die tonight – what a strange thought.'

'Please stop talking like this.'

Maggie got up on her elbow and looked at Katie.

'Why? It's an unescapable fact. I just want to relive the moments when I was happiest, like the feeling of freedom of running into the waves and trying to beat down the cold, feeling my blood warm up, munching bagels and chatting in the kitchen of Kilcashel House. Sometimes stepping in as a waitress when Anna was overrun in the café. Sunsets on the deck, sipping a favourite tipple... They were such good times, Katie.'

She lay down again and gazed at the sky.

'We should have paid someone to write my name across the clouds; that would be such fun.'

'I don't think Anna would approve,' Katie said, and Maggie doubled over, laughing.

'Gosh, that woman has infuriated me, and now I love her so much, and her silly outrage.'

'She has been good to you since...'

'After you, she's my best friend – along with Dan and Millie, of course. I was so lonely at the start. That's where Millie came in. I loved trekking alongside the wildlife meadow and the river and, when it was very hot, throwing off the saddle and wading bareback into the sea with Millie, meeting the waves and moving together through the water. Those were the good days of summer, when the living was easy.'

'And what about Dan?'

'What a lovely man; a great listener. The night he brought me to Dublin, he drove me up into the mountains so I could see the expanse of Dublin, the city lights twinkling below us,' Maggie laughed. 'When he wasn't listening to me, he spent most of the time talking about you.'

'Dan is a good friend.'

Katie was lost in following the clouds.

'If I were a cloud, I would be that long interesting one over there,' Maggie said, poking Katie in the side with her elbow.

When Katie sighed in exasperation, Maggie turned her head to face her.

'You will need Dan when I'm gone. You have my blessing; I want you to know that.'

Katie didn't know how to respond. Jumping up, she said they should have their picnic by the river.

Bending over, she took Maggie's weight as she pulled her to her feet.

'Do you think you can make the walk across this field to the river?'

'I can try.'

They trudged slowly on, Maggie leaning on Katie for support. Every few paces, Maggie had to stop to take a breath.

'Should I ring Dan to come and help?' Katie asked.

'No. When we've finished our picnic, you can call him. He will have to carry me all the way home. We don't need his help until then,' she said, pushing herself forward.

It took them fifteen minutes to hobble across the field, a journey which usually took Katie three minutes.

When they got as far as the river seat, Maggie sank down, grateful that she did not have to walk any more. Katie handed her the bottle of water.

Maggie pushed it away.

'You had better have Prosecco in there, or you're walking to Kilcashel town to buy some.'

Katie pulled out the bottle and opened it, the pop of the cork echoing across the water.

She poured the bubbly into plastic champagne glasses.

Maggie held hers up high.

'To Kilcashel House, our home, and a place where I am glad to be as I reach my last days.'

When Katie didn't move, Maggie frowned.

'That's the toast, Katie. Please clink.'

'I don't want you to go anywhere, Maggie.'

'Oh, come on, you will have Kilcashel and Anna and the rest of the gang.'

Katie dipped her head to hide her tears.

'I know you're crying, Katie, but I'm good with this. I'm not going to waste any precious moments that are left to me. I get so bloody annoyed when I get tired; when I can't stay awake. Shit, I'm going to spend forever sleeping.'

Katie clinked Maggie's glass.

'To your great spirit.'

'Don't talk crap, Katie.'

'I mean it; I wouldn't have picked you to be the person who was so brave in the face of adversity.'

'I will take that as a compliment, I think,' Maggie said, downing the bubbly, which agitated her throat, making her cough.

When she finished, she wiped her mouth with her sleeve.

'The indignity of this goddammed disease. That's what hurts the most.'

They sat quietly for a few moments until Maggie spoke again.

'I am not brave; I am just dealing with a situation here. It started with a feeling that something wasn't quite right. The feeling turned into a general air of disquiet that I could not shake off; there was a tiredness that pervaded, even after a night's sleep, and pain, which after a few weeks, I could no longer explain away. Remember, you thought I was avoiding work. I think I thought the same thing myself for a while.'

Katie made to speak, but Maggie put her hand up to stop her.

'I have a few things to say, sister, and I'm going to say them,' she insisted as Katie sat up and made a face.

'Can we not talk about cancer, please?' Katie said as she poured another glass of Prosecco. Maggie downed her glass in one go.

'You have to listen. It will help for after.'

Katie wiped away a tear as Maggie continued: 'When cancer invades the body, it is persistent, but it still took a while for me to accept that this cancer was my new life. Thanks to you and Kilcashel, I was a woman who had finally found contentment; a life I had built with the help of you all at the big house. And now cancer was invading, chipping away and stealing that contentment.'

Maggie reached across and swept a tear from Katie's right cheek.

'You have to know that I decided cancer may be trying to pull me down, but I would put up a fight – a battle I knew I had no chance of winning. That's why I wear the bright clothes, sit in the café and try to chat every day.'

Katie giggled. 'I thought you loved the attention.'

Maggie guffawed out loud. 'It was lovely, seeing Anna's reaction.'

They both laughed and Maggie hugged Katie tight.

'Katie, I'm fighting my way. I'm living with cancer my way; I want to do it, while I still can.'

Katie burst into tears and gripped Maggie so tight it hurt.

'Whoa girl, strong mind but fragile body here. I'm sorry I kept you out of the loop for so long, Katie. I was trying to deal with it by myself and then it dawned on me, cancer doesn't care. Plans, when they are confronted by cancer, crumble into insignificance.'

Katie took a napkin and dabbed her eyes, then handed it to Maggie, who wiped the perspiration from her brow.

'I kept my diagnosis a secret for as long as I could. A woman with a diagnosis is somehow treated differently and, while I knew I would be wrapped in a cloak of support and kindness, I didn't want things to change. You, Katie, once I confided in you, became my crutch to lean on.'

Katie pulled Maggie towards her.

'Lean on me; I can take the weight,' she said. Maggie slumped into her friend.

'I know it's not a battle I can carry on my own. From Stage 3 to terminal Stage 4 happened so quickly, just as the flowers in the garden become jaded by the summer months and let themselves fade away as the autumnal breezes roll in over the Irish Sea.'

'Please stop; you don't need to talk like this,' Katie said.

Maggie shook herself free.

'I want you to understand Stage 5 is me in the wicker basket. You, Katie, and my female tribe will carry me to the hearse that will take me to the crematorium. I need to know you will do it,' Maggie whispered. Katie nodded.

'I need to talk to you about it. I have told Dan some things too, so when I'm gone you two need to knock your heads together. Lean on each other and be there for each other.'

Maggie got up and kicked off a shoe and eased off her sock, dipping her toes in the water.

'Ooh, the pain of this cold is so satisfying; the pain of cancer, so debilitating.'

Katie got up and did the same, jumping back from the freezing cold punch.

'You're such a baby, Katie,' Maggie laughed.

They sat back on the bench. Maggie sipped a little more of her drink and tried a bit of the chocolate cake.

'I am grateful, though, for the time spent at Kilcashel House; for awakening my senses, for putting life into perspective, and for making me appreciate this rural life.

'If I have learned anything from this whole experience, it is to grab each new opportunity with both hands and give it everything. Life is short; don't run away from love. Eat the chocolate;

drink strong coffee and walk in those high shoes – well, maybe not on a farm. I ruined such lovely shoes.'

Katie reached over and put her arms around Maggie.

'I sound like a preacher, don't I?'

Katie nodded.

Maggie stared into Katie's eyes. 'Promise me you will enjoy every Kilcashel sunset and be thankful while you can.'

'I'll do my best.'

'And you are not to feel sorry for me. I'm lucky to be here at Kilcashel House with you, and surrounded by friends.'

They held each other, quietly sobbing until Maggie pulled away.

Reaching into her pocket, she took out the velvet ring box.

'If Harry did know he had cancer, he took a very lonely road dealing with it on his own. I have the whole of Kilcashel House behind me and it's still tough. Maybe it's time to forgive him,' she said.

'I don't have the energy to hate him anymore,' Katie said.

Maggie placed the box in Katie's hands.

'You're ready to take this back; hopefully, you can concentrate on the happy times together.'

Katie smiled and opened the box clasp, the sun sparkling on the diamond ring.

'I think so,' she said.

Maggie clapped her hands.

'That's enough talking for a lifetime. Ring Dan, tell him to bring Millie; it will be the best way to get me home,' she said cheerfully.

Maggie was awake most of the night. Katie sat by her bed and wouldn't leave.

'There will be long enough to sleep. Text Nora and tell her we'll join her and Leonie for the dawn swim.'

'Rowena comes along now too.'

'Great, a cancer lady who has to compete with a teenager,' Maggie said, and they both giggled.

'Are you really going to do it?'

'Yes, when Dan brought me back on Millie, he said he could join us this morning.'

When she fell asleep, Katie was loath to wake Maggie, but she knew when she heard Nora's car come up the avenue, she should.

She ran downstairs to let Nora and Rowena in.

'She's still asleep, but I'll wake her up,' she said, running back upstairs.

Maggie was stirring.

'You don't have to go to the sea; sleep on, if that is what you would prefer,' Katie said.

Maggie sat up, indignant. 'And miss my opportunity to feel the calm of the sea all around me? No way, I can do it.'

Katie helped Maggie get into her wetsuit and wrap up warmly for the walk to the sea.

When she heard Dan in the kitchen, she asked Katie to spray some perfume on her neck and turban.

'Dan said he would carry me down; I want his last memories of me to be good ones.'

When they got downstairs, Anna was in the kitchen preparing flasks of tea and coffee.

'That poor thing will need a hot drink the minute she comes out of the water, and I brought up a nice dryrobe my cousin sent me from the UK. I sure as hell will never use it.'

She held it up for Maggie to slip on.

Maggie planted a kiss on Anna's cheek.

'You really are a softie at heart, aren't you?' she said.

Nora asked Anna would she come down to the sea, but Anna declined, saying somebody had to keep the café running.

They set off, a small party filing along the garden path, led by Dan, carrying Maggie. The sun was rising, throwing streaks of gold across the sky, intermingled with pink.

They could just about see where they were stepping, the sound of the sea loud in their ears.

Dan took a break when they got to the shore, gently placing Maggie on a rock.

'You'll have to make sure they continue to do this when I'm gone,' she said.

He didn't answer.

'I'm being selfish, wanting to encroach on what, for them, is a necessary meditation on the day, but I need the healing power of the sea to prepare my brain for what's ahead.'

'Everybody understands. We're all so glad you are with us today.'

'I want to run into the sea.'

'Do you think you can manage it?'

'I don't know, but I want to do it.'

'I could carry you.'

Maggie shook her head. 'You'll have to carry wet me back to Kilcashel House; that's enough.'

'Are you ready to give it a go?' he asked.

She beamed with delight as he picked her up again, and carried her to where the others were getting ready to go into the sea.

Nora took a small foldaway chair that Anna had insisted she bring for Maggie and set it up.

'Sit here and we'll test the waters and see how cold it is,' she said.

'As if it will be different from any other time. I appreciate your kindness, but I want to do this; I need to do it.'

Dan undressed and got into the sea. They watched as he plunged into the waves and swam a few strokes.

Katie and Nora helped Maggie get ready.

It was a mild morning, but still she shivered when they took off the dryrobe.

'Can we run together, like we did that first time?' she asked.

'We can, but do you think you are up to it?' Nora said.

Maggie caught both their hands.

'Grab me under the arms so I don't fall. I need to do this,' she said.

Taking a deep breath, Nora said they would run on the count of three.

Leonie called out one, two, three and they supported Maggie, who managed a few strides before her legs went from under her. They carried her like you would a child, swinging her little weight between them as they sprinted into the waves.

When the first wave hit her, Maggie closed her eyes, letting the water push over her head; the noise of the surf surrounding her, buffeting her as she fell into its depth. She began to swim. Here in the Irish Sea, she wasn't a woman with cancer, but a sea swimmer.

After a few waves had crashed around her, she felt Dan lift her out of the water.

'Time for the mermaid to come ashore,' he whispered in her ear as he carried her out of the water.

Nora had a dryrobe ready and they wrapped Maggie in it.

Katie handed her a tea laced with whiskey.

Maggie held up her cup.

'To my tribe, thank you,' she said.

She could only manage a few sips before she started to cough again. Dan swept her up in his arms and reached Kilcashel House in just a few strides.

Anna fussed and got Maggie into a bath, all the time complaining she could have caught her death.

When she was safely tucked in bed, Maggie took her hand.

'I'm fine Anna; you can stop worrying now. Tomorrow, Dan is going to take me to the mountains,' she murmured, immediately falling into a deep sleep.

'Well, I never. That's pure madness,' Anna muttered as she tidied up the room, all the time keeping a watchful eye on the silly, brash American she had grown to love.

TWENTY-SIX

Katie pulled on her coat, because the harsh wind squalling about was making her shiver as they stood on the front steps watching Dan settle Maggie into the front seat of his Land Rover.

Anna was fussing, complaining that nobody went near the mountains in November.

'Stop them, Katie, they might listen to you. This is madness,' she said.

'Let Maggie do what she wants, she deserves it,' Katie said quietly.

Anna clicked her tongue, but gestured to Dan to wait. She ran into the kitchen and pulled a light blue cashmere shawl from her basket.

'I found it the other day; Bert bought it for me one Christmas and there's nothing like it to keep you warm.'

Maggie laughed.

'I'm toasty already, Anna, there's no need to fuss so much.'

Anna spread the shawl over Maggie's shoulders.

'It brings out the colour of your eyes and matches the blue on your headscarf.'

'You are such a liar, Anna, but I love you.'

Dan got into the Land Rover beside Maggie and placed a mohair rug on her knees.

'You do know, I might just pass out with the heat,' she laughed.

'It's cold up in the mountains at this time of year, you'll need every bit of it. And drink the hot chocolate, that bubbly will only freeze your insides,' Anna said as she waved them off.

Katie had stayed quiet, concentrating on packing the picnic basket and only came out to wave goodbye as the jeep trundled down the avenue. She snorted back tears.

'It won't be long now, Anna; it could be counted in hours.'

'So, we make the most of it. Let's concentrate on having a welcome home for her, when she returns. The bedroom needs a right going over and I thought a nice fire in the café with the armchairs all around, so we can sit and chat.'

Katie wasn't listening; she didn't want to make the best of it. Without saying a word to Anna, she hurried down the steps and the avenue. She needed time on her own. She liked to walk through the allotment fields to the horses. There was something about the allotments; the feeling that while everything looked ragged and dead now, renewal and new life was not far away. It gave her sustenance and a break from the drudgery of this cancer, which was eating her friend from the inside out. There was nobody on the allotments today; the wind was too cold, and the ground hardened by frost. Plants that had withstood the winter frost were blackened, others who had been cut down were cowering low, waiting for the spring sunshine to remind them to sprout again.

A bank of sunflowers which had not been pulled out or the seeds harvested, stood at an angle after doing their best to withstand the winds which swept in from the Irish Sea. But Katie knew that soon the plants would begin to thrive again, and the allotments would get ready for their summer display of colour.

She picked her way past the mini gardens, stopping for a moment to look at a lone rosebud on a bare rose bush; the petals never unfurled, the bud blackened from the cold and frost.

Scrabbling in her pocket, she felt for the carrot she always had there these days for Millie, and snapped it in two. When Millie saw her approach, she ambled over, nuzzling Katie's hands and pushing against her pocket.

Katie liked this time with the horse, when she could forget about everything else. Maggie had asked her to visit Millie every day, in the hope she could build a bond with the horse. Katie wasn't sure at first, but now she looked forward to this quiet time, when all that was required of her was to meet Millie's demands. Dan had offered to teach her how to ride, but there would be plenty of time for that.

She didn't want to think about life after Maggie, so she took out half the carrot and watched Millie crunch it, pushing at her hands for the other half as soon as she was done.

She knew Maggie wanted this bond to develop as much for Katie as for Millie. At first Katie had merely indulged her sick friend, but as the days went by, she had begun to look forward to this simple bonding over carrots and apples.

Katie found peace with Millie, rubbing her mane, fixing the collar of her rug where she had pushed it back and often even pulling a few twigs from her tail.

Holding out the last piece of carrot, she leaned in close to Millie and hugged her; the horse nuzzling her neck, taking some of the burden of her pain. When she turned away from Millie, she was ready for what the next hours and days would bring. It was time to get the house ready for the next phase of Maggie's life and death. Katie stopped, pain rising through her. She wanted to scream out loud, that it wasn't fair; that Maggie should be spared; they had only just become the best of friends, sisters even. Kicking a few loose stones out of the way, she welcomed the sharp pain in her toe. She would take on anything for her sister; she would even have sold this place that had brought them together, if she thought it could save Maggie. She looked at her watch. Maggie expected to be gone all day, but Dan did not expect her to last more than an hour on the mountain, which meant there was little time to get a lot done. She rushed back to the house, where Anna had already stripped Maggie's bed and was making it up with the most expensive silk sheets.

'Where did you get those? Maggie will love them!'

'I have my sources. A friend of mine works in a big department store in Dublin and I gave her the job of finding me the best set.'

'They must have cost a fortune, Anna.'

'Nothing is too expensive for our Maggie, not now anyway. And she got me the staff discount.'

Katie took a pillowcase and put on the silk cover.

'Remember how you used to complain about her being too fancy.'

'She was always that, but back then she was a handful. I'm glad I got to see the other side of her.'

'Funny the way life turns out. She didn't want to come Kilcashel, and yet it changed her so much for the good. For the bad too, unfortunately.'

'She was getting that cancer wherever she was. At least here she is surrounded by people who love her.'

They placed the top sheet and duvet on the bed and plumped up the pillows. Anna rearranged the dressing table and sprayed polish over the wood panels in the room. Katie opened up the windows, letting the cold air freshen out the corners.

'I'm off to organise the café. Do you think we should close for the day?' Katie said.

'No, Maggie wouldn't like that, but she would love to be in

her velvet chair in front of the fire where everyone knows her,' Anna said.

'Dan promised he would bring Millie up to visit her too.'

Anna looked at Katie. 'Did the doctor say how long?'

'He said once she gets worse, and that could be at any time, it might be long, a matter of days, or short, just a few hours.'

'So, this could be her last time downstairs?'

Katie nodded, her face pale and strained.

Anna walked across the room and grabbed Katie by the shoulders.

'Stay strong, darling, you have to. We all have to be strong for Maggie. There will be plenty of time for tears afterwards.'

Pulling her hand across her face to take away the tears, Katie made her way downstairs. It was time to bake Maggie's cake, even if she would only be able to manage a mouthful.

Dan drove along the narrow country roads leading into the Wicklow mountains. Maggie, cocooned in layers of cashmere and mohair, was comfortable, taking in the mountains covered in heather not yet flowering, and interspersed with faded, brown ferns. It was as if up here, time was on hold until the warmth of spring brought everything back to life.

'You're taking me into the clouds,' she whispered as they moved up the winding road into the mountains, where the clouds were pressing down in places almost onto the road.

'This is where I want to be, on top of the world; do you want to know why?'

Dan pulled into a small parking space, where they could sit and look out over the mountains.

'I loved to go up high on the Empire State Building on a cloudy day. It was like going up into the sky. I never went for the view, but to feel the clouds around me, and I usually had the place to myself too.'

'I wonder why,' Dan laughed.

'You can laugh, but in a big city to have a space to yourself is a rare gift, and to be so close to nature, just as rare. Call me silly, but I loved it.'

She rolled down the window and put her hand out.

'I can't touch the clouds but they are so close.'

'There are not great views here today; in summer it's spectacular.'

'I'll have to take your word on that.'

'Shit, that was insensitive; I'm sorry.'

'Don't be silly; I love this wild and rugged terrain. The air is like nectar and the silence; it was something I was never used to. I always rushed to fill in the gaps as you probably have guessed.'

'If we drive down to a spot overlooking Lough Tay, you'll be able to look down on the lake.'

He drove slowly so she could take in the blue and purple tones of the far-off mountains like beacons compared to the earthy tones of those closer. A stream by the road flowed over the rocks. She pointed to a small tree growing out of the bog.

At Lough Tay, he parked the car and walked to a spot overlooking the lake where they could sit sheltered from the wind behind two slabs of rock. Pulling a huge cushion from the back seat, he placed it in a sheltered spot then came back to the car and lifted Maggie out.

'I can walk.'

'Not on my watch; the ground is a little slippery,' he said.

She let herself be carried on the soft, muddy grass until he gently placed her on the cushion, the cashmere shawl over her shoulder and the mohair rug tucked in around her legs.

'Katie told me not to have you out for too long, and Anna said she was only packing the drinking chocolate, but I sneaked out a bottle of Prosecco and two glasses.'

Beaming a bright smile, Maggie clapped in excitement.

'It's not as if it will kill me, so who cares; something else has already taken care of that.'

'He took out two crystal glasses and a bottle of Moët champagne, standing up to push out the cork and pour the bubbly into the glasses until they overflowed.

'Careful, don't get any on the cashmere. I might be dying, but Anna can still get cross.'

She shuffled over on the cushion, and he sat in beside her.

'Can I make a toast?' she asked.

'Of course.'

Maggie held up the glass high.

'To us, here and happy,' she said.

Gently, he clinked her glass.

You're treating me like that crystal glass. I might be broken, but I'm not gone yet.'

'Maggie, I wish it could be different.'

'So do I.'

'He caught a stone and threw it over the cliff edge.

'You're angry.'

'At the bloody cancer.'

She downed the bubbly in one. 'You can't mention that today. That word is banned. Today, I'm Maggie the Manhattan chick, who is in the mountains drinking champagne on a bloody freezing winter's day.'

'And eating warm bagels made by the best baker around,' he said, opening the picnic basket and handing over her favourite bagel, with crisped onion on top and the cream cheese filling she loved. She managed only a tiny bite.

'You and Katie, you need to support each other in the months ahead.'

'I thought we weren't talking about it.'

'We're not; we're talking about you two.'

Maggie looked out across at the mountains and the lake

below. In the far-off distance, a bird cried out, maybe a hawk. She saw it hovering high, watching, ready to pounce.

'I have a hawk stalking me too; it's ready to swoop. That's why I can say what I want now, I will be forgiven anything.'

She turned to Dan, reached over and pulled his head towards her. Softly, she kissed him on the lips, but swiftly pulled away.

'I know you love Katie; I've seen the way you look at her. I've seen the way she tries not to respond. I know what you two have been doing and I thank you for it, but after I'm gone and the hawk has pounced, don't waste any more time.'

Dan shuffled uncomfortably.

'We didn't think you would notice.'

Maggie giggled.

'Tell you this for free. I have been sitting in that café watching the world go by and sometimes even from my bed. It's not that people don't notice me, but it's as if the filters are gone. I have seen everything, and I have been told everything.'

'Katie has been so stressed; she loves you dearly,' Dan said.

'I know, and to think at the start, we didn't really trust each other. Kilcashel gave us a new life, a new purpose and a deep friendship.'

He shivered.

'We should get you off this mountain.'

'Shut up, Dan.'

He poured another glass of champagne, and she sipped it.

The cold made the bubbles scrape more at her throat. She felt very cold, but she liked the feeling. The air was still, like the world had stopped, because she wanted it to.

'I wish I could stay here forever,' she said, and it was only when Dan hugged her tight, she realised she had spoken out loud.

'Will you remember me often at this spot?'

'Always,' he whispered, and she detected a shake in his voice.

She opened a café box which was tied with a pink ribbon.

Taking out her favourite raspberry biscuit, she took a small bite.

'Mmm, if this is my last meal, I'm happy,' she said. Grabbing the rest of the biscuits, she crumbled them in her hands and threw them into the air.

'Katie will be so disappointed if we bring home all the food. I know she got up early this morning to make these cookies, because she knows I like them almost out of the oven. I don't want to disappoint her.'

Maggie reached in and took out the other box, tied with a blue ribbon.

'These must be your favourite; you should do the same.'

Loosening the ribbon, she opened the second box and picked out the chocolate orange biscuits and handed them to Dan. He munched one, then broke up the others and threw them far down the mountain.

'The local wildlife can have a feast later,' Maggie said.

The seeping damp cold made her shudder, and she adjusted the cashmere shawl, hoping Dan would not notice. Closing her eyes, she listened to the silence curling about her, touching off her skin, kissing off her turban, and she did her best to preserve this memory, to draw on it, when times were worse.

A red kite high above them called out and she envied its freedom on this wintry day.

Dan asked was she all right.

'Maybe we should go,' she said, trying to hide that the pain had come back in the base of her spine, and she felt quite light-headed. She let him pull her to her feet, and she leaned into his broad chest as he kissed her on the top of her head, hard so she could feel it thought her hat.

'Take me home to Kilcashel House,' she whispered, and he

scooped her up in his arms and marched her across the grass to his Land Rover. She sobbed quietly as he tucked her into the seat. Looking out the window, she saw the mist rising on the far-off mountains; the clouds briefly parting and allowing the sun to break through.

'I wish I had known before this how beautiful the mountains were; I would have had you bring me here many times,' she whispered.

'Maybe better than any view from a highrise in Manhattan.'

She smiled.

Here there was the stillness and abundance of nature; there, the sound of the city which brought with it a sense of excitement and trepidation. They were both exhilarating in different ways.

'Nothing compares to today and being here with you,' she said.

He drove slowly down the windy mountain road, past the bog and the heather, brown now waiting for the warm spring air to unfold its full colour.

TWENTY-SEVEN

Katie and Anna were loitering on the steps waiting for the Land Rover to round the rhododendron bend. 'Do you think we should be here? Is it a bit much?' Katie asked.

'That poor girl will need our help after that madcap trip,' Anna said.

'We're fussing around like mother hens; I'm not sure Maggie would like that.'

'Nobody minds a bit of pampering,' Anna said, walking down the steps when she heard the Land Rover come up the avenue.

Anna ran to open the passenger door.

'What's wrong? I knew this would be too much for you.'

Maggie flashed a smile.

'Dan here is such a bore; I wanted to dance barefoot along the bog, but he wouldn't let me.'

She saw Anna look at her uncertainly, before she realised she was joking.

Nora and Leonie came out and called them in.

'It's all ready, we have a nice surprise for you' Nora said.

Maggie looked at Katie, who was hanging back.

'I know you organised all this. We can't fight the inevitable, but we can take pleasure in being together while we can,' she whispered to Katie, who took a deep breath.

'Yes, agreed,' Katie replied.

'I hope there is Granny's chocolate cake,' Maggie said.

'A special one, just for you,' Katie said. The Falveys were standing waiting for Maggie, and they clapped as Dan carried to her favourite velvet chair.

'You're looking good, Maggie,' Muriel said.

'And you are a good liar, Muriel Falvey,' Maggie answered as she settled into the armchair.

Rosie pulled out her accordion and played a reel. Katie made the coffee and Anna laid out a small table with different biscuits and chocolates. Rowena hovered and Muriel stoked up the fire, while Dan slipped off to saddle up Millie.

'Is this the wake I should be having?' Maggie whispered to Katie.

'We thought you would like to have your friends around you.'

'While I still can. I get it.'

Nora called out that Dan was outside.

'Do you think you can walk to the front door?' Rowena asked Maggie.

Maggie stood up, her legs wobbly. She leaned on Katie's shoulder. Anna slid in from the right and gave her another shoulder to bear her weight.

Millie, in her best saddle and bridle with a saddle pad trimmed in velvet, was standing waiting for her.

Maggie looked at the horse who had been such a friend all these months. When she was riding Millie, even just hacking around the estate, she felt she had a purpose in life; she felt content.

'Do you think you could sit up on her? I could lead you around and maybe down to the sea?' Dan said.

'I'm not sure I can,' Maggie said.

'If we go bareback, the two of us can fit. I can hop up behind you, Millie won't mind,' Dan said.

'Yes, we can all go to the sea,' Muriel said, but the others moved to hush her.

Maggie looked around at her friends.

'I want you all to come; you make me feel alive and that is a big thing right now.'

They grabbed their coats and Katie handed out spare pairs of hats and gloves, while Dan sorted out Millie and helped get Maggie kitted out.

When she was ready, Dan lifted her onto the horse and he got up behind her, his arms around Maggie and also holding the reins.

'She's no extra weight for the horse, she's only skin and bone,' Anna muttered to Katie as Millie set off around the side of the house and down the path to the sea, the party of women following behind. At the sea, Maggie also placed her hands on the reins as Millie trotted through the edge of the waves. The women, with Katie leading the pack, were jogging behind, trying to keep up.

'There's some life in me yet then,' Maggie laughed, and Anna said if she went near her with that animal, she would splash her.

Nora kicked off her shoes and socks and ran into the water, followed quickly by Leonie and Rowena. Katie marked out a huge love heart on the sand with her feet and called everybody in for a selfie beside Millie.

Dan jumped from the horse, threw off his boots and socks and rolled up his trousers before getting in the water. Maggie laughed out loud; it hurt to laugh, but she didn't care.

A passer-by waved and said they were all mad, and they giggled as Maggie manoeuvred the horse back on to the sand.

Muriel and Rosie, who had gone back to their car for their

wellingtons, were late, but insisted everybody huddle together for another photograph.

Maggie felt a little queasy and began to cough. Katie and Anna were by her side immediately.

'Time to get you home, kiddo,' Anna said.

Maggie nodded and they trudged back to Kilcashel House and the fire, which was glowing red warm.

Dan helped Maggie down from the horse and carried her as far as the armchair.

The others were taking off their coats and fussing about getting tea and coffee brewed, when Maggie said she was sorry, but she needed to get to bed.

Katie immediately put down the candles she'd planned to put on the chocolate cake and ran to her friend.

'Are you not feeling well?'

'Just a little tired. It has been such a busy day. Please, everybody, stay; have coffee, maybe I can join you all later.'

The others smiled and agreed it was the best thing to do, but watched with concern as Dan carried Maggie up the stairs. He beckoned to Katie to follow.

In the bedroom, Dan gently placed Maggie on the bed and loitered, not sure what he should do next.

'Thank you for a lovely day; it was perfect; you thought of everything,' Maggie said. She noticed his smile didn't quite reach his eyes, which were full of sadness. She called him closer.

He leaned into her, and she breathed in his aftershave. Stroking his cheek, she pinched it playfully.

'Enough with the sadness – cut it,' she said, pretending not to notice the glisten of tears in his eyes. She could not keep him there, see the pain on his face. She asked him to send Anna up.

Katie helped take off the layers of clothes which had been keeping Maggie warm.

'Can I keep the cashmere shawl? It's so soft,' Maggie said, after slipping on her pyjamas. She draped the shawl over her shoulders. When she pulled back the bed covers, Maggie let her hand run over the silk sheets.

'You guys are spoiling me so,' she said as she sank into the sheets and asked for her oxygen mask. When Anna came into the room, she sat at one side of Maggie.

'I rang the doctor, and the palliative nurse will be here shortly.'

Maggie lifted off the mask slowly.

'How I wish I could see your cherry blossom trees one last time, Anna.'

Anna, the tears streaming down her face, nodded and squeezed Maggie's hand gently, so she didn't hurt her.

Katie leaned over and stroked Maggie's forehead.

'The chocolate cake is our bestseller; everybody loves Granny's cake. And we have ordered a reprint of the menus, so it's now called Maggie's chocolate cake. You were right, it's a flyer,' Katie said softly.

'I told you so,' Maggie whispered and smiled.

Downstairs, they could hear the women gathering and talking quietly, shuffling their feet and waiting.

TWENTY-EIGHT

The house was quiet, languishing in the morning sunshine, its rays creeping into the room, when Maggie took her last breath. Katie, who had been asleep, had woken with a start to find Maggie looking at her.

She motioned for the oxygen mask to be taken down and pulled Katie close.

'Don't ever let Kilcashel House go; keep it for both of us,' she rasped, the words coming slowly and painfully.

'Promise,' she said.

'I promise,' Katie answered and slipped the mask back on.

When she heard another loud gasp, she knew Maggie was taking her last breath before her body slumped in death.

Katie prodded Anna to wake her up.

'She's gone.'

Anna touched Maggie's face and kissed her, then got up to close the curtains.

'I will go downstairs and tell the others,' she said, stopping to press Katie on the shoulders.

'I thought they had gone home.'

'They insisted on staying, every last one of them, for the last two days.'

Katie heard the crying downstairs. She didn't know what to do. Anna said something about a priest and there was talk of a wake, but she didn't want people traipsing around Kilcashel House, and talking about Maggie as if they knew her.

When there was a knock on the bedroom door, she was relieved it was Dan.

'Maggie reckoned you might be at sea, so she told me how she wanted this to play out. She does not want a religious service and wants to be cremated; her ashes are to be scattered in the mountains.'

'You talked about all this?'

'Yes, and a lot of other things.'

'Can we do that, in this country, no religious involvement?'

'Anna won't like it, but we have to respect Maggie's wishes. In her own words, she said she wanted to be sent off to the crematorium in a wicker basket and, when she returns as dust, you can have a café party and say a few nice things after she is scattered in the mountains.'

'Very specific.'

'Wasn't Maggie always? Do you want me to make the arrangements?'

'Please. I wouldn't even know what to say; who to ask.'

Dan leaned over and kissed Maggie's cheek. Afterwards, he stood in silence as if in prayer before leaving the room to phone the undertaker.

Katie walked to the window and pulled back one of the curtains a fraction to peep out. The allotments looked bedraggled and unloved in the winter cold. Nora was on the driveway talking to a group of people; no doubt turning them away from the café for the day. They stared up at her and she quickly moved back into the room.

It was selfish she knew, but how was she going to run this

place without Maggie? Without her tough as old boots attitude and her fake bolshiness, which cut right through any red tape. Katie felt lost and empty inside.

How was she going to get through every day without Maggie's drama, her dirty laugh and her brilliant asides. Every morning, she had listened for the appearance of Maggie; even when she didn't like her much at the start.

Even then, she looked forward to the kitchen door being pushed back too hard and bouncing off the wall, while Maggie announced that she couldn't spend another day in this godforsaken place. Even the dreary days at Kilcashel were eventful when Maggie was around.

Now she was gone, and Harry was gone, but Kilcashel House remained and she was the sole custodian.

The old Maggie would be furious at herself for falling out of the race at the last minute; the old Maggie would have attempted to wrap up the sale before she exited. But the new Maggie just wanted to stay at Kilcashel and continue this life they had built around them.

Anna came quietly into the room and straightened the bedclothes and gently brushed Maggie's hair so that it framed her delicate features. Katie did not move from the window. She wanted to remember the awkward Maggie, the stubborn Maggie, the soft as butter and hard as nails Maggie; she didn't recognise this dead person. Maggie was gone.

Anna came and stood beside her.

'The undertakers will be here shortly. We thought of saying a decade of the rosary at her bedside.'

'She didn't want anything religious.'

'For God's sake, how do you know that?'

'She told Dan; she said it might make you cross.'

'It makes me frustrated, but we must respect her wishes; we will do it in the café downstairs.'

Katie shook her head, but didn't say anything. There was no

point arguing with Anna, who needed to find some comfort in prayer right now.

'If you don't mind, I'll stay here,' Katie said.

Anna went downstairs and just a few minutes later, the rise and fall of the hushed prayers filled the house as the women bowed their heads and concentrated on the decades of the rosary to help Maggie on her way to the next life.

Katie wanted to go down and shout at them to stop, but at the same time, there was a certain comfort in the soft rhythm of the prayers as they wafted upwards.

Standing closer to the window, she pulled back the curtains further and leaned her forehead on the glass as grief overpowered her. Pressing into the cold glass, there was some relief from the pain she felt, but the empty chasm could not be lessened.

When Dan came and wrapped her in his arms, she leaned against him and let him lead her down the stairs, where Nora and Leonie brought her to a velvet armchair, and handed her a cup of hot, sweet tea.

'You drink that and we'll look after things,' Anna said as a hearse van pulled up at the front and a man in a black suit got out.

Dan had asked her did she want to say a final goodbye, but Katie was frozen to the spot, and could not answer. She was there for the last breath; she had made her promise. The others watched as she put on her wellingtons and coat and escaped out the back door before Maggie was taken from the house. She could not see her in a coffin. She wanted to remember her friend, the vibrant, colourful Maggie, the way she wanted to be remembered.

Making her way down the garden path, Katie didn't notice the pools of water being thrown at her by the crocosmia or the tall, bleached stalks of the fennel which hit against her wool coat.

At the entrance to the beach she stopped and raised her

head to the wind and the rain. The harsh December wind spit off her face, blasting her with cold. The rain ran down her neck and her back, but she didn't care. How was she going to go on without Maggie? Katie was afraid to think of the future without this woman, who had become a sister.

Falling to her knees, she buckled to the wind and rain, letting its power push her and tear at her. She didn't much care anymore. The chill wind ripped across her; sea spray clinging to her hair and coat. She closed her eyes, unable to fight off the sound of the sea or the harshness of the cold wind.

Katie was slumped on the sand when Dan found her an hour later. Scooping her up in his arms, he ran to the house calling out to the others to help.

'You stupid girl, you will get your death...'

Anna stopped herself and told the others to get some dry clothes and prepare a bed for Katie.

Nora and Leonie rushed off, while Dan poured a whiskey.

'No, she needs warm milk; the whiskey will be too much. Ring the doctor; she may need some medication to get her through the next day or so,' Anna said.

Pulling out a pan, Anna plopped milk with a few drops of whiskey in it and lit the gas burner.

Katie knew two things: Maggie was dead and she, somehow, was back at Kilcashel House. She found a strange comfort in Anna's cross mutterings to herself as she filled a mug with the warm milk.

When she handed it to her, Katie accepted it, though the taste was strong and not sweet as she expected.

As soon as Dan returned, Anna told him to carry Katie to her bedroom on the second floor. Nora and Rowena were ready with a pyjamas and soon had Katie sitting up in bed, Leonie using a hair dryer on her hair. She heard their voices, but she couldn't make out what they were saying. Nothing made sense anymore. She lay back on the pillows, closed her eyes and went to sleep.

They told her later she slept for two days and Anna had never left her side. When she woke up, Anna was asleep in the armchair beside her bed. She looked old, her black hair, which she normally had tied up in a bun was showing grey at the roots and it had fallen half over her face. Her hands were clasped in her lap; in front of her. Katie noticed for the first time, the gold band wedding ring and what looked like an eternity ring on Anna's left hand.

When Anna stirred, Katie clinched her eyes shut again, not wanting to talk yet about what had happened. She heard the swish of the curtains as they were pulled back and Anna opening the door to go downstairs. Katie knew she would bring back up a cup of tea. She had a vague memory in her sleep of the aroma of hot sweet tea tickling her nose.

She wished she could stay in bed and not have to consider how she was going to manage Kilcashel without Maggie.

When she heard Anna on the stairs, she sat up, her head against the hard headboard.

'Welcome back; how do you feel?' Anna said.

'Strange, everything has changed.'

'It's very quiet. I never fully realised the presence Maggie was here until now.' Anna stopped, her shoulders slumped. 'The crematorium are sending her ashes this week.'

'Oh.'

'Don't you worry about it; Dan can go straight up the mountains, if you like. He knows the spot; seemingly on that last day when they went on their trip, she picked it out.'

'Why didn't she want to be scattered at Kilcashel?'

'Maybe she thought it was a bit creepy and she knew you would be so sad.'

'Did she talk to you about it?'

'A while back. she was worried about you when she was gone.'

'I never knew.'

'You weren't supposed to, but Maggie asked me to help you keep Kilcashel House going. She said if you left here, you would be lost.'

'I am lost anyway.'

'She wanted me to get cross and tell you to snap out of it. I won't do it today, but soon, when you have had a bit of time. We all need time to adjust.'

'What about the café?'

'We put a sign up along with a black bow, so everybody knows we have suffered a loss and I have kept the gates closed.'

TWENTY-NINE

Katie spent another two days in bed, afraid to get up, afraid to face the world. When she finally slid out from under the covers, her head hurt and her legs were wobbly.

She rushed past Maggie's bedroom on the way downstairs.

Anna was in the kitchen reading a newspaper.

'It's good to see you up,' she said, slowly turning the pages.

'Anna, I don't know if I want to continue with the café,' Katie said in a rush.

'What? After all the work you two have put into it.'

Anna took off her glasses, folded the newspaper carefully and pushed it across the counter.

'It's not going to be the same; most people came to chat to Maggie or watch her high drama; I'm a poor replacement and you know it,' Katie said.

Anna looked to the ceiling. 'Maggie warned me you would say that.'

She got off the stool and stood in front of Katie.

'They came up that avenue for your baking, everything else is the support act. Yes, our support act has changed but the key ingredients, which brought people here in the first place are the same.'

'Nice words, but we both know everything has changed.'

'Well, that's a pity because right now, Nora is taking down the black bow, and I have instructed her to open up the gates from tomorrow morning. We have put up a new sign, saying normal hours from tomorrow, Tuesday.'

'I didn't sanction this; nobody consulted me,' Katie said, her voice cross.

'You were only going to say no.'

'Anna, this is my house; my café.'

'And if you had your stupid way at the moment, you would ruin the good work all of us, including Maggie, have put into Kilcashel. I'm not going to let that happen.'

Katie sat down on the armchair they had placed beside the Aga for Maggie.

'It's so hard; I can't imagine this place without her.'

'Do you think any of us can? Nora and Leonie haven't been swimming and the bloody horse is in an awful way.'

'What's wrong with Millie? Maggie asked me to look after her.'

'She needs a bit of company. She needs looking after. We all need looking after.'

Katie got up and grabbed Anna into a hug.

Anna wept. Katie held her, until she pulled free.

'You and Kilcashel mean so much to all of us. We need you to go back to what you do best: baking the bagels, the cake and cookies, and running the café. Everybody wants to get back to some sort of normal.'

'I don't know if I can.'

Anna stared at Katie.

'You can, you just have to start baking. Everything else will fall into place.'

Katie sat down, her head in her hands.

Anna arranged the stainless-steel bowls, the wooden spoons and the weighing scales in a row on the worktop.

'Start with her favourite raspberry biscuits. I bought fresh raspberries in the market this morning.'

Katie started to weigh out the flour.

Anna turned on the ovens and got the trays ready. Neither spoke very much as Katie got the mixer going and worked up the batter.

When it was time to scoop the mix into little balls and place them on the baking trays to flatten them into shapes, Katie turned to Anna.

'Did you mean it when you said everybody missed the café?'

'I did.'

Katie placed the trays in the ovens.

'Do you think many people will come tomorrow?'

Anna took a deep breath.

'Now is probably a good time to tell you,' Anna started.

'We're not getting a tour bus, I hope, don't tell me you didn't put them off.'

Anna looked away as she spoke, because she didn't want to see Katie's face.

'Two tour buses are coming. When people heard Maggie had died, they wanted to pay their respects.'

'What, when?

'Tomorrow morning at 11 a.m. We have all day to prepare.'

'You mean I have to bake enough bagels and biscuits for one hundred people, when I have just about got my head around the fact of opening up the café.'

Anna stared at her.

'Listen, girl, we all have it hard at times. Life is one long challenge. You can choose to lie down in the face of the challenges, or you can ride with them and move on. Over to you.'

Katie was surprised at the harsh tone of Anna's voice. She was right, if Katie let everything come on top of her now, she wouldn't keep Kilcashel, and what would she do then? Go back to Manhattan where nobody cared whether she succeeded or failed, and leave all of those she loved behind.

'OK, but we need to sit down and plan out the menu. Can Rowena come in too?'

'Already done.'

Katie shook her head.

'I should have known. You planned this all along. This casual you was all an act; I have never seen you sit in the kitchen and read a newspaper. You wanted me to agree to opening the café before you told me about the tour buses.'

'Maybe. Now, don't worry, I have got all the ingredients in. You just have to bake.'

Katie hugged Anna again.

'Thank you,' she whispered in her ear.

Katie rummaged in the vegetable baskets. She took out two carrots.

'I am just going upstairs to change into warmer clothes and get my wellies. I think it's time I paid Millie a visit.'

Anna smiled brightly.

'Good idea.'

On the first landing, Katie hesitated outside Maggie's room. She turned the brass handle and gingerly stepped inside. The bed was made with sharp neat corners. It was disconcerting, Katie thought, because Maggie never used to make her bed. The dressing table was the same. She couldn't find Maggie's Coco Chanel perfume, so she picked up the Chanel No 5 eau de toilette and sprayed a dash on her wrist; the aroma bringing back memories which made her smile, like the time Anna complained because there a stink all over the house because of 'that one's cheap spray'. When she was told it was Chanel, Anna said Maggie should have more sense than to be spraying expensive perfume all over the place. Maggie had challenged her and said she read once Jerry Hall sprayed it into the air after a shower and walked through the mist.

Anna had retorted if it was mist she wanted, all Maggie had to do was look out the window.

Katie sighed. She would miss the arguments that could go on hours or days, and the crazy ideas. The blue cashmere shawl was folded on the bed. She skimmed her hands along it.

Anna had never worn it. Her husband bought it for her as a gift. She found it, wrapped up and hidden in his wardrobe, after he died. She could never wear it, and now she didn't want it back. Katie imagined Anna on the avenue wearing the shawl and her heart hurt for what might have been.

When she heard a footstep in the hall, she knew Anna was checking for movement upstairs. Katie made her way to her own bedroom.

When she got as far as the kitchen ten minutes later, Anna was wiping down the worktops.

'The ladies used to come at night to keep us company; we took turns looking over you, while you slept. They could drink tea for Ireland that lot.'

'I guess I have a lot of people to thank.'

'No need, opening the café is thanks enough.'

'Are you sure we have enough ingredients for the week?' Katie asked.

'I checked the other day, and I kept up with the orders; you can settle up with me later.'

'Cool.'

It was then, she saw the chocolate cake pushed to the end of the counter.

'We never got a chance to show Maggie her cake.'

'I didn't know what to do with it. I just wrapped it in tinfoil. We didn't want to cut into it,' Anna said.

'I'm going to bake some more chocolate cake. We will call it

Maggie's chocolate cake. I sent out a new menu to the printers a while ago.'

'They came back. I have them all ready to go. You're going to have to go into town and get almonds and good organic chocolate,' Katie said.

'I'm ready to go, whenever you give me the list.'

Katie and Anna left the house at the same time. Katie walked across the allotment field to the second paddock. When she didn't immediately see Millie, she climbed the fence and called out the horse's name. In the far corner, wearing her warm winter rug, Millie lifted her head. Katie walked across the grass, calling out her name. Millie wandered towards her.

When they met, Millie nudged at her pockets.

Katie broke up a carrot and doled it out piece by piece, all the time massaging behind Millie's ears. Millie nuzzled into her, and Katie knew she had been forgiven for her tardiness since Maggie died.

Walking back to Kilcashel House, Katie felt more confident that maybe she could continue to make a go of the café. Maggie loved this place and so did she. She rushed along because she had to start baking. A fresh excitement seared through her to think that the Drawing Room Café would soon be up and running again.

Katie was up to her elbows in flour when there was a knock at the front door. She thought of not answering. It must be somebody who didn't know her or were looking for the café, because anybody from Kilcashel knew to come around to the back door. She lifted a tray of biscuits into the oven and, grabbing a tea towel, she wiped her hands as she walked down the hall to the front door.

The young man standing on the top step holding a box looked nervous.

'I am sorry to bother you, but is this the home of Maggie Flint?'

'Yes. What's this about?'

'I have her here.'

'Who?'

'Maggie Flint, her ashes, I work with Miley Carthy undertakers.'

He stopped, as if he suddenly realised he was talking too much.

'These are Maggie's ashes?'

'I am sorry, yes.'

'Can you carry them in for me?'

He stepped into the hall. 'Where shall I leave them?'

Katie walked down the hall to the kitchen.

'I don't know, this is too much like getting an Amazon delivery.'

Tears streamed down her face.

'Look, I'm sorry I messed it up; where can I put her down?'

Katie pointed to the side of the counter.

'She sat there every morning.'

Gently, he placed the box on the counter.

Katie looked at the package.

'Is there an urn inside?'

'I don't think you ordered one, so it's a metal box, like a mini casket, and a plastic bag inside with the ashes.'

'Maggie Flint, reduced to ashes.'

He dropped his head and clasped his hands together as if in prayer.

'Do you want a coffee?'

'Seriously?'

'There has to be a funny side to this delivery, Maggie would certainly have appreciated it.'

She poured a black coffee and pushed it across the counter.

'What's your name?'

'Ben, I am Nora's nephew from Bray.'

'Ah, Nora knew Maggie well.'

'Yeah. she still talks a lot about her.'

'Ben, you're going to have to work on your doorstep manner.'

'It's my first day on the job.'

Katie pushed a plate of cookies towards him.

'Lucky you came here then.'

'I'm sorry. I got so nervous; I was pumping sweat on the doorstep.'

'Too much information, Ben.'

'Right, sorry.'

'Did you ever meet Maggie?'

'I did, she gave me a lift in her BMW once. I was ribbed solid for a week by my mates.'

Katie laughed out loud.

'Maggie would have loved that.'

He got up to leave. 'I have another delivery to make.'

'Remember, learn from this one.'

'Thank you.'

She led him to the door.

When she got back into the kitchen, she walked past the box. Hard to believe that Maggie's big life could be reduced to a small brown package on the kitchen counter.

She pushed it in from the edge. When Lola burst into the kitchen and popped her paws on the counter to get a closer sniff, she ushered her out, and pushed the package further along the counter towards the middle.

Anna would have to deal with it when she came back, because she could hardly look at it.

. . .

Katie concentrated on the chocolate cake. It seemed fitting to be making the recipe Maggie loved as she sat on the counter. Maggie would have crowed about her grandmother's recipe and said her side of the family had such talent. Katie smiled to herself, thinking none of the baking talent made it as far as Maggie; she couldn't even scramble an egg.

When the postman called round, she gestured for him to step into the kitchen.

'There's a letter here for Maggie. I wasn't sure what to do with it, but I have to deliver it. I hope it doesn't upset you.'

He handed her a rectangular white envelope, the name of a big American publisher printed on the back.

'Thanks, Frank, I'm OK; the café is opening tomorrow.'

'Oh good, I'll spread the word if you like, when I'm out on my rounds.'

'That would be great,' she said, turning the envelope over in her hands.

She didn't know if she should open the letter.

Her hands shaking, she propped the envelope up against Maggie's ashes. Stepping out on the deck, she breathed in the cold and stood pummelled on all sides by the chill wind blasting in from the Irish Sea.

When she heard footsteps, she thought it was Anna.

'Good to see you up and about,' Dan said.

Katie jumped, opening her eyes.

'I had no choice; we have one hundred tourists making their way to us tomorrow.'

'Good start to opening back up.'

'Maggie's ashes arrived.'

'Damn, I was hoping to get here in time to collect the package.'

'It's on the counter; are we going to scatter them today?'

'There's a spot overlooking Lough Tay; she picked it out,

said she wanted her ashes spread there, across the bog and the mountains.'

'Shouldn't I go, and maybe Anna?'

'Are you up for it?'

'Would it be dreadful of me to put it off for a day or so?'

'It might be a bit windy, for what we have to do this week anyway.'

'Do you think you could move it from the counter? I'm afraid to touch it.'

'Of course.'

When Dan picked up the package, she watched him from the deck as his shoulders slumped.

'Hard to believe all of Maggie is there,' she said to fill in the silence.

He swung around.

'But it's not; it's all that she has left us, that is important.'

'I guess,' she said, joining him in the kitchen.

When Anna pushed in the back door, she dropped her shopping on the counter.

'What's this?'

Katie didn't say anything for a moment, but when she spoke, her voice was croaky.

'Maggie's ashes.'

'Did Nora's nephew drop them up?'

'Yes, Ben.'

'I told him to wait until I got home; he has a brain the size of a pea. I didn't want you upset.'

'I just don't know where to put it.'

'Not the counter.'

'We were going to scatter them in the mountains later this week. Will you come?' Dan asked.

'Of course I will. Somebody has to say a prayer and she's only dust, she can't stop me now.'

'Maybe her swimming pals can come too, and we can sip champagne and say goodbye,' Katie said.

'Sounds like a plan, but it will depend on the weather; a bright winter day's is best. Will we talk about it tomorrow?' Dan said, making for the door.

When he left, Anna took the package and carefully brought it to the café.

'I thought it could sit on the mantelpiece. She always like sitting beside the fire.'

Anna picked up the letter.

'Are you going to open this?'

'I didn't know if I should.'

Anna passed the envelope to Katie.

'It came to Kilcashel and you are the sole owner now; you open it.'

Tentatively, Katie unsealed the envelope and took out a typed letter.

She leaned against the counter.

'It's from a US publisher; it says they have accepted Maggie's manuscript for publication,' Katie said, her eyes wide and her hand shaking as she read the letter.

'I can't believe it; I didn't even know she was working on a manuscript.'

'What manuscript?'

'Working title, it says. "Waking Up at Kilcashel House".'

'Divine Jesus, what has she been writing about us now?'

'Anna, it's wonderful, a book about Kilcashel.'

'Why the hell didn't she tell us?' Anna asked.

Anna grabbed the letter from her and read it.

'They have been emailing and she didn't answer. They want to publish in the late spring. They want to talk money.'

'It's so unfair, she would have been so proud,' Katie said, wiping away a tear.

She looked at Anna. 'It will be a fine book. If she had

revealed she was writing a book, I would have been so worried, but now I know it is something I will treasure forever.'

'You can think that way, but I'm going to wait to read it. If she was around, Maggie would be insufferable. Now, of course, she's gone, and we will be overrun,' Anna grumbled.

Katie took back the letter.

'Maggie always blabbed about things she didn't care much about. When it was something she felt deeply about, she was more reticent. They will hardly go ahead with it now,' Katie said.

'Or maybe they will; it's such a tragic twist.'

Katie shivered.

'What has she done to us? it will put too much of a spotlight on us,' Anna said.

'Maggie would be so happy with this news.'

'God forgive me, but this makes me so cross at her.'

'I don't think she would have it any other way.'

THIRTY

They decided to scatter Maggie's ashes on a bright but cold December day; the mountains were stark and brooding. Dan arrived at Kilcashel House wearing a long black coat and a wool scarf tied at his neck.

'You look nice,' Katie said as she stood at the hall mirror and slicked on some lipstick.

'Is it too much?' he asked.

'Maggie would love it.'

He reached inside his coat and pulled out a bottle of champagne.

'If you have glasses, I thought Maggie would like us to sip champagne to remember her life.'

'Great idea, I had better bring the crystal or she'll be back to haunt us.'

Anna walked up the avenue. Nora, Leonie and Rowena arrived in Nora's car. The Falveys were the last to pull up at Kilcashel House.

'I brought some nice dried flowers, roses and camellias from Kilcashel. We can leave them on the mountain,' Anna said.

They set off in a convoy up past the village of Roundwood, and on to the narrow, windy roads towards the Sally Gap.

The blue sky reached down to tip against the mountaintops, and they rolled down the windows to drink in the clear air.

Just short of the summit, they pulled into a small car park.

'What is here?' Katie asked.

'Follow me across the road,' Dan said, leading the way though the soft boggy land to an outcrop overlooking the deep blue lake below. 'This spot was Maggie's favourite. It was here we poured the hot chocolate in to the ground and drank champagne that last day.'

Anna clicked her tongue and the others giggled.

'I never thought you were going to drink the hot chocolate,' Katie said.

Dan cleared his throat.

'On this spot, Maggie told me to go on living my life and to insist you lot do the same. She was happy in the moment, hiding her pain. She wanted to be scattered here, for her ashes to blow free like the birds, and maybe drift down to the lake.

'We can place the roses on the ground and I'll scatter the ashes from the top of the rock and let the breeze take them away.'

They watched as Dan climbed the outcrop and took out the casket carrying the ashes. Carefully he took out the plastic bag and popped open its seal.

Nodding to the others, Dan slowly tipped the bag over until the ashes fell out in a puff, whipped away by a mountain zephyr and carried across the hard terrain, finally settling on the earth to nourish the soil for the emergence of the bog cotton and heather in spring.

When he was sure every last speck had dispersed into the air, Dan called on Anna to say something, because he knew Katie was too overcome with emotion.

Anna straightened to her full height.

'I have nothing prepared, but I want to say, fly high my dearest Maggie; you did in this life, and I know you will in the next. We had our differences at the start, but a deep-seated affection grew. I will miss you so.'

Katie, swiping away her tears, popped the champagne bottle, the sound ping-ponging across the mountain. Quickly, she filled the crystal glasses and held her own aloft.

'To Maggie, my beautiful sister. Kilcashel House won't be the same without you,' she said, her voice cracking. Nora clinked her glass to Katie's, and the others followed; the sound like a new birdcall in the wild hills.

Muriel jumped up on a rock. 'To Maggie, the only woman I knew who insisted on working on a farm while wearing three-inch heels.'

Katie held up her glass again. 'To my best friend, I hope wherever she is, she has run down Harry to give him a piece of her mind and they are sitting now and catching up like old friends.'

Somebody laughed and the others joined in. When they looked around, there was no sign of any of the ashes, which had melted into the mountain air or landed lightly on the peaty soil.

It was cold and they weren't sure what to do next, so they began to troop back to their cars.

At one stage, Anna stumbled and Muriel caught her weight.

'Thank you, that could have been a nasty fall,' Anna said.

'I am glad I can do something for you, Anna; I would like if we could talk from time to time, like two women who know each other well.'

Anna fixed her hair and spoke quietly.

'I would like that too; the past is a long time ago.'

'Thank you,' Muriel said, linking Anna's arm the rest of the way back to the car.

When Anna got into the front seat, Katie said nothing.

'For Jesus' sake, can't we get off this mountain, I'm bloody perished?' Anna grumbled and Katie pulled the car out onto the road.

When they got back to Kilcashel, they trooped into the kitchen, not sure what to do next. Dan set off to catch up on jobs around the estate.

'Somebody go get the stupid man; there's a bit more to do,' Anna said.

'I don't think any of us are up to having a party,' Nora said, and there was a murmur of agreement.

'Maggie wanted this; I need everyone together,' Anna said impatiently.

'OK, no fuss, we're here,' Katie said.

Anna pulled out a chair and ordered Katie to sit down. She called the other women around her.

She took an envelope from her pocket.

'Somebody call Dan, he needs to be here too,' she said.

'What is that?' Katie asked.

Anna straightened as if she were addressing a crowd.

'As you all know, Maggie and I didn't hit it off at the start but by the end, we were pretty tight. Two weeks before she died as we sat there on the deck under the watery winter sun, she dictated a letter to me which she asked me to read to you all when the time was right. I guess the time is right.'

Leonie got out her phone to text Dan.

'Tell him it's urgent,' Anna said.

When Katie's phone rang, they all leaned forward to hear Dan speak.

Feeling embarrassed, Katie turned away and they heard her reassure him everything was all right and they would wait for him.

'Is he coming?' Anna asked.

'Yes, he'll be here in a few minutes. He was about to fix a side panel on the gazebo.'

Nora and Leonie said they would make some tea.

'I'm sorry I didn't bake this morning, but there are cookies left over from yesterday, if anyone wants,' Katie said.

They heard the heavy step of Dan in the yard. When he opened the door he seemed surprised that there were so many in the room.

Anna ushered him to sit down and pulled an envelope out of her handbag.

'This is a letter to all of us. It's Maggie's final farewell and I am honoured she entrusted it to me.

Straightening to her full height, Anna cleared her throat as she opened the envelope, and took out two handwritten pages and began to read the last words of Maggie Flint.

Katie dipped her head as the words flowed around her. Dan walked to the side and leaned up against the old dresser, his arms folded. The tribe of swimming women blew their noses and sniffed back their tears while the Falveys handed around a box of tissues.

Kilcashel House
Kilcashel
Co Wicklow

My Dearest Ones,

All good things come to an end – right?

I don't know what to say. It is time to say goodbye to my lovely Kilcashel House and all the friends I've met here.

I'm sitting on the deck looking out over the sea. I am tucked snug in a fleece blanket, and I am content. Remember when I came here, I found everything so strange, I wanted to find fault and I wanted to sell Kilcashel House. None of that matters now. This place changed me; this house and you, my dearest friends, have made me realise what is important in life.

I had to leave Manhattan and the city I loved and come to

this backwater to find the true meaning of life and love. To Katie, I say this; you have been more than a sister to me, but now you must live the life you want and deserve at Kilcashel House. We had hard times and fun times; remember me fondly, sweet Katie, but please do not allow yourself to get so lost in grief that you forget to enjoy life. Thank you for a great adventure, the best bagels in the world and the hand of friendship, when I needed it most.

I want you to learn to ride my Millie, to look after her; she loves to be brushed on her long neck, but when she turns sassy, at least pretend to be stern.

Out on a trail with Millie, going down by the sea was always when I was happiest with the world.

To Dan I say, follow your heart. Don't waste time grieving for what we didn't have. I know my lovely Katie and Dan that you have put your own relationship on the back burner to care for me.

Be together, have fun and know you have my blessing. Be happy in Kilcashel together and please, no grieving. I don't want to be remembered by tears and sighs, but with laughter and fun and big happy smiles.

Anna, you were my great adversary at the start, and now my greatest friend. As I approach these last days and hours, there is nobody I want closer.

To Anna, I say thank you for your patience; it would have been all too easy to dismiss me and walk away, but you endured and waited until I saw the light.

All that I ask is to remember me, please plant a cherry blossom by the gate of Kilcashel House.

Anna's voice cracked and there was a murmur of delight from the others. Anna continued reading the letter aloud.

It is at Kilcashel House I found myself and I found the friendship of Katie and my tribe of women.

My life without all of you annoying, funny and endearing women would have been so poor. In truth, until I came to Kilcashel, I lived a busy life, but not a very satisfying one.

To my swimming tribe I ask you to particularly remember me on those cool, summer mornings when the sun has not yet started to sparkle across the water and in the spring mornings when it is difficult to even step on the cold sand; remember your friend who would give anything to be there with you.

To Muriel and Rosie, keep the allotment going please and don't give up on the wildflowers, even if I am not there to pester you. Rowena, you are a wonderful young girl, please learn from all these women at Kilcashel House; this is your home too.

Goodbye and good luck. Think of me and smile.

Maggie xx

THIRTY-ONE

After the letter, nobody knew what to say. Dan ducked away, but texted Katie almost immediately.

Can we meet down by the sea; away from the others?

She answered yes and made to grab her coat from the rack at the back door.

'Hold on, I'll come with you,' Nora said.

Anna put a hand on Nora's shoulder.

'Maybe Katie needs some alone time.'

'Of course, I'm sorry.'

Katie nodded to the other women and stepped out into the damp morning. It was drizzling rain and she pulled up her hood.

Stepping down the path towards the sea, she dipped her head against the harsh cold wind. Stopping to take her breath, she looked back at Kilcashel House. Her heart skipped, expecting to see Maggie, a cigarette in one hand, a glass of Prosecco in the other at her special place on the deck, which Dan had installed for her, so she could sit out in all weathers.

She should ask him to dismantle the little hideout now, but she didn't have the heart.

In her last days, Dan had carried Maggie downstairs for an hour or two every day, and sat with her, watching the winter garden; the birds fluttering between the feeders; the waves falling to shore a constant backdrop.

Katie sometimes joined them and the three of them sat together, feeling no need to speak.

Pushing her hands deep in her pockets, Katie continued on her journey to the sea and the small outcrop of rocks, where she expected Dan would be sheltering and waiting.

She spotted him before he noticed her. She stopped to take him in. He looked taller and his hair was drenched because he was wearing his coat still. His shoulders were hunched against the rain, his hands in his pockets.

She stepped off the path onto the sand as he turned around to look at her.

'I'm sorry about the weather; do you want to go back to the deck?'

'No, too many memories there.'

'The gazebo then?'

He took her by the hand and led the way past the agapanthus, and the tall dead stalks of fennel silhouetted against the hazy, grey sky.

At the gazebo, Dan cleared the seat of old sodden leaves and took off his coat, spreading it for Katie to sit on.

'You will freeze,' she said.

'I don't think so.'

When he sat beside her, he put his arm around her and she leaned into his chest. He kissed the top of her head.

'What are we going to do now, Katie?'

She sat up.

'Take it slowly; we have to grieve first.'

'You have had to do a lot of grieving in such a short space of time.'

'I just never thought we wouldn't get further down the line; even when she was diagnosed with Stage 4, I thought she was too young to die.'

Tears choked Katie's voice. Turning away, she leaned against the side of the gazebo, the wet from the wood seeping across her cheeks.

'Maggie used to steal down here with a bottle of champagne in those early days. I thought she was a drunk, but I guess she was lonely. One night, I followed her to give her a piece of my mind, and I stopped on the path up there, and watched while she swigged from the bottle and just cried and cried. She was crying for Harry, but I guess also herself. I didn't want to intrude, but as I turned back, she called out to me. "Minnie Mouse, show yourself," she said, her voice strong and rather scary.

She insisted I join her, and she passed the bottle to me. When Maggie did that you couldn't refuse, so we both swigged from it, passing it between us.

I cried too. It was good for both of us.'

'I'm afraid I don't have any Prosecco or even a bottle of whiskey,' Dan said.

Katie turned to him and smiled.

'We need to give it time, Dan, and only then can we even think of ourselves and what we mean to each other.'

Catching her face with his two hands, he reached down and kissed her gently on the lips.

'I will wait for as long as it takes. I love you, Katie Williams.'

She pulled away.

'I love you so much, Dan,' she said.

'Let's get back to the house before the others decide to join us,' he said, taking her by the hand and guiding her up the overgrown path to the house.

As they stepped on to the deck, he pulled her close and kissed her on the top of the head.

'You and me, we have all the time in the world. I am ready to take the next step, whenever you give the signal.'

She nuzzled into him one last time then slipped across the deck to the back door.

When she got in, Anna looked at her.

'Everything sorted?'

Katie nodded and took down her stainless-steel bowls to begin making Maggie's chocolate cake.

THIRTY-TWO

Katie got up early to get her bagels ready. Now that the café was open every day, there was a steady stream of customers. She relished these quiet moments, before the swimming ladies stuck their heads in the door, on their way to the sea. Everyone seemed hell-bent on checking up to see how she was doing, when all she wanted was to be alone with her own thoughts.

It didn't mean she was lonely; she was grieving. She had been here before; she knew she would pull through, but there was no explaining that to anybody in Kilcashel. Dan was the only person who understood, because he was also hurting deeply.

The postman pulled up outside and tapped on the kitchen door.

'Just a small parcel this morning, Katie,' he said, and she was relieved it was not another sympathy card sent from far away. She laughed when she saw the small box in his hands and produced her own little café box.

'Your favourite bagel and Maggie's chocolate cake.'

He grinned and took the box.

I was hoping, but I wasn't sure that...' He stopped, blushing with embarrassment.

'That things are back to normal? Yes, maybe they are,' she said.

'My mum didn't know whether to leave the café this week or...'

'Tell her to come; we need to get a buzz going around here again. It's not the same with just the tour buses.'

The postman beamed.

'I'll ring her straight away; they don't know what to do with themselves, without their morning fix at Kilcashel House.'

Katie stood at the back door and waved him off as he manoeuvred past the raised flower beds and herb gardens Maggie had insisted on having installed last spring, which now seemed like a lifetime ago.

She was still standing at the door when she realised the postman had left, and she heard his van trundle down the avenue.

She placed the parcel on the counter beside a pile of white envelopes she had no inclination to open. In the first days after Maggie's death, she had found some comfort in reading the messages sent by people from all over who had been touched by her, in one way or another. Now, they were a reminder of her loss and the lonely road ahead, without the woman who brought so much energy to Kilcashel House.

Rolling out the bagel dough, she prepared three trays. Frank the postman probably had a whole gaggle of women set up to visit the café this morning, and she had better be ready. She worked quickly and when she had a moment she picked up the parcel again.

Turning it over in her hands, she noticed it was from the attorney in New York.

Curious, she got a sharp knife and slit the seal.

There was something wrapped in delicate tissue paper and two letters.

One was addressed to Ms Katie Williams and Ms Maggie Flint.

A pang of guilt seared through Katie that she hadn't informed the US attorney of Maggie's death. She'd thought about it, but somehow could not commit it to paper. There were days she got up early and sat in the kitchen believing that Maggie was still upstairs, or that she was sitting at the bay window in the café and all was well. She owned Kilcashel House now; she had stayed the course, but somehow that didn't matter anymore. What mattered was that she continued at Kilcashel for both of them and everything they had built up together.

She took the letter addressed to Ms Flint and Ms Williams and unpicked the seal.

Manhattan
New York

Dear Ms Flint and Ms Williams,

I hope this letter finds you both well and enjoying your time in Ireland. This may appear unusual to you both, but Mr Flint had put both of your names down as next of kin and nobody else. In that capacity, I enclose here the following item and the information contained in the enclosed envelope regarding Mr Flint's identity and heritage.

I feel you will know what best to do with it. If I can be of any assistance, please let me know.

I leave the matter in your hands, and will be in touch at a later date in relation to the transfer of full property rights to the owner/owners of Kilcashel House.

Yours sincerely

Miles Traynor

Attorney at Law

Katie reached in and pushed back the tissue paper. Carefully, she lifted out a soft crocheted bundle, letting it unfurl. It was a tiny gown, like for a doll or baby in a delicate crochet stitch with satin ribbons at the short sleeve cuffs and around the chest. There were four pearl buttons at the back.

The crochet was done in such a way that it looked like a delicate lace which was lined with satin. Katie laid it across the counter. It was a christening gown, she was sure of that.

She wanted to know its significance but a large part of her wanted to crumple it back into the box and forget it ever arrived. Her head hurt; what more secrets had Harry left to reveal? What else had he not told her in their years together? How had she ever thought she could marry this man? She didn't even know him. What did the attorney mean, his identity?

Harry never told her much, only that he was from Boston. She met his parents once, but they had died within a few months of each other, just about a year into her relationship with Harry. She went with him to the funeral in Boston; she remembered meeting aunts, uncles and various relatives, but Harry, she thought, never maintained contact afterwards.

Katie picked up the second envelope. Her heart tightened; she could hardly breathe. Here was a letter initially addressed to Harry Flint, but the name had been crossed out and THE LEGAL REPRESENTATIVE OF THE LATE HARRY FLINT was written in small capitals.

Katie tapped the envelope with her fingers; she was unsure of what to do next. The late Harry Flint; it was so formal, so final. Harry was gone. Maggie was gone.

It seemed like it was in a different lifetime when she was waiting for Harry in Bryant Park.

Stuffing the envelope in her pocket, Katie called Nora, who was passing by on her way to the sea, and asked if she could she hold the fort for ten minutes, until Anna arrived.

She didn't wait for an answer, but set off quickly through the back garden, past the gazebo and on to the fields that ran down to the sea. She turned her back on the water and headed across the big expanse of grass which Dan said she should let to a farmer, and towards the river.

She always stopped in the middle of the field and looked back at Kilcashel House resplendent against the dawn sky. There were days like this, when she had to remind herself that there was a huge world outside Kilcashel House and the Drawing Room Café.

Kilcashel House towered over the landscape, standing firm against the sea as if it was prepared to push it back. This was her home now, her safe place. What had made Harry want her to be here and Maggie too; the letter might give her a clue, but maybe she didn't want to know.

She turned towards the small hazel wood at the far end of the field. She hurried along to her favourite spot, the ferns whipping against her bare legs, a rabbit here and there scooting out of her way. She slowed down once she entered the wood, picking herself carefully across the ground, for fear of disturbing any otters that might be about. Dan had said there was a family of otters here with newborn pups that would soon be learning to swim.

Ignoring the letter in her pocket, she sat down on a tree stump, just a little back from the river's edge, and sat as still as she could. Her mind was racing with too many questions, but her body was statuesque.

Dan said he came here when he was troubled, because watching the otters concentrated the mind and gave his brain a rest, as well as making his heart soar with the wonder of nature.

A plop of water, and she saw the sleek adult otter swim across the river as if checking if the coast was clear. Katie strained for a better look, almost afraid to breathe as another adult otter sneaked out on to the riverbank, seven tiny otters carousing around her feet. Almost as if she were ignoring her pups, the big otter slid into the water. The little otters tentatively went to the edge, each too afraid to step out and into the unknown. The mother tipped her head up and gently nudged the first and second one, making them fall into the water with a splash. Another followed, though Katie was not sure whether it was by design or not.

The mother otter made noises as if coaxing the others to follow, and began to swim.

Another tumbled in and the second last one slipped into the water. The mother, almost impatient at this stage, jumped up and gripped her last pup by the neck, pulling it in to the water. They swam, dived and cavorted as if they had not a care in the world. Katie wanted to laugh out loud at their antics, but as quick, they were gone downriver, where a small pool had been created.

All that was left of their presence were the rings of movement in their wake, diffusing wide to the riverbank.

Katie took the envelope out of her pocket and opened it.

Boston

Dear Mr Traynor,

My name is Niall Pritchard, private investigator. As you may or may not know, I was engaged by Mr Flint to check on his heritage. Mr Flint had recently found out from a relative that he was in fact adopted as a newborn by Harry and Maude Flint of Boston. He knew nothing of his birth mother. He had in his possession a christening gown which he had been told had been crocheted by a woman from Ireland and which Harry and Maude had promised to keep for their son.

On examination of the gown, I found a reference to Kilcashel, Co Wicklow, which I believe to be in Ireland. This address was in tiny block capitals and somehow had been sown into something similar to a secret pocket at the back of the ribbon woven into the gown, where it could not be noticed, except if the ribbon was taken out.

When I told Mr Flint this and showed him the piece of paper, he was convinced his birth mother had placed it there and I was in agreement with him. So sure was he of the address that he travelled to Kilcashel in Ireland. He bought a property which he said was the grandest in the area because he said he felt a connection to that place. He decided we would continue investigations in the US and if they were not fruitful, we would move operations to Ireland.

On what I now know to be the day he died, I spoke on the phone to Mr Flint and gave him a summary of the information I had discovered as a result of my extensive investigations. We arranged that he would forward the remaining tranche of my fees and I would send all the information, including his adoption certificate, to him. Reminder notices were left unanswered until my office was informed by letter that Mr Flint had died and your attorney details supplied.

I have only recently found out that Mr Flint lost his life a short while after I spoke to him. I am sending on the below information so you may pass it on to his next of kin along with my sympathy on their sad loss.

As a result of the examination of the records I have included here an adoption cert for Harry Flint. He was born to an 18-year-old Irish girl, Catherine Walker.

She spent her confinement in a Catholic home run by an order of nuns in a suburb of Boston. She was described as a quiet girl and the fees had been paid upfront.

The note in the convent book which was to assist adopting couples said she was a good girl with good habits and manners and spent her days crocheting, sitting on a landing window seat on the first floor.

It had been intended that she would go on to find gainful employment after the birth of her baby and the nuns had already sourced a position as a nanny to a family in the city for her.

Unfortunately, due to complications at birth, Catherine Walker died after the delivery of a healthy baby boy, who was immediately handed over to his adoptive parents. Catherine Walker was buried in a grave paid for by her family in Ireland at Forest Hills Cemetery, Boston.

If I can be of further assistance, do please reach out.

Yours sincerely,

Niall Pritchard

Katie crumpled the letter and gazed out across the river. Everywhere was quiet, but inside her head, she was screaming. Why had he not told her he was adopted and searching for his birth mother?

It was too much. She could hear Maggie cursing and spitting fire that Harry had sprung yet another secret on them. How she wished Maggie was here now, to show her the way forward in her over-the-top way.

A heron flew low over the river, the sound of its wings swiping though the air. She saw it drop down quickly on the bank further down, where it must have a nest. A robin watched Katie from the branches of a hazel tree, and she stared back at it, as if they were playing who would blink first.

When she heard two cars on the avenue, Katie jumped up and checked her phone. It was opening time at the café and Anna would be so cross if she had to handle the first customers herself.

Stuffing the letter and envelope in her pocket, she dashed across the fields. Rushing through the garden, she heard a commotion at the front.

Walking around the side of the house to investigate, she heard Frank the postman's mother giving out at the top of her voice.

'He said it was definitely open; this is not good for business,' she said.

Another woman with her said they could wait a few minutes, and give Katie some time.

Katie took a deep breath and rounded the corner of the house.

'I am so sorry, ladies; I'm a bit behind this morning. Just give me a few minutes,' she said.

Frank's mother smiled and said no rush as Katie ran around to the back door to enter the house, and open up the café.

Anna should be here. The bagels had not been put on grids to cool and the coffee machine had not been set up.

Katie walked straight through to the front door and swung it open.

'We have free tea and some delicious chocolate orange cookies this morning, until we can get the coffee machine set up,' she said brightly.

'Ooh I fancy an Early Grey, if you have it,' Frank's mother said, and the ladies, chatting happily, helped get the chairs unstacked and set at the tables.

Katie set about making pots of tea and laid out the biscuits on fancy plates. When everybody was seated, she set up the coffee machine. She saw Nora wave as she passed by from the sea and she knocked on the window gesturing her to come in.

'Is there any way you can help me again in the café? Anna should be here and I don't know where she is.'

'That's odd, when I left for my swim, she was in the kitchen,' Nora said.

Katie folded up the christening gown and stuffed it back in the box.

'I'm sure she has her reasons,' Katie said.

THIRTY-THREE

Nora stayed all day in the café. They never mentioned Anna again, but worked side by side, Nora taking orders and Katie assembling back of house. At one stage, Nora called Katie to the counter.

'I think you should go around and talk to the ladies at the different tables; they have been saying how much they miss Maggie and her stories.'

'I'm no replacement for Maggie, but I suppose I could take a break and have a chat.'

'That's my girl,' Nora said, tapping Katie's apron to remind her to take it off.

Katie stood to one side of the counter, where she could observe the café floor. Every seat except Maggie's armchair was occupied. The velvet chair, she could see was taking up too much space beside the fireplace. Some customers glanced sadly in its direction, but nobody dared sit there; it was as if nobody wanted to acknowledge that the brash American they had all come to love would no longer visit the Drawing Room Café.

Katie knew she could never compete with the memory of Maggie, but just maybe she could begin a tradition of her own.

Reaching for the box containing Maggie's chocolate cake, she cut tiny cube-like sections and arranged them on a china plate with gold edging.

Taking a deep breath, she stepped out onto the café floor. She cleared her throat, but nobody seemed to notice. There was a loud tinkle. Nora had found a small bell which had once been tied around the neck of an old goat and she was shaking it furiously.

'Katie here has something to say,' she said loudly.

Everybody stopped talking and turned expectantly towards Katie, who flushed with embarrassment and self-consciously rubbed her neck, which she knew was showing red.

The postman's mother got up and stood beside her.

'We all love being here, Katie; we have missed our chats and the delicious fare served up in the café,' she said kindly.

Grateful for her words, Katie smiled.

'I wanted to thank you all and I thought maybe each day at this time, which was Maggie's story time when she entertained everybody with her New York tales, that we could remember our dear friend.'

There was a murmur of agreement around the room.

'It's such a simple memory, but Maggie always loved her grandmother's chocolate cake and insisted I bake it when we introduced cake to the café. It's our bestselling cake and was the one I baked for our last gathering with Maggie. It will always be known now as Maggie's chocolate cake, and we hope it will evoke a memory of one heck of a woman.

'So, if you don't mind, I will send a plate around of bite size pieces of Maggie's cake to please enjoy, with my compliments.'

The postman's mother started a clap, which turned into a strong applause, making Katie blush even more fiercely.

'What a great idea, and it will keep everybody here until near closing time,' one woman said as she kissed Katie lightly on the cheek.

'Mark my words, they will all come for the free cake; just make sure they pay for something else as well,' Muriel said.

Katie escaped back to the kitchen. Nora, who had stacked the dishwasher and wiped down the counters had left a note on the worktop.

I am off; I've to collect my young lad from school. Check in on Anna, just in case. X

Katie looked at her watch; there was just twenty minutes to closing time. There was no point phoning Anna; If she was so upset that she'd left her café for a whole day, this would require a face to face.

It was about thirty minutes until the last person had left the café. Katie hoovered the floor, and stacked the chairs on the tables, before adding the last of the cups and plates to the dishwasher and starting the cycle. She could do the till later; it was time to visit Anna.

Gathering up the box and the letter, she wandered down the avenue. After placing the closed sign on the main gates, she walked around to Anna's back door. Lola was lying out on the back step and didn't get up but wagged her tail.

Katie knocked, but there was no answer. She thought she saw a glimmer of movement, so she rapped louder with her knuckles.

'I know you're in there, Anna; I just want to check that you're all right.'

'Can't a woman be left in peace?

'Why won't you let me in?'

'That's my business. I'll be at work tomorrow.'

'Can't we talk? I'm sure it would be better than letting anything fester overnight.'

When there was no reply. Katie knocked on the kitchen window.

'Anna, I know you're upset about something, but I really need to talk to you. I don't want to leave it any longer than I should. It's important.'

The key sounded in the lock. Anna, her eyes red from crying, her shoulders hunched and her arms folded, stood in the doorway.

'Anna, what's wrong?'

'Child, will you just leave me in peace, for the love of God.'

There was something about Anna that made Katie hesitate. She didn't know what to say so she backed away. Anna swung the door shut with a bang, making the dog jump up and start whining. Katie turned to walk away, but the dog ran in front of her, jumping up, looking for attention.

Katie made her way slowly back up the avenue. Maybe she should leave Anna until tomorrow, but the thought of her remaining upset overnight was almost too much to bear. She shooed the dog away and told her to go home. What was she going to do if Anna cut off all contact? Katie knew she could not bear that; Anna was as important to Kilcashel House as Maggie had been.

When she got into the kitchen she took a box of painkillers from the drawer and swallowed one quickly, to quell the pain which was creeping up the back of her neck and in behind her eyes. Without Anna, the café would never survive.

Katie made her way to the empty café and sat in the velvet armchair. How she wished Maggie was here to take on Anna. She would have insisted on confronting her, but Katie wasn't able to do that. She closed her eyes, willing the pain thumping inside her head to stop. She must have dozed off, because when she heard the back door open, she jumped up.

Anna, who looked as if she had spent the day crying, was standing in the middle of the kitchen.

'I shouldn't have hunted you from the door.'

'I understand.'

'No, I shouldn't have done that. I know you're only trying to help, and we're friends.'

'I hope so,' Katie said.

Anna stepped into the café and lifted two chairs from a table.

'I think we need to talk,' she said, pointing to a chair.

'Yes,' Katie said, sitting down.

Anna sat opposite; her hands clasped in front of her.

'You know something about Catherine, don't you?'

'Your sister?'

'Yes, I saw the christening gown on the worktop,' Anna said.

'I didn't know I left it there; that was stupid of me. It arrived in the post this morning,' Katie said.

'I walked into your kitchen this morning – you were out with Millie, I think. I saw that crochet; my sister was the only person I knew who could crochet as well as that. That very pattern I bought for her, before she went away.'

'To the States?'

'Yes, how did you know?'

Katie pulled the envelope from her pocket and handed it across the table.

Slowly, Anna opened it and read down the page, tears wetting her cheeks and dropping on to the paper.

When she was finished, she carefully folded the letter and put it back in the envelope. Gulping back the tears, she looked to the ceiling as she tried to compose herself. Katie glanced away; she knew Anna didn't want her to witness her intense pain.

The large clock on the shelf on the café mantelpiece ticked loudly; the dog came and sat at Anna's feet and the cat slunk in the open kitchen door and jumped on the counter, settling down to sleep on a tea towel.

'Do you want me to leave you in peace?' Katie asked.

Anna shook her head and dipped her face into her hands. Katie, unsure of what to do, sat and waited. She should not have left the christening gown on the counter; there surely were better ways of dealing with this, she thought. After a few moments, Anna raised her head and spoke.

'I always hoped Catherine had a grand life in the States and chose not to make contact with home, even me,' she said.

'I am sorry you found out this way.'

'It gives a closure of sorts, I suppose. All these years, I considered writing to newspapers or maybe hiring a detective or something; but I never did. I suppose I just hoped.'

'Hope is a good thing.'

'Except when there's none. I have nothing to cling on to now. I never saw his face. We had the emails back and forth but to be honest, I didn't connect with him. He seemed on edge and constantly trying to wheel and deal. Maybe I wasn't fair on him, because I saw him as a bloody rich American who I thought to be an imposter taking over my family home. I didn't know he was family.'

'To be fair, he didn't know either.'

Anna moved over to the worktop and switched on the kettle.

'He wanted to know, and that's the tragedy, isn't it? He never got to find out that Kilcashel House was by right his home as much as mine. Maybe back in New York, he was happier. I think when it came to Kilcashel, he was almost trying too hard.

'If he had known the house was part of his history, I don't think he would have got rid of all the contents. I know he was my nephew, but that Harry was too swayed by silly interior designers, particularly that precious one from Dublin, who hadn't a clue.'

Anna threw coffee and hot water in some mugs and spooned in the sugar, before handing a mug to Katie.

She took a handkerchief from her pocket and blew her nose loudly.

Katie watched as Anna slurped her coffee, steeling herself to talk again.

'Dan Redmond's old man, Dermot, was the father. He was married, but Catherine had only eyes for him. She was young and he was such a handsome man.'

'So, Harry and Dan were half-brothers?'

'Yes, I hadn't thought of that.'

Katie shook her head.

'You're obviously attracted to a type,' Anna said, some of her old spunk back in her voice.

Katie didn't react.

'Tell me about Catherine.'

Anna sighed loudly.

'She was the youngest and really quite a shy girl. I was always surprised the way she took to Dermot Redmond, but love does funny things to you.

'She used to steal out to him at night. They met down by the sea. There was an old summer house down there, and it was their place. I used to wake up at four every morning to check if she was in her room. If she wasn't there, I would have to rush down and bang on the windows, and get Catherine back to the big house, before my father, when he got up early to tend to the animals, found out she wasn't in her bed.

'Catherine really believed Dermot was going to leave his wife and they were going to move to Dublin. She trusted him; I don't think I ever did, but Catherine was so happy, I didn't want to do anything to upset that.

'My head was telling me it couldn't last, but her heart was telling her other things.'

Anna slurped her coffee before continuing.

'She must have been three months pregnant when she told me she thought she was having a baby. I told her she had to tell

Dermot that if he was going to leave his wife, he had to do it before she started to show.'

'He didn't leave her though, did he?'

'He left Catherine, said he had to stay with his family. He had responsibilities. She was all on her own.'

Anna dabbed the perspiration from her forehead with her handkerchief.

'I was only two years older. I hadn't a clue what to do. When you're that young, you think it can be talked through, that a way can be worked out. We were clueless.'

She paused for a moment and swallowed hard. 'We had only ever known a good life; but we were forced to grow up fast. I confided in my best friend from school, Muriel Falvey. She swore not to tell a soul. I didn't know then what I know now. Muriel can't keep anything in. She told her sister Rosie, who blabbed it to her mother, and suddenly this was a huge incident, where the parish priest arrived on our doorstep late one night. Mr and Mrs Falvey had gone to the priest, because they didn't want to interfere in our business by telling my parents their daughter was pregnant.

'I will never forget that night. Catherine was in her room, crocheting a blanket – a throw I still have. It was on your bed that first night you stayed at the lodge. My father burst into the room ranting and raving. I had never seen him so angry. We weren't allowed outside the door the next day and school was forgotten about. We were told not to leave the house, and we didn't. My mother and father dressed up in their Sunday best to visit the priest at the parochial house.

'It was decided that Catherine would be sent to Boston. The priest had already begun making the arrangements. She was to spend her confinement with a nun's order and after the baby was born, they would help her get some sort of work.

'When my mother came and sat on Catherine's bed later, the poor girl was excited about the prospect of America.

'"What about Dermot?" she asked. I thought my mother would explode with anger, but she remained deathly calm. I will never forget what she said next.

'"That name will never be mentioned in this house again, and that family do not exist as far as we are concerned."'

Anna got up from the table and stood at the bay window.

'Catherine asked why she couldn't stay at home, but my mother didn't answer her. When she asked when could she and her baby return to Kilcashel House, I have never seen my mother so defeated, but her voice was hard. "The child will be given up for adoption over there; it's not welcome here. Your father has decided you will stay in America. He will send money every month to help you out, but you can't return here."'

Anna swung around. 'My mother left the room and she never saw Catherine again. I was the one who held that poor girl after she collapsed on the floor, crying her eyes out. My father knocked on the door, dropped a suitcase at our feet and barked at us to get it packed because Catherine was leaving in an hour.'

Anna walked over to the fireplace and put her hand on the mantelpiece for support.

'What do you pack for a girl who is never coming back; for a girl who never wanted to leave? I stuffed as much as I could into the case. I was zipping it shut when I saw the crochet pattern and her hooks, and I squeezed them in at the side.'

Anna came back and sat at the table.

'Maybe it's best Harry didn't know all this.'

Katie fumbled with the empty glass vase in the centre of the table.

'I think he would have been shocked and angry; I know I am,' she said.

Anna guffawed out loud.

'It's hard for you to understand, Katie, but becoming pregnant was the worst thing my sister could have done, and to have had an entanglement with a married man... One was unforgivable, but both meant banishment from country, community and family.

'If I wanted to contact Catherine, I didn't even know where she was. You know, I don't think my parents even had a proper address. I went to the priest so many times, up until the day he died, and each time he said the same thing to me.

'"Put her out of your mind. I couldn't help you if I wanted; all I did was help send the unfortunate away."

'He wouldn't give me any name or address in Boston. Even after I lost my Bert and my girls, I went to the parochial house and asked was there any record I could see, and they had nothing for me. I got a solicitor to write a few letters, but we hit a stone wall.

'The Church was very good at building walls of stone and now it refuses to help knock them down. It's the shame in every community; the shame of a whole country. Catherine was behind that wall of stone, until now. You brought her home to me; you have helped kick the wall down.'

Anna slumped into the chair and put her head in her hands.

Katie hugged her gently around the shoulders.

'Your sister was not at fault. Surely, Mr Redmond was the older married man, what happened to him?'

Anna smiled.

'Catherine was eighteen years old, though to us she was still a child in so many ways. My parents didn't want a scandal; I guess they put up their own wall. Catherine's name was never mentioned again and, when I tried, I was told off and threatened with expulsion from the house too.

'My father bulldozed the garden room and he never spoke to the Redmonds again. Mr Redmond had two more children with his wife. He died in a boating accident ten years later and she kept the farm until, years down the line, the children could help out in tandem with their schooling and his sister eventually took it over.'

'What about your mother? surely she wanted to know about her daughter?'

'My father was the boss in our house; nobody went against him. When I married Bert we went to Boston on our honeymoon. I tried every nuns' order I could find; I had a picture of my sister, but nobody would help me. More stone walls. Tell me, what should I have done? I thought that, after the baby was born, she must have moved to another part of the country. All I could do was hope that she was happy. I clung on to that hope, even when I knew there was no hope. I know now that my parents knew she died in childbirth. I think it was particularly cruel to leave me all these years without knowing she was gone; leaving me with hope for something that could never happen.'

Katie pushed the box across to Anna.

'The gown – you should have it.'

Ann stood and stared at it, gingerly lifting it from the box, the satin and crochet garment falling into place.

'I knew the minute I saw it, the perfect stitches, the attention to details. The bodice there in rows of trebles and the three-row lace shell pattern repeat with the Irish rose motifs forming a band or hem; that was the exact pattern I gave Catherine.'

She held the dress up to the light.

'So delicate and so beautiful; Catherine was very talented.'

Anna stroked the gown. 'We used to have long chats when she came back from being with Redmond. We were naive and silly, we thought she would be living at the Redmonds' farm next door and I would have Kilcashel House. It was innocent and sweet talk.'

'Don't you think your parents overreacted?'

'They reacted like any parents would in Ireland at the time. They packed me off to boarding school so I wouldn't have to face the Falveys. I ended up losing my sister and my home within the space of a week.'

She pulled at one of the ribbons of the gown which had become twisted.

'That was so Catherine, hiding the address under the thin bit of ribbon. She was very dainty in everything she did. Maybe I should have hired a detective like Bert suggested.'

'It wasn't going to make much of a difference,' Katie said.

Anna stood up and began to pace the Drawing Room Café. 'That's where you are wrong. I would not have spent all these years wondering why she hadn't made some effort to contact me, or be constantly looking for information nobody would give. I wished a lot of my life away, Katie.'

'I'm sorry, I didn't mean to minimise your suffering.'

'You have brought me answers, Katie. Otherwise, I would have gone to my grave not knowing.'

'Does Dan know?' Katie asked.

'He knows there was a falling out between the families, but not why. My father would have made sure to close that down. When Bert died, Dan came over to the house and offered to help me and I gave him the use of my paddocks for his horses.'

'That was big of you.'

'Not really, he offered to pay in cash and labour, and I needed help. It was practical and by then so much time had passed, there was no point continuing an animosity.'

Anna pointed to the chimney breast. 'The painting – my father had it taken down and sent to the attic the day Catherine was sent away.'

'Maybe it's time to put it back,' Katie said.

Anna shivered.

'I gave Maggie such a hard time about it. I'm sorry.'

'I think she would have worried if you didn't give her a tough time.'

Anna chuckled.

'Before you two turned up, things were pretty lonely around here. I may not have always liked it and my resistance was high, but you Americans did change things for the better.'

Anna stepped across to the bay window. 'I was so lonely here at the big house and everything was on top of me. I thought if I moved to the gate lodge, I could cope, but in truth I missed this old place.

'To think Catherine's son, my nephew, was here. My only regret is I didn't get to know him. For God's sake, I never got to look in his eyes.'

Katie got up and stood beside Anna. The evening was closing in. The horses were gathering at the far fence because they knew Dan would arrive soon to bring them into the stables for their bucket of feed. The person who had taken over the McDonald vacant allotment was packing up for the evening and he waved when he saw them inside the window.

Katie waved back.

'To think Catherine's son, Harry, saved Kilcashel House,' Anna said.

'I guess everything has come full circle.'

'I suppose it has.'

Katie moved closer to Anna.

'This will always be your home, Anna. We are family now.'

Anna reached out and squeezed Katie's hand tightly.

'I know,' she whispered.

A LETTER FROM ANN

Dear reader,

I want to say a huge thank you for choosing to read *Secrets of an Irish House*. If you did enjoy it, and want to keep up to date with all my latest releases, just sign up at the following link. Your email address will never be shared and you can unsubscribe at any time.

www.bookouture.com/ann-oloughlin

I love to write about ordinary people often dealing with extraordinary circumstances and women who, when they band together, can do the impossible.

I write stories that celebrate the enduring power of friendship and how family, friends and community can make all the difference.

At Kilcashel House at the end of the avenue which sweeps past the allotments and the paddocks where the horses graze, you will find a group of women who support each other through the toughest of times. They laugh and cry and hold each other up through the good times and bad.

At Kilcashel House, the women learn the true meaning of friendship and how we all need the support and love of those closest to us as we walk through life.

I hope you enjoyed your visit to Kilcashel House and the Drawing Room Café and if you did, I would be very grateful if you could write a review. I'd love to hear what you think, and it makes such a difference helping new readers to discover one of my books for the first time.

I love hearing from my readers – you can get in touch on my Facebook page, through Twitter, Instagram or Goodreads.

Thanks,

Ann

facebook.com/annoloughlinbooks

twitter.com/annoloughlinbooks

instagram.com/annoloughlinbooks

ACKNOWLEDGEMENTS

When the two beautiful words The End are written, it is not really the end.

It is more like the beginning of a process that takes a whole team of people to bring the novel to publication.

So when it comes to thanks, I must first applaud the team at Bookouture and particularly my wonderful editor Harriet Wade. Thank you, Harriet, for the sound advice, your keen eye and the words of encouragement which made the editing of this novel such a joy.

My agent Jenny Brown of Jenny Brown Associates has always championed my writing and for that, I am very grateful.

My biggest thanks go to my family, my husband John and my two children, Roshan and Zia. Without their constant support, the words would not come easy.

Finally, to all the readers who have taken my books to their hearts, thanks a million. And for any new readers who happen on this novel, I hope you enjoy your time at Kilcashel House as much as I enjoyed writing this story.

Ann

Printed in Great Britain
by Amazon

41778920R00202